Julia Fitzgerald was b
which, she says, inspi
passion for history fi
she would spend hou
historical costume. She wrote her first historical novel at seventeen, though she had begun writing short stories when she was six.

Julia Fitzgerald also writes under the names of Julia Watson and Julia Hamilton. She lives in Cheshire.

JULIA FITZGERALD

The Jewelled Serpent

Futura

A *Futura* Book

First published in Great Britain in 1984 by
Century Publishing Co Ltd
First published in paperback by Futura Publications 1984
This edition published by Futura Publications 1994

ISBN 0 7107 3044 6

Printed in England by Clays Ltd, St Ives plc

Futura Publications
A Division of
Macdonald & Co (Publishers)
Brettenham House
Lancaster Place
London WC2E 7EN

Whatever your faith shall be my faith,
Though Judgement Day break me tomorrow,
If I may kiss your milky throat,
Come near, my lovely one, come near . . .

Pir Sultan Abdal (16th century)

THE JEWELLED SERPENT is dedicated to Miss Rita Hayworth, in memory of her unforgettable beauty and grace in the film, *Salome*.

Contents

PART ONE

The Garden of Allah

Think not that you can direct the course of love, for love, if it finds you worthy, directs your course.
Kahlil Gibran

Sleep exists because my eyes yearned for it,
Love exists because my soul called for it.
George Thémelis

Chapter One

The silver and pewter castellated rocks of Pentrevick rode on the jutting promontory of coastland like the fearsome fortress of some long-dead medieval king – Arthur, perhaps, who was reputed to have ruled hereabouts with his variegated courtiers, some mystical, some black-hearted, and some incurably romantic.

The potent seas smashed and battered; driving into the hard, sandy shore, pummelling twisting black rivulets, then bounding out again into the thunderous maelstrom. Gulls circumnavigated the pockets of air with a grand finesse, eager for the sight of food, but this was the second storm in three days and all living creatures had taken refuge far out of sight.

The girl walking in the buffeting wind relished the savage Cornish weather. Tucked tightly into a russet woollen cape, its hood clasped firmly beneath her chin, her boots the strong variety worn by fishermen, she tramped across the muddy earth, bending into the gale, her mind alive with thoughts, her face sparkling wet and cold from the turbulent rain.

The violence of the sea had never frightened her, not even when, at the age of thirteen months, she had seen her first storm. Her nursemaid, Polly Hervy, had walked too far with her after lifting her from the dogcart, and they had somehow managed to get lost, the weather changing before they could find shelter. Polly had trembled and sobbed, while her tiny charge laughed gleefully at the barbarism unleashing its headstrong energy around her.

Not only did the girl now feel herself to be transmuted by the storm, she *was* the storm: bright, all-powerful – and unpredictable.

'Get her a husband? 'Twould be easier to marry Satan to the Pope!' Her late grandfather's premonitory words came into her mind. 'When she was baptised Allegra, against *my* wishes, her mother should have known what it would mean. The chit is lively to the point of a maelstrom! Why could she not be like Elizabeth? Now, there is a sweet maid, full of amiability, who'll be rushed to the altar before she can say St Michael's Mount!'

Her mother had loved to dance. It was her grace and radiant enjoyment of music which had first attracted their father to her, so grandfather had told them, and it was also why she had chosen Allegra's name.

'Dance throughout the night, she would, if given the chance. Fireflies on her heels, that's what she had, to light her through the dark.' Coughing gruffly, the old man had pretended that his gout was stabbing, the poignant memory of his only daughter being turned into a grimace of pain. Dour and irritable, his gouty foot had turned him from a blithe and fearless spirit into a hobgoblin who sat hunched and snarling in his chair, his leg elevated on a padded stool. Acid and turbulent though he had become, nothing had dimmed his acute perception, or his memory of the daughter he had loved so much, and who had died so young, leaving him with two grandchildren. One enthralled him, and one annoyed him, some of that impatience stemming from her 'paltry, foreign name' (as Grandfather called it), a name for 'she-demons and fallen women,' not for one of the patriotic Cornish Pens.

Pens had been famed throughout history, for Grandfather had not been the first to possess a sharp and shrewd business sense. Never renowned for their looks, the Pens had made up for that with a flair and spirit which had massed their fortunes over the centuries. Sea-pilots and navigators, merchants and adventurers, they had participated in the extension of England's boundaries and its possessions abroad. True, there had been some Pens who had exhibited a greater interest in the ale in their mugs, or the proximity of soft white thighs, but these wastrels were the exceptions to prove the rule that the Pens governed their domain with probity, acumen and a wise, good-hearted tolerance which had made them a deal more popular than many landlords and estate owners.

Not even Allegra's love of music, which she had inherited from her mother, would placate the old man. He could not forget that dispute with his daughter over the baptismal name, and the guilt that he had suffered afterwards; for they had barely spoken since and she had died so suddenly of the smallpox, being taken from him before he could make amends. It was easier to project the guilt and rage on to the child whose name was responsible than to face his own pig-headed nature which was the real cause.

No wonder that Allegra loathed her name. It had caused a family quarrel, a schism between her mother and her grandfather. The weight of guilt lay heavily on her, too, because her grandfather was not man enough to face the truth.

Her sister, Elizabeth, petite, with a heart-shaped face, hair the colour of sun-drenched primroses, and eyes of the most unusual soft blue, was betrothed to no less than Lord Nash Hamilton. One of the wealthiest and most powerful of Cornishmen, his ancestors had marked themselves as men of outstanding achievement. They had shone at the side of the Black Prince, of Hotspur, Raleigh and Hudson, returning from their travels with treasures, curios and the tolerant wisdom of the wordly who have been uprooted and who have learned to survive single-handed.

Elizabeth and Lord Hamilton were a perfect match, she so feminine, romantic, and accomplished at the most important female pastimes of embroidery, singing, the writing of honeyed verse and the making of scented pot pourris, and he so worldly, larger than life, renowned and dashing.

Allegra gazed out to sea, her eyes welling with the reflection of the convoluting ebony and emerald waves.

She had first seen Lord Hamilton when she was twelve, and he had visited her father on a business matter. Running into her father's library, her face limned with sunlight and excitement, she had been about to fling herself into her favourite chair when she saw that a man sat there. He was looking at her as if she had dropped from Heaven, his hands gripping the arms of the chair as if he feared it might eject him.

'I apologise for my daughter's impulsiveness, my lord. Allegra is still young, a mere chitling, you will excuse her I know.'

'This is not Elizabeth?' The stranger rose, tall and omnipotent before Allegra, the sunlight enamelling his silver-gilt hair. She could not see the colour of his eyes for the brightness behind him.

'Indeed not, my lord. This is my younger daughter, Allegra, a wild young creature but we hope to tame her before she is old enough to wed.'

The stranger and her father had then exchanged a glance which excluded her so totally that Allegra felt a coldness grip her. They were grinning, sharing a private jest, shutting her out. She was furious.

'Father, I came to inform you that Bernadette has had her foal. It is a girl, another wild young female for you to whip into shape.'

Then, cheeks pulsing with heat, she had bobbed a curtsey and rushed out, slamming the door behind her. Since that time, she had learned how to protest more stylishly. When roused, she still spoke with as much venom, making her point so cogently that none could argue, but now she closed doors quietly.

Elizabeth, easily shocked, took Allegra aside at least twice a month to lecture her on the qualities of femininity which must be tended unless she wished to become an old maid, for, at eighteen, Allegra was unbetrothed, unwooed and unsuited to every man, thanks to her fiery temper, or so Elizabeth would say with pertinacity.

'You cannot sew a fine seam, you cannot sing or compose verses, you have no inclination to learn housewifery. What are we to do with you?' Elizabeth had sighed impatiently. 'You should have been a man and then had you behaved in this way, everyone would have lauded you.'

'Yes, we agree on that, Elizabeth, I should have been a man.' Allegra tossed her gilded-russet hair. 'But I do not agree about the inability to compose verse. What of this?

'Women may be small or tall, but most of all they must be nice, while men may travel all the world and indulge in every vice.'

'*Allegra!*' How shocked her sister had sounded as the cause of her dismay flounced out of the house to walk by the sea.

An old maid. A spinster. One who sits by the fire spinning and weaving because no man has asked her to marry him. Plain, ugly, infirm, poor in possessions and spirit, that was what spinster meant to Allegra.

The waves heaved towards the sky, climbing, rolling, thundering down. Lord Hamilton was a famous discoverer who had travelled widely in the New World. There was a strait named after him, and a township, too, so her father had told her, far away in a country where the people had ebony skins and worshipped pagan gods. Lord Hamilton had brought back a little black boy called Juke, but he had died in the erratic climate of England. He was buried in the Hamilton family vault.

'A kindly and generous gesture,' so her father said, 'allowing one of the heathen to lie in one's family vault.'

'As he caused that heathen's death I think it was the least that he could do!' Allegra had cried, making Elizabeth burst into tears.

'If only your sweet mother were here,' their father had groaned, at which Elizabeth cried: 'Praise God that she is not, Father, for she would die of shock at seeing how Allegra has turned out!'

The girl in question smiled softly to herself. She could not remember her mother save for her name, Margaret Mary. There was a tiny portrait of her in the minstrels' gallery. A dignified and handsome girl, smilingly secure in her husband and family, her mother had not been pretty as such. Elizabeth was the beauty, but as to the source of her looks no one could say, yet it was she, Allegra, who was called the changeling.

Now she was in view of Redbeard's Creek, so called because there a famous fifteenth-century pirate, Redbeard Maltravers, had anchored his ship between voyages. During the battles between the Houses of York and of Lancaster, he had reigned supreme in the Channel, looting both Houses and enriching his own. He was an ancestor of Allegra's, and, as Elizabeth liked to remind her, she was the first in the family since Redbeard himself to have the famous Maltravers' russet hair.

Redbeard had married four times, outliving all but his last bride, Joan Margaret Pentrevick, who had borne him eleven children, all of whom had inherited the pale yellow Pentrevick locks or the caramel-brown colouring of Joan's mother's family, the Lornes. Now here was Allegra with Redbeard's blazing hair.

She could never live like Redbeard Maltravers, roaming the seas, looting and pillaging, stealing booty and preying on ships, then putting into port, here in this secluded Cornish cove, to recover from his escapades. Women were not allowed to behave like that. Women were delicate ornaments on which men feasted their eyes and, after marriage, their bodies. Human broodmares must be beautiful, serene, and wholly absorbed in such essential matters as sewing tapestries depicting Paris receiving the apple from the goddesses, or the Virgin Mary in the Garden of Paradise. Allegra had once spent five days learning how to goffer her father's ruff to perfection, without making mistaken creases which would not come out or singeing the fragile material. It was, of course, *vital* and important work, goffering ruffs. People might be dying of the Sweating Sickness or the plague, but women must know how to press ruffs. Heaven forbid that she might die in ignorance of such accomplishments!

Failing piracy and adventure, Allegra would have liked to be a physician, but that too was unthinkable. *Men* were physicians; women who dabbled in such matters were dubious characters, halfway to witches, without the qualifications which men could flaunt, and having no prestige. When her sister had been ill with a quartan fever, the physician had given Elizabeth a dead toad in a tiny leathern bag, telling her to hang it round her neck until she was well.

While Elizabeth was asleep, Allegra had substituted a live toad so that when her sister woke the bag was trying to hop off her bed. When Allegra rescued the bag and freed the toad, Elizabeth laughed so much that her fever vanished.

The storm was caressing the rocks nearby, tempting them to respond before rattling against their gritty surfaces with a supernatural violence. What would it be like aboard a ship in a passion like this, with the decks tilting, the seas smacking, the timbers grunting? She could almost imagine a tiny craft out there bobbing up and down. No, she was not imagining it, there *was* a ship in sight. It had strange sails, brightly coloured and variegated, and it was heading out to sea. By rights it should be seeking a haven. How odd. She watched until the ship had vanished and then she turned for home, oblivious of her drenched cloak and squelching boots.

'Saint Matilda!' her old nurse exclaimed when she saw Allegra. 'Where hev ye been, ye witless girl? I thought ye had drowned at sea at the least!'

'Or devoured by some enormous sea monster, but no such luck?' Allegra grinned, tugging off the sopping cloak and boots.

'Oh, there was a sea monster hereabouts, so they say. The Glooming Man they called hem. He'd pop out o' the water and pull naughty children down into the depths, and 'tes long overdue for hem to get his hands on you!'

'You're teasing me, Mattie. Where's Elizabeth?'

'She went over to Cuttley four hours or so ago. Went to see the shoemaker. No doubt she'll stay the night with the Allisons till this storm be passed.'

Roger Allison was one of the almost-suitors scared away by Allegra's tongue. When she told him that she dyed her hair, padded her stomacher, and had a twisted leg, he had paled so much that she thought he would faint, before mumbling excuses, he had leapt away. How could she have let him come so close to kissing her? He had a blotchy skin, foul breath and a broken front tooth. She knew that she could do much better than that . . . if she wanted.

But did she want to? No! Flinging herself in a chair by the fire she sipped at the cinnamon-spiced wine which Mattie had brought her, and toasted her bare toes in the hearth in a way which would have shocked Elizabeth. Allegra slumped cosily in the chair and gazed into the flames. She wanted to see the face of the man she would marry. They said that if you gazed in the flames on May Eve then you would see that very face, and today was May Eve.

For a time she saw nothing and then the flames shimmered and began to take nebulous shape. Gold hair, a strong, powerful face etched with character, reliability and passion. Full, sensual lips made for kissing, and piercing blue eyes which held the skies in their depths.

Lord Nash Hamilton, her sister's future husband.

Scowling, she picked up a fire iron and smashed it into the logs so that the flames dizzied and dissolved.

Next morning the skies were black and smouldering, and Allegra surveyed them with disdain. If only her father were here and not at court. It was marvellous that the Queen thought so highly of him, but this meant that he spent many months in London. Elizabeth had met the Queen, who, she said, was vigorous and overbearing. She had eighty wigs and one thousand dresses, one of which was embroidered with eyes, ears and mouths to show that she saw all, heard all, and knew all that was being said in her kingdom. She was a great age now, yet she still danced much of the night away, tiring far younger companions, for she had inherited her father Harry Tudor's immense energy. He had exhausted eight horses before Mass every morning, so Allegra had heard. No amount of brilliance, perception or power was of use if there was not the vigour to it.

Allegra stepped back from the casement. She would make an entry in her diary after breaking her fast, some sharp words about the subjugation of uncrowned females while the Queen herself was worshipped like a goddess and was omnipotent. Yes, that described it exactly.

She heard a sound behind her. Turning, she saw Mattie, her face chalky white, her eyes distended.

'Mattie, what have you done? Are you ill?'

Helping her old nurse to a seat, she chafed her small red hands.

'Can I get you something, a posset, your tincture?'

Mattie shook her head. It seemed to tremble on her neck as if it might collapse to one side.

'The news . . . A boy 'as come from Cuttley. Oh, what are we ter do? If only the master was here!'

'Cuttley? Elizabeth has not had an accident? Oh, tell me, Mattie, tell me!'

'I thought them days wuz past. Oh yes, so did we all. Not for ten year or more 'ave they been this way.' Mattie seemed to choke, unable to breathe.

'Who have not been here, Mattie, who?' Allegra pressed the rough red hands.

'The pirates, the pirates! Oh, Saint Matilda save us, save us, she be gorn, gorn, that lovely young thing with all that streaming hair like the sunlight . . .' Bending double, Mattie sobbed heartbrokenly.

Allegra had to wait until the old woman regained some control, and then she learned what had happened late the previous day and the moment that she heard it she thought of the strange, foreign-looking ship which she had seen spearing its way out to sea. A pirate ship, a pirate slaver's ship . . . It had harboured near Cuttley, in Demon's Cove; the villains had crept up on the village while honest people were sitting snug by their fires, and all the women and many of the men had been abducted. The boy who had brought the message was returning from feeding his uncle's horses, when, on seeing the swarthy-looking strangers, he had hidden behind a barn, from where he watched in horror as women and children were dragged from the farm at knife point. Unable to help, he had sped towards the next homestead, only to find a repeat scene of abduction and his godfather, James Bowles, lying dead in the mud, his right hand sliced off and lying stiff and ashen a few yards away. It contained a lock of his daughter Frances's hair.

Allegra took charge instantly. Never had there been such a furore in Pentrevick Manor.

The boy, Philip, was lying on a pallet by the kitchen fire, shivering uncontrollably. He was betrothed to James Bowles's daughter, and he was convinced that he would never see his Frances again.

Allegra knelt beside him, mindless of the grime and grease splashes around the hearth.

'Do you know if my sister is taken?' Philip's eyes rolled upwards wildly as he began to sob, cutting, painful sounds.

'She was staying the night at the Allisons' because of the storm. Did you see her? Did you?'

'Gone, mistress, gone, all gone . . .' The boy let out a wail, and one of the cooks hurried to him with the spiced wine she'd been preparing. Lifting his head, she tipped the steaming liquid down his throat. That would take his mind off his self-pity. A burnt mouth allowed little room for thought.

Allegra got to her feet. Hands gripped together, she paced up and down the steamy kitchens which smelt of dough, roasting meat, saffron, spices and herbs. Here she had lived for eighteen years, in this solid, mellow and beloved house, so sure of her destiny as a daughter of the Pentrevick line, bored sometimes, yet soon revived by communing with the sea and the rich world of nature outside. Now she was sure of nothing. The world had been tipped upside down and she felt as if she had fallen off it, was still falling, to land she knew not where.

Word must be sent to her father at once, but the journey would take all of a week in this weather, even with their best horseman taking the message. Jesu, her sister taken by pirates! She thought the full horror of it had settled on her, but it was increasing, tightening round her, striking into the pit of her stomach.

The messenger dispatched, Allegra went back to question the boy. Did he know the name of the pirates' ship, where they had come from? Did he hear any names being mentioned, or recognise any of the men?

He looked perplexed, questioning, trying his utmost to reply carefully.

'Heathens, they wuz heathens I know that, mistress. Not Christians. Dark skins, nasty black eyes like crazed beasts, bright clothes – I don't recognise colours that well. Green I think, mebbe red. Dark hair, and great curved knives in their hands.' His teeth rattled in a sudden memory of Master Bowles's severed hand. 'Boots, too, but they ain't no rarity in sea dogs.'

'Did you see their ship, Philip? Did it have striped sails?'

'Running o'er Peace Hill I wuz when I saw the ship. Sails with strips across them, like leddies' ribbons pulled taut across. A mark, I saw their mark!' His face brightened. 'The wind got up, like a devil rushing out o' the earth at me. Gave me the horrors et ded, but I saw the mark flung out flat by the wind!'

'The mark? Do you mean their ensign?'

Philip nodded vigorously. 'Yes! The sea monster with a flaming tongue coming from its jaws. I've heard men talk on it. Infamous it is. Terrible . . . the sign of the Devil.'

Allegra absorbed this with a sinking feeling. The sea monster. She and Mattie had been jesting about just such a creature only a few hours ago. She had said that Mattie might have been wishing a sea monster would run off with her, and instead it had taken Elizabeth . . .

Biting back her tears, she rushed to her bedchamber. Elizabeth, oh Elizabeth, would she ever see her again? Her beautiful, fragrant, feminine sister in whose shadow she had grown up. She tried to pray but her thoughts were too tangled to settle into the routine pattern. She had never been one for piety anyway. How could she wait here in this tragedy-stricken household for two weeks or more until her father came? And what could he do when he arrived? Elizabeth might be dead even now . . . abused and assaulted by the vile heathen men who had captured her.

What was the answer? What could she do alone, a mere woman? Had she been a man she would have commandeered a fast ship and sped after her sister, first having found out all she could about this fiend who displayed the sea monster ensign. When she found him, she would kill him with her own bare hands, woman or not!

A violent hammering at the front door shocked her from her thoughts. For a moment she believed it was the pirates come for her, and she shook with rage at the thought of seeing them face to face. They would wish that they had never confronted her!

It was not the pirates, however, but the man who made her heart twist and silvery chills flee along her spine in an entirely different way.

In the salon they sat facing one another, he thinking that if she were not so frigid and arrogant, then she would be almost as beautiful as her sister, she thinking that she was truly cursed to have any tender feelings for this presumptuous and bumptious man, her sister's future husband.

Years before, Nash's father, Greville Hamilton, had loved the Queen. It was no secret. When she was imprisoned, a terrified young girl, flung from pillar to post by her sister Mary and the Catholic faction, Princess Elizabeth had found a loyal and true friend in him. He had volunteered his fortune and his lands to finance her during those difficult years when she was kept so desperately short of money. On taking the Throne, the Queen had returned it all to him with interest and a new title, that of Earl of Cornwall, but he had died of the Sweating Sickness a few months later, when rumour had it that the Queen was about to marry him. How true that was, Allegra did not know for there were a thousand rumours surrounding the Queen; that was how she herself liked it. Only the monarch knew the truth.

Allegra was sure that the first Lord Hamilton must have been a warm and marvellous man who had failed to pass on any of these qualities to his arrogant, illegitimate son, the posthumous child of his union with a Cornish girl of good family who had died when Nash Hamilton was born.

Normally, the Queen blazed with fury when her suitors so much as cast an eye at another woman but in this case she had forgiven Greville totally, passing an edict that his son would inherit the title despite his bastardy. Such a thing had never been known before. It was an alarming precedent, counselled the Queen's ministers, but she ignored them.

Heart thudding, Allegra broke the silence which had settled between herself and Nash Hamilton.

'What – what is to be done, my lord? Have you – that is, do you know who has taken my sister?'

Lord Hamilton rose to his feet. 'I do. One of the most evil and powerful men in Islam. The Amir Adem Ali, Lord of the Incense Road. He and his family before him amassed their fortunes by controlling the incense routes of Arabia. They deal in myrrh and frankincense, silks, gems, spices, pearls – and slaves.' His Lordship's bright blue eyes gazed steadily into Allegra's.

'So my sister will – will be a slave?'

'I have no doubt of it.' Hamilton clenched his jaw. 'However, it shall be over my dead body, for I intend to get her back.'

'You will go after her?' Allegra's eyes blazed with excitement.

'What else did you think I would do, sit around wailing and weeping? I am no morbid female.'

'If women are prevented from taking such action, it is because men forbid them!'

'Only because they are unfit for it, wild, emotional, irrational creatures that they are. Thank the Saints your sister was more composed and temperate than most.'

'Which is of course why you are betrothed to her.'

'Of course. Do I detect sour grapes, Mistress Allegra? Would you have liked to race her to the altar? You always were the one who had to be first and best at everything, were you not?' He turned his back, to gaze out of the casement with hollow, unseeing eyes.

'Yes, there you have it, and that is why I shall be coming with you on the voyage, Lord Hamilton.'

He whirled on his heel, his face awash with an astonishment which turned to bitter laughter.

'A little, hysterical chit like you? Even if you were male I would not take you on as my cabin boy! I would needs spend the entire voyage patting your hands and rinsing out your sick bowl.'

Allegra flushed a painful scarlet.

'I said that I am coming with you, Lord Hamilton. I assure you that I shall be no trouble. I shall behave in the most constrained fashion at all times, but I must do *something*, I cannot just stay here for weeks, perhaps months, not knowing what has happened to Elizabeth. My mind would be unbalanced by . . .'

'If it were not so already, and by far lesser matters than chasing after murderous pirates,' Nash Hamilton intercepted coldly.

'I – I do not know what you mean, my lord . . . We barely

know one another yet you pass judgement on me as if I were a shrew.'

'I am a fair man, Mistress Pentrevick, and I do assure you that I give merit where merit is due. If you appear to think that I am condemning you, then perhaps it is because your reputation has gone before you.'

Allegra felt the blood sweep away from her head. His cruelty was unbelievable. She had been prepared to forgive his acerbity because of his distress over her sister's abduction, but this was too much. Shaking, she turned on her heel and walked to the door.

'I see that my words have hit home, Mistress Pentrevick,' he called after her. 'If you could not face up to the truth about yourself here on your own home ground, how do you think you could face the hazards of life at sea? There are far more important matters than drawing attention to one's self yet again. The time has passed for such childish humours.'

Not looking back, Allegra half ran, half stumbled, up the stairs to her chamber where she flung herself on her bed and pounded the pillow in a fury.

Chapter Two

The *Tudor Raven* slipped through the seas like a vast amphibious beast, the sun blazing above, and the reviving tang of the salty waters reminding the crew of past voyages, past memories.

Nash Hamilton stood on the fo'c'sle staring at the fast disappearing wedge of Cornish coastline. The last few days had been tortuous, his every move hampered by the screaming hysterics and insulting accusations of his future sister-in-law. Once he had pondered briefly on Allegra's character, thinking that she might have been the preferable bride, but not any more. She was a vixen, and her temper would have done justice to the most notorious villain. She had hounded him, demanding to be taken on this voyage; she had shouted insults after him in the streets and kicked his shins when he called her a minx and a hussy. How the people of Pentrevick had relished the last few days of scenes and trials!

Having escaped the brazen wench by sailing two days earlier than the date which she had been told, he managed a cold grin of relief as the last of Cornwall shrank to a misty veil on the horizon. There would be peace of a sort now that he could carry on with the rescue of his betrothed.

The hasty preparations had taken his mind off the worst of his fears but now they crowded back and he thought of Elizabeth, crushed in the arms of a vicious blackamoor, sold into slavery for the depraved lusts of an Eastern potentate, perhaps even the notorious Sultan himself.

He doubted that she would survive such a life, for her nature was gentle and innocent, her temperament lacking in bellicosity. Allegra could survive a lifetime in a harem, he was sure, and he wished with all his heart that it had been she who was taken and not his sweet Elizabeth.

This would not be the first time that he had ventured to Arabia, and he knew all too well how badly Islamic women could be treated. Slaves and broodmares, subjugated by their men, doomed to annual childbearing in the harshest and most ignorant conditions, their youthful freshness soon dimming. Draped in the dark veils of purdah, and wearing hideous masks, these heathen women were never allowed out of their homes, and only their husbands, sons and brothers could see their unveiled faces. By comparison with the women of his homeland, their lives were wretched, and he could not bear to think of Elizabeth suffering in this way.

He had circled the known world three times and he knew what dark-skinned men of uncontrolled lusts could do to gentle girls with white flesh and sunny-coloured hair, and his heart shrank at the thought.

The *Tudor Raven* was a new ship, strong and beautiful, built light and streamlined for speed. He deplored the fashion for heavy ships which had led to such disasters as the sinking of the *Mary Rose* in the lifetime of the present Queen's father. Ships were, above all, made for voyaging, for reaching far destinations; to make them weighty was madness. The infamous pirates on the Barbary Coast and Arabia used the lightest of ships, which skimmed the sea's surface; they were not the easiest to pursue, but Nash knew where he was heading. He was making for the amirate of the man whose emblem had been seen on the ship which took Elizabeth.

The Amir Adem Ali, reputed to be one of the most powerful men in Arabia, controlled the major trading routes and their abundance of frankincense and myrrh, gold, ivory, silks and spices, gems and ikons, exotic beasts and luxuriant carpets. For a comparatively young man, he was immensely rich, boundlessly powerful, displaying his emblem of the flame-spewing dragon with an arrogance which chilled the hearts of those who came into his thrall.

Nash had tangled with him twice before. Once, when six of his sailors had been keelhauled by Adem Ali's slave dealers, he had pursued the slavers himself. During a violent fight, all the slavers had died and soon Nash and his men were safely back on board his own ship. The second time, he had lost a large cargo of hides and curios and, after extensive enquiries, discovered where they had been diverted: to the home of one of Adem Ali's slave masters. Nash and his men had laid siege to the house, a low-roofed, snowy white building standing in the vast swells and dips of the desert.

After days in the blazing sun and chilling nights, his water supply and food cut off, the thief had surrendered and thrown out the stolen goods. Nash had helped his men load their camels with the sacks of curios and as many of the hides as they could carry. Adem Ali was intolerant of such bold tactics, so Nash fully expected to be attacked during the return journey, but, much to his surprise, they were left in peace. He doubted whether he would get away with that again. They said all dogs were allowed one bite, and he had taken his.

His thoughts turned to the Pentrevick sisters. How was it that two girls could be raised and educated in the same family and yet turn out such opposites? He was not a man who gave time to such arts as astrology, yet he knew that many in his time, and most particularly the Virgin Queen herself, consulted astrologers as others went to their dressmakers and to market. Some could not survive without knowing what lay round the next hedge, yet he had always been more interested in the hedge itself than in what lay in its shadow. Elizabeth was born under the gentle, feminine sign of Virgo, like the Queen herself, while Allegra was a tempestuous Scorpio. Once, he had read a passage on the failings of those born under this dark and stormy sign and he considered that she possessed all of them, the arrogance, the disputativeness, the reckless disregard for any destiny but her own, the secretiveness and the ruthless will. Yet surely upbringing had some importance in the scheme of things, or else every sign would end the same, whatever the childhood and home life?

He had disregarded the passionate Scorpion and wooed the gentle Virgin, knowing that he did the right thing. As a man who courted danger and adventure, he needed a gentle and nurturing wife, not a hussy who spat brimstone at him. Jesu, where would that gentle virgin be now?

Dusk clasped the sea in tender, misty arms as the sun dipped out of sight. Even in spring it was chilly at night out on the ocean, not that the weather ever troubled him. He had first gone to sea at the age of eleven, with his late cousin, and everything after that had been an anticlimax.

The Queen always made much of him when he appeared at Greenwich or Windsor, but that was not his ideal mode of life, posturing in emerald silks and gold-barred satins with a ruby dangling from one ear and exotic oils dabbed at the wrists, though many gentlemen of the court favoured such apparel. It was the French influence, allied with that of the Italians. However hard one tried to be conservative, these foreign embellishments managed to insinuate themselves. As a sap to fashion he had begun to wear the new type of knee breeches called Venetians. They went down to the knee instead of puffing out at the thighs (a design which he had always disliked, reminding him as it did of women's puffed sleeves). Venetians were smooth, unfrilled, and warmer at sea.

Out of the corner of his eye he was absently watching a

young sailor scrabbling with a coil of tarry hemp. The lad seemed to have poor sea legs – and how small he was for the width of his shoulders. Malnourishment most probably, for that was rife amongst the poor, and that was where young sailors mostly hailed from.

Forgetting the boy who was fighting the rope as if it were a living snake, Nash turned his thoughts back to his quest. In a pouch, tucked safely against his chest, was the famous emerald necklace of the Hamilton family. It was handed to every new Hamilton bride on her wedding day. He planned to barter for Elizabeth with its priceless stones. If she were in the hands of Adem Ali, then he would offer the entire necklace in exchange for her freedom. If he caught up with her in Arabia at some point on the Incense Road, then he would offer one emerald at a time to whoever held her captive.

A shout made him turn. In the dusky light he could see little save for a tarry tangle of rope into which a small figure had fallen. He was about to turn, knowing that the boy would be more embarrassed if he, the master of this vessel, saw him blundering than if he were left to pick himself up alone, when he heard the groan of someone in pain. The dratted boy had injured himself. Short of hanging, how could a simple coil of rope damage anyone?

In seconds he was hauling the boy out of the tarry spiral, his grip hard and uncompromising. The lad was hobbling, his head bent and face screwed up with pain.

'What's your name, lad?'

'Rafe, 'tis Rafe,' the boy mumbled huskily.

'When you address me, you call me Captain, is that understood, Rafe?'

' 'Tis, Captain.'

'Is your ankle sprained?'

'Don't know, Captain.'

'Let me feel it.'

The boy's bones were skinny as a child's, but the ankle seemed in one piece. It was swelling rapidly, and would need bathing and bandaging.

'Come to my cabin, Rafe, and I'll bandage your ankle, otherwise you'll be no use whatsoever.'

'No need for that . . . no need, I'll be all right . . .' the boy said breathily.

'No need, what?'

'No need, Captain.' The husky voice was gritted.

'To my cabin, Rafe, and we'll look at the damage.'

Somehow, the boy managed to knock over the lamp as he hobbled into Nash's cabin so they had to make do by candlelight while one of the crew fetched more oil. All the same, even by candlelight, Nash could see that the leg which was spread before him on a bunk had the delicacy of the female lineaments, even though the hose in which it was clad had been roughly padded to bulk out the muscles.

Rafe gave a very female scream when the captain's hand gripped the swelling ankle and pressed deep.

'You cunning young whelp!' Nash growled. 'You're going straight back home in a long boat.'

'I'll kill you if you make me go back! Besides, we're too far from land now.'

'You'll go back if I have to swim back with you myself!'

'Try, just try! You *bully*! I'll make sure everyone in England knows what a savage you are! I'll tell the Queen – she'll listen to me and have you flung in the Tower where you belong, you – you traitor!'

Allegra, hat askew, sat with clenched hands, glaring up at the man she hated and despised most in the world. Her ankle was pounding with pain, and she could feel the impression of his fingers where he had pressed so brutally into her tender flesh.

'So now I'm a traitor, am I? Well, I may be many things but not that, you little vixen.'

Before Allegra knew what was happening, he had upended her over his knee and was slapping her bottom so hard that the screams died in her throat. Scarlet and enraged, she lashed out with her fists, and feeling the collision of her knuckles against Nash's face, once, twice, three times, while he went on calmly dealing out her punishment with the air of a man who has long waited for just this moment.

Finally, exhausted and shocked, she collapsed over his knee in a sobbing heap and that was when he tipped her on to the hard oaken floor and slammed out of the cabin, locking the door behind him.

Hours later she woke in the strange and eerie silence of the night at sea, wondering where she was for long moments before she remembered what had happened. She had dressed as a cabin boy, padding an old jerkin and hose, pinning her hair flat against her head and cramming a round, floppy cap down over her face. Having brushed her eyebrows the wrong way so that they looked thicker, and practised what she considered to be a young boy's bored and passionless expression, she had crept aboard the *Tudor Raven* late one night, tip-toeing along the deck with her heart rattling while she searched for a hidey-hole. On finding a dark, damp cavern between two wooden sections, smelling horribly of fish, she had curled up there to sleep.

She would never have believed that wooden planks could be so mercilessly hard. Waking was like being thrust into a world of premature old age, muscles and bones screaming with pain. She was chilled, ravenous, even more thirsty, and her head felt as if it had been kicked. Sliding out from her cubby hole was even more alarming. Men were padding everywhere, their huge bare feet silent on the boards, then one paused near her hiding place to do something over the side of the ship which left her speechless. Her mind filled with thoughts of saving Elizabeth and hiding away on this ship dressed as a boy, she had not considered what it would mean living as a member of the opposite sex amongst a riff-raff of hoary sailors.

Cheeks burning, she had clamped her eyes shut and wished she was back on land, the latter feeling lasting exactly two minutes. This voyage was all that she had dreamed of and longed for since she was twelve years old, and the fact that she had undertaken it to save her sister from a terrible fate was all the more exhilarating. What better chance to prove that women could be as fearless and adventurous as men? If there was a river named after Nash Hamilton in some far-off land, then why not a Pentrevick Harbour or Creek?

This thought consoling her now, she searched round the

dark cabin for something to eat or drink. Finding nothing, she sank with relief on to the bunk, her ankle throbbing. There were two locked cabinets, and no doubt Lord Hamilton kept his treasures in there, away from thieving hands. She could imagine the food, pink-rimmed roast beef, juicy and heart-warming, a succulent capon stuck with spicy cloves and served with fresh fruit sauce; syllabub, frothing and creamy, to follow. Her stomach gurgled with hunger at the memory of such meals. Even a slice of fresh-baked bread would have served her well at that moment . . .

Unable to read any of the volumes piled high on the captain's escritoire, because there was no taper to light the lamp, Allegra had no option but to lie on the bunk and wait for dawn's light. When it came, she would hammer on the door and demand to be freed. Then she would insist on being treated as befitted her station and her future relationship-by-marriage to the monster who ruled this ship . . . That was, if her relating of Hamilton's despicable treatment did not entirely change Elizabeth's intention of marrying the man. Her rump still smarted from the rude punishment he had delivered. What would Elizabeth say when she heard? She would be shocked that her betrothed had laid hands on such an intimate area of Allegra's anatomy.

The key turned suddenly, the cabin door burst open. In the small, cramped quarters, Nash Hamilton appeared like some enormous entity risen from the past and Allegra could not help but shrink back.

When he did not speak to her or acknowledge her presence, she sat there fuming, fingers tapping on the coarse linen sheet. When he looked about to leave, without having said one word, she called out, 'Oy!' but he neither faced her nor replied. Next minute, having found the objects that he wanted, he had gone, locking the door behind him.

'Oy, you, Hamilton, where's my breakfast?' Allegra yelled, banging on the oaken door with her fists. 'Where's my breakfast? I want my breakfast! How dare you lock me up, you cur!'

It was quite startling how painful wrists and hands could become after such a hasty usage of them and soon she was rubbing the bruised areas and drawing in her breath in a loud hiss. She would make him pay when he came back!

Two hours passed, then three. Straining her ears, she heard the creak of a board. He was returning! She had the surprise ready for him.

When the door swung open, the pile of heavy books crashed down onto his head, followed by the lamp which broke into large, glassy slivers, oil spilling over his head and shoulders.

The first burst of laughter was on her lips when she read the look in his eyes and then she tried to run past him to freedom, wincing at the pain in her ankle, but he caught her by her flying arms and again she was flung over his knee. This time, the beating went on for a considerable time, as did the curses, some of which were so profane that she would have paled had she heard them under normal circumstances. As it was, the imprint of his hand was emblazoned on her buttocks, probably for all time, she thought, which would be just as well when she told her tale to Elizabeth.

'I do not like spoiled children on board my ship,' Lord Hamilton was saying. 'The place for you is the nursery and that is where I shall put you with my own hands when we return to England.'

'So I'm a child now, am I? You called me a hussy before, you skunk!'

'A child hussy then, you infantile monster!'

'You, Nash Hamilton, are a knave and a poltroon of the lowest, vilest order. My father will whip you when we get back to Cornwall! When he finds out what you've done to me, you'll regret it. He'll never let you marry Elizabeth now!'

'I'll tell you what he will do, monstrous minx, he will shut you up in a nunnery in some foreign land and you will never see any of your family again. You will be the disgrace of the Pentrevicks, by God you will.'

Allegra struggled to swivel round on Hamilton's knee, the better to punch him, but her rough, loose shirt chose that moment to twist open, revealing one plump, soft white breast which gleamed like polished porcelain in the dawn light from the casement window. Letting out a scream, Allegra struggled to cover herself, while Nash Hamilton watched her efforts with a sardonic smile on his bronzed face, his blue eyes alight with satisfaction.

Then, before she could stop him, his broad, tanned hand was palming her naked breast and squeezing it with more than a little curiosity.

'So, not a child after all,' he mused.

'No, a woman, as if you did not know!'

'You are fortunate that I am a man of honour or you would be losing your virginity at this very moment.'

'No man of honour would subscribe to deflowering his future sister-in-law.'

'That is why I am not planning to deflower you, you vixen.'

The intense excitement of the encounter vanished at that moment, yet his hand was still clasping her breast and, to her dismay, she knew then what she wanted. She wanted him to tear off her shirt and breeches and make savage love to her. She had wanted it from the first moment they had met, when she was little more than a child, yet only now could she recognise her feelings for what they were. Shaken, she slid away from him, tugging at her shirt and grimacing as she stood on her swollen ankle. Perhaps there had been an ulterior motive in her determination to stow away . . . ? If so, she did not know how she was to handle it.

Nash Hamilton seemed reflective, too, as he ordered his servant to fetch her food and wine. When it arrived, it was not the succulent meat she had visualised, but tough and salty beef in a leathern strip, with a kind of gritty, baked biscuit which refused to break when she bit on it. The wine was sour and she could not swallow more than one gulp, yet the salt in the beef created a burning thirst and she would need something to assuage it. She asked the servant, a meek-faced man dressed in a plain brown doublet and breeches, if he would kindly fetch her some water.

He returned with a battered tin mug of the most vile-tasting water that she had ever failed to swallow.

'Do we not have fresh water on board ship?'

'I am sorry but we do not, m'lady,' the man replied courteously.

Allegra was enjoying being called by that title when Nash Hamilton growled from his corner, 'Mistress will do, Barkesworth. She is no lady.'

So this was to be her fare for the voyage: leather beef and murky, brackish water or sour wine! How did sailors stand it?

Later, when Barkesworth, Lord Hamilton's body servant, handed the captain clean linen, the latter proceeded to strip off to all but his hose while Allegra kept her eyes almost averted. What a broad, powerful back he had, bronzed to the most glorious russet by working uncovered at sea. There was a satisfactory bulge in his hose, too, which did not need the assistance of a cod-piece, that padded assemblage of male vanity which was worn to project the masculinity of the courtier. A blaze of heat washed over Allegra as she remembered the hand on her breast and the swirling whirlpool of emotions which had consumed her, and was doing so again now. What would he be like at kissing, at more intimate embraces . . . at the arts of love-making?

Swallowing, she thrust such passionate imaginings from her mind, but with difficulty. She was wishing that he had stripped off all his clothes and leapt on top of her, and in that ardent moment she forgot all about her sore bottom and her painful ankle.

Turning away, she concentrated on tucking her shirt into her breeches and ensuring that there was a good overlap of the coarse linen so that her breasts were thoroughly enveloped. This was, after all, her dear sister's future husband, and she must remind herself of that constantly. She had stowed away on this ship so that she herself could find Elizabeth, or help to find her, instead of pacing up and down in Pentrevick Manor, chewing on her fingers and sighing at the stars. He is Elizabeth's betrothed, she now told herself firmly. Elizabeth loves this man, for all that he is a brute and a savage, and, presumably, he loves her, for he asked her to wed him quickly enough. Elizabeth and Nash Hamilton love one another passionately, yes, passionately and, even if they do not, it would be a heinous sin for me to think of this man as anything but forbidden to me.

Over and over she said these words to herself until her passions cooled and she was able to keep her thoughts on the matters in hand.

Dressed in fresh clothes, Lord Hamilton faced her, his expression quizzical, yet stern.

'As it is too late for you to be taken back to land, you realise that you will be expected to carry your weight while aboard this vessel?'

'Carry my weight? What do you mean?'

'There are many sailors who fear the presence of a female on board their ship. They say it brings ill fortune and danger. Many would be hostile to you if you were to walk on deck, especially dressed in that ridiculous garb. So far, only my servant and I know that you are here.'

'And what does that mean?'

'It means, Mistress Pentrevick, that you are to stay here in this cabin and be locked away for your own safety. I cannot protect you day and night, so I have no alternative. Your father would never forgive me if I allowed anyone to harm you.'

'No one is going to harm me! I am more than capable of taking care of myself!' Allegra squared her shoulders.

'I was not aware that you had ever been attacked by a pack of sex-crazed sailors, and succeeded in fighting them off. When did this unfortunate event take place, Mistress Pentrevick?' Nash looked at her scathingly.

'It, that is, it never has, and well you know it! I am sure that your crew would never attack me. How would they dare do such a thing?'

'Men behave like wild animals when they are together. Another few days at sea and they will fall on you like ravening beasts if they are given the chance.'

Nash Hamilton was now so close to her that she could see the sparkle of gold where the morning sun enamelled his eyelashes and the thatch of crisp hair which grew on his chest. She was having difficulty breathing. A hand was crushing her lungs, preventing air from reaching them.

'Do I really need to go out of this cabin to face a wild animal?' She flung her head contemptuously. 'Is it not your own ungovernable lusts of which you speak?'

'What do you know about such passions, little girl? I wager that you have no knowledge of anything more serious than a kiss on the cheek, if that. When you grow up, you will learn that you know nothing now.'

'Can you read my thoughts then? If so, what am I thinking now?' She filled her mind with a string of insults, a gentle smile playing on her lips.

'I speak from my own experience. When I was thirteen . . .'

'I am eighteen years of age, not thirteen!'

'Eighteen, eh? And still flat-chested as a child and without any hips. No wonder no man has sued for your hand. 'Tis plain that you will end your days a spinster.'

She could not believe what she was hearing. She, flat-chested? Never!

'How would you know what any man has done? You profess such great knowledge, yet your words are empty prattle, the mouthings of a boy in a man's world, an ignorant boy who has not yet found the strength to tilt!'

'I, a boy?' He threw back his great golden head, his laughter booming around the cabin. 'I, an ignorant boy?'

'Not only a boy but a yellow-legged knave no more fit for captaining a ship than for running after hounds with a water dish! Or, or, clearing up the filthy straw from the place where beasts have slept!'

'What spirit, what imagination . . .' Nash Hamilton came closer still, leaning over her so that she felt small and fragile as a rosebud about to be crushed by a giant. 'Why are you not writing sonnets, child-woman? Stories of unrequited love and heartbroken maids pining for their knights . . . Would that not be more suited to your enfeebled talents?'

She kicked him so hard that she almost fainted with the jarring pain which cut through her toes, while the pain from the swollen ankle on which she was keeping her balance chose that moment to stab violently. Paling, she fought for control, not wanting to break into tears in front of him.

'Did the little infant hurt her tiny toes, then?' Hamilton crooned, taking her arm as if to help her to a seat but instead tugging her close to him. Eye to eye, they stared at one another fiercely, while, amazingly, all the pain in Allegra's limbs ebbed away as if she were cured by a miraculous healing touch. As it was impossible to drag her gaze away from his, she sagged against him weakly, feeling every ounce the foolish, conquered female.

'We must not forget why we are on board this ship, Mistress Pentrevick. We are searching for your sister, my future bride. She is in the hands of the Amir Adem Ali, or one of his men, and I shall not rest until I have found and rescued her.'

'That is why I am here, too,' Allegra whispered. 'I want to find Elizabeth as much as you do. Do you think I would have stowed away dressed as a boy for any other reason?'

'I know very little about you, Mistress Pentrevick, except what I have heard from others and none of that was favourable. Termagant, baggage, dragon, vixen, those are only a few of the words which I have heard used to describe you.'

'I see. And you listen avidly to gossip, you let it sway your judgement? Really, I had thought you more intelligent and perceptive than that. Those who are swayed by gossip flow to the left then to the right, then back again until they are dizzy, and all this over lies, exaggerations and half-truths. They deserve what they get!'

'The little philosopher, now, eh? How quaint in one so young, and how unexpected in *you*.'

'If it is unexpected then it is because you are inept at judging character, Lord Hamilton, but believe me, I have *your* character judged most accurately.'

At this, to her disappointment, he withdrew, locking the door behind him as before.

'*Oy!*' she called after him, like a country yokel herding sheep, but it was too late. She wanted to know where she could attend to nature's demands and how it would be possible if she were not allowed to leave this cabin knowing that asking him would cause her intense embarrassment, but that not asking would cause an even greater problem in the near future. She hoped that Barkesworth would return. His face was a little softer than that of his intransigent master.

Eventually, she used a silver-gilt dish which stood on the escritoire, then, pulling open the casement window so that a blast of salt-laden air blew in her face, she emptied the contents into the sea, sighing with relief that no one had entered the cabin while she was thus occupied.

The coarse linen of her shirt was beginning to inflame her skin, but that was nothing to the pulsing throb in her sprained ankle. Hobbling to the bunk, she rested her leg high on a wool-covered hassock and tried to calm her thoughts. She had come in search of her sister, *hadn't she*? She would have had to be moon-fevered to stow away because she was in love with Nash Hamilton. He was brutal, insensitive, cruel, abrupt and ruthless; he was swayed by idle gossip (a most contemptible quality) and he had no regard for her feelings. Besides that, he believed that a woman should bow and scrape to her husband, produce an infant annually and spend her entire time tending to her family's needs and ensuring that their home was bright, spotless and shining. How did she know this? Because her sister had told her so. Elizabeth fully supported this view, which was why she and Hamilton were betrothed.

Oh, poor Elizabeth, where would she be now, what would she be doing? One heard appalling stories of slave ships, the filth and hunger, the lack of fresh water, the darkness of the hold where slaves were packed. Would they treat her lovely sister like that? Surely not, for she was so delicate and fresh, yet how did anyone know what those heathens were like? Men who bartered with human flesh would hardly be possessed of compassionate, civilised natures.

She began to pray for Elizabeth's safety, succeeding in gathering some semblance of serenity into her mind, deciding then that it was the enforced inactivity which was making her feel so restless and wretched. Normally, she rode for three hours every morning, or walked on the shore, burning off the tumult of nervous energy which drove her.

At midday Barkesworth appeared with food, the same fare as breakfast, a strip of leather beef awash with salt crystals, a rocky biscuit, and a choice of sour wine or murky, warm water. Looking at the tray in dismay, she felt her gorge rise. She could not do battle with such food again, yet there seemed to be no alternative.

'Is there no fresh food aboard?' she asked the manservant,

who looked at her askance. 'No fresh-baked bread, butter or fruit, no cheese?'

'And where would we find such things aboard the *Tudor Raven*, Mistress?' Barkesworth said. 'Weevils and mould and the rats get everything as it is, without us putting down such delicacies for their bellies.'

'Weevils and rats . . . ?' Allegra looked at her tray. 'Will . . . Have rats been near this?'

'Well, I cannot say, mistress. They may well have been. 'Tis not easy to keep them and food apart on board a ship.'

'I see.' Allegra pushed the tray back towards the man. 'Is there . . . I mean, could you arrange that I make a visit to the – the closet, please?'

'The closet, mistress? Oh, but we do not have closets aboard ship. 'Tis a rough, tough world for a leddy to understand I'm sure, but that is how it is, ye see. Men are able to make do and mend in a way that leddies find highly improper.'

'No closet? Then what shall I do!' Allegra wailed.

'Well, ye'll have to do like we menfolk do, mistress.' Barkesworth pointed to the bowl on the writing table and gestured towards the window.

'You mean I must use that during the whole voyage?'

' 'Tis better than the men do, mistress. Over the side without the bowl is for the likes o' the rest of us, and dratted uncomfortable it can be when there's gales blowing and the rain dashing against our . . . Ahem, my apologies, mistress. I quite got carried away there, if ye'll forgive me.'

Allegra slumped on her bunk when the door closed behind Barkesworth. This was not how she had imagined life at sea. But she would make it exciting and challenging if only that savage, Nash Hamilton, would let her out of here. The crew falling on her indeed! What balderdash! Other women had travelled by sea and not been attacked by sailors, not that she knew of anyway. Time stretched before her, boring and empty, while her ankle seemed to be swelling before her eyes.

'Go to sea and find adventure,' she muttered to herself. 'Out on the ocean wave the whole world of thrilling delight will fall into your lap. Storms, pirates, sea monsters, uprisings amongst the crew, finding lost treasure . . . all this and more to delight you, Allegra Pentrevick, if you were not a prisoner in this stuffy room!'

By late afternoon she was so ravenous that she nibbled at the leather beef and rock biscuit once again, sipping the murky water and wrinkling her nose. What if a gigantic rat had scuttled across this very plate and touched this food with his dirty feet? Her stomach turned, and she put a hand to her mouth.

'Enjoying the tranquillity of my cabin?' Lord Hamilton loomed over her. 'Not eaten your beef? You shall never make a sailor with an empty belly. Here, let me cut the meat for you. This is a real sea delicacy. On some ships, the food is contaminated with rat droppings and quite inedible, but this is not.'

'Barkesworth said that rats were everywhere on this ship!'

'Did he? Oh, not everywhere, I do assure you. Come, taste this beef.'

'I do not wish to, thank you!'

'You will regret it by nightfall if you do not eat.'

'Shall there not be an evening meal?'

'Of a sort. Gruel and ale. Does that appeal more than this?' He pointed to the nearly black beef.

'Decidedly!'

'Then we must ensure that you receive extra large helpings of both. Barkesworth will see to it.'

'Where will you be?'

'About my business. Why do you ask?'

'I thought that you might dine here with me.'

'I would eat in here were it not for you. It is not seemly that we eat together alone. Would you not agree?'

'Why not? We seem to have done everything else!'

'Not quite.' His eyes glittered menacingly. She thought she knew what he was thinking: he would like to tear off her clothes and rape her.

'Please, I need some company!'

'Barkesworth can dine with you.'

'I meant you, intelligent company!' She hung her head.

'So now you seek my company, eh?'

'Only because there is no one else!'

'I see.'

He stared down at her white face for a moment and then suddenly his fingers were trailing in her reddish-gold curls and brushing against her cheek almost as if by accident, a dart of flame spearing into her face where his hand touched her. Furious, she turned her head away and then wished that she had rushed into his arms. Jesu, but she must not think like that! Was she a wanton, as he thought? Near him, she lost all control and her thoughts were flooded with sexual longings. How would she hold back during the long weeks ahead? God forgive her if she weakened! But she must not, she must not. He was Elizabeth's.

Chapter Three

During the first weeks at sea they were fortunate where the weather was concerned, even escaping the infamous Channel storms. Fate was shortly to make up for that.

'I shall not be seasick, I shall not be seasick!' Allegra muttered beneath her breath as she clung to the bunkhead to save herself from being tossed on to the floor. Now it did not matter if they brought her a whole cask of beef, for she had never felt less hungry in her life.

For seven hours the seas pushed and thrust at the *Tudor Raven*, the rains crashing down relentlessly, drowning the creaking protests of the woodwork, drenching the sails and rigging.

When Barkesworth came in to see how she was faring, she sat up, putting on a bright face, but the moment that he had gone, she lay down again, the cabin pitching and tossing before her eyes, her stomach following suit. Darkness swallowed them and she did not get up to light the lamps. The mere thought of the cloying scent of oil upset her. She had heard of sea voyagers praying to die when assailed by seasickness and she had never understood how it could be so bad. Now she did. She would never look down on such poor travellers again. Her stomach was on the far side of the cabin, shaking like syllabub, and she might never be able to walk again.

She tried to remove her mind from the sick dizziness by counting the weeks since they had set out and recalling what had happened. She should have kept a journal and noted down all the fiery dialogues she and Lord Hamilton had exchanged. What sportive winter reading that would have made when she got back to Cornwall! What arguments and tussles they had had, all caused by her, of course, which brought a pallid smile to her face. He had insisted that she exercise with him, saying that her legs and muscles would grow flabby from her enforced inactivity.

'And why is it enforced, Lord Hamilton? Because you keep me prisoner here!' she had snapped, tossing her head.

'That is a thought, Mistress Pentrevick. The decks need swabbing . . . Wonderful exercise, shall you begin the work now? Barkesworth will have a mop and bucket nearby, I am sure, and you can be out on deck in no time at all.'

'Swabbing? Is that washing?' She eyed him suspiciously.

'Yes, it should not take you longer than two or three days. The decks are somewhat large, but I think you will cope admirably.'

She did not trust him. He might be planning to have her thrown overboard!

'I would prefer a more ladylike exercise, if you do not mind.'

'And is not washing floors ladylike? Indeed, I had thought women were made for such homely chores.' His eyes twinkled.

'Not this woman!'

'Then shall we try out the exercises in the cabin?'

Silently, she nodded, and that was how they came to be standing before the open window, breathing the sea air in large, fresh gulps, swinging their arms up and down and running on the spot. After that, it was twisting to the left and right, swinging down to touch the toes and reaching up high, to stretch the shoulders. Allegra was pink and breathless after that first session, but determined not to surrender. Every morning, they had carried out the exercise programme, she continuing resolute that she would not say it was too demanding. In time, she was glad of the strengthening of her muscles, and she began to feel more alert.

A fresh gust of wind buffeting the ship, she gulped and clapped a palm over her mouth.

When she had sneaked on to the ship, she had not realised how long the journey would be. Not a few weeks as she had envisaged in her ignorance, but month after month, leaving far behind England, the Channel, the Mediterranean and heading for the Arabian Ocean and Cana, the nearest port to the palace of the Amir Adem Ali.

Had it not been for her frequent lively wrangles with Lord Hamilton, and her determination to prove that she could equal him where stamina was concerned, the voyage would have dragged interminably. Eventually, he did allow her out to walk a space, but only while he and Barkesworth kept watch to ensure that none of the crew saw her, and in between, she was still locked in the cabin. She found the sight of the ring of ocean surrounding them, and the blazing sun above highly exhilarating. The sea was like another world, the one which had enthralled so many of her ancestors.

She was woken from an exhausted sleep by a hand on her shoulder. A lamp was dazzling in her face so she could not see who held it.

'Are you recovered?'

It was his voice. How dared he appear after leaving her to suffer alone all this time!

'Would you care if I had died during the storm, Lord Hamilton? This might well be my shade that is talking to you now.'

'I doubt it. Spirits do not sleep naked, revealing large quantities of bare pink flesh.'

'Oh!' Furious, she tugged up the rough sheet which she had pushed away because of the heat and the material's coarse texture. How long had he been staring down at her breasts before waking her?

'I take it that you are unharmed, then, and in your customary fine fettle and bursting with health?'

She stared up at him, wondering what insinuations lay behind his words.

'Why did you take so long to enquire after my condition? No one has been near me for hours!'

'There is the little matter of keeping the ship afloat, small I know by comparison to asking after your health, but nonetheless somewhat vital to the dozens of men on board.'

Ignoring his barb, she said, 'Where are we now? Cathay?'

Throwing back his golden head he roared with laughter, the lamplight making a shining nimbus around his hair.

'Jesu, but you have a wild imagination! Cathay? Why Cathay?'

'You said the East . . . You said the man who had taken my sister lived in the East! Is not Cathay in the East?' She scowled, feeling an idiot.

'It is, but on the other side of the world when it comes to navigation. We head for Arabia . . . the land of Islam and Mohammed, of veiled women and unlicensed men. If you ever conjectured that English women were housebound and prevented from exploring the world, then wait until you reach Arabia. Black robes and a lack of freedom they call purdah, for the God of Islam frowns on women revealing their beauty before anyone but their husband, and he is allowed four wives if he so chooses. Of course if he is a Sultan, then he may decide that he wants five hundred concubines as well.'

'What are concubines? Children?' Allegra asked innocently.

'Unmarried wives is the politest description I can give.'

'Unmarried? Living unlawfully, out of wedlock, you mean? But what of their poor children?'

'Their children are as likely to be the next Sultan as are those of the legal wives. There is none of this illegitimacy and stain of sin in Islam. Not for that cause, anyway.'

'Five hundred concubines! But how does the Sultan . . . I mean, he cannot possibly have time for so many wives. Can he?'

'Much of it is show. Power and riches displayed by the large number of wives a man can afford, but there is no doubt that many of them will be with child at any given time, and not by the eunuchs who guard them, for they have been emasculated.'

Seeing her about to ask what that meant, but not daring, he added: 'They have had their sex taken away, so that they cannot father children or behave improperly with the concubines.'

Allegra remained silent. Men having their sex taken away? It sounded barbaric, and she did not wish to ask how it was done. All those women – five hundred of them – belonging to one man. She could not imagine anything less like the Virgin Queen with her vows of marriage to her kingdom and her refusal to wed even one prince.

The night was calm now, almost ghostly in its serenity, after the tumult of the storms. Allegra lay silently in her bunk, the sheet tucked under her chin, while Nash Hamilton stared down at her, the lamp held stiffly in his hand as if it were frozen. She was sure that he was going to move closer, try to kiss her perhaps, and she had her knee ready to lash out at him. If he touched her he would regret it for ever! She would tear out his hair, stab his eyes, scratch his face . . .

Moving swiftly, he was gone before she could summon her next words. Then she felt such an emptiness that she almost called him back. If he had kissed her . . . If he had tried to touch her, she was sure that she would have gouged out his eyes. Wouldn't she?

Barkesworth brought her breakfast. A log of bread, a plank of beef and a mug of sour wine.

'None of that fresh, sweet water is left then?' she said acidly.

'No, mistress. Ye'll have to get accustomed to the wine. 'Twon't hurt ye. I drink it.'

'Then you are a stronger man than I am!' Allegra muttered into her mug.

Barkesworth went out, closing the door carefully behind him. Not hearing the grate of the key this time, Allegra leapt to her feet, almost spilling the tray's contents to the floor. Creeping to the door, she turned the handle and the door opened. Such excitement swept through her that she almost forgot to breathe. Stepping outside was like being born anew into a wonderful world of thrilling delight. Turning a corner of the narrow, dark and tarry-scented corridor, she came to an abrupt halt. There was Nash Hamilton speaking to his servant. Straining her ears, she heard what they were saying.

'She accepted the food?'

'Aye, sir. Not a word of complaint this time.'

'Continue to give her the same fare. 'Twill do more for her rebellious spirit than a lifetime in a nunnery.'

It was at that moment that Allegra smelt the most divine odour of roasting meat wafting down the corridor towards her. Beef? No, a different yet equally delicious scent. Her stomach growled so violently that she was sure they would hear, but they did not. Meat was being cooked somewhere on this ship! But had Lord Hamilton not said that they all lived on stony biscuits and salt beef?

'Shall ye be wanting the Malvoisie or the Burgundy tonight, my lord?' Barkesworth was asking. Her ears tingled.

'With the lamb? Burgundy I think, please, Barkesworth, but make sure it is not chilled.'

'And fruit syllabub to follow, my lord?'

'Yes, excellent.'

Allegra felt her legs turn to tissue. They were talking of the most luscious food, real, normal, fresh and beautifully cooked food while she had been living on leather and stones for weeks, washed down by foul water! Such a burst of rage followed the weakness that she almost leapt towards the two men to hammer their heads together. With extraordinary self-control, she padded back to the cabin to prepare her revenge.

By dinner-time, she had fashioned herself a dubious gown from the coarse linen sheet. As it covered her in the most important places and would have done justice to a Grecian nymph, she combed her hair into a wild, loose style, as befitted her virginity. There was nothing she could wear to alleviate the plainness of the cut, but she hoped that her smile would suffice.

When Barkesworth appeared with the tray of leather and stones, Allegra smiled sweetly.

'Would you tell your master that I shall dine with him tonight? I am ready, as you can see.'

Scooping up the blood-red tapestry cloth which covered the back of the carved bench, she donned it like a gypsy shawl, stalked to the door and waited there for Barkesworth to escort her. He, red-faced, did not know what to do.

'Well, am I to wait here all night? Tell your master!'

The man was back in a few minutes, his hair sticking up in spikes, as if he had run his hands through it in agitation.

'Lord Hamilton will dine with ye, mistress, if ye'll follow me.'

Triumphant, Allegra stalked after the man, and soon she was entering a small cabin not unlike the one she had been locked in for many weeks. Softly lamplit, it was scented divinely with roast meat, juices and sauces, and there was a flask of red wine on the table.

Seating herself, her smile sweet and mild, Allegra gazed up at Hamilton. He was dressed in a rich, dark blue doublet embroidered with a darker blue silk, and his Venetians were of old-gold corded velvet.

'Is this some special feast day?' she asked innocently.

'Indeed it is. My birthday, mistress.'

'Of course, and you were going to invite me for dinner, were you not?' She looked up at him from beneath thick, dark lashes.

'But of course.' He looked uncomfortable. Good!

'It is a little warm in here. Might we have the casement open, Lord Hamilton?'

'Of course.'

Allegra relaxed back in her seat, eyeing the enormous platter of juicy red meat swimming in succulent juices, and the flask of French wine.

'A man of taste I see.' She nodded towards the wine.

She was waiting for the right moment and it came as Barkesworth distracted the captain's attention for a moment. In one movement, Allegra had scooped up the platter of meat, piling the wine bottle on top, and emptied the entire contents out of the window. When she had done it, seeing their shocked expressions, she could not stop laughing. She laughed so much that her side hurt and she had to fall on to the chair, gasping for breath.

If he put her over his knee again, well, that was just too unfortunate. She had gained her revenge and it was very sweet.

Barkesworth went out of the door, returning a few minutes later with another platter of meat looking remarkably like the first. Allegra gaped, but was ready to repeat her revenge.

'If you would care to look out of the window, mistress, you will see that this cabin looks on to a lower deck and not the sea, so our dinner is saved.' Hamilton's eyes were glittering.

Barkesworth tittered, then guffawed and then both the men were bellowing with laughter.

'The wine bottle broke though, did it not?' Allegra scowled, tapping her foot.

'Yes, but then I have forty more bottles aboard, so that does not bother me unduly. Actually they were a gift from your father to celebrate my betrothal to Elizabeth.'

Allegra clamped her lips shut and watched as the servant carved the meat, her stomach beginning to gurgle and rumble most embarrassingly, her face turning pink. When her serving of meat was placed on her platter, three days seemed to elapse before her eating implements were provided. Falling on the meat she devoured it ravenously, shocked at how sore her mouth felt after days of tugging and chewing on salt beef. Another bottle of wine having been brought by the obsequious Barkesworth, this was opened and wine poured out for Allegra. Lifting the goblet to her lips, she had a vision of sipping this same Burgundy at home, her father and Elizabeth sitting with her at table. Her heart twisted. Would she ever see either of them again?

The wine tasted like nectar and went straight to her head. When she replaced the goblet, she missed the edge of the solid oak table and the delicate Venetian glass smashed.

'Mistress Pentrevick is feeling contumacious again,' Hamilton explained to his servant. 'Perhaps you would fetch her a tin mug next time? The battered one in my medicine cabinet should be ideal.'

'Of course, my lord.'

They were laughing at her; jeering because she was a woman and they thought women stupid and ignorant. She knew what they were thinking and she despised them for it, this infuriating gilt-haired lord and his obedient servant. Rising in one swift, haughty movement, she somehow found that her dish was on her knee, the meat juices splashed on the sheet which was serving for a gown. Did it matter? She did not care. Heading for the door was not as easy as she had thought. The room seemed to be curving and swaying around her, as though she were looking into a glass bauble. The door refusing to come closer, she paused, not sure what to do.

'The lady requires assistance back to her chamber,' Lord Hamilton said. 'Shall you do it, or shall I?' Master and servant exchanged glances while Allegra's rage swelled. How dare they discuss her as if she were a side of ham!

'I need no one's aid!' she snorted, then, stepping on the rough hem of the gown, she felt it being tugged from her breasts, rushed to support it, and tripped over a small embroidered stool. Stars wafted past her vision as her head made contact with the carved cabinet in the corner.

She lay there stunned for what seemed to be an age, while Hamilton did not so much as approach her. Nothing would urge her to beg for his hand, however. Head aching, she grappled with the sheet and, after an unladylike tussle, managed to get to her feet, glaring at Lord Hamilton accusingly. There was a smile of amusement playing round his lips, and that sparkle in his eyes which made her three times as angry as before.

'The entertainment is over now, gentlemen!' she snapped, 'You may return to your mundane amusements. What is it to be tonight, Lord Hamilton? Watching one of your poor sailors walking the plank, or whipping some young cabin boy who has annoyed you?'

Barkesworth brushed past her, the tray laden with dirty platters, and closed the door behind him, his face a mask.

'My good friend will be washing those dishes and I shall be writing in my journal, if that is of any interest to you.'

Allegra's eyes glittered. So he kept a journal. Now that was something she would love to read! She was positive that there would be ample material therein to turn Elizabeth against him for ever. No doubt he bragged of his many conquests and wrote of them in detail. Her cheeks flushed at the thought. She believed that nothing would protect a woman from this man's lusts, not even the fact that she was to be his future sister-in-law.

'Shall I escort you to your cabin?'

'No thank you. I can manage alone.' She tossed her head.

'It would be wiser if I came with you.'

The return journey seemed longer, but then she did not have anticipation to lighten her way. Lord Hamilton kept close behind her, and she was glad, for the corridor was darker now and leaping shadows grimaced on the walls where the lamps threw a pallid gold patina. The wheezing creak of the ship was deafening here, and the scent of salt, tar and oil quite suffocating in places.

'I suppose you are going to lock me in again?' They stood just outside the door of her cabin.

'It is a question of locking others out as much as ensuring that you do not get yourself into any mischief.'

'What do you think I plan to do, try and swim home?'

'Hardly, but ships are dangerous places for the unaware. A sudden tilt when the wind rises and you could be flung overboard.'

'That you would relish, I know.'

'Scooping pieces of your flesh and bloody limbs out of the sea after some ravenous shark has attacked you is not my notion of enjoyment.'

'Sharks! They eat people, do they not?'

'Yes, decidedly, and we are in their waters now. They prefer the warmer seas. If you took it into your head to try and swim, or to set out in one of the longboats, then you would last perhaps one hour or two – in the boat, that is. Only a few moments in the sea itself. I once saw a man devoured by a shark. I watched him being swallowed, until I could see only his head, the eyes fluttering and the screams choking in his throat. That was a monster, but there are smaller sharks which are happy with a few inches of leg or arm for their first course.'

'You did not try to save the poor man of course?'

'I was fighting off a second shark at the time, so no, alas I could not. We were afloat on a raft after a shipwreck.'

'You were the only survivor?'

'I was.'

'So you let everyone else die? I thought captains were supposed to go down with their ships!'

His eyes flashed with anger, but his voice stayed calm.

'The ship did go down with me, but as I was still alive, I swam away, holding on to the mast which had broken in the storm, so I was not sucked under with the vessel.'

She wanted to know more. What was it like to be shipwrecked in tropical seas? How had he survived? What had he felt like, what had he eaten? But she was too busy assuming the haughtiest expression of disdain which she could muster.

Turning, she opened the door and stepped into the cabin, finding him close behind when she had planned to slam the door and put a cabinet against it.

'Did you require something, my lord?'

'It is my cabin after all.' He raised one dark-gold brow.

'I am tired, so if you would please make haste.'

'Make haste? What were you expecting me to do?'

He stood over her, towering and omnipotent, intimidating her, although she would not admit to that.

Cheeks rosy, she prodded him in the stomach with one sharp-tipped finger.

'If you would collect whatever it is you want and go!'

'This is what I want!'

To her horror and delight, he pulled her close, clamping her with his arms so that she could barely breathe and then crushing her mouth with his. It was fortunate that he was holding her tightly for she would have fallen, such was her excess of passion and dismay. To be kissed like this was rapture, paradise! How had she survived all these years without such kisses? Modesty and morality ran laughing hand-in-hand out of the window, and she responded as lustily as the most ardent young woman could.

She took herself by surprise, but she surprised him even more so. He had planned to infuriate her, to show her who was master and that she had better be wary of him, yet now here she was, responding more searingly than any girl he had ever kissed. Now it was he who was taken aback, knowing that her passion was rousing him beyond the point of sensibility and wisdom. They clung together, demented with longing, kissing repeatedly, she gripping his waist and he gripping hers so that their bodies were pressed, curving together, his roused, hers waiting for the beautiful finale.

'You swine!' she groaned.

'You hussy!' he snarled.

'How could you do this to me?'

'God only knows!'

'This is wrong, so wrong, we must not do it!'

'But it is what you want, is it not? You want me tearing off your clothes and kissing your breasts, your thighs. That is what you came for, is it not, little she-wolf?'

She slapped his face so hard that her hand went momentarily numb.

'You are the most evil, selfish and immoral man I have ever met!'

'That is not saying much at your age,' he retorted, ruefully rubbing his cheek.

'How could you take advantage of me like this?'

'Am I the first then?'

'But of course! What do you think I am? No, do not answer that!'

'Admit it, my little she-wolf. You followed me because you wanted me, is that not so? You thought Elizabeth would never find out if we made love on my ship.'

The implications of his words struck her to the heart.

'You are vile and arrogant, and I wish you to go! Now!' Opening the door, she pointed out into the corridor.

'No one need ever know if I spend the night with you, little she-wolf. I shall tell no one. Admit that is what you want, admit it!'

'Get out you – you shark!' she cried, reaching for the lamp to throw at him, but he had gone.

She pushed the cabinet against the door, then curled up on the bunk and stared into the darkness. The nights were hot now and she could not sleep. She yearned for a flask of cool spring water, but even more she yearned for Nash Hamilton to be lying beside her, to make love to her through the night as the ship sped along through the glossy, shark-infested waters.

Chapter Four

It was dawn when she woke to find the ship tilting again and rain smashing against the window. Groaning, she staggered to her feet to smooth out the crinkled sheet. She had fallen asleep after hours of pitching between longing and guilt. Her eyes were red from sleeplessness so the room was blurred.

The wind was raging, a frightening sound which made her think of wolves, howling and ravenous for blood. Lying down was the safest thing to do, so she climbed back on to the bunk and tucked the sheet firmly at either side to provide some security.

She had thought the earlier storm bad but this one was terrifying. It was a wonder that the glass did not shatter; any moment she feared that the screaming wind would spear into the cabin and beat her to death. A crash made her jump in alarm. Was the ship breaking up? Jesu, where was Nash? What if they all drowned, what if . . .

The door was flung open and there was Nash as if summoned by her wishful thinking. Crying his name, she reached up to hold him.

'Shall we die? Is the ship sinking?'

'It is bad. Pull on some clothes, warm ones. Breeches and shirt would be wisest, and wrap yourself in a blanket. I have food and a cloak. There is not much else we can do save wait and pray.'

She felt the ship judder then, as if it were surrendering its ghost. There was an eerie sighing sound which made her heart pound, as it grew to a piercing wail.

'A cyclone. It is heading straight for us.'

'Holy Mother!' She fell against him, her legs shivering with terror. Oh, how brave she had planned to be, but there were moments when courage was stupidity.

'We have done all that we can on deck. The men are prepared. Some have lashed themselves to the mast or the helm. Loose or free, the risk is the same. Tied too tightly you go down with the ship. Untied, you at least have a chance of swimming free. I have done it before, remember?'

Blue eyes, as bright and comforting as speedwells, gazed into hers.

'The – the sharks . . . ? Will they be waiting?'

'We shall make a raft. Land is not too far away,' he lied.

The piercing wail was very close now. The ship seemed to be held aloft, waiting tautly for its aggressor. When the whirling wind drove through, twisting, coiling like a dervish, it would scoop up the ship as if it were a toy and fling it down again on its side, hammering it into the water so that it would be submerged before half of it would bob up again, broken and reeling.

On their way up to the maindeck, Allegra and Nash were flung into the air, the wind scorching their faces, tearing at their hair and clothes, sweeping their feet from under them, and blasting them out into nothingness before they smashed down into the sea, yards from the drowning ship.

Allegra could not swim. It was not on the curriculum for Elizabethan ladies. She dipped beneath the waves, shocked and struggling, fighting to keep her head out of the water, her eyes scouring the sea's surface for her saviour. Long, terrifying hours seemed to pass before she saw him swimming towards her with smooth, powerful movements. He called her name and she sobbed out his. When he reached her, they clung together. She could see little for the salty wet hair in her eyes, and she had swallowed so much water that she felt green. Tucking her beneath his arm, Nash swam in search of a plank or spar to use as a buoy. In the far distance was a tiny black dot: an island of a sort, too small to be on his charts, but there all the same.

Swimming around in the flotsam-dotted sea, the rain drenching their faces, and the fear of sharks paralysing Allegra's legs, they eventually found a spar which had broken loose. Clinging to this with one arm, and with Allegra tucked under the other, Nash began to swim. They had not seen another soul, nor heard a human sound. Not one cry. It was chilling, and best not dwelt on as Nash swam the long, arduous distance to the tiny black dot.

Allegra fainted from shock, and fear of the sharks which she was sure would eat her legs at any moment, then when she opened her eyes, she thought she was having a nightmare. The sky was inky dark, the stars low and sparkling like watchful eyes, the moon glowing opalescently. Her body was freezing, so cold that she could not feel her limbs, and she began to sob.

'Weeping? After I have gone to all this trouble to arrange an idyll for us? A beautiful, tropical island just made for lovers . . . golden sands, palm trees, strange birds with brilliant plumage . . . and here you are crying your heart out!'

She wept all the more at his courageous badinage. How long had he been swimming, supporting her dead weight without a murmur of complaint nor any sign of weariness? Yet his face was pallid in the moonlight and she knew that he must be exhausted.

Something bobbed against her leg and she screamed with terror, but it was not a shark. Kicking it out of the way, Nash told her to look in the opposite direction, for a corpse was more frightening than a piece of flotsam. Barkesworth must have tried to swim, or else been caught in a current before his strength had deserted him. If he had not had to save this headstrong little minx, then he might have been able to help his loyal servant. They had been together for thirteen years. Clamping his jaw shut, he continued to swim. In the name of God, where was that accursed island?

Birds! He was half asleep, leaning heavily on the spar, his legs too weary to paddle any more when the bird-song jarred into his consciousness. The island was close!

A shimmering figure bathed in celestial light leaned over Allegra, offering her crystal-cool water to drink. Greedily she swallowed, the water restoring life to her freezing, wooden limbs.

'Go back,' said the angel, 'go back. Your time is not yet come.'

Her eyes snapped open then to furry-black darkness and the touch of grit scraping against her body. Fear filled her when she could not recall what had happened. Then, remembering, she looked around in terror for Nash. Had he drowned while saving her life? Mother of God, she would never forgive herself . . . How would she live without him?

'Nash!' she cried. 'Nash!' Her entire heart sounded in her voice.

'I am here.' The voice was close by and she gasped. Turning, her eyes becoming accustomed to the darkness, she saw him lying a few feet away.

'Is it really you? I thought you had drowned. I thought I was alone!' She began to sob.

'Cry all you want, little one.'

Dragging his exhausted body towards her, Nash enveloped her in his strong brown arms, covering her icy body with his so that his warmth flowed into hers and was her.

'I am sorry, so sorry, this is all – my – fault!' she hiccoughed.

'I think God and destiny may have had more to do with it. A cyclone out of nowhere, a storm such as I have never seen before. Yes, it was fate.'

'What are we going to do? We shall die here!'

'That seems a little on the gloomy side. I have no immediate plans to stop breathing. We shall find food when it is light and build a shelter. You will change your mind when you see this island in the baking sunlight with the glittering seas and the sparkling, silvery sand. You will enjoy every moment then.'

Having digested his words, Allegra said: 'What about fierce natives? Will they not kill us?'

'I think this island is uninhabited. In fact, I am quite sure it is. It is too small to be charted, but if it is the one I think it is, then it has been given a name by a learned philosopher: the Garden of Allah, so it must be beautiful. He was shipwrecked here about seventy years ago, and he was rescued. So you see, there is hope for us. I read the account of his survival.'

'The Garden of Allah. Does that mean I shall have to dress in purdah and wear a veil?' Allegra attempted a jest although she was shuddering with the cold.

'Only if some kindly Sultana has left her wardrobe here. As for myself, I would be more than happy to see you go naked.'

She punched him hard, right in the neck, and then was pitifully sorry. In return, he kissed her, knowing that roused passions are the surest way of avoiding death by freezing, and they went on kissing and hugging tightly until they fell into an exhausted slumber.

The cackle of a bird woke them. It was an almost human sound, and Allegra leapt awake, shaking with fright, expecting to see a massive black man standing over her with a spear. She had seen paintings of them in the book on explorers which was in her father's library. They wore feathers like fans in their hair and their eyes were big and white, their noses flat and broad, their mouths thick-lipped . . . and they wore very little in the way of clothes, just a strip of cloth between their thighs.

The sun was already hot, and the birds were swooping in search of food. Close by was the soothing swish of the waves, and an exotic array of plants and vegetation met her eyes as she took in their surroundings. This was the Garden of Allah indeed.

Getting to their feet, they rubbed life back into their cold, stiff limbs. Allegra critically surveyed Nash, his clothes sodden and salt-stained, his gold hair blackly wet against his head. She did not realise what a sight she looked, her cabin boy's clothes similarly drenched and crumpled, her long russet-gold hair sleek as sealskin down her back. There was dried salt on her lashes and brows, and thick on her mouth as she licked it off, wrinkling her nose. As she did so, a large, domed stone on which she was just about to sit began to crawl away. Leaping back, she gave a cry.

'That is a turtle. He has more right here than us, and he will do you no harm whatsoever.'

'He is enormous! Are you sure he would not bite?'

'No, but we might bite him if we have no alternative. Turtles make excellent soup.'

'But that thick shell . . .'

'The flesh inside is good. Now, you must stay here while I explore the island.'

'Where do you think I would go?' Planting her hands on her hips, she scowled at him. 'I am coming with you.'

'Let us not argue, Mistress Pentrevick. We got on so well last night. Can we not continue our truce?'

'Is that what you call it?' Then, remembering that he had saved her life, swimming for hours to carry her to safety, she hung her head in shame. 'I shall stay here, do not fret.'

'No, on second thoughts, come with me, just in case . . .'

'In case what?' She glanced over her shoulder, still half expecting devilish natives to appear.

'Come, follow me, and keep an eye open to your left. I shall watch the right.'

The island was perfect, a gently-sculpted jewel filigreed with verdant foliage. Dazzling birds flew to left and right as they passed, and Allegra could hear the chatter of unseen, exotic creatures coming from the clumps of dipping palms. As they neared the top of the island, they could see the ocean all around them, a circle of cerulean cloth-of-silver, its surface gemmed with a hoard of rhinestones newly polished by the sun. Nothing else was in sight except the distant ellipse of the horizon.

The enormity of the world struck her at the same time as the realisation that they may never leave this island or see other humans again. They might die here with the turtles and the dazzling birds, lying in one another's arms on the cloth-of-gold sand. Absorbed in that sad thought, she stumbled over a root.

He caught her arm instantly, and she saw concern in his eyes at her sad expression, and a look which in anyone else she would have known was tenderness. Her heart gave a jolt. If no one ever found them, they would surely die together . . .

He held her close, brushing away the tangles of salt-streaked hair to kiss her forehead.

'For a wild heart you are the most delicate plant I have ever known. I was convinced that you would chew tobacco and wield a sword by now, and be cursing like a mercenary.'

She could not help but giggle. 'The time for that may not be too far away.' Her stomach let out a yowl of hunger.

'You will feel much stronger after we have eaten,' he prophesied.

While Nash went in search of birds' eggs, Allegra collected brushwood and ferns to make a fire. She watched him light it, taking in the rapid twisting and scraping of the thin twigs, as he rubbed them together until sparks appeared. Placing the eggs in the ashes at the side of the fire, they waited until Nash judged it right to push them out and toss them from palm to palm to cool them.

They tasted fresh and fluffy and delicious, and Allegra forced from her mind the thought that they would have grown into dazzling scarlet or yellow-plumed birds if they had not been stolen and cooked.

While Nash went in search of fresh water, she lay back replete, revelling in the feel of firm land beneath her back after all these months. How did sailors live at sea for year after year, coming home so infrequently, only to set out again with such optimism, knowing that storms, sea monsters, hurricanes and sharks lay in wait for them? Was it courage or foolhardiness? She had thought that men were favoured by being allowed their freedom but now she was not so sure.

Nash reported that he had not yet found fresh water, but he was confident that there would be some. They would search together. Until he had explored the whole of the island he did not want to leave Allegra alone.

'Sharks cannot walk on land, can they?' she asked, curious at his caution.

'No, but cannibals can. As far as I know we are not in their country, but so much of the world remains uncharted that one never knows what will turn up next.' Seeing her frown, he explained what cannibals did. 'Now will you see why you must stay close to me?'

'Yes, so that they can have two courses,' she grinned, looking braver than she felt.

The sun was even hotter now, drumming against their backs and faces with a persistent, scorching heat. Allegra felt burned already and Nash cut down a fleshy leaf for her to hold over her head. She felt silly walking along with a huge piece of vegetation flapping over her face, but it served its purpose. Nash said that sunburn could cause a decimating fever and she quite believed him.

'If we do not find fresh water, then we are in worse trouble than we know,' he said when they had been walking for some time, without success.

The miniature island possessed pyramids of golden rocks, tiny mountains which rose up from the thatches of palms and vines. The earth was dry and dusty, the creepers twisting along by their feet and hooking them by the ankles. Bright butterflies gyrated past, their wings so wide that Allegra wished she could immortalise them with her paints. Such colours . . . If they could only make material of that shade.

At noon they rested, their throats parched. Little creatures scuttled away as they lay down, and had Allegra known more about the insects and reptiles which lived in this climate she would not have sunk to the earth with such careless abandon. Nash did know, and he had ensured that nothing dangerous threatened them before they relaxed.

'What do we do if there is no fresh water?' Allegra asked.

'Die of thirst, or drink sea water until we lose our minds.'

'You paint a very gloomy picture!'

'But an accurate one. I have been on a voyage where we were forced to eat the oxhides from under the yardarms, as well as ship's rats. The water was foul and those who drank from the sea went mad. Those who chose thirst survived.'

Turning on to her stomach and leaning on her elbows, Allegra gazed up at Nash. How rich and brilliantly blue were his eyes beneath that aureole of glittering gold hair, his face already touched by the sun. She did not know it but her own nose was rosy red, and very soon she would be tanning like this hardy man.

She had begun this adventure for two reasons: to find her sister, and to show the world that women could succeed in such matters as well as men; if not better. When Nash had refused her permission to sail with him, she had decided that nothing would stop her. They had been at sea for less than half a year and yet she felt so very different from that capricious, headstrong and wayward girl who had dressed in boy's garb and stowed away aboard the *Tudor Raven*. Perhaps sailors aged fast during their first voyage and became so hardy that nothing ever frightened them again? This iron-nerved man lying beside her seemed as unperturbed at the thought of death at the hands of cannibals as from the lack of fresh water. He had eaten oxhides and rats, explored the New World since he was a boy. How could she hope to compete with such experience and stoicism?

'What are you thinking?' His question took her by surprise.

'If there will be enough water to bathe in as well as to drink – when we find it,' she said, reaching out to snap off a piece of brightly coloured vine. She was about to chew on it, as she would on a juicy stalk of grass, when Nash pushed her hand from her mouth so suddenly that she gasped with anger.

'Do not eat that!'

'How dare you! There will be sap inside this vine! Why do you always have to interfere with everything that I do?'

'Go ahead then, eat it, but there is no known antidote.'

'Antidote? What do you mean? This is poisonous?'

'One of the deadliest poisons.' He looked so serious, so assured, that she obeyed. 'See those berries attached to it a little way along? Those are even deadlier. Eat one of those and death by paralysis will follow in moments.'

'You are jesting with me! How would you know that?'

'I have explored the world, do not forget. The first thing explorers learn is to how to recognise nature's deadly fruits as well as her beneficial ones. Often the prettier are the most fatal.'

Allegra jumped to her feet, cheeks flushed. When would there be something that she knew and he did not? She had always regarded men as poor things, second to women in virtually everything. To survive they needed a house filled with servants to wait on them, a large family of sons to indulge their pride and vanity, and a wife to worship them. All that a woman needed was the man she loved . . .

Allegra was out of sight of Nash within moments, hurrying into the tangle of vegetation. Being told what to do and how to do it had become intolerable. Elizabeth was far cleverer; she could appear to dangle on a man's every word while going her own sweet way, undismayed. Yes, Elizabeth suited this arrogant, overweening man admirably.

Allegra thought back over their months at sea. Running around the cabin and swinging her arms, stretching and twisting, had not been her idea of jollity, but she had complied because she did not want to become feeble. Nash had shown her how to breathe deeply, inflating her lungs to their fullest before the open window. To humour him, she had done it all, although not without complaints at times, but now she was glad. When she was twelve she had been bedridden for a month with a fever and, when she had tried to walk, her legs were so shaky and weak that she could barely hobble across the room. This time, she was strong and healthy, despite the tedious diet aboard ship.

Lost in thought she did not notice the labyrinthine shape lurking in the trees ahead, nor see it as it arched its way down towards her. Not until it knocked against the side of her head in one swooping, scything movement did she even realise that the thick entwined vine was not a vine at all but a gigantic snake.

Vines did not hiss and dart at one's face . . . yelping with horror, she watched the snake steady itself for a second onslaught. This one would be the last . . .

Nash moved as stealthily as the serpent, leaping towards it in one flashing, agile bound, gripping it behind its elliptical head and squeezing, squeezing, until it grew limp and dropped to the ground.

Seeing it lying at her feet, Allegra realised that she would never have survived its attack. It was vast, and whether it was the breed which bit or crushed, she would have been dead by now.

Nash executed a flourishing bow before her, as if doffing a feathered cap.

'At your service, m'lady. Just scream at any time and I shall save your life.'

She did not know whether to laugh or be furious, but decency told her that she should thank him for his fearless deed. There lay the villainous serpent on the ground, quite dead and harmless now, and all because of his speed, his cool nerve and his extraordinary strength. In her father's books about the New World she had read that man rarely survived a confrontation with the beasts of the jungles, yet here was one woman who had – thanks to Lord Hamilton. She tried her utmost to thank him, her mouth opening in preparation as she summoned her most gracious manner, and then, before she knew what she was doing, she had burst into noisy tears.

It was too much, the shipwreck, the torment in the seas without land in sight, the cold, desolate night, and now this enormous serpent deciding that she should be his next meal. The tears would not stop. They flooded out of her eyes, salty and fierce, yet, when Nash swept her into his arms to comfort her, she bunched her hands into hard little fists and pounded at his face and neck.

'No, no, leave me alone, leave me alone! This is all your fault, all of it! I want to go home, I want to go *home*!' She screamed hysterically, and then, turning on her heel, she ran back the way she had come.

Somehow she would get off this island and away from him. She did not care how she did it as long as she succeeded. He could stay here as long as he liked, mooning over the vines and the sands, but she was getting away, now, now!

Chapter Five

There was the spar lying on the beach, the same spar which had helped keep them afloat after the shipwreck. Giving a cry of triumph, she tugged at it, pulling it towards the waves and running into the water to catch it as it bobbed buoyantly in the sparkling sea. She heard Nash shout as he saw what she was doing, but she did not listen. Nothing would keep her here in this accursed place, nothing! Tears blinding her, she clutched at the spar, pushing with her feet against the shingle and spiky little stones until the ground gave way.

Clinging to the spar, she bobbed out into the blue, not thinking beyond that blissful moment of escape. Nash was a tyrant, a monster, who tried to control her as if she were an infant. Every word he said and every move he made was directed at making her feel a witless fool. Well, he would be sorry when she was dead! Let him explain that to her father and sister!

She did not get far before his arms caged her like iron, and she was swept against his chest to be pinned there like a fluttering moth.

'You are the most idiotic and dull-witted female I have ever had the misfortune to tangle with! Had you forgotten that you cannot swim, that there are sharks out there, that you would be burnt to a crisp by the sun even if you survived for more than an hour?'

'Lemme go! Lemme go, or I shall hurt you where it hurts most, you spiteful boor, you poxy oaf, you curmudgeon!' Allegra screamed, wriggling and slapping, and biting when her teeth met flesh.

'I think another punishment is in order, little she-wolf,' Nash growled. 'Risking both our lives with your witless behaviour. Jesu, when I get you to land!'

'You are a savage, a cannibal savage, Nash Hamilton,' Allegra yelled, pinching him viciously as she could not punch him from this angle. 'What you need is a horse whipping and I would love to wield the whip!'

'And I know what you need, Mistress Pentrevick.' Reaching the beach, Nash dropped her on the shingle with a painful thud. Crying out, she gathered her strength to kick him with both feet, but as she did so he dropped to the ground beside her and kissed her, pinioning her arms so that she could not move.

She tried to shout, but he continued to kiss her, so hard, so ruthlessly and passionately, that she was shocked into submission.

Then, when she was beginning to respond, when gentility and restraint were about to be flung overboard, he thrust her away, made a sound of disgust, and disappeared up the beach and into the tangle of vegetation.

Allegra lay on the sand, her feelings resembling those of a landed porpoise, or so she imagined. She was both dazed and mystified. Why had he done that? All those months confined on the ship and he had not stepped too far across the boundaries of decency, although she had sensed at times that he wanted to do so. Now he had kissed her as if he wanted to make love to her, and she had begun to respond. That was what was so shocking. There was something about this island, a primitive, primordial aura, as if they were suspended in time and no longer of the real world. A time lock. Could there be such a thing? She had read of an island where men were shipwrecked and when they were rescued, five years later, none of them had aged by so much as one wrinkle.

It was a delightful supposition, yet fanciful. She remembered her father saying that there was only one thing which kept one from ageing, and that was the laughter of the young. Her old nurse, a trenchant Cornishwoman, had believed in the fairies. If they were generously fed with cream, and tasty treats set out for them regularly, then they would keep away the years from their supplier.

Cream . . . Juicy meat, fresh, sparkling water . . . What she would give to have any of those! The sun was high now, burning overhead, and she could feel her face tightening. She got up to follow the track which Nash's feet had made in the sand. Entering the mossy green shade of the island's foliage, she could not see any trace of him. She was wary now, keeping a watchful eye open for snakes and anything which crawled about her feet, but having no intention of shouting Nash's name again. She did not need him, here or anywhere else for that matter. He was a greedy and ruthless savage, his methods barbaric and self-seeking; she hoped that when the next serpent appeared, it would be ravenous and aim straight for the man who had been ordering her around for the past six months . . .

The palms overhead created a glowing luminosity of silvery-green shade. Beneath them it was humid, yet many degrees cooler than on the beach. How thirsty she was now; her throat was tightening, a malaise gripping her limbs. She did not see why she should not drink sea water if no fresh could be found. That tale of Nash's was probably yet another of his exaggerated stories to frighten her, or to punish her by keeping her thirsty.

She thought that she had his measure now. He was a fortune hunter who, seeing that her sister Elizabeth was amiable, sweet-natured and biddable, wished to marry her so that he could enjoy her wealth and estates, not to mention the prestige of an alliance with the Pentrevick family. That Nash was an earl, and greatly in Queen Elizabeth's favour, did not enter her thoughts; nor that her sister Elizabeth, for all her beauty and grace, had a way much employed by older sisters, and which had kept Allegra rudely suppressed on many an occasion. Having lived in her sister's shadow, possessing little of her bright charm, radiant blonde looks or aptitude for all matters feminine, not until Elizabeth was abducted by slavers had Allegra realised that she loved her.

Thinking that she heard the rustle of some hideous jungle creature, she paused. What mythological beast was about to confront her, teeth gnashing, claws extended?

On seeing that it was Nash, she breathed again, even if the description fitted him perfectly. At least he had no plans to kill her . . . unless, of course, he truly was a cannibal. The notion brought a faint smile to her curvaceous mouth, but did nothing for her increasing thirst.

He held something in his hand. It looked like an upended shell, large, round, and streaked with rosy-silver pearl. Then, lifting the shell to his lips, she saw him drink deeply.

'Have you found water?' Eagerly, she took a step towards him.

'Why, are you thirsty?' His eyes glittered above the edge of the shell, daring her to admit to human weakness.

Tossing her head, she turned on her heel to retrace her steps. What did she need with him, the boorish renegade? For all she knew, he too was a pirate slaver and trying to tempt her into his net. Nash Hamilton was a pirate slaver. It was he who had abducted Elizabeth, and not the Arabian hordes! When he caught her, he would chain her to the ground and beat her . . .

the cat o' nine tails, that was what sailors used to whip people, was it not? She could almost feel the sting of the lash across her back, cutting, piercing, and the blood pouring, cold, cold blood, the pain, the agony . . . *Mother!*

The sand smacked her hard in the face, the jolt of her body against the earth thumping the breath from her lungs. That was where Nash found her, breathing like a child with croup, her limbs trembling and her eyes rolled up into her head. Sighing, he hauled her up into his arms as if she weighed no more than an ashwood pike and made his way back into the glimmering opaline shade of the undergrowth.

He had made a hide-out, sturdy palm branches interlocked over the mouth of a small, neat cave, so that he could sit in the open air without burning. The cave was clean save for a dusting of gilded sand, and nothing ominous had nested there. At the back, as if it might have lingered there for centuries, was a tiny pool of what he had found to be clear, sweet water fed by a rivulet which flowed through a fault in the rock wall. Drinking deeply, he had felt refreshed. Later he would find a shell to use as a drinking cup, and if the quixotic minx whose life he had saved twice cared to join him, then she could share his newfound treasures.

High above his head, he had made out small elongated green shapes, the fruit of the palms, but as yet hard and unripe. There would be berries and other fruits, there always were on these warm, temperate islands. Fish too, if not in the sea then in the sparkling pools which must surely be somewhere nearby.

When he found the proud Allegra Pentrevick in a huddle on the beach, displaying all the signs of sunstroke, he did not know whether to be relieved or angry. It was true that he would have peace while she was unconscious, but he had no medicines with which he could alleviate her illness. He thought of the locked cupboard in his cabin, where he had kept all that was needed to treat a variety of ailments, herbs, dried, or ready-made into tinctures, the juice of the poppy for those in intolerable pain, brandy for the shocked, and a flask for examining the body's waste fluids, for the condition of the latter said much about the patient's state of health.

Had Lord Hamilton not discovered early his passion for the

sea, then he would have become a physician, which was what his late cousin had wished him to be. For years he had thought medicine a tedious, restrictive career; where in that was the excitement and the adventure of captaining great ships? And then during a long voyage, the ship's surgeon had died of blood poisoning after an insect bite, and he, Nash, had taken on the care of the crew. Strangely, he had found it a satisfying labour. To treat a man who was in pain and fearful of death, and see him recover to vigorous health within a few weeks, because of one's own ministrations, was marvellously encouraging.

Reflecting on this, he had compared himself with Chiron who rowed the dead to the Underworld, only in his case, he had captained the ship which took the sick away from death.

So here he was now, with an unconscious woman in his care, half blessing, half cursing the problems which her fever had brought him, yet nonetheless anxious about her chances of survival. Thankfully he had found fresh running water, but the choice of food would remain limited until he had explored further.

He looked at the ashen face, beaded with sweat, the generous gloss of the dark russet lashes, the waterfall of glowing scarlet-gilt hair cascading down from the pale neck. But for her sharp, shrewish tongue and contumacious nature, she would have made some man a useful bride. She was inordinately healthy – bar sunstroke, so no doubt would bear a large brood of children and raise them to strict disciplines and the reciting of their catechisms twice daily. No child of hers would answer her back or dare to flout her maternal authority, he was sure. It would not matter if the man she married were a nervous weakling; she possessed sufficient strength and spirit for two . . .

Placing her gently on the ground at the mouth of the tiny cave, he ensured that there was a protective shadow across her, before stepping to the rear of the cave to fill the shell with water. There was no cloth save what he wore, and little enough of that for he had torn off all his outer clothing to make himself lighter in the water. A brief search disclosing some soft, fluffy leaves, he bunched them up, dipped them in the water and gently wiped them over the she-wolf's face. Not even when silent could she free him to go about his business. Even now she demanded his full attention, just like a child.

She did not make a sound as the water dripped over her, trickling down her neck and into the deep cleft between her breasts, where now a bright red V displayed her sunburn, although occasionally she shuddered. There were two methods of treatment available to him: an Armenian physician had told him that fevers would not abate unless the body were kept chilled, because the accumulation of the patient's vital humours would increase during fever, swelling in the veins and causing a thickness and a poisoning there. Yet another physician, an inebriate Greek, who, when sober, was brilliant at diagnosis, had told him that fevers must be kept warm or else the heat – which was the body's way of healing the sickness – would escape, taking with it the patient's spirit.

Both were convincing arguments; the choice was his.

He decided on a combination of the two, which meant that he must strip, but as they were alone in the Garden of Allah, that did not matter greatly. No one would be offended, save the birds. His shirt and Venetians removed, he shook them free of sand and dust and tucked them round the she-wolf. Then, having collected some palm leaves, he placed these on top of her, compressing them tightly round her arms and legs. At regular intervals, he bathed Allegra's face with cool water from the cave, noting that the hollow was swiftly emptying and not refilling, which meant that he must institute a grand search for water soon.

Having found some bulky rocks, he placed them round the patient, forming a protective wall just in case any beasts took a liking to the sight of her vulnerability, then, aware that he would suffer for walking naked in the searing sun, Nash set off to search for fresh water.

Apart from stepping into a clump of stinging plants which scorched his ankle and halted his progress while he scratched energetically, his exploration went without hitch. Men who had been with him on previous shipwrecks had died from eating the pretty, bright-coloured berries which looked so like the appetising ones growing in England, but which contained a fatal, swift poison.

He viewed the scene ahead. This was almost an atoll, but for its preponderance of vegetation and wild life. Strangely shaped rocks rose high before him, some pointed, some twisted, some curved like hunched-backs. Here and there palms, tropical vines and bushes flourished in the baking heat. His skin was burnt already, especially those delicate areas which had never been naked under a tropical sun. Shrugging ruefully, he walked on, the rough gritty earth stinging and stabbing at his feet.

Breaching the top of the slope, he saw the sea spread out before him, a gentian-blue, glittering silk veil. The urge to leap into its sparkling cool depths was powerful. Reminding himself of salt-soaked skin, which was even more prone to sunburn, he tore off a clump of heavy leaves which he knew to be succulents. Splitting open the pulpy flesh, he sucked at the juice inside. Heaven! One mouthful of fresh, tangy-sweet juice, but afterwards his mouth felt even dryer. His back was tight with sunburn, and he knew that he would suffer tonight. What would he lie on? Sand pressing against scarlet, burnt flesh . . . not a cheering thought.

A dip ahead looked promising. Twisted trees encircled a dark hollow, their heads genuflecting over what must be precious water. A wild creature skittered past him, and another, and then he saw a graceful, supine head and neck the colour of palest caramel. A tiny deer was drinking at a pool, pawing the sandy edge with delight. Waiting until the deer had finished, Nash crouched in the shade, keeping himself as still as possible while the wild life, whose home this was, frolicked and scurried around.

If he were Adam, he supposed that he would rush to the palms and cut himself some form of edible loincloth, but the notion did not appeal. Clothes were for decency but, in his view, mainly a protection against the elements. What did it matter what he wore now? There were no prelates to censure him, not that he would take notice if they did. For a man of his era, he was extraordinarily separate from dogma, choosing to think things out for himself and frequently failing to come to the old, hidebound solutions beloved by synods and the Church. Strange how formal and artificial appeared the world that he had left behind, as he sat here in the midst of such a natural, wild and uncultivated Eden. Stiff, starched ruffs, breath-nipping wooden corsets, and enormous padded cod-pieces to project the male's vanity, carmine rouge, white-lead face creams, feathered hats with ruby brooches and high-heeled slippers . . . and they were for the men! When he turned his thoughts to the dress of the Elizabethan courtesan, he laughed out loud. Twenty layers of petticoats, vasquines, the inane little edifice popularly called a bumroll, which was tied about the waist, and padded so that the skirts stood out around the hips like a cock's comb; embroidered hose and garters, shoes and ostrich-feather fans, bodices and basques, stomachers rigid as wood, jewelled earrings, clusters of carcanets at the throat, bleached wigs and sprays of flowers . . . the heavy, musky perfumes and multitude of artificial aids which courtesans cultivated; the coating of egg white, powdered eggshell, alum, borax and white poppy seeds which the Queen herself employed to improve her complexion. Now Nash saw all these as extraneous, unnecessary, possessing no worth in the world which man had created for himself.

Time was passing, and with it memories, ambitions and longings, some never to return. It was the very *naturalness* of this place, the fruitful untempered ambiance. Suddenly, he had a notion to live here for ever, becoming the wild man of this island until his beard grew long, down to his knees at least, thus removing the problem of how to cover his sexual organs. Laughing again, he leapt up, and bounded down to the pool, where he flung himself into its cool, shaded depths and swam gloriously until he was thoroughly refreshed.

Draped over his head as he swam were curlicues of vines and creepers, emerald, dark agate, the browns of rust and peat, the colours of primordial nature, earthy, powerful, timeless; the pool, a shadowy luminescence, haloing his limbs as they struck out to left and right. Easy now to think of sorcery and spells, of being enchanted, part of another world, perhaps even another planet.

He was not a man given to thoughts of anything but the

important and immediate. Stoic and practical, he had a generous, perceptive sense of humour, and it was this which alleviated what might well have been a nature far too serious, an imagination totally unsuited to magicians, wizards, astrologers and their ilk. Yet here he was pondering on the meanings of life and death, eternity and religion, conscience and principle.

Bounding from the pool, where he had drunk his fill as he swam, he refilled the shell which he had brought with him. He seemed to have been in this glade for hours, yet by the position of the sun he knew that it was not so. Mindful of why he was here, he thought of the sick girl sleeping in the cave, and he knew why he had been entertaining such strange and unfamiliar ideas. The spitting she-wolf was unlike all other women he had ever known. She was no proud courtesan, vain and obsessed with rouge pots, scented oils, the latest padded basques, and embroidered shoes; nor did she spend hours maintaining a false edifice comprised of all these accoutrements and artifices. Had he been a man of a more superficial cast, he would never have come to realise what struck him now.

Allegra infuriated him because she was not of the traditional female mode. Many times in the past he had rebelled against the brittle façades which women presented to him, refusing to allow him beyond these. How that had incensed him! Yet now, when he had met a woman who refused to be dishonest, deceiving or pretentious, he was enraged by it.

'It is your own failings which are incensing you,' he said aloud to the silent glade. 'You do not know how to treat a woman who refuses to comply with tradition. *You* must learn how to treat her . . .'

Knowing that the learning would be a long and arduous task, he retraced his steps at a faster pace than before. Whatever lay before them, he would strive to do his best for her. She was not like her sister Elizabeth: who was? The woman he loved was gentle, natural and affectionate, yet distant. These were virtues which he preferred in his future bride, after all, for they spoke of modesty and chastity and who would wish to marry an immoral woman? They were ten a penny in the streets of London, beautiful while young, but swiftly becoming sick and diseased. Not for his bride one of those unfortunates. Sufficient to satiate his powerful desires when he was a youth, but not the proper material for a wife and the mother of his sons.

But this one . . . She was complex, different. He did not like it; it unnerved and unsettled him. God be thanked that he was betrothed to her sister so they could never become close, for he feared that he would get the worst end of it. Marriage to Allegra She-Wolf Pentrevick would be like bedding with an active volcano . . . When they returned to civilisation, which he was positive they would, then he must forget this strange enchantment which had come upon him in the Garden of Allah, for it boded nothing but ill.

Ships passed this way regularly. One day he would see a vessel on the horizon and attract its attention, and then he would sail to the nearest port, organise his affairs, obtain some money and set off again – without the she-wolf tagging along, claws unsheathed.

Allegra lay where he had left her. He was very close before he saw that her eyes were open, surveying him. Her gasp was loud; then he remembered why. He was naked.

Chapter Six

Night fell suddenly, scooping out the light and bringing with it a coolness which was dangerous to those recuperating from fevers. Nash had retrieved his Venetians from the patient, who had closed her eyes while he was doing so. They felt hot and heavy in the slumbrous heat.

Seeing the tall, naked man standing over her, Allegra had

almost forgotten to breathe. Over six feet of bronzed, beautifully sculpted manhood, broad, powerful shoulders, slender waist and hips, strongly shaped calves and thighs . . . and between these, surrounded by an aureole of gilded, curling hair, the one thing which she had never seen before, and which she had never imagined she would behold until her wedding night. She closed her eyes at once, but the memory remained, brightly imprinted, so that she could recall it at frequent intervals, which indeed she did.

So glorious, so perfect, like Neptune rising from the surf, he stood before her, hands on hips, legs thrust slightly apart. Her imagination raced.

What sprang from that sudden, shocking and thrilling sight was an ungovernable curiosity, a powerful wave of feeling which she had never experienced before. Oh, she had dreamed of men, the young, handsome page her father had taken to court with him, knowing that she would never be allowed to marry beneath her; later, Nash himself, all previous dreaming paling to nothing beside her longings where he was concerned, all firmly suppressed because he was out of reach. There was something wild and uncivilised about him, stirring and ancient, a primitive force which appealed to her and towards which she gravitated, without really knowing why or to what it would lead, but only knowing that she must go. She must. Yet it was forbidden. He represented authority, dominance, masculinity and the male force . . . all of these qualities smiting her to the heart and fashioning a sharp and aching longing. She wanted to know how that soft, tender and pendulous manhood would change when they lay together . . . She wanted to touch and caress it, squeeze and hold it, and see what happened to it then. Most of all, she wanted to be there at the magic moment when it began to grow and harden, so that she could see with her own eyes and feel with her own body . . .

'Your face is flushed. Is the fever returned?' Nash's voice made her start. He was squatting beside her, peering into her eyes.

'No, I am quite all right, thank you, Lord Hamilton. The earth is uncomfortable, but nothing can be done about that. May I have another drink?'

Gently he held her head while he placed the shell at her lips so that she could drink. His hand felt very hot, almost burning through her hair, while the water tasted icy, although it was warmed by the sun. Closing her eyes to drink, she allowed herself the indulgence of imagining that he was close because he wanted to be, and that in a few moments he would take her in his arms and then the magic change would take place . . .

Water sputtered from the side of her mouth.

'I cannot drink so fast!' she exclaimed, at which he sighed patiently, waiting for her to catch her breath. If only he knew what she was thinking! If this was a symptom of sunstroke, then she wished that she could live here all the time. It was a delicious sensation, deliciously shocking. Never could she have guessed that such passion could be forged by her own mind, her own body.

Out of the corner of her eye she could see that he now wore the Venetians again. How tedious. She wanted an excuse to see him strip off his breeches . . .

'I trusted the fever had gone!' Consternation filled Nash's eyes as Allegra began to shudder violently. 'Do you feel nauseated, thirsty?'

Silent, Allegra continued to shiver and even managed to make her teeth chatter convincingly. When she saw Nash looking around for something to cover her, she moaned as if in pain. He stepped away, his bare feet making no sound in the sandy earth, and returned with an armful of enormous, curving palm leaves which he placed over her from shoulder to toe. As if she did not know what she was doing, she thrust out her arms, flinging aside the leaves, but he only replaced them, doing so a second and a third time when she flung them off.

It was then that some semblance of virtue returned to Allegra, joining the accumulation of exhaustion and hunger, so that she fell asleep with an almost forceful deliberation. If this were indeed the island called the Garden of Allah, after the Muslim paradise, then might she not be sinful Eve, and Nash poor, innocent and unsuspecting Adam, waiting to be tempted by her lustful body?

It was dusk when she woke, roused by the scent of roasting flesh. Her stomach gave an enormous rattle of hunger as she lifted her head to see what Nash was doing. A fire flickered merrily only a few feet away and across it was fixed a pole on which were hanging tiny, round creatures; birds, perhaps. The scent of roasting was so marvellous that she forgot to feel sad for the plight of the beautiful birds who had not, after all, asked them to invade their paradise.

'Hungry?'

'She-wolves always are, are they not?' Allegra retorted.

'When they have young to feed, yes.' Nash's sea-blue eyes glittered, but she could not make out their proper expression with the light from the fire behind his head.

Allegra sat up, apparently recovered, refusing to admit that the top of her head seemed to float away quite frighteningly when she was upright, and that there was a great hollow in her stomach. Nausea gripped her and she feared that she would vomit all over Lord Hamilton's sandy, yet expensive Venetians, but it vanished as rapidly, to be replaced by a fervent hunger.

Moments later, she was clutching one of the tiny hot creatures in her hands, tearing at its luscious flesh with her teeth and swallowing as ravenously as any she-wolf. Nash shook his head at her haste, warning her that she would be ill if she swallowed so fast, but she tossed her head and continued to gulp, then started on a second roasted bird.

There was water to follow and it slithered down her throat in the most glorious fashion. Now she knew what manna was: any food which was eaten by those who were half-starved. A gift from Heaven.

She lay back, replete, happiness soaring through her. Happiness came from such simple things in the wild: enough water, enough food, and the nearness of a man who had given her more sleepless nights than she cared to recall, because she had hated him so much, not so very long ago . . .

She must have dozed, for she was filled with sharp pain when she woke, a great, slicing pain cutting through her middle. Next moment she knew that she was going to vomit and that Nash Hamilton would say, I told you so! Struggling to her feet, her head swimming, she ran into the undergrowth and pleaded with the pain to go before she collapsed. Leaning against a gnarled tree, she deposited her dinner on the ground while tears streamed down her face and she turned from hot to cold and back again. Then, swallowing, feeling as if her legs were made of cotton, she assumed an air of composure before returning to the cave entrance. She knew what he would say, cutting words about her being headstrong and disobedient, and, if it was the last thing she ever did, she would find an answering retort from somewhere.

He was waiting with the shell filled with cool water which he held for her while she drank, her body trembling.

'Now is the time to take in water, when your belly is empty,' he said, his voice displaying none of the animosity she had anticipated. 'If you do not drink, you will become dehydrated and then your troubles really will begin.'

She wanted to dash the shell from his hands at these condescending words, but managed to show him nothing of her true feelings. The water filled her like a bubble of ice and she wondered if she would vomit again. Lying down, she said nothing as he covered her with his shirt and the palm leaves.

'If we are fortunate, then some casks may be washed ashore from the wreck. You may be able to make yourself something out of old shirts . . . or a sail.' He grinned at the thought of her draped in the vastly heavy canvas, tripping over its hem as she struggled to walk. It would not be easy to cut up canvas without the correct tools.

'And you may be able to make yourself a ball and chain from the anchor!' she snapped. 'They say that wild savages should be kept shackled!'

She thought that he was going to slap her across the face and she shrank back. But he was laughing, loud, uproarious laughter, laughing at her, at her words and her distress, she was sure.

'You are a barbarian!' she gritted through her teeth. 'This island was made for you and your kind.'

'Indeed, that may well be so, but if it is, where are you going to spend your time, Lady Nose-in-the-Air? If there is a more comfortable cave on this island, with servants to wait upon you, then I bid you find it and enjoy yourself there. The comforts at this wayside inn are intolerably meagre, but they are all I have to offer.'

'When I am well, I shall go, do not worry! I cannot wait! Staying here in your odious company is insufferable. You make me sick . . .'

'So I noticed, so I noticed.' And with that, he retreated into the cave and the silence of sleep fell upon them.

The island wildlife more than made up for their silence as eerie twitters, chirrups, squeals and scuffles reached Allegra's ears. It was easy to imagine an enormous serpent slithering towards her across the sandy ground, and now and again she woke with a start, imagining that a snake was poised above her, ready to strike. Otherwise, the night was uneventful, and there was some minute comfort in knowing that she could shout for Nash should the need arise, although that was the very last thing she wanted to do. What would please her more would be for him to shout for *her* help as some hideous creature tried to kill him. Evening the score was a sparkling idea to sustain her through the fears and isolation of her new existence.

Dawn was noisy and bright, the sky a multitude of gold, apricot, silver and carnation pink streaked with ivory. Such beauty! If only there were nothing else to do but contemplate it, Allegra thought as she lay on her back, slowly waking up. Sleeping on the hard ground was not conducive to proper rest but anything was better than rocking to left and right in a storm-tossed ship. How had she endured those long weeks at sea, or ever thought that such a life would suit her marvellously? Sailors must have constitutions of steel.

Glancing into the cave and seeing no sign of Nash, Allegra stretched to ease her stiff and aching limbs. Her insides felt as if they had been stolen in the night; she was empty and dizzy. There was the shell, devoid of water, but she did not dare drink from the almost empty little pool to the cave's rear not knowing if the water was safe. Nash had warned her that waters in such places could be poisonous, and she did not trust herself to test it.

There was no sight of food and the fire was a tiny pile of ashes. She could see berries and peculiar-shaped fruits on bushes nearby but they too might contain deadly poison. Nash had been shipwrecked at least once before and navigated his way through the rigours of such an experience. She wondered if that accounted for his extraordinary detachment, his air of self-sufficiency.

Having decided to explore, and search for eggs, she made her way along a path through the vegetation which loomed like three-dimensional tapestries on either side. Squawks and twitters clashed in her ears as birds and tiny animals ran out of her way. She kept a sharp eye open for snakes or beasts. If there was one conveniently-shaped cave here, then there might well be another and she would not need to shelter with the arrogant and odious Nash Hamilton. That thought driving her on, she walked for some time, until she found the pool where miniature deer came to drink and the waters of which tasted sweet and pure as she drank deeply. Animals had been munching some plump, pale green plants, so she reasoned that they must be safe to eat. Tearing open the flabby leaves, she sucked at the juicy centres. They tasted rather like watery lemons, without the tang. She tried chewing the succulent centres, but the fibrous quality rendered them virtually unpalatable. In the end, after swallowing all the juice, she had to spit out the fibre.

Walking on, she found a smooth path so neat that it looked as if it had been shaped by human hands. The path was part shiny, slippery rocks and part beaten-down earth; no vines had grown across it, as if a gardener were tending it. She was enjoying the walk, as far in front of her she could see a narrow carpet of glittering blue, like a ribbon of sapphires. The sea! Her eyes were bright with anticipation when she felt the earth give way and she vanished from sight.

Chapter Seven

Allegra landed awkwardly, pain stabbing through her shoulder, but that was nothing compared to her alarm at finding herself in an ebony-black subterranean pit. Snakes! She thought of them instantly, and struggled to her feet although her back hurt and her body felt as if it had been rudely shaken by a monstrous hand. This might even be the lair of a creature more dangerous than a serpent . . . A brutal wild animal, perhaps even a sea monster which lived on this island when it was not swimming . . . The hair at the back of her neck stuck out like prickles and she wrapped her arms round herself for meagre protection.

The ground was uneven, wet and slippery in places, earthy in others. She trod with great care, dreading the feel of something coiling furrily against her bare foot. She held out her arms for balance, although it took all her courage to extend them in this thick, black darkness. From far off she heard the dancing trickle of water, plip-plopping its way downwards, perhaps into a pool, guessing from the sound that the water was falling in a large, echoing cave.

The darkness seeming to ease a little as her eyes became accustomed to it, Allegra could make out the tall sides of this labyrinthine place. As she did so, she spotted a circle of faint light ahead. Making for it, her toe stubbed a rock and she bit her lip at the agony. Long moments passed before the pain eased and she could walk on.

The circle grew brighter and her heart lifted. Now she could see that she was in some sort of narrow corridor, weaving its way towards the light of a large cave. She prayed that there would be an exit there through which she could escape this frightening underworld.

Stepping into the cave, she was instantly bathed in the drumming sunlight of mid-morning. It encompassed her like a blanket, soothing her aching shoulder and brightening her considerably, inside and out. Somehow the sun reached down here, although she could not see where it was coming from, for above was craggy, arched rock.

She was about to move forward again when she saw a dark, cloaked figure standing at the opposite end of the cave and her blood turned to ice.

Nash returned to the hideout with a brace of birds whose size was a great improvement on last night's dinner. No doubt Lady She-Wolf would be groaning with hunger by now. He had tried to catch some fish, but failed, for he had not yet made the correct implements. Tucked in his belt was a collection of edible fruits which would change the patient's whole perspective on life, he was sure. There was nothing like a nourishing meal to cheer the spirits.

She was not waiting for him, so he began to prepare their late breakfast. No doubt she would be back as her hunger increased, for he had warned her against eating berries and fruit without asking him if they were safe. He had no fears for her safety, for, after her escapade with the snake, he did not think that she possessed the stoic courage needed to explore on her own.

Time passed and the birds were roasted and ready to eat, the fruit split open and awaiting its fate, yet still she had not returned. Nash made a quick exploration of the surrounding area, calling her name, but eliciting no reply. Returning to the fire, he picked up the fruit and covered the roast meat with shells to keep off predators. Eating as he went, he began to search for the troublesome girl who had managed to interweave her fate with his . . . but not for one moment longer than it took them to get off this island!

He walked for an hour, and then two, yet still there was no

sign of her. Could the illness have turned her mind, so that she had walked into the sea and drowned? His heart pounded painfully at the thought. Why, he did not know. Probably because he would have the responsibility of telling her father and sister, and that task would be the most difficult he had ever undertaken. 'She was in my care, yet she died . . .' He could imagine their faces.

That was the only reason for his uneasiness. The stupid, witless, infuriating bitch had made his life hellish for the last few months and he would be well rid of her when he handed her back to her father, yet, however much he loathed her, he did not want to think of her at the bottom of the ocean. She would make some hapless, dull and dreary man a scintillating, earth-shattering wife one day.

Midday passed, and his fears grew stronger. Something had harmed her, he was sure of that now. She might have been bitten by a snake and be lying in her death throes. If it took him all day he would search the island until he found her. He *must* find her.

As Allegra stared at the dark, cloaked figure, the strangest sensation tingled under her skin. It was as if all the hairs on her body had twisted round to lie in the opposite direction.

'Nash, is that you?' she called, but she knew that it was not. He had no cloak, and he was taller than the figure she could see.

She could turn back into the darkness – but how did she know that the figure would not follow and kill her in the dark? Summoning her courage, she took the first faltering steps towards it.

Halfway across the cave, she laughed out loud, but it was uneasy laughter. How had such a thing found its way here, to an isolated island which was considered the property of Islam? She knew enough about Muslims to know that they did not worship a female god, but only the one male god whom they called Allah. Why then was this statue of a woman standing here in this underground cave?

Stepping closer, she found herself standing in a pool of the brightest sunshine, as if the glowing and gilded apricot light were channelled cleverly to fall directly upon this life-sized figurine. Now she saw that the cloak hung like wings, yet the entire body beneath could be seen clearly. It was of a naked woman, shapely, distinctly female, its generous curves, the full, heavy breasts and wide hips fashioned to make a direct statement: this is woman, fertile, sexual, omnipotent. Round the carved neck was a torc of a shiny gold colour which fitted the neck to perfection, as if carved out of the stone. Allegra reached out to touch the torc, and realised that it was solid gold, rich, beautifully and incredibly ancient. Time spoke to her through her fingers, a shiver of delight and primitive memory soaring in her mind. She half remembered being a part of this same primitive past, but nothing clarified in her brain. She felt, without knowing, that women who had lived at the time that this statue was carved were proud, powerful, the authority in their land, possessors of life and fecundity, spinners of destiny, rulers of men's lives, founts of wisdom and of knowledge.

In England there was a queen who was deified as a goddess and who was all but worshipped by her people. She was now a great age, yet immortal, so it seemed, vigorous enough to live for ever, and radiating in that agelessness such an omnipotence that her people were strengthened by it and were joyful and optimistic.

Instinctively, Allegra felt that this carved statue in the feathered cloak was a representation of a goddess or queen who had once held sway as successfully as Elizabeth did now. How old would this statue be? The face was far from beautiful, the features blunt and displaying a maternal homeliness which reassured, and yet, at the same time, possessed a grandiose authority. Having touched the thick gold torc, the carved stone curls which billowed down past the plump, sloping shoulders, Allegra felt that her next move should be one of obeisance. But why? Kneel to a stone statue? That was Popery, firmly and brutally dismissed by Henry VIII. *Worship no pagan idol.* Surely the Bible said that somewhere, or words to that effect? She could not remember exactly what was the admonition.

Something was reborn in Allegra as she caressed the stone

curls, the snub-nosed face, the wide, sensual mouth and the glittering torc. How it shined, as if it were regularly polished by adoring hands! Now she saw something which had eluded her before. The goddess, queen, or whatever she was, rested her stone feet on a coiled serpent. From the distance it looked like a footstool, or a circular dais, but now that Allegra saw the coiling shape, the raised elongated head with the darting, bifurcated tongue, she felt suddenly chilled.

A woman standing on a snake . . . Why? What did it mean? That she was so powerful she could kill such creatures? Or was the snake somehow her familiar, like witches and their cats? Was this a statue of the famous Egyptian Queen Cleopatra, who had died by placing a poisonous snake to her breast? Allegra had seen a performance of the play by William Shakespeare, but she had thought that an asp was a tiny serpent . . .

All her conjectures came to nothing, for she knew nothing beyond what eye and instinct told her. This woman represented here in stone was – had been – very important, and her people must have hidden her statue down here before they died. Perhaps they were all destroyed by a natural disaster which had overtaken the island centuries before, or perhaps they had loved this queen so dearly that they had made this place her temple, carving this memorial statue and giving it pride of place here where the sunlight streamed through from a secret crevice, illuminating their beloved monarch?

It was a cheering thought. Allegra smiled to herself. No more did she feel the aches and discomforts of her body, not even hunger. In finding this sacred memorial, ancient temple, it was as if she had found herself.

Allegra found herself humming a strange, lilting tune and then she was dancing before the statue in the most abandoned way, as if she had been doing that all her life, a dipping, swirling spiral dance which made her feel light-footed and graceful, weightless and happy. Long-lost memories were pouring through her, ancient ceremonies and sacrifices, the flares of torches in the night and women singing sacred songs, initiation ceremonies which were secret to all save the chosen few, all of whom must be virginal and dedicated to their beloved mother goddess . . . Artemis . . . the name was in her head, bright and happy, and there were tears on her cheeks, when she heard the voice of Man calling her, summoning her back with a sharp, painful shock from the dear and familiar ancient time.

'Jesu, woman, how in the name of the Virgin did you get down here? I heard you singing . . . Why singing for Heaven's sake?'

Worship of the Virgin might be secret in her homeland now, but the old phrases held fast. 'Sweet Virgin'; 'Mother of God'; 'Holy Virgin'; the people still said them as they had done for centuries. What words had they used for this stone goddess? She wished that she knew.

'*Allegra!* Are you sunstruck again? I asked you what you were doing here. I have been searching for you for hours, you witless mamekin. You've spoiled my dinner and yours too. Are you not hungry?'

She smiled up at him winsomely. How big and powerful he was, blocking out her vision of the stone goddess. He did not even seem to have noticed the cloaked figure in the corner, but he would, for she would show him now.

'Look!' She pointed, and watched as his eyes fell on the statue, first on the hair, the face, and then the thick gold torc.

'*Jesu!*'

In two strides he was touching the stone exactly as she had done, his fingers sliding over the gold with pleasure and disbelief.

'I had not thought that this was one of those places. Imagine this being here all these years, hundreds of years and no one knowing. If those greedy Arab slavers had found her, she would have had her head hacked off and her pretty trinket would be gracing some concubine's throat by now.'

'You will not deface the statue, will you?' Her heart twisted in her breast. She thought that she would kill him if he harmed the goddess.

'I? Never. These things are sacred. I would no more steal from this than I would from the Virgin Mary. Oh, you did not guess that I might have a certain fondness for the Lady in the blue cloak? You took me for a cold-eyed Protestant, did you?

These matters cannot be cast aside in one generation, if that.'

'She is like the Virgin Mary, but not like her.' Allegra felt stupid after speaking in that ignorant way. 'Someone worshipped her, did they? Many years before?'

'One of the ancient Mother Goddesses. There were many in this part of the world. Possibly in ours, too. I have spoken to men who have found the temples still holding their sacrificial bones and even blood stains where the temperature is right for preservation. One man brushed away the sand and discovered a complete skeleton, with the dagger still embedded in its heart, and every limb heavy with gold bracelets and collars.'

'Sacrifices? Humans killed, you mean? What for?'

'To make the earth fertile for new crops, to placate the gods of nature, to shed fresh blood which would feed the soil and create new strength out of which the harvest would spring. They say that our own ancesters were head-hunters, but I find that hard to believe myself.'

'So I was not far out in calling you a cannibal!' Allegra cried triumphantly.

'They were your ancestors, too, Lady She-Wolf, the tribes who lived in our homeland before the invaders came, the Saxons and the Norsemen, the Normans and the Jutes.'

'So did our ancestors live here centuries ago, the same who lived in England, I mean?'

'They may have done. They were great travellers. Who knows? But our ancestors were not the only ones to worship goddesses and sacrifice humans. It was quite the fashion before the Son of God brought light out of the darkness.'

'Or brought darkness where once there was light . . .' Allegra's eyes glittered, and she felt light-headed. When Nash took her by the arm and began to lead her towards the outer world, she did not stop him. She could come here any time, now that she knew of it. She would come here and dance and sing and remember when woman reigned . . .

The glare of the sun, the heat and the birdsong shocked her senses. Seeing that she was about to faint, Nash scooped her up into his arms and began the long trek back to his camp. Her eyes closing at once, she relaxed in his embrace, half-fainting, half-sleeping, yet recalling nothing when at last they reached camp. For a moment she could not think of why he was holding her and then she knew, and gazed up at him with alarm and astonishment. Her head was resting on his breast, her body limp against his, her lips only inches from his mouth, such a soft, curving, yet powerful mouth, that she ached to kiss it a dozen times.

The delicate moment was ruined by her stomach letting out a loud and angry growl of hunger. Cheeks flushing, she wriggled to freedom and watched in silence as Nash removed the shells to reveal the roast meat he had prepared. Cold, it went down better than steaming hot, and she took her time in chewing. While she ate, her thoughts settled themselves from a wild, ungovernable tangle, becoming more of the kind she was accustomed to, well-ordered, if not always serene and confident.

As she finished the last of the fruit, she said, 'Why did they put her in the dark ground like that, hidden away? Why not in a temple above ground or some kind of church where everyone could see her?'

'If they had, her gold collar would have been torn from her neck by invaders, and her statue smashed to pieces by hordes of non-believers, exactly as happened to effigies of Mary in the days of Henry VIII. Mother Goddesses are fated to be worshipped in secret. Have you not noticed how the Virgin's followers do so even today in England?'

'But only because Mary Stuart was a Catholic and kept insisting that she was the rightful Queen of England in place of Mary, and because Elizabeth's sister made Catholicism obligatory while she was queen, and it turned everyone against her.'

'And those who did not obey were burned, were they not? It is better to let man worship as he wishes, surely you agree to that? How can people be bludgeoned into believing certain facts, and what happens when those facts are changed at the whim of a monarch? Does man change too, change those beliefs which are the strongest and most powerful in his life? In the fields and hamlets of England where life is hard and the living lurches from one poor harvest to the next, with fortunes destroyed by storms and cold weather and nothing certain, not even life itself, people need their Virgin to love and worship.

She brings them warmth and comfort; she is their mother, their sweet mercy, their intercessor before God.'

'You are a Papist, Nash Hamilton, a Papist! What would my sister say if she knew? You want to marry into one of the staunchest Protestant families in England, yet you worship idols!'

'I am giving you the other side of Catholicism, Lady Sharp-Tongue. There was a very ancient religion here long before Christianity, and the Mother Goddess was the God before Jesus came, and she was suborned so that Jesus could take her place.'

'You are moon-fevered!' Allegra sprang to her feet, her heart beating wildly. 'You are a heretic, you should be . . .'

'Burnt at the stake?' he suggested, lifting one dark-gold brow quizzically. 'Tortured by the Inquisition, perhaps? They are so good at these things. Or would My Lady She-Wolf prefer beheading? For me, I mean . . .' He threw back his head and roared with laughter.

Angry beyond words, she looked about for something to throw, a large rock or a heavy stick. She wanted to stop him laughing, to knock the breath from his body. He was pompous and supercilious, and she loathed him with every fibre of her being.

'Over there.' He pointed to a large chunky rock and she ran towards it. It was in her hands, raised above her head ready to throw, when he leapt at her so suddenly that she let out a scream.

'You are the pagan around here, Lady Proudheart, not I,' Nash growled as he knocked the weapon from her grasp and gripped her by the wrists, her hands still raised in the air so that she could not bring them down. They were aching now, her back straining, but he manacled her as tightly as if he were torturing her.

'You will break my arms . . .' she gasped, tears starting from her eyes. 'Let go, let go!'

'Would you not agree that you would be safer with one or two limbs broken? As it is, you run around like a madwoman, doing whatever takes your fancy. I have never known anyone with so few wits.'

'Except perhaps yourself,' she gritted, struggling to remove her wrists from his grasp. It was useless. 'You are right. You should have been in the Inquisition. They tortured women, did they not?'

'And still do if they have any sense. All women should be beaten at regular intervals to keep them sane, and to show them who is master.'

'You are the lowest and most foul monster I have ever met, Nash Hamilton! You are a bully and a brute who tortures women for his own delight. You are enjoying this, you barbarian!'

He freed her so hastily that she lost her balance and felt herself falling over. To save herself she scrabbled wildly at his body, but it was impossible to get a grip on naked flesh, as she found. To her dismay, her fingers lodged in the belt of his breeches and, as she fell, she pulled them open with him on top of her.

'That is the first time any woman has been quite so obvious,' he murmured in her ear as she screamed and kicked to throw him off, 'but now that we are here, it was quite a pleasant notion of yours to seduce me, and I applaud you, my lady.'

'How dare you! Get off me, you pig, get off, or I shall hurt you. I shall, I shall!'

Roaring with laughter, his arms tightened round her, his body crushing hers.

'Yes, feathers are very painful, and so are the breeze. Which will you hit me with first?'

Bringing her knee up as savagely as she could, she enjoyed intense satisfaction as he grimaced. Then she saw such anger blazing in his eyes that she wished that she had not hurt him.

'Normally, I would not touch you with the tip of an anchor, but I think that I have earned this, Lady She-Wolf.'

He clamped his mouth on hers so suddenly that the breath shot from her lungs. She tried to scream and to kick, but he was weighting her down with his considerable strength. She could not breathe, she could not move, she could not escape. Unable to shriek insults at him was the worst thing, but being his prisoner ranked a close second.

The kiss went on for a very long time, far longer than her breath, but he would not release her mouth. The limit of her strength passing, she went limp beneath him, hoping that her lack of response would rebuff him. Small chance of that! He paused, watching her as she gasped for air as if she had been running, and then, when she was gathering strength to shout, he silenced her again in the same, efficient fashion.

The first kiss was a punishment, ruthless and painful, a way of telling her that she was nothing more than a helpless chit of a girl and that he was very strong indeed and could do whatever he liked with her. The second kiss was different. For a start, she enjoyed it more and more as each moment passed, and, what was more, she could feel that he was enjoying it too.

The magic moment had arrived; she had not been able to watch the metamorphosis, but she could feel its result pressing into her thighs, steely hard and determined.

It was stark danger, of course. The declarations had been clarified, each now knowing what was possible between them: she realising that he desired her, he realising it too for the first time. Before, she had been an infuriating little minx and his future sister-in-law, but now he realised that she was tempting, exciting and responsive.

Unable to restrain herself, she began to pull him closer instead of pushing him away. Ancient primeval feelings were gushing through her, worthy of those who had once worshipped at the shrine of Artemis-Diana, and those other goddesses with different names but all being the same earth mother, extensions of her multiple nature. Slowly, as if she were spellbound, she lifted her knees so that he lay inside them, the instrument which fascinated her lying between her thighs, the sacrifice waiting at the entrance to the shrine.

Her mind was jumbled. As a handmaiden of the goddess, she would give her maidenhead to any man who wanted it. That was the most sacred custom. As the handmaid, she would freely give her body . . . as she was doing now. Curving against Nash's flat stomach and thighs, she revelled in the sensation of intimacy which this brought. He was hers and she was his. This was no stranger come to the temple but her lover, her dearest lover, the man she longed to marry . . .

She could feel his rasping breathing in her ear and knew that he was eager yet surprised. She wanted to laugh out loud, for now she was the aggressor and he must do what she demanded. Her hands reached down, pushing away his breeches, so that she could feel the lean hard power of him, and hold the velvety stiffness in her palm. How soft and warm it was and yet how rigid! Now there was the problem of her own clothes, but he was tearing at her shirt and tugging down her breeches as if he could not wait. Nothing could stop what came next. Nothing.

She curved against him, thrusting to meet *his* thrusts, feeling the hardness battering at her maidenhead. It could not get past, although he was trying valiantly.

'You are a virgin!' He sounded amazed.

'Should I not be?' she gasped.

'You behave like a harlot!'

'Have you seen me begging men in the streets then? I do not think so!'

'A hussy, then.'

'No one else has ever accused me of that. Only *you*. You are so used to mixing with villains, Nash Hamilton, that you see villainy in everyone.'

Then it was impossible to speak. They were consumed by their passion and the glorious moment of consummation. Minutes passed and the pressure increased, the entrance refusing to give way although their fervent desperation should have achieved what they wanted by now. Undaunted, Nash continued to thrust, his arms clamping her tightly, the sweat from his forehead dripping on to her face and neck. She was burning, searing, beginning to throb, yet he still could not gain entry.

Overhead a shimmering, effulgent moon was watching, symbol of the earth mother who had once reigned supreme in the world, above all gods. Ripe and silver, its radiant glow enamelled the two lovers as they lay locked together, mindless of everything but their surging passion. A few yards away, the silver-tipped surf, filigreed with moonlight, swirled and crashed, retreated, then rose to squirm along the darkening sand as if searching for some ancient truth. A nightbird skittered, its sharp cry of alarm making no impact on the man and woman.

'It is a blessing that we have no way of getting off this island, for I think that this is going to take some time.' Nash spoke lightly yet with a suggestion of disbelief. This had never happened to him before, this inability to pierce through a maidenhead, not in all the years that he had been pursuing and making love to women. There was no feebleness on his side – far from it – but this infuriating minx, who had been scorching his senses for months now, had yet again beaten him. She was responsive, ardent, and eager, as was he, but they were getting nowhere. Night had fallen and he had not noticed. The moon was high, and they should have prepared their camp for sleep, but he doubted if he would sleep tonight, not after this.

'What is wrong? Do I displease you?' Her instinct was sure, yet it could not counterbalance the ignorance of the maiden. Allegra knew what she wanted, but how one went about it was another matter, and as for the accepted method, well, perhaps this was it, although she thought not. Nash, scowling furiously, was lying silently beside her, his brows thunderous.

'There is nothing wrong! *Jesu*, this is one way of bringing us to our senses!' Leaping to his feet, he wrenched up his breeches, tied them firmly, then marched off into the undergrowth.

A chill washed over her. She was deformed; there was something terribly wrong with her. Now she knew for sure. Either that or she repulsed him. Tears filled her eyes so that the moon appeared to be washed in molten silver. Sitting on the ground, her arms crossed over her raised knees, Allegra pondered on the male sex and on what had just happened – or failed to happen. She felt sick and unsure, shaken and dismayed. Where had her chastity gone, and her morals? What of her strict upbringing regarding the behaviour of unmarried females with men? It was as if she had donned a different nature for the past few hours, that of a pagan girl who had never been inculcated with right and wrong, with the strictures of piety and chastity indigenous to the Christian religion.

'Elizabeth.' She spoke her sister's name as if it would retrieve her virtue. She was here because of Elizabeth. How could she have forgotten her sister's plight, the sufferings that she must be enduring under the emblem of the flame-breathing dragon? Somewhere, in the blazing, burning desert, her sister might be tramping along one of the incense roads, where slaves and pearls, frankincense and myrrh, spices, ivory, jewels, gold and silks were taken, to be sold for the further enrichment of the man whom they called Lord of the Incense Road, the Amir Adem Ali. Yet she, Allegra, had been thinking only of her own bodily needs, lying with Elizabeth's betrothed, a man who could never ever be hers, for betrothals were as binding as marriage in the eyes of the church.

What had possessed her? Flinging herself to the ground, she pounded the earth with her fists until her body was raw with the blaze of angry self-recrimination.

Chapter Eight

'Here, at the feet of the goddess.'

It was the evening of the following day and Allegra had returned to the underground cave, this time by a less bone-shaking route. There was a track of sorts, veiled by bushes and vines and she tore at these, pulling them aside to reach the low opening which would lead to the statue. She had to think. She and the impious Nash Hamilton had not spoken since the previous night. He had caught and prepared their food, they had eaten in silence and he had then gone on a sortie to search for wood and casks or anything else which might have been washed ashore from the wreck of the *Tudor Raven*.

What did he feel like, having lost his ship and apparently all his crew, for no one else had reached this island? He was a wealthy man, that she knew, but how wealthy she was not sure. Would the loss of one ship make him a pauper or would its material value mean little to him? He had said not one word about the fate of the crew, yet he must have grieved for them, surely?

The magic between them, a temporary bewitchment, was now lost and it was an attempt to revive it that had brought her back here to the cave. At the feet of the goddess she would feel happy.

The sun was falling, and she sat in shadow this time, glancing up now and again to observe the roughly carved yet compelling face. She wanted to observe the face constantly for she had an eerie feeling that the eyes might suddenly sparkle, the mouth open to speak to her. Perhaps she had visited this place before in her dreams, for, now that her first alarm was over, she felt at home here.

The coiled serpent was enormous and fat. She touched his coils with misgivings, for if he sprang to life, then her own life would be brief. Why a serpent? Was it because they crawled deep in the earth and this statue was of the earth mother, or because they appeared out of holes in the ground, and worship of the earth mother took place in caves and underground hollows? Nash said that the spiral shape was sacred to the goddess, so perhaps that came from the coiling snake, or the snake was used as an emblem because it was a spiral shape? She wished she knew all these answers; she felt so ignorant. Her portals on the world had widened quite shockingly, and too swiftly for her to keep pace. How had she thought herself clever and knowledgeable when at home in Cornwall!

When would they be rescued from this island? Nash said that ships passed regularly and it would be a matter of weeks, or even less. They must keep a watch from an uppermost rock and light a fire as a beacon if they spotted a vessel. She was supposed to take her turn to keep watch but she had run away today. It was too dark to see the ocean anyway, and the sight of so much black water chilled her. Sharks or whales or sea monsters may rise out of the waves and come for her.

The stone cave was cold tonight, and darkening rapidly, but she was not frightened here. A shallow stone bowl lay at the side of the goddess and she had brought berries and brightly coloured flowers to place in it, as a meagre offering. She wished that she could bring more, to show her goodwill. Somehow, that seemed important. Offerings were brought to the Mother and Child at harvest time, bread, fruit, sheaves of gilded wheat, eggs and vegetables to be placed before the altar of her local church, so it seemed quite normal to do the same here.

Hearing the scrunching sound of feet on the gritty earth at the entrance to the cave, Allegra leapt to her feet, looking round for a hiding place. There was a dark shadowy corner close to the goddess and into this she sprang, clamping her mouth shut to silence her breath. That interfering man could not leave her alone for a moment. He had to follow her everywhere and interrupt her peace.

'Allegra, are you there? Allegra, answer me! You must let me know where you are going, for safety's sake. I am no nursemaid, but I shall feel quite within my rights to treat you like a naughty child and put you over my knee again.'

Her heart thudded. Did he get some kind of spurious, misbegotten pleasure out of slapping her? She was not scared of pain, but she did not want him to discover her here. This was a secret place, for women only, not for the noisy, blustering intrusions of men.

'Allegra, I am going now. You had better be careful on the return journey as it is dark and you will not be able to see what lies in your path.'

Hearing him retreat, she breathed a grateful sigh and stepped out into the cave.

It was a trick. He had not gone. He was beside her, grasping her wrist and glaring down into her face.

'I thought so, you scheming little vixen! You should be glad that you have someone here who will look after you, for I warrant you would be helpless without it!'

'You are so arrogant that you think no one can manage without you, Nash Hamilton, but I assure you that *I* can look after myself. I can cook and I can do other things too.'

'Embroidery, you mean? And weaving? Collecting petals for pot-pourri and herbs for beauty creams? They are hardly talents which will be invaluable here.'

'Your derision is unbearable, and so are you!' Allegra kicked out with her bare feet, remembering that such a move could hurt her most and minding how she placed her toes against his shin.

'Wildcat! If I run short of animals to catch for food, I can always start on you!'

'Yes, you would, you bully! If your whip were here, I suppose you would relish using that on me too.'

'Whips were designed for keeping stubborn mares in order, yes, so I probably would.' He had neatly side-stepped her kick and now had hold of both her wrists. Her skin was scorching with the pain.

'Stallions are the ones which give most trouble, so I was led to believe,' she spat. 'Running wild, refusing to be broken, treating mares like sluts and abandoning their foals when they are born!'

'That is hardly the case, my little mare. It is man who separates the foal from his father, not nature. In the wild, horses live happily together and there is no abandonment.' Stepping closer, he looked down at her, his eyes glinting in the darkness. 'So you think that I am a stallion, do you? Tell me, was it last night when you formed that opinion in your mind?'

Her heart was juddering as she tried to twist away from him. The arrogance of the man!

'Last night was a failure, if I recall, a total failure. If you are a stallion, then it is long past the time when you should have been put out to grass!'

He gave a roar of rage, and she thought that he was going to knock her down. Flinching, she waited for him to strike her, but instead, he swept her up and off her feet, placing her swiftly on the ground, all in one sinuous movement, and then, before she could scream out or fight, he was on top of her.

'This is where you want it to be, is it not? Here, at the feet of the goddess, symbol of pagan rites, blood sacrifice and the dark primeval world . . . This is what you need, is it not, you scheming little temptress . . . ? You brought me here deliberately for this, didn't you? Admit it!'

She would have screamed denial had his mouth not been crushing hers, his body slamming into hers in the most painful way. Barely able to breathe, she wanted to scratch and kick and scream, but at the same time she had never been so excited in her life. Every part of her was throbbing and tingling, her flesh sparkling, glittering. All the same, as she would die rather than admit such a reaction, she did her best to struggle free. He pinioned her to the earth floor of the cave, there beneath the statue of the pagan goddess who had seen a thousand pagan rites in her time, man conquering woman and impregnating her so that life would continue, seed falling on both female and the earth itself to refertilise it.

This time, nothing would stop him, and nothing did, for he was beyond sense or wisdom, knowing only that this woman roused him as no other woman ever had, not even in the earliest years of his sexuality; she stirred him, she moved him; he could not rest until he had conquered her body. He must have her now, take her, enter her, in the old, time-honoured way, surge into her body and rouse her as he himself was roused.

Allegra was burning from brow to heel, a tingling, scorching heat too powerful for cautious analysis. Her passions and emotions were surging, she was woman, he was man, and nature, the goddess or destiny, had decreed that they were to become one. Opening her legs, she locked them round Nash's narrow hips, this move taking him so much by surprise that he paused momentarily . . . but not for long. Both were desperate now, exultant, overwhelmed by desire, consumed by the self-same longing: to be joined to one another.

The struggle was not too long this time, and after four or five powerful strokes, the barrier broke and Allegra felt herself invaded by the steely instrument which had so intrigued her. Now she had what she wanted. She could feel it inside her, hard and stabbing, thrusting against her, and the sensation was intolerable ecstasy. She gripped at his hair, tugging at it for leverage, to pull him even closer as he kissed her, over and over, kiss after beautiful melting kiss, while his slender hips moved sinuously up and down, propelling him deep within her womanhood.

She gasped, and cried his name, tears of joy sparkling in her eyes; and then she knew why the goddess was worshipped in dark underground caves, for they represented the most secret part of woman, where Nash Hamilton was now, the invader, the conqueror, the male. From this part of woman came all joy, all fruitfulness, the love, the child, the feeling, and, in that moment of consummation, she herself became the goddess.

'Do not worry, I shall not stop yet.'

His voice surprised her. Did gods speak like mortals?

'I said I shall not stop yet, although you might have thought I would.'

'Why would I think that?' She was puzzled.

'Because I have finished.'

'Finished? What do you mean?'

He whispered in her ear, as if to conceal his words from a multitude of watchers, and then she understood.

'It is customary for the man to stop at this point,' he grinned in the darkness, 'but I shall not, so relax, little one.'

Sighing, she pulled him closer, not telling him that she was hugely, enormously ignorant on such matters and all that she must learn would come from him.

He was as good as his word, continuing for a long, long time with as much passion and hardness as before. It was her first time, so she was growing a little sore, but that was not going to be allowed to interfere with their need. Their bodies had been created to be used in the way in which they demanded, not the other way round.

'Women can do it too,' he said, whispering in her ear. 'Not quite the same as men, for there is no outpouring, but with the same sensation.'

She blushed hotly, which seemed odd in the circumstances, so gently he explained to her what he meant, and that he wished her to experience the same enjoyment. As she did not know how this would be done, she said little, waiting for him to explain more, his kisses falling like velvet on her breasts, his fingers gently exploring between her thighs, his touch both sensitive and masterful. He touched something there which made her feel dizzy and excited at the same time, sending an unbearable tingling sensation right through her so that she gasped.

'You see, even the oldest stallions have their uses,' he grinned. 'A hoof here, a hoof there, and anything can happen.'

'What did you do then?'
'This.'
He did it again and this time she squirmed with delight for it was too thrilling to endure, and yet she must have more of it. As he planned to give her more, she lay back while he stroked her expertly, and within a few minutes, she was writhing and gasping in his arms, her face flushed, her head twisting from side to side.

'I guessed that you would be the responsive kind,' he said. 'Those curving breasts and flashing eyes are hardly the façade for a prude.'

'If I am a prude, then you are a bishop!' Allegra retaliated swiftly as the flush of heat spread from her cheeks and down across her neck and breasts.

Laughing, he slipped inside her again, and this time when he entered she was ready, clutching at him frantically, urging him on to a blissful repetition, and then another . . . and another.

It was after midnight when they finished, lying stiffly on the hard floor, the cold of the sea blowing in on them, and hunger insisting that they attend to it.

They walked back, hand in hand, the silver moon lighting their way, feeling as if they had known one another for centuries, as if this moment had been carefully arranged for them, predestined in God's scheme of things – or in the goddess's . . .

Their dinner had been stolen by some hungry creatures, so they had to make do with water and fruit, but it did not matter. Love was the most satisfying meal of all. When they had eaten, they curled up together in the cave, arms wrapped round one another like protective shackles and there they slept as the waves crept and sidled across the sand and the stars pulsed with glittering energy.

Nash had found some shattered casks and pieces of wood washed up on the opposite side of the island, along with slivers of driftwood, ragged shirts and a boot, a metal casket which was locked but with no key, and a soggy box made of cheap wood and which had once contained food. There was nothing which they could eat, and nothing to drink. He had hoped for some alleviation of their diet, but no luck. Nor were there wearable clothes so they must stay in the creased shirts and even more creased and shabby breeches. One thing was sure: they would now be able to wash their clothes and not worry about seeing one another naked while their linen dried in the sun. In fact, that sounded like an excellent idea. Washday. Nash's eyes sparkled at the thought.

He did not speak of the bodies which he had found. Four of the crew, drowned. Two had tied themselves together and, unable to free themselves, had been drawn into the depths. He recognised them all. They were his men, his crew. Tom. James Bastnett. Stephen Adey. Malachy Dare. His men; and the storm had taken them. Making the sign of the cross, he had fallen to his knees and prayed for their souls. It was the least that he could do and he knew that they would have done the same for him. Then he dug graves for them all, shallow, as he was digging with his bare hands, but efficacious all the same. Over the graves he piled rocks and stones to keep away the buzzards, and then he prayed again. When he got back to England – when! – he would see that these men's families wanted for nothing, as he would see to the families of all those who had failed to survive the storm. He truly hoped that some had survived, being picked up by a passing vessel, or clinging to a raft or driftwood which had taken them to safety. This was not the only island in this area; there would be dozens like this.

He had prayed, at the start, that other members of the crew would reach here alive. To think of his men all dead had been intolerable. Now that he and Allegra were lovers, he knew that he was delighted they were alone. *Lovers.* He stood staring out to sea, legs astride, hands on hips. Not a ship in sight. Nothing but the bare, bright-blue horizon and a speckle of white clouds. God help him, that was how he wanted it now. He wanted them to be marooned here for as long as possible because he knew that the real world would want them back all too soon and when it claimed them, he must say goodbye to Allegra for ever. He would not break his betrothal vows: what decent, God-fearing man would do that? Elizabeth loved him; she had been first and he would never betray her publicly even if he had done so privately, here on this pagan island. Having found her, he would marry her instantly, and then he must never, ever see Allegra again, whatever problems that caused in the family.

Chapter Nine

The surface of the moon-dappled rock pool shivered and then split as two heads burst into view. Laughing, Allegra and Nash kissed, hugging one another's wet bodies tightly. They were naked: what need did they have of clothes here? The cool and silken waters were their robes, love providing the ornamentation which made them glow. Twisting, touching beneath the surface of the pool, they revelled in their intimacy, holding, squeezing and laughing when their heads split through the silvered icing of the water's surface.

They had eaten well, Nash having caught two plump fish with a long spear which she had helped him to smooth and polish against sharp stone. He had stood for more than two hours, barely moving a muscle, waiting for fish to dart near enough to the shore for him to stab, all the while considering more efficient methods of obtaining food. If he could find some netting and drape it across poles, forming a trap, then the fish might swim into it, become entangled and be waiting for him to retrieve them. Fresh water from the pool had helped them to wash down the succulent roasted fish. Then, after resting while their meal digested, they walked hand in hand in the moonlight until they came to the pool which seemed to invite them to jump in.

Allegra tore off her shirt and breeches first, leaping into the water without a second thought. She knew it was not very deep and Nash would save her if she got into difficulties. He had promised to teach her how to swim, if they had time before they were rescued.

When he spoke of their being rescued, she fell silent. She did not want the world to intrude. After their heady days here, she could never return to the suffocation of her former life with its hidebound customs and limitations. She did not want to go back to the moral lectures, the strictures and disciplines which she now realised had been crippling; heavy gowns and wooden stays which grasped like mailed fists, rigidly starched linen and collars, tightly curled hair stuck with pearls and feathers, all the paraphernalia of Tudor life. How tedious, debilitating and artificial it all was. She would never go back to it. Never!

She wanted to be alone with Nash for eternity, just the two of them; surely they could hide in some foreign land and live as man and wife? Everyone would think that they had gone down with the *Tudor Raven* so no one would imagine any the worse of them. Surely he felt the same as she?

Next time they hugged in the water's silky depths, she clamped her knees around his hips and wriggled against him invitingly.

'Tell me that you love me, Nash Hamilton, tell me!'

Laughing, he lifted her on to him, so that he plunged into the very depths of her, a perfect fit as though they were fashioned for one another. Gasping, her neck fell on to his shoulder, her arms clutching round his neck. He pushed deep and hard, a bee searching the blossom for pollen, and she gasped again, speechless with desire and lust and yearning. No one else had ever loved like this, nor felt such a powerful longing, she knew. This was fate, destiny, call it what you will, but it was theirs, entirely theirs. Nash said that the Turkish used the word kismet for fate, and she liked the sound of it; like their love, it began with a kiss, and ended with a meeting.

The moon seemed to swell in its efforts to peer down closer at them, watching, meditating on their love-making, while the ebony sky billowed like a veil transformed into cloth-of-silver by the stars. All was beauty; ecstasy was here on this pagan island where they had forged their love for all time.

'Tell me that you love me, Nash Hamilton,' she whispered, but he kissed her into silence and thrust against her, palming her breasts and gently squeezing them so that she shuddered with bliss. Hours seemed to glide by and yet he did not stop, for here in this place he had the strength of gods. Then she felt the start of that disturbing yet urgent sensation. How strange it was, so new and overwhelming, springing from her and yet she had no knowledge of it before meeting Nash. Welling, the sensation spread through her thighs and stomach, to her breasts and back again, settling where Nash was filling her. There it danced and twisted, so that her breath vanished and she gasped out loud, over and over, her legs weakening, her head thrashing. It was sheer ravishment; how had she lasted all these years without it?

'There, you did it all by yourself that time,' he grinned as her whirling sensations began to slow and she could see him clearly again.

Now she felt limp, falling against his tanned body so that he carried her safely to the edge of the pool, and there, after placing her gently on their bed of ferns, he entered her again, as they lay on their sides, staring into one another's eyes, her leg curving over his hip. This way, she could touch his face and look deep into his eyes, feel the strength of him fitting inside her in a different yet equally exciting way.

He had not told her that he loved her, but she was positive that he did. She loved *him*, madly, wildly, irrevocably. She would go anywhere in the world with him, live anywhere, endure any conditions – privation, poverty, destitution, anything to be with him; surely he would respond in kind? Destiny had brought them to this pagan island, this Garden of Allah, to make them face what they had been fighting so hard: that they were made for one another.

'I have never felt like this before, Allegra,' he sighed, his eyes glittering. 'Never before, ever. That is the greatest compliment I can pay you, so take great care of it, sweet little minx.'

She laughed, feeling proud and joyful, not fully understanding.

'I can say the same, Nash Hamilton, the very same, but for different reasons from yours. I never did go a-whoring as men do, and no doubt as you did too, for it is in the nature of men to be thus.'

'On that we are agreed. I am glad you think that way, sweeting, for it will make things so much easier when we are rescued.'

'Why, do you plan to search for a whore when we reach land? After this?' She giggled.

'You do not understand . . . Perhaps you never will. Come, let us enjoy ourselves while the moon is bright. We are heathens come here to take part in pagan rituals, to worship the earth goddess and to revel in these fertility rites. We have journeyed a very long way, so let us make it memorable.'

'It is, it is already. How could I ever forget it?' Allegra spoke from the heart.

'That is it . . . enter into the spirit of it. You are a quick-witted girl . . .' He stopped speaking then, for speech was impossible at that moment.

This time, they were even closer, revelling in their peak of ecstasy at the very same moment as they cradled one another, mouths pressed together. After, they lay until they began to feel chilled in the breezes from the sea. Leaping to their feet, they pulled on damp clothes and half-ran, half-walked, hand in hand back to their camp.

There the ashes of the fire were soon provoked into flame so that they could warm themselves, steam flowing like a vaporous mist from their clothes, before they curled up to sleep, tightly crushed together, Allegra's head on her lover's shoulder, his head cushioned by a pillow of ferns.

As Allegra sailed into sleep, it was easy to imagine that this enchantment would last for ever, that they were sweetly caged in a time long past which encapsulated this island but nowhere else. That being so, the very last thing Allegra wanted was to leave . . . Go back to the world of morals and piety, the obligations of chastity and early marriage to a man selected for her by her father because his name was right or his fortunes pleasing? No, she wanted her freedom, the freedom to love and cherish this man above all others.

Her dreams were tormented and unsettling. Wild figures, shrouded and dark, were creeping through the vines towards her and her lover. She knew what they were: frightening and oppressive beings from the ancient time of the earth goddess.

Were she and Nash to be their sacrifice? She jumped awake, seeing the dark faces draped in some kind of dull-coloured veiling. She knew that they brought death and she was terrified.

'Sweeting.' Her lover's arms enclosed her, his kisses gentling her mouth. 'It was only a dream. Nothing shall hurt you while I am here.'

She slept again, reassured, and this time the dark and ominous figures did not return.

The days mingled together so that time, or the man-made meaning of time, faded and vanished. Their days were spent in searching for or catching their food, cooking and eating it, fetching fresh water from the pool, bathing and washing their clothes, which dried swiftly in the hot midday sun, cleaning out their cave and making fires, gathering brushwood and ferns to burn. That was the practical side, vital to their survival but nowhere near as delightful and satisfying as their love-making.

Their bodies were in harmony. They slept and woke together, felt hungry and thirsty together; rarely was one bursting for adventure when the other was weary.

Allegra had grown up with a father, who, being an early riser, believed in his family following suit, for he did not like to be alone at dawn. His hearty singing, of hymns and soldiering songs – in particular the Agincourt Victory song – would ring round the house until everyone was awake and yawning. She had considered that a husband like that might well be tiresome. Here was the man who woke when she did, or, if he woke before, would go about the morning tasks silently so as not to wake her. Breakfast would be ready when she opened her eyes. To her, that tender thoughtfulness was love in its finest form.

Once she had grumbled at being woken at five in the morning by her father.

'Father, if only I could sleep a little longer then I would not take all morning to wake up!' she had complained.

'My cherub, be like your sister who wakes with me and thus

has more hours in the day for her devotions. You females take so long a-dressing that if you woke at midday, you would never have time for your prayers. A virtuous woman is equal to the finest rubies. No child of mine is ever going to neglect her godliness by staying overlong in her bed!'

In winter it had been hardest, when the night was black and dawn came hours after their rising. The icy night could not be appeased by the largest fire or the thickest gown, and their fasts would be broken with freezing hands gripping mugs of mulled ale, their breath steaming as thickly as that from the liquid.

Here she woke to shimmering dawns, and temperatures which were as hot at mid-morning as they were in the middle of the hottest summer day in Cornwall. Once she tried an experiment. At midday, choosing a rock which was heated by the sun, she washed it clean and broke their dinner on to it: four eggs, which she had climbed a tree to find, grazing hands and knees but determined to succeed in her quest. She was right. They did begin to set and whiten with the heat from the stone. Watching, she saw them forming into plump ivory circles before she pushed them on to the flat shell which they used as a platter.

They were not fully cooked, but they tasted delicious and were a welcome change from fish and meat.

That night there was a storm. It blew up out of the calmest evening to gush and howl around them with a terrifying fury. They lay in the cave, locked in one another's arms, listening to the smash of the waves and the whipping, wrenching sound of the wind. Plants and bushes which lacked deep roots were being hurled through the air and dispatched to oblivion, driftwood and shattered casks following them. During the night, an ear-shattering crash woke them. Something had blown on to the roof of the cave, where it jutted out from the rock, and from the sound of it, it may well be a tree trunk. They were grateful for the screen they had made from piled stones and wood at the entrance of their cave.

Nash did not tell Allegra of the old sea legend that the storm which followed a shipwreck would bring the bodies of the dead out of the waves to confront those who still lived. He would never admit to it, but the thought gave him the shivers.

When it was light they went out to see what damage had been done. The shore was littered with streamers of seaweed, grotesque and black, and here and there a dead creature. Strips and splinters of new wood and old, battered barrels and casks, a frayed length of tarry rope, a silver dish, a candlestick, another boot, hats, and a weed-entwined crucifix of a cheap metal, the sort favoured by the poor – perhaps from the neck of one of his own crew. Thoughtful, Nash pocketed it. Then seeing a mound in the distance, he suggested to Allegra that she start their breakfast while he went on exploring.

Allegra too had seen the mound, and she thought that she knew what it was. Bodies. She did not want to take the woman's part while Nash did the manly thing, so she followed him to the spot where the two men lay. The sea had placed them on the sand with their arms locked together as if they were lovers. It was a grim parody of love, for the bodies were bloated and hideous in death, their faces swollen so that their eyes were no longer visible, their mouths gaping for air, their skins a sickly greenish-white, luminous in a strange surreal way.

'Do not look.'

'I must.'

She wanted to see what death was like, this mortality which took men away from all that was dearest to them. There was nothing left here but distended, horribly coloured bodies, rotting flesh, weed-flecked hair. Their spirits had gone long ago, leaving empty shells.

The muscles at the back of her calves convulsed as she stood, transfixed, unable even to turn her head.

'Mule-headed woman. I told you not to look!'

Taking her by the shoulders, Nash turned her away and propelled her back to the camp.

'Would – would they have suffered terribly?' she whispered when he had made her drink some water and seated her by the crackling camp fire.

'It is never easy to die, so they say, but when the first moment is over, I imagine that there is a great peace, a serenity which would be difficult to describe, even if one had experienced it.'

'How near have you been to death – I mean, have you thought that you were about to die?'

'I have nearly drowned twice, if that is what you mean. The first time I remember nothing; the second time, I was welcoming death for it seemed beautiful, a reward, and then I was rudely shaken awake and brought back to this life by someone who had some skills at saving lives. To this day I do not know whether I would have preferred to die or not.'

Allegra's distress surprised her as much as it did Nash. She burst into uncontrollable sobs, tears spurting out of her eyes.

'Oh, if you had drowned, I would never have known you . . . We would not be here now! My life would have been a desert, a desert without you . . .'

Holding her close, Nash stared unseeingly towards the shore until she stopped weeping. Tomorrow he must begin to collect enough brushwood to build a huge fire on the highest rock, and they must keep it alight, night and day. The longer they stayed on this island the worse it would be for her to return to life's realities. As soon as they reached a port, he would put her on the first ship back to England, and then continue his search for Elizabeth. The sooner the better.

The dream figures were as dark and forbidding as before. Leaping across the shore, they surveyed the scene with practised eyes, taking in the graves which Allegra had helped to dig, topped by roughly fashioned driftwood crosses, seeing the footprints embedded in the sand when they held their torches aloft, the flames flickering in the gloom.

A look-out had seen the fire on the rock, burning low. Shouting warnings to his fellows, their captain had ordered their vessel to head towards the island.

Allegra woke on hearing the sandy scrunch of many feet. Thinking that she was dreaming, she nestled close to Nash, but the sounds went on, and then a whisper of guttural, foreign voices made the hairs rise on the nape of her neck. Someone was close, very close, and they were not hailing them, as honest rescuers would . . . They were muttering in a strange tongue, low, throaty words which sounded savage.

'Nash, wake up! Quickly, quickly, I can hear voices . . . Arabs, I think?'

But he was awake, and hoping that she had not heard the approaching footfalls. Now he ordered her to hide in the back of the cave while he behaved as a decoy and drew the Arabs away from her.

'No, I will not do that! I stay with you!'

'And end up with Elizabeth, in some desert harem . . . ? Or worse, raped and beaten by these men? You do not realise what they would do to you, my love. Death would be the better choice.'

'I stay with you! They could kill you! What would I do then?'

To argue further was impossible, so when Nash tiptoed to the entrance of the cave, she was behind him, a stout stick in her hand. All they could see at first were flaring torches held aloft, but Nash knew all too well that guttural tongue, for he could speak it fluently, as he could five other languages. Adventure and exploration were severely hampered by the lack of such knowledge. Nash had sailed after Elizabeth, because her life in the hands of men like these would be a torment. He could not see Allegra taken, too, watch her being raped by these men, one after the other, beaten, whipped or even stabbed to death when they had finished with her. If they were of the better kind, she would be sold into a potentate's household. Even now, they were talking of the unexpected fortune at finding life on this deserted island, for the selling of slaves was their way of life.

'Arabs, slavers, looking for plunder. In the name of God, hide while I speak to them!' Nash whispered in Allegra's ear, pushing her behind him.

'No! If they harm you while I am hiding like a coward, then I would never forgive myself!' she hissed back.

Roughly, he pushed her back, but she had no intention of allowing him to command her in this barbaric, male way, so she fought vigorously.

'If the worst comes to the worst, light the fire each day, keep it burning . . . There is food here to sustain you until a friendly ship arrives . . . But make sure that it is not a slaver before you show yourself! Do you think that I would leave you if I had the choice? I shall be back, you will see . . . I can talk to them and spin them a tale. Hide now. Hide, and be silent!'

'No, I am not letting you go alone! *No!*' Allegra's voice rose, and it was then that Nash knew that he must take action, for the voices were almost within a few feet of them.

If he let these men see her, a beautiful, white-skinned girl, the most prized booty in the world, she would be condemned to a terrible life. Two sisters in bondage . . . No, he must not allow it to happen.

Closing his mind to what he must do, he punched Allegra neatly on the jaw, so swiftly that she felt nothing and lost consciousness immediately. Then, scooping her up, he ran to the rear of the cave where the rocks were rough and uneven and tucked her body down behind them. Pray God she would be safe and stay silent there until the Arabs had gone. If they killed him, or took him into slavery, both of which were possibilities, at least she would be alive still, plucky little wench that she was, and a rescuer would come along eventually to take her back to England.

Fired with his determination to save her from multiple rape followed by a life of slavery, or a brutal death, he did not pause to analyse the emotions which were pounding inside him at the thought of separation from her – if it came to that. He would be the decoy. He would make the Arabs think that he was alone on the island. Whatever happened to him now, she would be free and alive.

He hastened towards the Arabs, hoping to distract them from the cave, speaking rapidly in their tongue to disarm them. Such was the rarity of a non-Muslim speaking their language that they were momentarily stunned, looking at Nash as if he were an Arab spirit locked in a Westerner's body. One or two, thinking of jinns and fearful magic, stepped back in alarm, but others did not react so primitively. They saw a tall, strong and vigorously handsome man before them, his hair an aureole of silver-gilt in the torchlight, his body bronzed a rich russet brown. There were pashas and princes who would pay vast sums of money to possess such a beautiful man with such extraordinary colouring, pashas – catamites – whose preferences were for male lovers.

Husain, who led the band, saw his fortunes made. Prince

Qasim would pay highly for this man, as would the Pasha of Omir. Then there was their own master, Adem Ali, Lord of the Incense Road. He, too, would be grateful for such a man whom he could sell to the highest bidder. Husain's thoughts ranged over these three possibilities, coming back each time to the fact that if Adem Ali discovered he had cut him out of the arrangement, then he, Husain, would be cut in a different way, tortured and hacked to death as an example to all those who might be considering betraying their master. Adem Ali controlled the Incense Roads in Arabia, decided the fate of all the treasures which travelled along them, human or otherwise. His anger was dreadful, as bad as evil jinns, and Husain knew that death would be a pleasant relief after the tortures to which Adem Ali would submit him if he discovered his deceit.

On the other hand, if he sold the gold-haired man to Prince Qasim or the Pasha of Omir, he would be so rich that he could sail to anywhere in the world and live in luxury for the remainder of his days.

A babble of discussion amongst his men brought Husain's thoughts back to the present. He waved to them to be quiet, then he voiced his idea: he would share his riches with them, he said, and none would ever have to work again, or fear their master. He could see their faces brighten at this prospect, then darken with remembrance of Adem Ali's terrifying revenge on those who disobeyed him.

Last year, three men had tried to trick Adem Ali out of the full payment for a cargo of damasks, china silk, and cloth-of-gold, and he had ordered them to be tortured, whipped on the soles of their bare feet until they fainted with agony, after which they were chopped to pieces, little by little, in the most skilful manner, so that they remained conscious until near the end. Who would volunteer for such a fate? Adem Ali ruled in savage times, and savage punishments must be meted out to keep order.

Nash gritted his teeth, listening to what they were saying and weighing up the situation. Then, when they thought that he was relaxed, he began to run, speeding away from them before they knew what he was planning. On, on, he ran, faster and faster, as far from the cave as possible, along the beach, farther and farther away.

Behind him he heard raucous shouts, and the thudding of dark feet, but he did not think of anything except leading them away from Allegra. What man would prefer his beloved to be savagely raped by foreign devils, or sold into slavery, if he could prevent it?

Ahead, he saw the slavers' trireme, and fluttering aloft, although it was too dark to make it out now, the ubiquitous emblem of the Lord of the Incense Road, the flame-spewing dragon.

'Please God, if you save her, I will do anything . . . submit to anything, any cruelty or barbarity in Your name, as penance, if only You let her escape these devils . . .'

He did not see the twisting outflung root of the tree, concealed by sand, and his foot locked into it. With a breath-crushing thud, he fell to the ground. Within moments the Arabs were on him, kicking, spitting and threatening. Turning on to his back, stars flashing across his vision, he saw a myriad heads, like a monstrous hydra above him. Before he could summon his strength, his hands were bound behind his back, his ankles shackled, and he was being lifted up and carried towards the sea.

He was flung on board the trireme with a loud smack, the cracking sound of skull and spine on wood, but he righted himself instantly, clutching at coils of rope to pull himself up. They brought heavier shackles, but he fought them continually, then, when his arms and legs were burdened by irons, they looped a chain from these to the main mast against which he was forced to stand, facing the island as the sailors prepared to leave.

There was a fine wind, perfect for propulsion, and they intended to make good use of it. Shouts and movement detailing their labours, the trireme began to move, slowly, gracefully, as yet giving no hint of the sinuous speed with which it could move.

Into the wind, as they turned, Nash made out the shape of another trireme a little way away, also preparing to sail, and he bowed his head in a wave of relief. They were leaving. She was safe. God be praised! God be praised! What happened to him now did not matter, nothing mattered save that his darling little she-wolf was safe. Until the day he died, he would give thanks to God, and everything that he did would be dedicated to the Holy Spirit in gratitude.

'*Nash! Nash!*'

The voice speared through him. *No!* God, no! Don't let it be her, let me be imagining it . . .

'Come back, wait for me! Nash! Nash!'

Allegra had recovered consciousness, at first too dizzy to move and then, summoning her strength, she had run down to the beach in search of her lover, following the churned up sand until she saw the departing ship. How could he leave her like this? How could he *do* it? She would die without him, surely he knew that? Her heart banging wildly, her eyes pouring with tears, she screamed his name, over and over, not caring who the ships belonged to, not caring for anything except being reunited with the man she loved.

The second trireme, which had been waiting for its partner sent out a longboat immediately. They had heard a woman's voice, a young, terrified woman. If she was as golden-haired as the man, then they would please their Amir enormously; he would rain gifts and coins upon them.

Allegra continued to scream, then struggle and kick out as the slavers leapt to the shore, ran to her through the shallows and took hold of her, lashing her hands behind her back so that they could survey her. The men, evil-eyed and dark-skinned, were the frightening figures of her nightmare, and they took full advantage of her helplessness. Sickened, she felt them touch her, tearing off her shirt and leering at her naked breasts, pushing, prodding, squeezing as if she were farm produce.

Screaming at them to leave her alone, she found her words ignored. They fingered her hair, pulling and tugging at it and muttering over it in exultation. Then they stroked her face and neck almost wonderingly, before returning to her breasts, each man squeezing and prodding them most painfully. No knowledge of Arabic was needed to translate the look in their eyes, four men all lustily roused by her nakedness. She yelled Nash's name, but in vain, for her lover was chained and manacled on the first trireme.

The first Arab looked at the second and they exchanged knowing glances. Who would guess if they raped her now? It need not take long. These slave traders prided themselves on their ability to be roused and satisfied in moments. The woman's feelings did not matter, not even when she was their wife. Coming to silent agreement, the first man pushed himself against Allegra, his rough dark hands gripping her at the back of the neck while he thrust at her thighs. Terrified, she kicked out, delighting at seeing him groan and double up in agony.

The second man, laughing at his companion's discomfort, leapt at her, taking his place. Something small, very thin and hard was stuck between her thighs, while the third man locked his arms round her ankles so that she could not kick again. She heard her attacker groan suddenly, for he had been unable to control himself sufficiently to penetrate her. Falling away, he took his turn at holding her ankles while the next man jumped at her.

It was worse than her nightmare. It was heart-stopping terror. Exhausted from trying to struggle free, her heart was hammering explosively, her head splitting from the shock. Now and again, when she could summon her breath, she screamed her lover's name, not knowing that she made him wrench against his manacles so that they sliced deep into his wrists and ankles, his blood flowing as freely as his tears.

Just as the third man was launching himself upon her, a shout was heard. The wind was changing. They must hurry now or they would be becalmed. The man whose groin she had so successfully bruised, urged the others to leave, for it was no loss to him. It would be some time before his parts worked properly again; at the moment they felt as if they had been paralysed.

Red-faced from frustration, the last two men exchanged glances before dragging the struggling Allegra to the longboat and tossing her in so that she crashed into its bottom with a sickening thud. Barely conscious, she lay helpless while the two cheated men did their best to satisfy their roused lusts before the longboat came in sight of the trireme, but it was a failed effort, for one was so anxious now that he could not summon an erection and the fourth could only thrust feebly against her side to satisfy himself, for a stronger movement would have tipped the little boat.

She hardly breathed as he pushed against her hip, panting and groaning, his fingers gripping her breasts savagely as he brought himself to a climax, his companions watching enviously. If only they had more time they would all begin again, and do the thing properly, she could tell that from their eyes.

Clothes smoothed, their breathing forcibly calmed they came to the side of their ship. Allegra was pushed and thrust towards the rope ladder which had been let down. Her limbs were shaking violently, but she was pinched and punched from the rear so that pain alone made her ascend. Longing to faint, to turn back, to do anything except climb over the side and into the slavers' ship, she could not see for tears. Where was Nash? What had happened to him? Had they killed him? Oh God, would no one save her from this horror?

The captain of the slaver stood on deck waiting to see their prize. He was very small, very dark, with tightly screwed eyes and a pincer mouth. As she lay gasping and sobbing at his feet, her head swirling so that she could not rise when he ordered her to do so, she could think of nothing save her lover's whereabouts. She had not seen the second ship, for the night was now fully ripe, nor could she hear him shouting her name above the noise of the oars and the shouts of the crew.

Not knowing was unbearable. If he were dead . . . If they had killed him as ruthlessly as they had assaulted her, how could she go on, what would she do? She did not want to live if he were dead.

Summoning her strength, she asked haltingly, 'What have you done with Lord Hamilton? Where is he?' But the slave captain did not show that he had heard her. He was prodding her thighs and breasts with his booted feet, and smirking to himself.

'Where is Lord Hamilton? Tell me where he is!' Allegra cried, lashing out with her clenched fists at the prodding foot.

A volley of rage was her answer as the slave captain leaned down to strike her hard across the face, so hard that she felt her neck click. Stunned, she lay down again, hiding her face in her arms, wanting to die, wishing that her life was ended now.

In the first trireme, his wrists and ankles scarlet from rivulets of blood, a pool of blood at his feet, Nash Hamilton gave heart-twisting sobs. The boat was gaining speed now. He had heard the orders being issued. The two vessels would continue together for the next few hours and then they would separate: his ship to the Bay of Lions, the port which was governed by the Amir's sister on his behalf, and Allegra's ship to the port of Shirh which gave access to the major incense roads into Arabia and the palace where Adem Ali held court. After much arguing the Arabs had decided that betrayal held too much risk. This way, there would be no deceit and their rewards should be magnificent.

The ships gathered speed, spinning along the water's surface, one carrying Nash into lifelong slavery, the other bearing Allegra towards the harem of the Amir Adem Ali, all-powerful Lord of the Incense Road.

PART TWO:

The Incense Road

How long still will my lover, kindling fires of longing, make me burn?
And still how long must I keep watching for a sign of his return?
With love my heart set out upon the road which leads to him;
Will not that door be opened which is knocked on in love's name?

Kadi Burhanettin, 1344–98

Ah, for the time when my star rode triumphant, good fortune its mount,
Keeping abreast with the dream of your fleetly elusive embrace!

Ah, for the time when I lived in the sheltering dust of your path,
Shaded from evils, as though by the wings of an angel of grace!

Ah, for the time when each lofty recess in the place where you dwell
Offered the fluttering bird that my heart was a nest and a base!

Cem Sultan, 1459–95

Chapter Ten

It was impossible to keep track of the days in this black and stinking hold crammed with captured slaves, all black, brown or coffee-coloured, save for Allegra, the only white woman. The stench was intolerable. Chained to the iron rings hammered into the oaken walls of the hold, there was no freedom even to relieve oneself in private or to sleep peacefully in this choking, blinding hell.

Allegra had wept for two days, before slowly emerging from her swollen-eyed misery. Strangely, she was not chained; nor did she know why she was allowed to move freely. Perhaps they thought that white women were too stupid or too feeble to fight back? All round her were women in various stages of heartbreaking discomfort and grief. As her eyes adjusted to the dark, she saw sights which would haunt her for years to come. The corpses of two little girls, twins, chained together, who had died together. They could not have been more than five years old. After her experience on the beach with the slavers, Allegra felt that these children had enjoyed a happy escape, tragic though their death had been.

One woman sobbed loudly, hour after hour, calling out the names of her children and her husband. She knew she would never see them again.

Disgust at the smells and the filth gave way to a spurious acceptance after a few days. It was either that or curling in a corner eyes shut, ears shut, like an unborn infant hiding from the world. As that was alien to Allegra's nature, she began to help those around her, despite the language problems which, with those possessing little intelligence, proved insuperable. Some of the women were black as sea-coal . . . she had never realised that skins could be so dark. Their native tongue was rapid and jolting, their flattened noses, wide eyes and protuberant lips only serving to exaggerate their shocked and fearful expressions. Their hair, black and frizzled, was tightly spiralled against their skulls and they had long, thin legs and arms and sinuous bodies.

These long limbs were proving an encumbrance in the narrow space and the black women wriggled constantly, trying to find a comfortable position.

Allegra was treated with distrust and fear. The women were as startled at her colouring as she was at theirs, so she failed to make any verbal contact with them for some days. She kept trying, however, those of a paler colouring responding more rapidly, in as friendly and open a manner as was possible in such vile conditions.

Food was thrown down at them twice a day. Stale loaves, half-cooked salt meat, battered fruit, ship's hardtack. There was always a most upsetting fight for the food, the women tearing and shoving, screeching and clawing, reaching as far as their chains would allow. When the buckets of water were let down on a rope, they were often tipped over in the rush.

Having watched this disorderly pantomime for two, or three days, Allegra knew that she could not sit back without trying to improve the arrangement.

A little time before the midday food was flung down at them, she positioned herself near the hatch and began to speak to the women, slowly and carefully, in the simplest English she could summon. Unlike many who wish to make themselves understood, she did not think that shouting would make the words easily translatable, so she kept her voice at mid-level. That way, they had to remain still to hear her. When she finished explaining what she had in mind, there was a brief silence before the wailing and rustling, gabbling and chatter burst out again.

Once more she said her piece, and then a third time. Finally, a tiny girl came towards her, pushing back her shroud-like veiling to show that she was fully adult, but amazingly petite in build. As she understood a little English, she now tried to speak to Allegra.

'You – woman – you have caring?'

'Yes, I want to help you all!'

'You – woman – not do. Here woman not care.'

'It does not matter if woman here cares, I care enough for you all.'

'Never get woman here to obey. Stupid, ugly, vile beasts. No heads . . .' The tiny woman pointed to her temple.

'That does not matter. I want them to line up when the food comes, instead of trampling on it and spilling the water!'

'Never you get woman here do it. Never.' The tiny woman smirked, seemingly delighted at this impasse.

'How many speak your language?' Allegra asked.

'Few, not many.'

'Would you like to explain what I want? If you are right, then they can ignore me, can't they?'

'*Me?*' The woman gaped.

'Yes, *you*. Whyever not?'

'They 'neath me. Poor fools.'

'I would speak to them if I could, and I do not think that they are beneath *me*. You speak to me, so what is the problem?'

The woman pondered this for some time. It was plain to Allegra that if anyone here was slow-witted then it was this dwarf-sized female.

'You speak to woman here. I not,' the woman said eventually, her nose held high.

'All right then, tell me what to say!'

And then began the laborious task instituted by the dwarf-sized woman's snobbery. First, Allegra told the woman what she wanted to say, then the woman translated it into her native tongue, repeating it for Allegra to say after her. Having managed this, Allegra then spoke to the women in the hold, dearly hoping that she was indeed passing on the correct suggestion, and not a fabrication invented by the proud dwarf.

The women who could understand what she was saying looked taken aback when she suddenly spoke to them in their tongue. One shrieked and held her hands to her ears, making Allegra falter. Was she insulting them?

'Are you sure that I am telling them the correct message?' She turned to the dwarf woman who was standing by her elbow, shifting from foot to foot.

'Yes, is. Go on. Do you think I lie?'

'No, of course not!' Allegra allowed herself the benefit of a white lie. Hoping that she remembered the foreign words properly, she spoke again, then again. By now she was hot-cheeked and thirsty. The smell and the suffocating heat were too much. No wonder these women lay around looking ghastly, only moving when food arrived. God alone knew how long these poor souls had been shut in this seaborne Hades.

The food arrived, crashing through the hatch at speed. Then came the buckets, six of them, with a single pitcher.

No one moved. Allegra was amazed. They had jabbered among themselves after she had finished speaking, and somehow the message had got through. Having gathered up the food, the rock loaves and biscuits, the rotting, bruised fruit, Allegra gestured to the women to line up and then she found herself with the unenviable task of sharing out the rations equally.

Somehow, she managed it, so that everyone had food and water. Having doled out everything available, she sank down on her haunches, exhausted, only to remember that she had kept none for herself. A wry laugh broke from her lips. A clear case of being too clever!

Then one of the black women shuffled towards her, holding out a piece of bruised fruit, a tropical variety which Allegra had never seen before. Thanking the woman, she sank her teeth into the rotting flesh, hoping that the strange, sickly sweetness was due to the unusual flavour and not to an incipient and poisonous decay.

It was growing hotter and more suffocating by the hour, and the fruit having come to an end, they were given only rock biscuits and strips of salt beef. Unable to break her biscuit with her teeth, one woman cracked it open on an iron ring, then screamed as a mass of maggots fell into her lap. There was general horror as the maggots squirmed, gyrated and jumped in the air, reaching startling heights in their panic. Those who had been attempting to break their biscuits between their teeth now threw them away in disgust. Retrieving these, Allegra broke them open, reasoning that some might be clean and that they could not afford to abandon what little rations they had. Seeing that some were clean, she decided to save a little water and place the broken fragments into this to see if they would soften.

On the third night, she woke at the sound of noisy guzzling. One of the women was devouring her little store of soaking biscuit. Angry, she pushed the woman away, receiving in return a savage punch in the breasts which made her gasp with pain. Seconds later, to her surprise, the thief was being held down by four of the women while Allegra retrieved the stolen bucket and leaned against it for the remainder of the night, the women acting as guards around her.

Next day they shared out the soaked biscuit. Even after all this time, it was still rigid, yet the outer crust was soggy. Nothing could improve the flavour of sawdust chippings.

How much longer would this journey continue? She was experiencing freakish emotions which were totally alien to the normal Allegra. After the first two days of bitter, disbelieving sobbing and grief, she had flung herself into organising the women, while her own feelings rose and fell, sometimes icy with her shocking memories, and then fiery with anger and yearning for Nash. Where would he be now, if he were still alive? She clung to the hope that he was not dead, that thought giving her some spurious courage. If he were alive, one day they may meet again. One day. But if he were dead . . .

She had outraged all morality, all decency, when she stowed away on the *Tudor Raven*, more than half aware that she loved its captain. True, she burned to rescue her sister, and that was the major motivation behind her stowing away, but would she have been so eager had the captain been portly, red-faced and three times her age?

At some point in the sweltering, dimly lit and half-starved hours in the hold of the Arabian trireme, she faced the truth about herself and her actions, realising that she was now being punished for her lustful and self-seeking behaviour. Her new understanding disturbed her powerfully, yet she tried to find the answer to the next question: would she, if the chance arose, do it all again?

And the answer came. Yes, for Nash Hamilton she would do it all again, and again, into eternity.

Dehydrated and dry-throated, her tears were little more than a blur of the vision, but they came with determination, so she rested her head on her bent knees and crossed her arms to conceal her misery.

The woman who called herself Ullah, was suffering from a fierce racking pain, and Allegra did not know how to help her. Water brought no easement nor did a change in her position, or massaging the side of her stomach where the pain raged. Ullah twisted up into a foetal position, her mouth widening with shock and this way she struggled through the night. By morning, she was limp, her hands outstretched, the fingers stiffly splayed, a rivulet of scarlet ebbing from the side of her mouth. By midday, she was dead, her death silent and serene, while Allegra held her hand and whispered prayers over her, knowing that they were not of the woman's creed, but that could hardly be helped.

They told the crew that a woman had died, but the men shrugged, as they had when told of the twins' death, saying what of it? So the women gently carried Ullah's body to the nearest dark corner, covered it in rags and said their own prayers over it while Allegra thought about the heat and the corpse and the possibility of contagion. Ullah might have died of an internal complaint, or a form of Arabian fever: how did she know? Nash would have known . . .

Only by the changes in temperature could they guess whether it was day or night, their clothes sticking to them with the heat and weeks of being unwashed. There were lice, too, as Allegra found to her horror. She had a vivid memory of her sister carrying home a louse in her clothes, after a visit to the city. Elizabeth had screamed as if the devil had hold of her, and

Nash had knocked if from her collar and stamped on it firmly. Would that he were here to do that for Allegra now.

There was a heavy feeling about being unwashed, the dust and dirt sticking like a layer of foetid cloth to the skin, and the squalor and misery increased as the corpse in the corner did what all corpses do in hot countries and began to rot. The smell was intolerable, a choking breath which filled Allegra's throat at every moment, a sweet yet sickening scent which fouled the air.

The women who could speak the slavers' language begged them to remove the body, but day after day they rejected the request.

'When do we reach our destination?' the women asked, but the slavers did not see why they should reply.

'That is in the hands of Allah,' was all that they would say. It was Allegra's first taste of the fatalism of Islam.

She had picked up one or two words of the women's language, deciding that she should learn the one which the majority of them spoke, and soon finding herself able to speak a pidgin version. She had always been a speedy learner. Some spoke Arabic, which she found clumsy and guttural, falling around on her tongue in the most ungovernable fashion. A phrase which sounded like '*Inshallah*' was frequently spoken, both by the prisoners and the slavers. She learned that it meant, 'the will of Allah.' In her own country, the clerics spoke this way, as did some of the older people, but the younger generation were more likely to believe that their fate lay in their own hands . . . with God's assistance, of course.

Was it the will of Allah, this strange pagan God, that she be wrenched from her lover and stolen by pirates? Was this god more powerful than the Christian God? How could he be, he was a heathen god, a mirage created by the ignorant and primitive people of Arabia. She was being contaminated by their pagan beliefs. With that thought came the memory of the statue of the mother goddess with the golden torc round her neck and the snake twisting at her feet. She was a pagan goddess, yet Allegra had identified with her in the most reckless way, and felt no regret. But a male heathen god was quite another matter.

When the sudden shudder of the vessel woke them towards dawn, the women cried with fear. After the shudder came a powerful thud against the ship's side which terrified them. They were being rammed by another ship! The women flocked towards Allegra, as far as their chains allowed, almost crushing her, begging her to save them. White-faced, she sat in their midst trying to soothe them with words which could mean nothing, for she had no power here on this vessel. If an enemy were attacking them and they sank, who would even known what cargo went down into the sea's depths?

Taut, she waited for shouts, for more sounds of ramming, but none came. Then she and the women realised that the ship had stopped moving. That bobbing, creaking sound and the plash of the oars had ceased. Were they becalmed? No, they had docked at one of the many major trading ports under the rule of the infamous Adem Ali.

In a few minutes, Allegra would discover what her fate was to be.

Chapter Eleven

She had grown weak during her dark imprisonment, and when the slavers ordered her to climb the rope ladder which they flung down into the hold, her arms and legs trembled and shook convulsively as she struggled to obey. Some of the women sobbed and said that they could not, or would not, climb, and when Allegra had made her ascent and stood blinking blindly in the stunning sunlight, the slavers leapt down to haul out the rest of the prisoners.

The tangy scent of the fresh air almost crippled her lungs. It hurt to breathe. It hurt to see. Water lapped around her, cruelly dazzling, a platinum glitter which blurred her gaze. But while her vision was impaired, her hearing over-compensated. The creak and complaint of timber, the thud of tarred ropes, the flap of sails being lowered, the gibber of foreign voices, the moans and screams of the women who were clutching the nearest support and sobbing out their fear.

Clamping her palms over her ears, she sought equilibrium. She was so disorientated that she did not look down, or remember that she wore filthy, tattered rags, roughly knotted together to conceal as much of her body as possible. On the island, she would have flung away her clothes and not thought twice; now it was back to so-called civilisation and men's eyes.

The women were herded together at the quayside by two grim-faced slavers where, to their delight, they were given fresh water and a sack of food, fruit, loaves and lumps of salt. The scent of the sack reminded Allegra of church and home, and then she knew why. At some time it had contained frankincense. That brought her thoughts to the Lord of the Incense Road, the man whose slave she now was, or so she presumed. Then nothing mattered except for the taste of the fresh food in her mouth, rushed down by the clean water and a twist of salt between her fingers. Nothing had ever tasted so magnificent.

It seemed that they were not to go ashore straight away and as Allegra's eyes adjusted to the sun's dazzle and took in the surrounding sights, she saw fluttering flags bearing the emblem of the fire-breathing dragon, dozens of them, on ships, on the tiny white buildings with their flat tops, on the larger, bone-white dwelling which had an imposing aura about it: a customs house, or the town hall, possibly, if they had such places here.

The quay resembled those in Cornwall, built for convenience and the daily unloading of tons of goods. Barrels were heaped in one place, sacks in another, and then there were hides, piled high in a chocolate-coloured hillock, baskets of spices and fruit, silverware, gleaming with luminous splendour in the sunshine. She could make out bowls and jugs, vases and religious vessels, a censer, crucifixes, and even a glittering monstrance flung on its side on the pile. They had not found *that* in any Islamic church.

She turned away, thankful that the women were silent now that they were fed. Had Elizabeth been brought to this port, had she sat here and seen the dragon flags, the ships being loaded and unloaded with their booty, wondering where she was to be taken next?

Nash, oh why was he not here to rescue her? She tried to visualise him running down the quay towards her, scooping her into his arms, pushing aside the pirates and riding off with her to freedom. If he were here, he would have done it, she knew, but it might be his shade that she was imagining; he could be dead, she did not know. The uncertainty was the worst. It engulfed her at times. Did they make the healthy male slaves work until they dropped dead? She fancied that they might, having seen how ruthlessly cruel they could be to women. Where would her companions go now? Looking at their haggard faces, quill-thin arms and lank hair, she could not see them gracing the bedchamber of one of the lustful Islamic lords of whom Nash had told her so much. Perhaps these were to be household slaves, dressed in cheap robes and forced to clean and scrub for their livings? If that were so, would that be her fate?

Some Arabs were snarling at them, kicking and stabbing with their sticks to make the women rise. Allegra pushed them away angrily, protecting the young girls who were being hurt, but was shoved roughly for her pains so that she almost plunged down the unsteady gangplank on to the quayside. Two of the women, screaming, caught her and helped her to regain her balance so that she could descend with care.

On the quay they stood uncertainly, feet shuffling, until the men leapt down to join them, their faces impassive. They had seen thousands of slaves standing there. The sight meant nothing to them. The women were herded towards the large white building with its flat roof and the flame-breathing dragon pennant, and there they were met by two very small, bulging-faced Arab merchants who were so alike that Allegra thought they must be twins. They had the same scouring black eyes, flattened noses and pursed, protuberant mouths and both had black moles on their chins. For a time, they examined the women, looking first at hands and palms, then teeth, then calves. Next, to her dismay, came breasts and thighs, then genitalia.

Allegra could not believe what she was seeing. The two men dragged open the women's robes and probed between their legs with an expression of total boredom. Now and again they mumbled something to one another, but that was all. Eventually, having reached Allegra where she stood to the rear, their jaws dropped open.

Determined not to be alarmed, she glared at them, her brows knotted together as fiercely as she could manage.

'Do you know who I am?' she snarled. 'Can you speak English?'

Gasping, they babbled to one another, then turned back to gape at Allegra.

'Surely you have seen a white woman before?' she sneered. 'What is different about me?'

'*Eenshallah!*' It was a phrase she recognised well.

'Why is it the will of Allah?' she snapped, at which they fell back, as if she had displayed a third head or serpent's fangs.

The two men did not reply, but went across to the slavers to enter into what appeared to be an excited dialogue with much arm swinging and head bobbing. They then returned to examine Allegra thoroughly. They looked at her hands, first the backs and then the palms, and then they looked in her mouth. Their fingers were soft and slimy and smelt of rancid butter so she could not help but gag as they touched her. She almost bit them, such a powerful desire filling her that she controlled it only with difficulty. If she bit their fingers, would they kill her straight away? Probably.

Now came the hellish part. The rancid fingers were pressing her breasts, then her thighs, stabbing at the delicate inner flesh of her legs so that she winced and kicked out. At once two of the slavers gripped her by the arms to clamp her into immobility while the merchants' revolting, flabby fingers explored her most private place. First one, then the second, and how pleased they looked when they had finished. Did they think that she was still a virgin? If they did, then they could not be very experienced at examining slaves.

How delighted all the men looked, their eyes bright, their

smiles broad, yet she did not know why. Was it simply the enjoyment of humiliating a woman?

Next came the separation. Some of the women were led away, about a dozen of them, the thinnest and most haggard. Heart sinking, Allegra watched them trudging off. Where were they being taken? For menial work, or to be drowned? Nash had told her that slavers were ruthless in destroying the sick and infirm slaves who could not earn their living. The women turned, wailing to her to help them, holding out their arms in supplication and crying her name in their broken English.

Tears flooding her vision, she could not look any more. Turning away, she sobbed, filled with a bitter, icy helplessness. Not to be able to help those in need, these women who had put aside their differences and done their very best to befriend one another in the most hellish circumstances!

'Why do women always weep? If they put their minds to other matters with as much effort as they do to tears, then the world would be a glorious place. Instead they wail and screech like demons at the least little thing.'

Allegra turned to face the speaker. He was very tall, tending to good looks rather than ugliness, his shoulders narrow and hunched, his hair wild and black like a goat's. He wore a white robe, open sandals, and a striped turban with a flap which looped over one shoulder. He had spoken her language, roughly it was true, but distinct. His face, coarse and stained brown by the sun, had black and tiny eyes, and a nose so hooked and jutting so that one could not help but concentrate upon it for it almost obliterated the rest of his features, not so much by its size as its omniscience.

Having hoped to see one of her own countrymen, a saviour, she sank into gloom again. She had thought that he was English, that he would help them, but he was not. His name was Abdul and he was to take her and the other women through the desert, to the palace of the Lord of the Incense Road, so he now told her, his black eyes betraying not one glimmer of compassion for her plight.

'We go now, white mistress, and the sooner the quicker. The Lord and Prince Adem Ali awaits these slaves, and no one would dare to delay us. Those who enrage our all-powerful

Lord and Prince meet with the most violent deaths . . .' The man made a savage cutting gesture across his throat, his eyes glinting.

'Where do we go, and how far is it? Shall we have horses or be taken in carts?' Allegra asked.

The man threw back his head and burst into a bubbling fit of laughter.

'Horses, for women? Carts, for women, for *slave* women? You have feet, so you can walk like the camel. If only Allah had made woman as mute as the beasts of burden . . .'

'So your sacrosanct Allah is not always total perfection?' Allegra riposted scornfully, at which the merchant glared at her with narrowed eyes. He did not know the meaning of sacrosanct; yet he knew that she was being insulting.

'There is but one God and that God is Allah the all-powerful, the infinite and the all-merciful,' he replied, in what was obviously a well-rehearsed litany. These were phrases which were to become all too familiar to her in the coming days when the trek across the desert would tax her strength to the limits.

The searing heat was digging into her skin, scraping away all the fluid in her body and drying out every infinitesimal hollow and vein. At first she had found it strange to walk on stable ground again, the world seeming to tilt dangerously at unexpected moments, then, as the dizziness passed and the hours wore on, she became desperately unhappy again. She wanted Nash; she wanted to be back on the island where there was serenity and joy and love, and her captain's protective arms cradling her. Had Elizabeth gone through this very same torture, the sea journey, the arduous desert trek? Oh Elizabeth, how it would add to your sufferings if you knew that your sister and the man you are to marry had become lovers! We betrayed you, Elizabeth, when you could do nothing to prevent us. The moment that your back was turned, we bedded with one another. I let your future husband take my virginity, Elizabeth . . .

The dry, stinging heat was affecting her mind, she was sure

of it. She felt melancholy, elated and guilty by turns. Their water was severely rationed, and their food was dried figs and more dried figs. But one night one of the guards emptied a pouch into the cooking pot and the sizzling scent of boiling cabbage trickled into the air.

Cabbage! At home she would have rejected such tedious food but here it was a blissful treat. When the man stirred the pot, tasting the contents to see if they were ready, her stomach growled with hunger.

Each woman was given a small wooden bowl, and then soup was ladled into it, generous helpings by comparison to earlier meals. Allegra almost wept as she scooped up the steaming vegetable mixture with her fingers, cramming it into her sunburnt, cracked mouth. Cabbage, fresh and sweet, just like they grew in England. Where had they found it? Surely it could not have survived the blazing desert heat?

The women were allowed one hour to rest following their midday meal, and then it was back to the trudging, foot-grinding journey. How soft the sand had felt at first, but now it grated against the tender and bruised soles of their feet, and there was always a spiky stone hidden by sand and on which they would unwittingly tread. Allegra had a festering sore on her heel.

The women were chained to one another, and joined by a linked chain which was looped through the rings on their wrist manacles. Travelling with them were camels, traders with a cargo of hides, some dozen nomads who were sharing this part of the journey with them, and a rich merchant who was borne in a litter protected by shimmering shot-silk curtains. Now and again, his face would appear, his eyes would catch sight of the women tramping along, heads bowed, faces seared by the sun, and he would hurriedly withdraw.

The camels were the oddest creatures, stubborn and lethargic when immobile, yet able to travel for miles without water or food. Abdul had pointed to the oldest camel and rubbed his stomach appreciatively. When it dropped, which would not be long now, they would eat it, he said, and the women would be given their share. He had thought the alarm in Allegra's eyes was due to fear at the thought that she might not be given any of the meat, but it was horror at the knowledge that these strange, noisy and ribald animals were eaten after their life's work ended.

'The wiry sinews, and the muscles like leather . . . we eat it all, white mistress.' Abdul bubbled with laughter. 'Boil and boil it for a very long time, and even then it is tough as stone, but who will say no at this fine meal? We drink the milk, too, and wash in the urine. You think that is shocking, white mistress, raised in your clean and narrow culture? The urine smells sweetly, of aromatic herbs, and desert women use it for their beauty treatments. They wash their hair in it, and their children's hair, too, and on cold mornings in the desert, we warm our hands in the fluid. New infants are covered in a plaster of camel dung and old linen, and when first born they are baptised with the urine, to be ushered into the great brotherhood of the wilderness. So it is with all the desert peoples and so shall it ever be, praise be to Allah.'

Allegra looked up silently at Abdul. Somewhere he had learned English; somewhere he had developed an almost poetic train of thought, rudely interrupted by his strong feelings regarding the woman's place (beneath a man's heel, of course) yet here he was living what seemed such a hardy, humble existence.

'We are practical in the desert; survival is vital. Even you must know this. Everything we find in the desert we put to good use. Like the food we ate not long ago.'

'The cabbage soup? It was quite tasty, especially after five days of dried figs.'

'Cabbage soup?' Abdul laughed again. 'Cabbage soup? Locusts, white mistress, locusts!'

'We . . . that was locust soup?' Allegra's stomach turned an energetic somersault as she recalled how she had munched and swallowed her way through the pulpy concoction.

'Yes, do you remember the swarm which came over us yesterday? That whirring sound, and the red veil which they made when settled? The ones which were too stupid to be beaten away were trapped and crushed for the midday meal today, and for dinner tonight. Will you join us then?' Abdul stomped off, bubbling with mirth, while Allegra, longing for privacy, vomited her locust lunch into the sand beside her.

She felt light-headed and wobbly when they set out again. She supposed that she should have been hardy and indomitable, as would a man, and kept down her meal, but how could she? Those whirring, enormous winged insects which were so frightening when they settled on the face and hands, and she had eaten them, crunched their insides and . . . Oh, it was too horrible to think about.

Birds fed on locusts; buzzards and bustards, ravens and storks followed their swarms; even the camels would eat them should there be no choice. How very practical, and how nauseating . . .

There was a shortage of herbs and greenery after the locust festival, so it was back to the eternal, chokingly dry figs with their hard seeds which caught infuriatingly in the teeth and would not be moved. Sometimes a hard, dried date or two was thrown in, a sweet and pleasant surprise.

The effects of the sun were so powerful that Allegra never felt free of the glare, not even during the cold, dark nights. Lying slumped in exhaustion in the hollowed-out sand, she would stare up at the stars and think of her lost lover. The sky here seemed vast, wide and low, the stars so big and glittery that she felt she was close to Heaven. Perhaps the skies were lower here, closer to the earth? The moon was nearer, too, shining with an eerie, silver-pearl light which mesmerised her to sleep if she stared at it for long.

One of the guards had given her a bernouse, a voluminous brown cloak with a hood, for they did not want her pale skin destroyed before they reached their lord and master. The bernouse was stiflingly hot and flapped round her calves, becoming heavy and damp with her sweat. But it was useful to sleep on at night, padded into a roll.

The other women, all dark-skinned and accustomed to the heat, did not suffer from sunburn but only from thirst and exhaustion. Generally, they seemed more resigned to their fate than Allegra, although sobbing for loved ones left at home was regularly heard. Allegra tried to comfort them. It was not easy because of their chains. Movement in anything but a crocodile could only take place with the agreement of everyone, for the chains and manacles were heavy and when one moved, the manacles dug and scraped the skin of those who stayed still.

Blessed now to think of the freedom she had left behind at home, possibly for ever, and to regret her railings at what she had believed to be restriction and repression. The emerald dips and rises of Cornwall, the flourishing sapphire sea, the cerulean skies, the fearless winds, they all lingered in her mind like a radiant dream which had little substance but was sustaining nonetheless.

Nash was always there, of course, beside her on the greensward, striding through the multi-hued wild flowers or the gilded sands, his hand clasping hers in such a way that nothing could ever separate them. Yet something had . . . Coming back to reality from those fragrant, romantic dreams was appalling, and it was no wonder that Allegra drifted away into fantasy as frequently as possible.

No one told them how long they would be tramping through the hostile desert, nor what would happen to them when they arrived at their destination. Abdul, who would often pause to chat with Allegra, displaying his knowledge of so much of the world, yet telling her nothing that she needed to know, became distant and silent when she pressed him for facts. He was a dismaying mixture of knowledge, ignorance, and philosophy, and widely experienced; yet threaded through everything he said or did was the narrow view of womankind which she was learning was deep-rooted in Islam. Women were like camels: they had their uses. They could carry food and water, trudge for miles with the family's belongings, survive all weather and all conditions, while their intrinsic value rested in their ability to bear children and prepare food. It was not expected of them to offer wise counsel or great philosophies, any more than it was expected of a camel. Anything in Islam which was connected with the very basic and mundane needs of survival, cooking, washing, fetching water, was treated with little more than contempt because it was woman's work.

Allegra had been misled at first into thinking that Abdul liked her company, that he was trying to lighten her burden, but in the end she realised that he was taking this rare opportunity to impress upon her how right he and his fellow Muslims were in their treatment of the female sex, and how stupid, ignorant and wrong were her own people.

'What is it you get for treating woman like human being? Why, you get queen who rules over all, who gives laws, who tells man what to do!' he raged one day, his face flushed. 'When woman tells man what he must do, then the devils are loose in the world and evil and disaster will come of it.'

'England is doing very nicely under our Queen, thank you very much!' Allegra retorted.

'Hah! Stupid! She has no children. One day man will take her place and imprison all English women in revenge for her reigning over all so long.'

'I hardly think so. Everyone is very happy with matters as they are and Queen Elizabeth is greatly loved.'

'Hah! Stupid!' Abdul riposted, turning on his rough brown heel and storming away, arms swinging energetically.

They had been travelling for five days when one of the women collapsed, a choking sound in her throat. Forgetting that she was shackled, Allegra tried to run to her, being pulled to a painful halt after a few feet. Shocked, the others moved into a circle so that she could examine the woman, but it was too late, she was dead. The guards approached, glanced down in critical disinterest and then unlocked the woman from her imprisonment and left her where she lay in the sand.

'Are you not going to have her buried?' Allegra cried. 'What of the carrion birds?'

'If you want her buried, you do it,' Abdul said, his voice surly.

And so Allegra and three of the other women scooped out a hollow in the sand, gently placed the body into it and piled it high with stones, sand and any flotsam they could find. Allegra said a prayer, the women mumbling their own prayers with her, then they were marched off at high speed to make up for the lost time.

Two more died before the week was out. They had looked strong enough, and they had not been suffering from sunstroke, so Allegra did not know why they had died. Both were buried in the same way. No one would have guessed how hard it was to dig sand by hand in the blazing sun. Nails clogged with rough dry grit became red and inflamed, and there was no water to clean them. The inflammation worsened, and became septic so fingertips throbbed constantly. Allegra tried everything she could think of to soothe the infection, rubbing her fingers together, shaking and swinging them, and finally, having found some parched twigs during one of their rest periods, she chewed on these until they were pulpy, then pressed the pulp against her sore fingers, clenching her hands to keep the balm in place. She had once seen a horse cure itself of an abscess in the gum by chewing branches, albeit fresh green ones filled with sap.

Strange, she thought, how each new agony was almost refreshing, an alleviation of the suffering and monotony of this long trek. Her feet seemed to be hardening to the walking, but her back twinged and ached, and the relentless dazzle of the sun made her dizzy. The pulsating pain in her fingers took her mind off her other discomforts, if nothing else.

She reserved, for rare moments of longing, the sight of the camels lumbering behind the walkers. Extraordinary and ungainly these creatures might appear, but she would have given anything to ride one of them. Instead of human cargoes they were burdened with rolls of silk, paniers of gold angels, coins found in a stolen treasure hoard along with plates, goblets and knives, spices and leather hides.

When Allegra met Adem Ali, she would tell him what she thought of the way she and the women had been forced to trudge through the hostile desert while the camels could have carried them. She would make the so-called Lord of the Incense Road wish that he had never dabbled in the buying and selling of slaves. How dare anyone traffic in human cargo? It was bestial, brutal and unChristian. The Muslim religion must be in the hands of the Devil if it approved of such atrocities.

As night drew in with the startling swiftness of the desert, a camp came in sight, roughly erected dark tents made of goatskin and propped on poles. Seeing fires glowing scarlet and gilt in the dusk, Allegra's heart lifted. Here they would be able to rest in comfort, with roofs over their heads even if they were only made of skins. When wafts of roasting meat reached her, she began to walk more quickly.

They were to spend the night at the camp with the tribe who were sleeping there, the nomads indigenous to the Arabian desert, travellers who rarely settled for long. Hardy, a law unto themselves, the Beduin feared little and spent their waking hours pursuing the arduous task of survival. Faithful to their leader, and to their ancient customs, lawlessness was rare amongst them, nor would they allow unbelievers to dwell with them.

Their diet comprised whatever could bc found, and on the night that Allegra arrived, they were roasting an old camel which had dropped dead from exhaustion, and were drinking milk and chewing on coarse bread spread with strong-smelling goats' cheese. At other times they would eat locusts and truffles, birds' eggs, honey, the seeds of wild herbs and roots, bulbs and sometimes game if they could trap it, or if they owned a hound which could be trained to catch hares, sand grouse, bustards and occasionally gazelle. Always on the move, always underfed, the Beduin were lean, tough and self-sufficient.

Abdul vanished into what must be the leader's tent for it was larger and two veiled women sat before it, infants on their knees. Allegra and the other thirty or so women sat in the sand, waiting to be unshackled and praying that they were to spend the night here. When Abdul came out, he was grinning broadly. Pausing to pat the head of one of the babies, the boy, of course – he strode back to the women, telling Allegra that they were fortunate indeed. They could stay within sight of this camp during the night, and their guards would be able to sleep, as the Beduin would keep watch for them. There would be fresh food, camel meat, bread and milk, and no one would interfere with them, providing that the Infidels stayed well away from the camp.

He glared at Allegra, who flushed hotly. 'The Beduin do not mingle with the unbeliever,' he explained. 'There is too much risk of the contamination of their evil.'

'Their faith cannot be too strong if talking to a Christian will seduce them from it!'

'You do not understand. How could you, a woman?' Abdul shrugged. 'The very hem of your robe is foul with the evils of the unbelievers, as is your mind, your body, your heart.'

'Better stay well away from me then, Abdul, or I might turn you into a slimy toad!'

Later, food was carried out to them by the Beduin girls. They were bright-eyed and attractive, jangling with bracelets and rich ornaments, gold glittering in layer upon layer of coins and trinkets. Their faces coloured with blue and green, they wore rouge and a scarlet dye was painted on their petulant mouths. These must surely be the young daughters of the chief himself, thought Allegra, noticing the small fortune in gold which each girl was displaying on her neck, breasts and wrists. If so, the chief was a fortunate man. They were lovely young girls, she guessed them aged between nine and fifteen, and with very pleasing manners. Having brought them steaming hunks of meat, leather bladders of milk and coarse bread, the girls sat watching as the women devoured the food ravenously. Now and again they would giggle and dig one another in the ribs, but in the friendliest manner with no hint of malice or condemnation. Allegra decided that she liked the Beduin, if these were a fair example.

An hour passed, and the girls began to jabber excitedly and point at the veil of dust announcing guests. The riders halting and dismounting, they were seen to be darkly handsome young men, maybe the husbands or the betrothed of these young girls. Allegra watched the joyful reunion, and her heart ached with her memories of Nash. If only he could gallop to her out of the arid savagery of the desert, scoop her up on to his horse and ride off with her to freedom . . .

There was much squealing and giggling, and one or two of the young couples were entwined in passionate embraces. From what Allegra had heard of the Beduin this behaviour was most unusual for unmarried men and women, and even more so in public. The girls, their gold necklaces, earrings and bracelets gleaming in the dust, took the men by the hands and led them towards a tent which stood by itself to one side of the camp. As they approached, an old woman pushed back the tent flap, her face split in a toothless grin. She wore a brown robe and her body shimmered with gold, like that of the young girls, but it was plain that if she had ever been anyone's beloved then they must have died a lifetime ago.

Allegra watched with interest as the girls led the men into the tent. Was this some kind of Muslim marriage ritual, some strange, nomadic method of husband selection?

Night drew in and all around her the women snored and murmured in their sleep, heads cushioned on the tattered hides which the gold-decked girls had brought them. From the lone tent the sound of giggles and excited chatter was followed by the sound of appreciative groans and moans.

Allegra went hot with embarrassment. If it was a form of marriage ritual, then the men and girls were at this very moment consummating their unions, and with little regard for what everyone outside must be thinking.

Suddenly a tiny figure fled squealing out of the tent. It was one of the youngest girls, possibly only nine or ten years old, and how diminutive and fragile she looked devoid of her flowing robes and glittering ornaments. Her body was sinuous and too young yet to display even the merest curve, but the young man pursuing her seemed undeterred. Having caught and trapped the girl in his arms, he pushed her down into the sand, only a few yards away from the sleeping slave women. And there, uncaring of his sleeping audience, he clamped his hand over the girl's mouth to crush her screams, and rammed himself into her body. He did it with all the lustful carelessness of the ardent young male, and with a determination which looked to Allegra both ruthless and barbaric. She flinched, biting her lip as the man continued to ram the girl, once, three times, four, then five, at which point he let out a groan and sank on top of her, apparently unconscious. The girl, who had wanted to scream all along, could now do so as his grip on her mouth weakened, her yells bringing out two or three of her companions, all of them naked, and the ancient, gold-decked toothless crone, who dragged the screaming girl back into the tent by one arm, scolding all the way.

Two of the girls stayed with the young man who was now recovering and eyeing their naked breasts. Within moments they had returned to the tent, arms linked.

Fertility ritual, thought Allegra. That must be what it was. These wild matings would ensure the crops and a good harvest for these desert people; that was how pagans thought, wasn't it? Yet the girls were so very young . . . Could it be that virgins were needed for this rite? And yet in such a lawful, secure tribe, could not older virgins be found? The thought of men taking such vicious advantage of girls of that age sickened her, even if all but one had appeared to be relishing every second.

Finally, aching with longing for Nash and the loving weeks they had spent together, she fell into a weary sleep to dream vividly of pagan beasts and pirates, and fertility rites from which her darling Nash rescued her with daring and courage.

Next morning, the girls had gone, complete with their old crone and all the glittering, musk-scented clothes and gold coins. The lone tent was taken down and the young men galloped off, their robes flaring in the morning breeze. It was a stirring sight, yet Allegra wondered why they were leaving their wives behind.

Abdul gaped when she mentioned the girls, the daughters of the chief, as she called them, because they wore so much valuable gold ornamentation.

'Daughters of chief? Daughters of chief?' Abdul doubled up, slapping his knees and pointing at Allegra as if she were an imbecile. 'They are not daughters of chief, they harlots come from mountain village where girls are trained for harlotry from the moment they are birthed. They travel around desert selling themselves, that is why they are covered in so much gold, a coin for every time, you see, and sometimes more than one if they are skilled.'

Allegra was bright red. 'Harlots! But they were little more than children! How could those men do that!'

'Same way all men do that, to all women. It is the will of Allah, the all-powerful, the all-mighty. When girls have earned themselves enough, they return to village and take husbands and live life of chastityness, as also is the will of Allah, the one true and only god, so be it.'

'You mean, after – after . . . When they have finished with this sort of life, they find men who will marry them?'

'Indeed yes, it is so. They will then be rich, you see, and still so young, and so able to bear many sons to please Allah, as it is said in the true book. You will grow used to our ways, white mistress, and find that they are of the most sensible and convenient.'

Allegra turned away, thinking of the little girl pinned to the sand so brutally the night before. What a way to learn about the realities of life! Would her experiences colour her marriage, turn her away from her husband's arms, make her cold and unyielding out of fear and resentment? She was sure that she would react in that way if she were forced against her will, and she was twice that girl's age.

This was a strange land. There was much talk of chastity and honour, of women being veiled and secluded from the world, of the will of Allah the one true god, and his many laws. Yet children were raised and trained to be whores and were paid handsomely for their bodies, then went to find themselves husbands who would not (so she would have thought) so much as glance at a wife who was no longer a virgin. Perhaps the laws of Islam were at their weakest when they seemed to be at their strongest. Everyone spoke so vehemently of them and yet they were changed to suit whatever man desired.

She vowed then that she would never allow herself to adjust to this foul country with its barbarous and contemptuous attitude towards women. The gentleness of these people was as rare as greenery in the desert; mostly they were dry, arid and as harsh as their land, and she hated them, every one. She hated this country, this savage life of slavery and subjugation and she wanted to go home, oh how she wanted to go home!

Chapter Twelve

The Lady Rouhkia was one of the wealthiest and most powerful women in Arabia, although none of it was due in any way to her own efforts. Proud, avaricious and highly sexed, she was the half-sister of the Amir Adem Ali, and flourished on the power of his name and authority. No one dared to refuse her anything, for, being typical of Muslims of the higher order, her half-brother would defend the women of his family to the death, their honour, reputation and virtue being sacrosanct.

Rouhkia was only three years old when she began to understand how men feared her half-brother. She had fallen and grazed her knee, and in her fright and pain she had pointed at one of her servants, a young boy who waited upon her and carried her messages.

'Zenar pushed me! He pushed me!' she had sobbed.

Ordinarily, that would have been the moment when her mother scooped her up into her arms, telling her that Zenar had done nothing of the sort. But this was not an ordinary situation. Any who laid hands on a relative of the Amir Adem Ali would be executed without trial. How innocent she had been! After seeing Zenar beheaded for daring to touch her, she had wept, shaking and bemused, thinking herself guilty, then, by the time three days had passed, she understood what it meant. She was as powerful as Allah himself; she had sovereignty over all people in her brother's land; she was suzerain, and mistress, with but the need to say 'That man, or that woman, offended me', and they would die by command of her half-brother.

From that day she had never wept nor suffered a pang of conscience. Power was too exhilarating, too thrilling, sensational and consuming to be spoiled by guilt or second thoughts.

Five men had since died for daring to try to kiss her or catch her hand in passion, or so she told the Amir. The truth was that they had failed to satisfy her endless sexual demands; they had tired of her, and she had arranged their deaths out of disgust and venom. No man who failed to achieve an erection on seeing her naked body would be allowed to live; it was as simple as that. She had secretly vowed that to herself and she always kept her vows.

Rouhkia was Adem Ali's equal in many ways. She too relished the excitement of trading in silks and spices, gold, jewels and curios. When new shiploads arrived at her gleaming white palace, she would examine everything herself if it meant staying up through the night to do so. Unpacking ivory figurines studded with coral and pearls, throwing back the lid on bronze-bound caskets crammed with glittering gold coins, or unrolling bolt after bolt of fabulous, gleaming silks – all of these held the same thrill however many times she did them.

With every new arrival there would be something so breathtaking, so exquisite that she would fall silent at sight of it. Once, there had been a black pearl so enormous that she wept when she took it into her hands. Gazing at it, she reached a peak of rapture which was equalled only by the final moments of sexual ecstasy in the arms of a man skilled in the arts of seduction. Now the black pearl, caged in thick serpentine coils of gold, lay between her breasts. She never took it off.

She did not care if men, women and children had been brutally slaughtered to gain her these treasures. Many were looted, pillaged or stolen, for the same pirates who worked for her brother worked for her. Many times she was sent the packages which her brother did not require; sometimes they were a gift, sometimes she would send him gifts in return. On her last birthday he had sent her sixteen camel loads of gifts – jewels, gold angels, frankincense, myrrh and precious oils and unguents, gold cloth to make herself a ceremonial robe, slippers bound with rubies and emeralds, three silvery-white horses of the purest Arabian blood, a casket containing a ruby bracelet and rings to match, and a sapphire-studded copy of the Koran, the holy book of Islam.

On his birthday, her feeble husband was sent a plain edition of the Koran, a pair of kid slippers edged with gold thread, and a pair of cushions tasselled with black silk. Rouhkia could not hide her mirth when she saw them. Adem Ali knew the truth about her impotent and inadequate spouse: he was good for nothing save reading while sitting on a cushion in a husbandly pair of house slippers.

She had been married to Youssef at the age of twelve, but the marriage was not to be consummated until she was fifteen. She was twenty now, and Youssef had still not achieved the consummation. He made excuses, a thousand of them, but everyone knew the truth: he was impotent and sterile, a blundering, inept and witless man who could not even get his wife with child. She might have forgiven him had he been ancient and in delicate health – (in which case she could have anticipated his death and married again) but he was only thirty. He looked healthy. He was pleasingly attractive, his manner courteous and charming, yet he could not achieve an erection even when Rouhkia laboured over his body for hours at a time. She did not try any more, of course. Do not throw good labours after bad . . . How often her mother had said that before she died bearing her thirteenth child, all the others having died except Rouhkia.

Sometimes, looking at Youssef's pleasant features, the bright dark eyes and curling black hair, the broad shoulders and slim hips, she lusted after him momentarily, but of what use was such passion? He could not satisfy her; he could not impregnate her; he must have tried hundreds of times and the trying had not even been pleasant. He was flawed, her handsome, comely Youssef, flawed.

Rouhkia's latest lover was called Amid. He was six feet three, a giant, and indefatigable in the arts of seduction. A slave, a gift from her half-brother, she had enjoyed many hours of sensual delight with him. Youssef did not appear to care however many lovers she took, and she laughed to herself at the knowledge that here, in the domain that she ruled, woman had the upper hand.

Amid had satisfied her so thoroughly that she had asked him to name any gift he wanted. To her anger, he asked for the black pearl.

'No one has that, no one!' she spat at him.

Amid scowled. 'Do I not deserve it, great lady?'

'No one deserves that. It is mine, my treasure. My soul resides in this pearl. Allah, would you ask me to part with my soul?'

Amid, biting on his lips, bowed his head meekly. He had spent hours panting over Rouhkia, his eyes fixed on that lustrous jewel; not surprisingly, he had grown very attached to it.

When he was sent away, Rouhkia surveyed herself in her hand mirror. This, of solid gold studded with rubies, was held before her face by a Nubian slave girl whose blackness was so dense that she was invisible in the dark when she closed her eyes.

The face which stared back at Rouhkia was far from beautiful. She had not inherited her mother's brightly glowing vitality, nor her delicate features and large soft eyes. Now she stared in frustration at a heavy nose, a straight mouth which was too wide, thick dark brows, a square, determined chin, narrow forehead and a far from radiant complexion. Yet there were compensations. She enjoyed bedding, and how many women could say that? Any husband but hers would have revelled in her lusty sexuality, and she might have mothered four sons by now. Because she could not take the risk of conceiving a child by one of her slaves (especially not the black ones!) she employed various contraceptive devices, a plug of beeswax and honey, or a sticky mixture of honey and bitter herbs mixed together into a glutinous mass.

She recalled the tale of the Egyptian pasha who was mortified to discover that his wives were giving birth to ebony infants. How could this be so when his skin was the usual dark-honey colour of his race and his wives were lighter-skinned? Eventually, he found out. The cause was his chief eunuch who was black, yet how was it that he, a eunuch deprived of his organs of fertility, could impregnate the pasha's wives? Examination had proved that the eunuch had been castrated as a small boy, when only one of his sexual organs had descended. The other, tucked away inside his body as sometimes happens with boys, and having descended later, had made him as fertile as a normal male.

Rouhkia had roared with laughter in the most unladylike manner when she first heard this tale, which was true, her prime minister assured her. There were other similar stories concerning castration, and she loved to hear them all repeated over and over again, however gruesome and gory. She loved to hear how King David, the great holy man of the Christian bible, had taken his new bride a loving gift. What had it been? The severed sexual organs of one of his enemies. And these same Christian holy men, David, and Solomon, too, had kept vast harems of women with castrated men to guard them chastely. So much for the Christian religion with its talk of charity, humanity and forgiveness!

When she was alone, Rouhkia would look through her private collection of sexual organs of men who had displeased her in some way, or of famous men who had offended her brother and been castrated as punishment. The sexual organ of Amil Pasha was the most intriguing, and she wished that she had known him when he still possessed it. It was enormous, the skin like silk and the colour a rich dark brown. True, the last months had caused it to dry out and shrivel somewhat, but it was still the largest. Next, she would be adding Amid's. It was not proper that a slave who had made love to her, the Lady Rouhkia, should be free to penetrate the body of any other woman.

She giggled at the thought of Amid's shock. He thought he was going to have her pearl, but instead she was going to have his.

Waving away the mirror, she prepared for her bath, throwing off her saffron silk robe, jewelled sandals and the bevy of necklaces, earrings and bracelets which she wore, all except the black pearl. Stepping into her steaming hip-bath, she allowed her female slaves to massage her body with pungent, exotic oils, particularly enjoying their skilled hands on her breasts and thighs. Sometimes she would let them go further, touching between her legs in the gentle rhythm which she adored. Then, when they had roused her, she would summon one of her male slaves – whoever happened to be in favour at the time – and he would complete what her women had begun. Had she been anyone but the sister of Adem Ali, she would have been forced to satisfy her urges with her slave women, that outlet being all that remained for the neglected wives of Muslim men. She had seen the wives of her brother, and pitied them. He had so many and he was always adding to their numbers, and what man, even one of his incredible lust, could satisfy two hundred women each week, and what woman could survive for a week without sexual conjunction? Certainly not she! Female slaves were sufficient to partially rouse her, but those final ecstatic and heart-shaking minutes must always be completed by a man who was generously endowed. Nothing could match the feel of the male sexual organ penetrating deeper and deeper into her body . . .

Her cheeks were flushed, her lower lip hanging open when she came out of her reverie. Mariam, who had such sensitive hands, was caressing her breasts in the most delightful way. Rouhkia's breasts were her most beautiful feature. Large, full and heavy, they did not sag, nor did she believe that they ever would. What was more, they were extremely sensitive so the merest wisp of a touch could arouse her.

Mariam's fingers were pressing into the furry black down between her thighs, probing and finding the tiny pearl which brought her so much pleasure. With the gentle rhythmic pressure came the storms of sensual delight which made Rouhkia squirm and bite her lip.

'Fetch Amid,' she whispered, then remembering his truculent avarice, she said, 'No, send in the new slave, the one that arrived this morning. He is ready, is he not?'

'Yes, *Ya Sitti.*'

'Then let me see him now, now, do you understand?'

Salaaming, Mariam rushed away to have the new slave summoned. There were tears in her eyes. She wanted to play the man for her mistress, oh, so very much, but her mistress was cruel and would not let her. Now she would have to watch from behind the curtains while this new slave pleasured her mistress and she would hate every second and want to dig out the man's eyes.

The new slave, having bathed and dressed in the spotless white robe given to him, was sitting on a bench in the gardens beneath the shade of a gracefully spreading fig tree. Startled at the breathless approach of the slave girl, he leapt to his feet.

'Come now, come hastily, our lady mistress is eager for you!' the girl gasped out in Arabic, without thinking that the man could not understand for he had come from a strange and foreign land. It was only later when the man had obeyed her, that she remembered that he was not Arabic and yet he had done as she ordered.

Racing after the slave girl, Nash wondered what he was about to see. He had been told that he now belonged to the great Lady Rouhkia, sister of Lord Adem Ali the Feared and Dreaded, but no one had told him what his new life would entail. Knowing that Muslim women lived in purdah, heavily veiled before all but their husbands because it was believed in Islam that women were brazenly seductive and that men could not control their lusts, Nash could not see how he would be able to help the Lady Rouhkia.

Rouhkia's suite coming into view, with its sumptuous silk furnishings and the fragile lace of the trellis-worked partitions, the scent of exotic blooms drifted out to meet him. Next came the pungent odour of incense, for Rouhkia burned eternal braziers in every corner. It served to remind her how her half-brother and his family had made their fortunes.

The shining silk of the almond-green hangings framed Rouhkia like veiling, and beneath the bed covering, which was translucent, Nash saw that she was naked, her breasts rising and falling as if she had been running.

'Kneel before the great lady!' he heard the slave girl crying behind him. 'Kneel, you must kneel!'

'I will kneel, if she will kneel to me,' the man said, and that should have been the moment when Rouhkia decided that he would lose his sexual organs, or his head, or perhaps both, had she not been entranced by his beauty.

She had rutted with brown and honey-coloured slaves,

slaves with sallow skins and black skins, with yellow and with rust, but never a man who was sun-bronzed and yellow-haired, his fair skin tanned to the most stunning colour so that his eyes glowed the brightest and most unbelievable blue. Such was his effect on her that Rouhkia sat up, the translucent coverlet falling away from her huge breasts, the black pearl bobbing between them.

She leapt out of the bed to survey Nash with awe-filled eyes. Walking round him, she stared at his face, at every line and curve, at his neck and the sun-coloured hair which aureoled his features, at his broad, powerful shoulders above the slender hips, and the solid, muscular legs partially concealed by the white *shalwar*, down to his bare, bronzed feet, then back to his hands which she touched as if in wonderment.

Impassive, Nash allowed her to examine him. He knew who she was, and that her reputation was vile. He had heard the pirate slavers talking of her. They called her the collector of men's sexual organs, and he believed that he knew what they meant. It was a way of saying that she would sleep with any man who took her fancy, and, to judge by what had been said, many men did. He had been surprised to hear of such behaviour from a Muslim woman, behaviour which went unpunished by all accounts. The men could and did such things, for that was how Allah had made them, but for a woman to be unchaste, unless she was a harlot, now that was something strange and mystifying.

The woman was staring between his thighs as if she wished her eyes could strip off his clothes.

Next moment, lithe as a tigress, she leapt towards him, stabbing at the silk of his *Shalwar* with her sharp nails and tearing them open over his genitals. Still impassive, he did not flicker an eye as she cradled his sexual organs in the palm of her hand, her mouth hanging open.

The jewelled hand continuing to caress him, Nash stared above the lady's head as if she were not there. She could never rouse him, not with any artifice, for he had left his heart and soul with his little she-wolf, wherever she was now, God help her. He would love that passionate and impulsive Cornish girl until the day he died and possibly even after, and no one else would ever be able to stir any passion in him, whatever they did. If this lust-crazed woman ordered his execution, then so be it. It would be the will of God, the Christian God. Until then, if that moment came, he would do all that he could to try and free himself from this odious bondage and go in search of Allegra and Elizabeth, through fire and brimstone he would search for them, if necessary.

Rouhkia, who was accustomed to men quivering at her feet in terror if they could not please her, was amazed at the stony silence of this man. It was his race, perhaps. They said that the men of the English Isles were cold and hard, without feeling or emotion, yet surely if they were truly thus, their breed would have died out?

'What is your name?' Rouhkia said.

'Hamilton, Nash, Captain, and Earl of Cornwall.'

'When you speak to me, you salaam, low, down to the floor, and you address me as *Ya Sitti*!'

'I believe that we are of equal position,' Nash said coldly.

'No one is equal to me, no one, nor to my brother the Amir Adem Ali, Lord of the Incense Road, Lion of Arabia, the richest man in this land!'

'You are sure that he is the richest?'

'How dare you question my word! Mariam, send for . . .' Rouhkia swallowed. If she had him beheaded, then she would never know how large he became when erect and she would never feel him plunging deep into her body; she wanted that desperately, the excitement of the foreigner inside her, the novelty and thrill of his lovemaking. She knew that she could make him erect if she tried, it would take a little time that was all. She must not let her temper get in the way and spoil everything.

'Do you have a wife in your own land?'

'No.'

'Are you to be be married?'

'Yes.'

'Do you have love for this woman you are to marry?'

'Yes.'

'Is she gold-haired like you?'

'Not as fair, but similar.'

'Are her breasts as large as mine?' Rouhkia thrust her bosom against Nash's chest, rubbing against him like a starving cat.

'I do not know, I have never seen them.'

'Never? What a strange land you have then. Do your women of the English Isles wear veils until after they are wed?'

'Not in the way that Muslim women do, but they wear their hair loose and then bind it up when they marry.'

'Their hair? How odd! Would you like to make love to me? You can, you know. I will not be angry. If I lie on that bed and tell you to make love to me, you can go ahead, and enjoy every moment, for I shall. Do you want to do it?'

'No.'

'*No?* You do not realise what you are saying! You will regret saying that. I can have you killed, hacked to death in the most painful way so that you must watch the blood flowing from your body and not until the last few drops have gone will you die. This is no empty threat!'

'So be it, I have no will to live.'

'No will to live? Does life need a will? We are alive because Allah has decreed it, not because we will it. What vanity, what ignorance, you insulting cur, you hound!' Making a fist, Rouhkia slammed it into Nash's side, but he did not flinch. Head down to hide her tears of frustration, Rouhkia returned to her inner sanctum leaving Nash to be taken back to his new quarters.

She would try again with him, but only once. If he persisted in insulting and offending her, then there was only one way in which it could end. If she did not punish him, then word would speed everywhere that the great Lady Rouhkia had turned feeble and now even the most unimportant slave could rail at her. She revelled in her reputation as a woman of merciless passions and vengeful punishments, even though she knew full well that she would have no power whatsoever without her brother's wealth and despotism behind her.

If the Christian slave did not change his attitude, and prostrate himself before her publicly, blessing her name and that of her brother, then she would have him castrated as an example to any who might think that such rebellion was acceptable to her.

Chapter Thirteen

The rabid bitch would get her deserved reward when she was handed over to the Amir, Abdul thought as he kicked at a tuft of parched grass jutting from sandy rocks. She was not right in the head, that was easy to see. Now, having memorised some Arabic insults, words which she had heard the men use to their truculent camels, she was shouting these at him and the other guards. It would do her no good. Tongues had been hacked out for less. Slaves were abundant; had she not been so white-skinned and possessing glorious hair the colour of the sun-burst, he himself would have struck her down days ago. She did not know the meaning of the words she spoke. He had been called a barren, two-humped bastard, and others were shocked to be called stinking hillocks of leather, or knock-kneed, impotent devils. Muslim women would never have voiced such phrases. They were raised properly, so they knew their place.

Their role was to worship, revere and wait upon their husband, and he in his turn could take as many women as he desired, for had not the Prophet said that a man might take four wives, if he could care for them as commanded, which was equally? Of course this was open to misinterpretation, and what man anyway was capable of treating four wives with equal kindliness and attention? The Prophet had made this ruling to enable the widows and orphans of battle to be taken under a male wing, an excellent idea at the time, but as far as Muslim men were concerned, it was always *après* battle in their country and any woman they fancied could be swept into their harem.

Abdul had two wives, Zikita and Maryam, and he loved

them both, especially Zikita who had borne him twin daughters. Maryam had not produced a child in five years of marriage, which was grieving him, but if she continued childless, he would divorce her and take another wife. It would distress him, because he loved her, but sons were more important. To whom would he leave his fortune, if not a son? No daughter could handle such an amount of money and make her way in the business and trading world.

Ever since Eve had sinned so grossly in the Garden of Eden, tempting Adam with her debased lust and showing her naked body to seduce him, women had been punished by eighteen curses which they could never escape. One was the monthly flow of blood from their bodies; another was the agony of childbirth; the third, their separation from their mother and father and marriage to a stranger; the fourth, the burden of carrying children for many months; the fifth, being under the heel of their father, husband or brother; the sixth, receiving less of an inheritance than their male relatives; the seventh, their vulnerability to divorce, for their husband could cast them off comparatively easily, while they could not divorce him; the eighth, the law which said that a man might have four wives, but a woman only one husband; the ninth, a woman's enforced seclusion in her home; the tenth, the ruling that women must keep their heads covered in the house; the eleventh, one man's testimony was worth the testimony of two women; the twelfth, a woman was not allowed out of her house unless chaperoned by a close relative; the thirteenth, men may participate in Friday prayers and those on feast days and funerals, while women may not; fourteenth, women were forbidden to be rulers or judges; fifteenth, merit has one thousand elements, nine hundred and ninety nine of which are found in men, but only one in women; sixteenth, sinful women who betray their husbands will receive only half the punishment given to men at the resurrection day; seventeenth, widows must mourn for four months and ten days before remarrying; and eighteenth, having been divorced, a woman must wait for three months before remarrying.

Abdul would never forget the joy which these rulings brought to him, by virtue of the great wisdom and holiness of the Prophet. He knew that poor men could not subdue and incarcerate their wives and so, naturally, the women fell into sinful ways and lay with lovers, women possessing no self-control and desiring to seduce all men with whom they came into contact. It had been Abdul's one ambition to make himself so rich, so informed, that he would be able to keep his wives where they belonged when he was absent on his long trading journeys.

Zikita and Maryam had a comfortable home, which they owed to him, and they were grateful for it, eager to show their gratitude, yet he knew that had he been poor, they would have had the freedom to seduce lovers and conceive sons by them, so he would not have known whose son was his. His fists clenching at the thought of such vileness, he kicked at the tuft of grass again, heedless of the stabbing pain in his toes.

When he was absent from home, his wives were guarded by four of his most trusted male relatives along with his mother, his three sisters and their children, all of whom depended upon Abdul for their financial survival and so were loyal and trustworthy.

Turning, he could see the white bitch who had made this desert journey so difficult. She was refusing to eat the stewed locusts which had been brought to her, kicking the dish out of the hands of the guard who had offered it to her. Christian women were ungrateful and savage, proving to him what he had always known, that the female sex needed firm discipline, lashings and severe punishments to keep them in their place. Well, she would get all that and more from the Amir his master. He would either make her his concubine, adding to the hundreds he owned already, or sell her for a vast sum to a wealthy ally. Then she would discover what it meant to be a woman in Islam . . .

He wished that he could observe her progress from barbarian and tigress to meek, submissive and subservient concubine, for he knew that the Amir was an expert at subduing females. There was a tale which his master had told him when they first met, and he was being instructed as to the variety of woman which his master required to be purchased for his harem.

'Have you heard of Abu Hanifa?' the Amir had asked him.

'Of course, master,' Abdul nodded, racking his brains. Was Abu Hanifa the one who had helped to found one of the four recognised legal systems, or was he the one who had sired three hundred sons?

'Abu Hanifa would rock with amusement whenever he heard this story. It concerns the advice given to an Arab by his father when selecting females. "Beware three kinds of women," the father said. "One, the woman who waits for her husband to die so that she can inherit his wealth, and two, the woman who has a quick temper, and three, the woman who scowls."'

'I see, master. I am never to bring you a greedy woman, a hot-tempered woman, or a scowling woman. Regarding the former, I shall have to make some enquiries at source.'

Adem Ali had laughed, his eyes glinting. 'A man who is faithful to his God and who obeys the laws of the Prophet will have no trouble finding me the right type of woman.'

Abdul heaved a quivering sigh as he remembered that scene. In so many ways she was exceptional with that pallid skin, the sunburst hair and the brightly coloured eyes like silk flowers embroidered on a prayer cushion. It was true that her nose was scorched by the sun, her hands were rough and the fingers red from infection, her feet blistered and rough after the long journey, but that could all be put to rights by the ministrations of harem slaves.

What made him uneasy was the thought that this woman undoubtedly displayed most of the failings which his master had warned him to avoid.

There she was, not only scowling, but raging with temper. Now she was screaming at one of the guards and calling him a gutless eunuch, pray Allah be hard of hearing at that moment! Should he send the girl with the other women, none of whom were handsome or attractive enough to present to his master, not even as house slaves? Or should he take the risk, and present the girl when they arrived at his master's palace in two days' time?

What if he told his master all of his misgivings, in fear that the Amir would think him stupid and disobedient? If he said that the girl might bring his master some enjoyable sport, but only if he kept her mouth tightly bound? Turn it into a jest and make his master laugh?

Or he could prostrate himself before the throne of his master and tell him that the girl embodied all that was most vile and hideous in the Christian world, and that she might be used as an example to the Muslim women, or given as gift to some relative or ally who had offended his master in some way. Yes, that was it!

'She will make a suitable gift for one who has tricked or deceived Your Highness and whom you wish to condemn to a punishment too vile to sustain . . .'

Grinning, Abdul returned to the crocodile of slaves, his step jaunty, his eyes narrowed with hidden mirth. As he passed the Christian girl she yelled at him, calling him a barren she-camel, but he clamped his mouth shut so that she would not see that he wanted to grin.

'Do you lust after boys?' Rouhkia was lying on her bed with Nash beside her, where he had been commanded to rest. 'Is that why I do not rouse you? Would a young boy please you now if I sent for one? Then, when you are roused by him you can make love to me?'

Nash turned his head away, sickened.

'Why do you not speak? Why do you lie there as if you are dead? Am I not attractive? Look at my body, is it not handsome?'

Rouhkia thrust her enormous breasts into Nash's face, but he winced as if they were offensive.

'Tell me what is wrong with you! You look so strong and healthy, you cannot be ill, yet you lie there with such empty eyes. Why? Why? Are you mourning someone you love, some young boy perhaps?'

She was almost at the truth, but in a way which nauseated him. Her debauchery and blatant lustfulness were like nothing he had ever experienced before, not even in the most forward Christian harlot. She spoke words which he did not think any woman would know, and she had told him things about sex and sexual relationships which a hardened traveller might know after a lifetime of journeying the world, yet she was only twenty years of age and there was not a line or a wrinkle on her face.

'My dancing girls will entertain you now. If they do not rouse you, then we must find some fitting punishment. Does the thought of the blade frighten you? Imagine the icy steel cutting through your sexual organs . . . That would be fun, would it not? I find it very entertaining, and why not? Men may have the upper hand elsewhere in Islam, but not here in my palace. Have you seen my husband? He is impotent. He has never achieved an erection, not with a boy or a girl or a sheep . . . If he were not my husband I would have punished him long ago, but I cannot, for it would offend my brother who chose him for me. But I can punish you, you see, and I shall. Do not think that I am making threats I shall not keep, for I shall, oh yes, I shall . . .'

Rouhkia's glowing dark eyes filled with steely determination and she tossed back her cloudy black hair, the loops of decorative seedpearls making a tiny clicking noise. Heavy gold rings dangled at her ears, and she wore a thick gold collar buttoned with emeralds which exactly matched the shade of the diaphanous silk robe which was lying over the back of a nearby chair. She had removed it swiftly, positive that such boldness would make her new slave erect, and that he would lunge at her and force himself into her body, but he had not reacted, much to her chagrin. Now, she rang the bell for her dancing girls, and then lay back to watch them in silence.

Six of the most beautiful girls, all of whom she had chosen herself, were kept to entertain male visitors whom she wished to impress and delight. One of the girls was pale-skinned, another the colour of honey, another black, another brown, the other two a darker honey brown. Wearing silken *shalwar*, the baggy trousers of Islam, with jangling bracelets round their ankles and wrists, their knee length hair billowing around them, filling the air with the scent of musk, rose and ambergris, they gyrated to the wailing music of drum and tabor, their hips shimmering and twisting, their breasts, naked save for henna-painted nipples, shivering in the most sensual way. Watching them, she almost wished that she were a man and could plunge into their voluptuous bodies. Watching them made her long to be penetrated . . .

Glancing sideways, she watched the Christian slave who could not fail to be impassioned by such a sight.

He was asleep! Or he looked it, for his eyes were closed! Screaming, she slapped him with her henna-painted hands, catching him with her rings so that tiny scarlet eels of blood sped out of his skin.

'Make love to me, make love to me now, or you will die!' she screamed in his face, and the dancing girls, legs shivering with terror, fled from the chamber before their mistress' wrath turned on them.

The palace of the Lord of the Incense Road was brilliant white, flat-topped and disappointingly plain from the outside. It lay in the midst of the vast sandy plain like a doll's house dropped out of the sky, yet as they came nearer, Allegra could see that it was enormous, and that lying just behind it were other buildings (where, she learned later, lived all those who served the Amir) and that beyond them was the township named after him, Adem.

Men were running towards them excitedly, gabbling to Abdul and scanning the crocodile of slave women with interest. Abdul glanced at them, raised his eyes heavenwards and splayed out his hands as if to say, 'These are not worth the time spent on them,' before he turned towards the camels which were being unloaded of their treasures.

When the women had been left in the searing sunshine for more than an hour while the men continued to unload the camels, Allegra shouted Abdul's name, but he ignored her. Again she shouted, her cheeks blazing. These poor women were faint with thirst and desperate for somewhere comfortable to rest their weary and aching bodies, yet they were forgotten. How different it would be if they were gold coins, myrrh or frankincense, or the precious spices and oils of the east . . .

Finally Abdul came over to them, but it was not because he wished to ease their plight. Instead, he looked down at Allegra as if she were a lowly and repugnant dung beetle crawling in the sand.

'We say goodbye now, and we shall not meet again. Our great lord prince has decided that he will see you for himself. Pray Allah that he never regrets taking a vixen into his palace . . . I, for myself, would rather marry a venomous snake . . .' His mouth twisted with disdain.

'Why keep a snake when you can poison yourself?' With that, Allegra turned her back on the man for the last time.

There was no release from the midday heat. Not until the evening shadows crept along the sandy earth did someone remember that there were slave women lying chained outside.

Last to be remembered, thought Allegra. All the baskets of gold angels, the ambergris, civet and musk, the soft leather hides, the floating silks of every hue from crimson to buttercup to cerulean to rich fig brown, the fragrant oils and unguents from the eastern coast of Africa, the monstrous ostrich feathers, ivory, indigo and cinnamon. Along this route since ancient times had come an abundance of such exotic riches, pearls from Ceylon, tortoiseshell from Malacca, cinnamon leaves from the Himalayas, spikenard from the Ganges, sapphires and diamonds, cotton and ivory, lapis lazuli, indigo, cinnamon and pepper from India, gold, wine and succulent dates from the Persian gulf, and all of them more precious, more protected and more desirable than the slaves who were stolen or bought in all parts of the world to be dragged here either for resale or to grace the glorious sanctum of Adem Ali, the Lord of the Incense Road.

When the servants scurried out to fetch them, the women were too broken and exhausted to speak and had to be helped into one of the palace outbuildings reserved for new slaves. There the women would be able to bathe, and wash their hair, and pungent oils would be poured over them to destroy the lice and fleas which they were likely to have brought with them. Then, naked, they would be herded into the examination chamber where Adem Ali's *wazîr* would inspect them, but at a distance, for the belief in the contagion borne by slaves was strong and not without foundation. A decade ago a slave had brought a murderous foreign fever with him and Adem Ali's favourite concubine had died of it, along with her son, who had been everything that was joyous to the Incense Lord. The boy, aged only seven months, had been his only son and heir and there had not been another despite the long passage of time. Such tragedies must not be allowed to happen again.

Consequently, the women would be kept in enforced seclusion until sufficient time had elapsed to prove them free of disease.

After two or three days in the cool seclusion of the slaves' reception chamber, Allegra began to feel more like her usual self. The sun constantly beating into her eyes and the strain of trudging mile after mile had grated badly on her nerves, but worst of all had been the deep and bitter hollow inside her at losing Nash. She had passed both the stage when she woke in shocked dismay, realising that her tortured nightmares were reality, and the phase of blank disbelief. Now she was angry, angry at everyone and everything.

On the fourth day, while the women were sleeping on their rush mats, a man entered the chamber. He was black as basalt, his face pug-like and cruel. Allegra's heart jumped when she saw his eyes. She felt instinctively that, given the chance, this man would commit murder.

The next hour left Allegra shaking and tearful, for Akhmar was there to decide what would become of each woman. Abdul had reported that they were unfit for his lord's palace, except for the crazy Christian girl, but Akhmar would be the final arbiter of that. His jaw jutted as he examined each of the women, for he was thinking that any attributes nature might have given them had been destroyed by the long desert trek. Yet there was no other way of getting them to Adem. By litter, it would take hundreds of beasts of burden, which they could not spare, and the time taken would more than double. More than once he had issued warnings to the pirates that he would not consider slaves who had been starved in their ships' hold for long journeys by sea, yet he was aware of the problems caused by lack of fresh food in the heart of the oceans. He had been assured by Abdul that these women had been properly fed, but looking at them now, he could see little evidence of a nourishing diet.

Bones projected, cheekbones jutted like bent fingers, breasts had dropped or flattened, hips had narrowed. Hands were rough and bruised, feet in a disgraceful state, with callouses, lumps, and suppurating sores. The physicians could cure all this, and food would bring back the curves, but only if it were worth the effort.

There was much squealing and struggling as he pinched breasts and stroked thighs, testing for evidence of a future blossoming. He did not speak. What was the point? These were females, stupid, erratic, emotional and unreliable. When they reached their eventual destinations they would settle down and, with the blessing of the one true God, would appreciate and grow grateful for the roof over their heads and the food on their platters. Kitchen work for at least twenty of them, Abdul was right. The others were not so easy to place. One glared at him with wild eyes and when he pinched her breast, she lashed out with her knee, trying to slam it into his groin. Surprised at such spirit, he shoved her backwards so that her head cracked against the wall and her eyes glazed. Women of spirit must be treated with spirit.

Having made his decision, taking into account what Abdul had told him (although nothing would ever make him admit that he listened to the slave trader), Akhmar gave the bevy of women a last, cursory glance, then left.

The moment they were alone, the women rushed to Allegra, grabbing at her hands and arms, trying to clutch her tightly, tears rolling down their sunburnt faces.

'We shall be all right,' Allegra whispered, her eyes still blurry from the bang on the head. 'God is taking care of us.'

'God? Which God?' The dwarf woman who could speak some of her language spoke up. 'The evil god of the Western Isles or the evil god of the Muslim, which one? Are not both devils to let us suffer like this? What have we done to hurt man?'

'I would say that we are being put to the test,' Allegra began haltingly, thinking of the church's teaching in England. So much of it rested on suffering for Christ, enduring agonies of fasting, self-denial and endless prayers so that the soul would be elevated to Paradise.

'Test? Why us? Thousands at home in peace and happiness with their families, yet we are stolen away and put through misery. I cannot go on, I cannot!'

'What choice do we have?' Allegra's voice was empty of emotion. Perhaps this vapidness was better than anger? She did not know. For a second, she remembered how she had felt about life just a few months ago, with such hope and joy and delight, yet that was because of her darling Nash. In his arms she had learned why she was born and what life was created for; everything uncomfortable or disturbing had been cast out of her mind.

'You give up, I not give up!' the woman screeched, and then suddenly she ran to the table where their breakfast was being laid and, smashing one of the slender glass pitchers, she slashed the jagged glass slivers across her wrists, first one, then the other, her terrible screams echoing round the chamber.

Allegra leapt across the room to try to stop her, and, for her pains, was drenched in a great spout of blood which flew from the ragged gashes. Allegra did her best to try to staunch the flow, although she skidded on the slippery tiles and almost fell. Tearing at her robe, she made strips of cloth with which she bound the woman's arms, just above the cuts, to halt the gush, and then she bound the gashes themselves, as tightly as possible.

'Leave me . . . I die. It is my choice!' The woman glared up at her in fury, but Allegra cradled her head in her lap and, from somewhere, found the serenity to soothe the dying woman, stroking her forehead and assuring her that she would go to Paradise, that the angels were waiting for her and she would see them soon.

A faint, twisted smile came to the woman's lips and then her eyes began to cloud, like frost on a window, while the bandages became more crimson and sodden as the blood continued to flood.

The others watched in horror, either silently, or gabbling prayers, and when the guards entered the chamber, having heard the commotion, they found the Christian slave drenched in blood, with a dead woman in her arms, her face was waxy-white and hollow.

The women were removed from the blood-soaked chamber to another, with a view of the harem gardens which were colourful and exotic with fragrant blooms. There they were kept for the next two days, during which Allegra did not say one word. How was it that something so exquisite and beautiful could become the instrument of death? She had admired the graceful, fluted shape of the crystal water flask, she had never seen anything so delicate in the way of glassware; the sun had flowed through it in the most brilliant and eye-catching way, yet what was a preserver of life, a water carrier, had become one woman's death.

Beauty. Death. The words echoed in her thoughts until she clapped her hands to her ears. All that blood, so much from one small woman. She had never realised how much blood there was inside people; it was shocking the way it had poured out; every time she shut her eyes she saw a bright scarlet veil in the darkness and the gashed wrists, the flesh zig-zagging and broken. Shuddering repeatedly, she would not eat or drink. She knew that the woman had taken the right way out, the only way; why did she not have the courage to do the same?

Chapter Fourteen

The room was elaborately beautiful, the floor tiles sparkling white with a blue design snaking through them, the walls cool ivory and screened by ornamental trellises, diamond-shaped and bright with encircling blooms. There was a pungent, exotic scent in the air: incense, the odour both redolent of the old Roman church mass and something threatening and barbaric.

Allegra had been alone now for two days and a night, carefully tended it was true, yet knowing nothing of her fate. Her attendants, although they could not speak her language, were amiable, quick to please and obsequious in their manner. She had been bathed twice a day, massaged with strongly scented unguents and oils, plied with Arabian foods and sherbets, and encouraged to rest on the luxurious padded cushion bed which filled the corner of the room.

Nonetheless, or perhaps because of this, Allegra was restless as a young hart, padding about the chamber, biting on her lower lip and sighing heartrendingly. She could not forget the way that Zora, the dwarf woman, had chosen to die in such untidy agony, nor the sobs of the other women when she, Allegra, had been taken from them and brought here. None of them would ever meet again, she knew, yet who but God had the right to separate those who longed to be together?

Nash was in her mind constantly, and in every dream at night. Sometimes he was bounding along the earth, surefooted as a young god and gleaming as if his flesh were gilded. He would turn back to smile at her, comfortingly, his arms rising to reach out to her, yet she knew that they would never touch. He was no longer within her reach. From that dream she would wake calling his name, her heart aching. Sometimes, he was holding her, his arm tightly and cosily round her waist, and she would be revelling in his closeness, longing for him to kiss her, and then suddenly the pressure of his arm would weaken and when she turned to look up at him, she would see that he was crumbling into ancient grey dust. Surely that could only mean that he was dead?

The uncertainty was torture, and she was sure that she would never rest easily again. Even hope had deserted her since the death of Zora.

Outside there may be arid, stark and merciless desert stretching for mile after mile, and the heartless shrivelling sun, but here inside this sumptuous residence there was nothing but perfume, luxury and indolent pleasure. If Adem Ali sanctioned all this, then he must be the greatest hedonist ever born, Allegra thought. She believed that she knew what he would be like. Gross and button-eyed, he would have a slack, blubbery mouth and damp hands. He would be disgustingly fat and coarse-mannered. He would gobble his food, washing it down with a wave of sickly sherbets, gulping so fast that the sticky mixture flooded down his chest to stain his robe. While he guzzled, dancing girls would entertain him, yet he would have little attention for their efforts until his belly was filled.

She wanted to know what they planned to do with her, and why she had been brought to this room alone, but no one could or would understand her questions. The slaves simply shrugged and smiled and looked apologetic.

'Where is your master, the Amir Adem Ali?' she asked, but they continued not to understand, although two of them, seeming to comprehend the name, quickly concealed their reactions.

That morning in the middle of the usual ritual of bathing, being massaged with scented oils and having her hair shampooed until she was sure that it would dry out, she heard the wailing screams of someone in mortal terror.

'Is someone being punished? What is happening out there, please tell me!'

No one looked at her, but hands trembled as bowls and jugs were tilted into the hip bath, and one girl bit on her mouth to stop it quivering.

The screams grew louder and more terrified, and they went on and on, until Allegra's nerves were tattered. A tap came at the door, and in hobbled an old wrinkled woman, propped on a stick, and accompanied by attendants. Their eyes narrowed as they took in the newly bathed Christian slave, standing in the gilded light from the trellised window, wearing a robe of sea-blue silk embroidered with silver thread which dazzled the eye as the sun caressed it.

'I am Husaina, keeper of the female slaves,' the old woman said, her voice gentle and cultured, which took Allegra by surprise. 'I am sorry that you have to hear such a fearful sound when you have not been here for long, but a man is being punished for threatening our prince's life. He was a stupid, vicious man. He thought that he could lie with one of our prince's concubines and not be found out. He has been tortured and soon he will be dead. It is an example to all. The concubine, a greedy, vain and corrupt woman, will be strangled in private. It is not fitting that one who enjoyed the favour of our prince be executed before the public eye.'

Feeling faint, Allegra looked round for a chair and sank on to it. At once the old woman ordered her to stand, the genteel tones becoming raucous.

'None but the favoured of our prince sit before the mistress of the slaves!'

'Does that include the favoured one who is to die today?' Allegra riposted, fingers clenched.

'She is no longer favoured. She is a witless, debased woman, sinful and corrupt as Eve, seducing man and tempting him beyond his endurance.'

'So why are you executing the man if he was not to blame?' Allegra's jaw jutted.

'No man who has insulted our prince can live! Even to touch one of the prince's favoured women is the greatest offending to our lord. Vile, vile!' The woman banged her stick on the tiles and shook with indignation.

'Then perhaps your prince should take better care of his favourites?'

'Pah, this has gone on long enough! I come to see you, *nasrani*, and decide what we are to do with you. Abdul said you were a sick camel, a crazy dog, but all that need be said of you is that you are *nasrani*, Christian.'

Smarting at this insult, Allegra boiled with rage, straightening her back and meeting the old woman's gaze.

'I have seen little in your land to convince me that you and your people are saintly and of a temperate nature!'

'You are ignorant. You will find out the truthing. We had a Christian girl here once, with hair paled of colour and blue eyes not unlike yours. She was sunstruck in the head; she would not let our prince lie with her. Such stupidity is beyond the understanding.'

Allegra thought her heart had stopped beating. A Christian girl with pale hair and blue eyes . . . Elizabeth? Could it have been Elizabeth? For some moments she could not find the breath to speak, she was so sure that she had found her darling sister at long last.

'What – what became of the Christian girl?' she asked, her voice a croak. If it was Elizabeth, was she still here? Would she be able to see her, talk to her, make up to her for all that she had done in the past few months?

'She ran away, into the desert. We did not see her again, but one of the guards found her bleached bones two moons ago. He brought them here and they are to be mounted in gold so that everyone can see the fate of those who disobey our *saiyid*.'

The blood had rushed from Allegra's head; she could feel its torrential, streaming sound in her ears. Elizabeth dying alone in the desert . . . her bones brought back here! Her sister dead! *Dead!*

Only with immense effort did she stop herself from fainting. She must know if it was Elizabeth: she must find out!

'The girl's name . . . do you remember the girl's name?' she gasped. 'It might have been, have been . . . my sister.'

'Your sister? Pah, it is true that she had your mulish spirit. She screamed and fought and accused us, just as you have done. Crazy *nasrani*! In your country men are feeble women, and women strut like men, like your queen. We have none of that here.'

The old woman drew herself to her full height, which could not have been more than four feet and eleven inches, and with one arm swept the pleat of her custard-coloured silk robe back over her shoulder. Her feet were encased in gilded leather sandals gemmed with sequins, her neck decorated with a glittering collar of gold leather, sequins, diamonds and tourmalines, her hands chunky with rings displaying every possible jewel. Over her dark head lay a veil of silk edged with silver tassels, and beneath it her face was multiply wrinkled, dozens upon dozens of tiny lines like nature's trellis work ornamenting her skin. Her eyes were small and pouched, but her mouth was full and curved, with not one wrinkle upon it, so that it might have been the mouth of a sensual young girl. Her teeth were white and perfect, and from the brown wrinkled ears, the lobes of which sagged almost to the shoulders, hung enormous thick gold hoops, six in each ear.

None of this Allegra noticed. She was gripping the woman's

arm, wildly, and shouting in her face, in a strange, hoarse voice which she did not recognise as her own.

'Tell me the girl's name! Tell me, tell *me*! *Tell me her name!*'

Husaina, trying to shake away her hands, but failing, was beginning to panic.

'Her name was . . . Ah, how can I think when you shake me so, you vixen? It was . . .' She gulped, her mind blank.

'Yes? Yes?' Allegra cried, pulling savagely at the woman's veil, at her sleeves, her hands.

'It was . . . I recall her harem name! That was Baida, because of her white skin and pale hair. Oh, creature, stop pulling at me or we shall both fall over!'

'Her real name when she came here . . . You must know that? Did she not tell you? You asked me mine when I arrived . . . Surely you asked her for hers, too? Tell me what it was! If you cannot remember, surely someone else can!'

'I shall ask if you take your hands away from me. Do you hear? I shall ask!' Husaina struggled to maintain her balance and unclasp Allegra's hands at the same time.

By now, Allegra felt as if she were losing her mind. The uncertainty was too much. To find her sister so close, and yet for ever out of her reach. She could not bear it, she could not!

The other slaves might sink to the ground when Husaina appeared, and find her tiny form terrifying in its extraordinary ugliness, but not she. Nothing terrified Allegra except the thought that her sister was dead, that she was too late. This malnourished grandmother, unfairly punished by nature, could have been anyone, for all she cared. Anyone.

'Was her name Pentrevick, like mine? Surely you recall an unusual name like that? You must!'

The old woman sighed, and stumbled to the nearest seat to sit down with a gasping breath.

'I cannot recall. My head is filled with cotton.'

Husaina halted there, amazed at herself. She was not angry with this girl; she was not screaming for the guard to come and beat the *nasrani*. Instead, she was making excuses to her!

'Then who else will know?'

'The Amir, that is all. I accept the female slaves. I decide what will become of them, what roles they will fill.'

'Would she have spoken to anyone who might remember her name?'

'Ask, you can ask, but few speak your language.' Tears beaded Husaina's lashes; she could not understand why. Sisterly love, why should that perturb her? She had never had a sister. She could not even remember if she had ever had a family.

'The Amir will know? He *will* know?'

Husaina nodded. 'If she told him her true name, then he will know. His memory is excellent.'

'Then I shall ask him!'

Allegra's face had some colour again, but she felt shaky and sick at heart. She must know the truth, and yet what if she learned that it *was* Elizabeth who had died? She would have no reason to live.

'You *nasrani* are crazy fools,' Husaina said hoarsely. 'You behave like wild demons when you want something, or you do not want something. You have learned all your evils from your queen: she has taught her women to be proud and selfish.'

Now that Allegra had some hope to cling to, she snapped a tart reply.

'No one flings themselves to the floor when Queen Elizabeth appears, as they do before you. They bow or curtsey, but they do not prostrate themselves in the dust.'

'Then they are fools, for she will cut off their heads. That is what she does. We have all heard this. Favourites and enemies alike, she cuts off their heads, like her father before her!'

'It is not quite like that . . .' Allegra began.

'Do not argue, do not lie, do not try to trick and deceive me, *nasrani*. I have seen all the tricks and heard all the lies a thousand times before, and Allah has shown me how to outwit all those who would cheat and delude me.'

'Then you are extremely fortunate.' Allegra's cynicism was lost on the old jewelled crone who sat smiling smugly, her wrinkles overlapping quite startlingly.

'When do I meet the Amir?' Allegra asked in the silence which followed. 'Will it be soon?'

She could not wait to question him, to find out the name of the Christian girl who had died in the desert, but she must try and have faith that it was not Elizabeth. Other Christians must have been here . . . The Amir would know their names and be able to help her.

She had tried to question Abdul during their desert journey but he had laughed in her face, telling her that if her fair-haired sister had come this way, it was not with him. 'The carrion feed on fair, white-skinned females in this desert heat,' he had sneered, and she had felt ill at the knowledge that he was most probably right. Would the delicate and fragile Elizabeth even have survived the arduous sea voyage? She had not questioned the man again. Knowing was almost as bad as not knowing.

Husaina got up and hobbled towards Allegra, leaning heavily on her stick, to stare straight up into her face.

'The sun has beaten your skin to the texture of a lizard's back. Your nose is the colour of sun-dried sand. Your forehead hairs are bleached to silver by the heat and so are your lashes. They must be darkened with colouring and antimony must circle your eyes. Precious oils must be massaged into your flesh until it returns to its former softness. Then, and only then, may you be presented to His Highness.'

A crinkled brown hand came out to touch the clouds of russet-gold hair in an almost reverent gesture, and there was a gleam of something like covetous admiration in the tiny, pouched eyes.

'The hair needs no artifice to improve it. Such hair is a lesson to all.' The old woman glanced behind her at the gathering of attendants who were listening keenly to her every word, even though none could understand English. 'As for the feet . . . they have been through the grindings of hell. Look at them, blistered and scarred and red! And the hands are as raw as a warrior's! No member of the harem of our beloved and feared Prince, Adem Ali, can be in possession of such hideous physical flaws. Attend to this creature and put right these flaws so that she will please our master in all things, and thus shall we all please the one true God, Allah the all-merciful, the all-powerful.' Having completed her admonishments so that Allegra understood, Husaina repeated them in Arabic for the benefit of the listening slaves.

Later, Allegra's 'hideous physical flaws' were treated by the harem beauticians, women who seemed to know what they were about, despite the crudeness of their equipment. As she lay with her arms hanging on either side, her hands resting in dishes of thickly glutinous oils, and bandages entwining her feet which were plastered with a foul-smelling cream, she reminded herself continually that she was only allowing this to be done so that she could speak to the Amir all the sooner.

While the women were working, she tried to question them, repeating her words in as simple a form as possible, but they could not comprehend, shaking their heads from side to side and shrugging.

'Do you know of a girl, a *nasrani*, who has been here in this harem? A *nasrani* with white skin and bright, pale hair, and blue eyes, this colour!' She pointed to the robe of one of the slaves. At least she had remembered the Arabic word for Christian, and this she kept repeating, over and over. But the women did not respond and eventually became impatient, tut-tutting, and slapping at her hands when she lifted them up out of the cream in a gesture of frustration.

Finally, Allegra gave up. Now that she knew she was meant for the Lord of the Incense Road, if her 'hideous physical flaws' could be corrected, she did at least have a thread to grasp, tenuous as it was. She was also experiencing a violent unease. It appeared that she was to be perfected and then placed before this Amir as if she were a rich new foreign dish for his table. How difficult it was to accept the customs of his country, customs which were irrevocably entrenched and which were the very opposite of all that she knew and loved at home. Hardest of all to face was that she had no choice; she was now a slave, the lowest of the low, without rights, without freedoms, without hope.

'*NO!*' She would not accept all this in silence, like the thousands who had gone before her. Knocking the delicate oil jar out of the hands of the nearest slave, Allegra leapt to her feet and headed for the door, making no sound because of the bandages swathing her to the ankles.

Her hands were slippery with oil, her fingers sliding helplessly across the door handle. Clenching her teeth in frustration, she struggled for purchase, bunching up her robe to fold round the handle so that her fingers would grip. Suddenly the handle turned, the door opened and she was free.

Outside in the corridor stood two of the most massive guards she had ever seen. They were naked except for saffron-coloured *shalwar* and bright yellow silk sashes round their waists, into which were tucked huge, curving scimitars. Their ebony bodies gleaming as if polished with oil, their flattened faces like lions, they turned to face her, swivelling on naked heels.

If there had been any breath in her lungs it vanished now. In slow, practised movements the two guards reached for their scimitars, fondling the jewelled hilts lovingly. With empty lungs, she stared in horror, too shocked to move, to scream or faint, as the scimitars, their terrifying glistening blades like murderous crescent moons, swept towards her.

The steel did not touch her, yet she felt as if her throat were cut, so near had come the blades and so unexpected the attack. Pain clamoured in her chest, her eyes fluttered and she fell to the floor unconscious.

The mistress of the slaves was standing over her when she woke, the bright, pouched eyes twinkling with cruel amusement.

'Thought your time had come, did you? That is for Allah to decide, not those sexless men out there.' She spat with laughter, the gold rings in her ears swinging. 'Eunuchs they are, Nubians, black as midnight, cruel as death, vicious as the day of Judgement.'

'They – they tried to kill me!' Allegra croaked, putting her hand around her throat.

'They do not try, they succeed, *nasrani*,' the old woman cackled. 'If they had wished to kill you, then you would be dead now, split into tiny slivers of bloody flesh. They wanted only to frighten you back into this chamber.'

'They succeeded!'

'Why are you so reluctant to join us here? There have been women so grateful for our prince's favour, for the safety, luxury and comfort of this harem, that they have blessed our name and showered us with gifts.'

'Their lives must have been truly wretched before they came here then!'

'And was yours not? Shipwrecked on a distant isle without food or water, alone and persecuted by wild beasts. Was that not wretched?'

'It was not exactly like that . . . My . . . the man I . . .' There she faltered. There had been much talk of virginity, of the fate of unchaste women in Islam. If they knew that she had lost her maidenhead, would they behead her?

'What man is this?' Suddenly the sloe-dark eyes were glittering with menace.

'The man I was to marry. He . . . I left him behind in England, that is all.'

She had visions of them tracing her beloved after learning that he had made love to her and thus, by their circuitous thinking, having insulted the Lord Adem Ali. Could they view that as an offence against the Amir even though it had happened when she was free? Yes, in this hellish land, anything was possible. Oh God, she wished she were free of it!

'You are loving him? Always the crazy *nasrani* must love her man.'

'No, I no longer love him,' Allegra lied, the words searing her tongue. 'He means nothing to me and never did.'

She hoped that her rebuttal would keep Nash safe, that was, if he was in the household of a Muslim who knew Adem Ali. Did they discuss their slaves? She did not know, but if they did, then Nash must be protected. If he were still alive . . . Her stomach churned at her denial and she managed to swallow the choking sound which would give her away. With Nash dead or in slavery, her life meant nothing, nor ever would.

'That is meet. When you are in our Amir's arms, you will see nothing but the golden glowing of the sun and the glory of being close to the one true God and you will forget for ever your Eenglishman.'

When the old woman had gone, hobbling on her stick, sucking on her teeth and shaking her head from side to side, Allegra slept, drained of energy and emotion. But there was little comfort in the darkness of oblivion for she woke aching and heavy-hearted. Before the end of the week she was to be presented to the Lord of the Incense Road, just as if she were a sack of spices or a casket of precious myrrh or frankincense.

A free gift, she thought mercilessly, a free gift . . . And yet the longer she fought, the longer it would be before she could question the Amir about her sister. All her questions so far had met with the same barrier. No one knew anything, or would admit that they did. It was not easy to tell if they were being honest or not.

She had repeated her questions to Husaina, hoping that she might have remembered something, but she had not.

The hours passed and the conflict within Allegra increased. She must speak to the Amir, and yet she was being presented to him as a slave, a concubine. Oh, how could she tolerate this impotence? Searching for food on a wild ocean island was a thousand times preferable to being a prisoner.

Oh, Nash! Where was he now? How could she smile and pretend friendship to the Amir when he had destroyed the lives of her sister, Nash, and herself? Yet she must find out more about the Christian girl . . . Only the Amir could tell her.

Chapter Fifteen

This part of the palace was so gloriously beautiful that it befitted God alone, not a mere mortal who had elevated himself by cruelty and oppression. Even the narrowest corridor was lustrously tiled in blue, white and amber, and at regular intervals there were niches in the walls, each painted in the brightest colours, the most perfect designs, and displaying a gold or silver incense brazier or perfumed lamp from which drifted the mesmeric, twisting, cloudy fragrance of priceless incense. Here, fresh clean air was unknown, or so it seemed to Allegra as she was escorted through the twisting corridors towards the apartments of the Lord of the Incense Road.

She felt confused, almost befuddled, and there was a weariness in her limbs, but nothing intruded upon her thoughts except for the approaching confrontation with Adem Ali. She had convinced herself as to what she must do, and do it she would, whatever the outcome.

This monstrous man had destroyed her life and happiness, taken Nash from her and caused the persecution and ill-treatment of the women with whom she had been brought to this place. For their suffering she would do it, as much as for her own.

Gradually, the chambers became larger and more opulent, their walls immaculate white or glowing sunny yellow, the designs of the lozenge-shaped tiles vivid and intricate. Trellises alleviated the stark beauty, their fragile frames woven with vines, blossoms and flowers which filled the air with heady scents. Here, too, were the ubiquitous incense burners and the scented lamps, their chubby swelling middles gracefully curving to narrow necks from which hung delicate gold filigree chains to support them.

Progress was slow for the mistress of the slaves was with them, hobbling along on her stick. Now and again she would glance at Allegra as if she were the fount of all that was miraculous.

They had dressed her in extravagant silks, rose, rich-blue, lemon and a deep sea-green, which billowed around her as she walked. Her hair was twined with seedpearls trapped in a gold filigree chain, and over her head there hung a thick silver-grey veil which she had been ordered to keep in place, Adem Ali himself being the one who must remove it.

Round her wrists and ankles were thin gold bangles; they had even put jewelled rings on her toes so that she could not walk at any great speed (which was probably their intention). They had painted her feet and hands with a thick ginger-coloured paste which stained them a russet colour. This was beautiful, she was told, and it would protect her from evil jinns. They had oiled her hair and plaited it so that it tugged on her head like a weight, and her ears had been pierced in the most terrifying way. A man had advanced on her with a great curving needle, and she had struggled wildly. Pierced ears were not a vanity to which she had ever been atttracted, nor did the result do anthing to remove the pain.

Her nipples too had been painted with henna, as had her navel, and into it was stuck a large glittering jewel. It was bright red, yet she did not believe that it could be a ruby for it was enormous and would have been worth a small fortune.

She had been multiply bathed, massaged and oiled, the hairs plucked from between her thighs, every single one, until her skin throbbed, and then they had done the same beneath her arms, explaining that it was all for cleanliness and the evasion of disease and vermin. She laughed bitterly then, for she had never had a flea or a louse upon her body until she was sold into slavery.

Her finger nails and toe nails had been painted a deep, rich red, which made her skin glow palely, this colour contrast causing the beauty attendants to gasp with delight. She knew that they had been imagining the effect her scarlet nails and white fingers would have upon their lord and master.

She wanted it to have one effect only: to repulse him.

Allegra walked stiffly, her mouth trembling beneath its lurid coating of scarlet rouge, her ears throbbing, for the piercing had set up an inflammation which might take weeks to fade. Having seen that some of the women had their noses pierced and adorned with a complicated display of gold rings and glittering chains, to which filigree and spangles were attached, she thanked God that at least they had left her nose alone.

'Not much farther to go,' Husaina hissed. 'Recall what I told you: when you see the mighty Lord of the Incense Road, you prostrate yourself at his feet until he raises you and removes your veil. That is his privilege, his right. Then, hold your breath while he judges you. If he does not take to you, then you will be sold elsewhere as is the custom, perhaps given to one of His Highness's loyal allies as a gift. If he takes to you, then you will be more fortunate than any but the first wife of Mohammed the Prophet.'

The tinkling sound of music reached Allegra's ears. It sounded like bells, harp and flute all rolled into one. She had heard that Adem Ali adored music, song and dance, and that his musicians were the finest in the world. After this, Husaina said, her nose wrinkling, that if she, the *nasrani* had displayed any gifts in the way of dancing then her fame and glory would have become vouchsafed along with her life and security for the rest of her days. Allegra had not replied. They did not ask her if she could dance, or how, they had merely assumed that she could not.

The music was growing louder and now came an eerie, wailing Arabic song, piercing, nasal and little more than a drone to foreign ears. Up and down and roundabout went the droning, without any definite tune. Thinking of such delicacies as *Greensleeves*, and the other verses and music written by Henry VIII, Allegra suffered a stabbing pang of homesickness. She longed for the delight of a Pavane, or the energetic Volte, or one of the other dearly familiar dances from home.

'Soon now you will be before our master,' Husaina hissed, and then the stately little group came to a sudden, swaying halt.

The grand audience chamber was before them then, lush colours stunning the eye. Scarlets and peacock blues and greens, bright emeralds, dazzling yellows and ivory, crimson and wine, all embroidered into massive silk brocade cushions and hassocks, tapestries, carpets and hangings. A vast plump and padded mound of cushions was against one wall, their covering crimson silk. Scented lamps stood at either end of this, and over it was suspended a huge filigree lamp from which came regular silvery-white clouds of incense. Two Nubians, tarry black and gleaming like satin, stood at each end of the bed, holding ostrich feather fans and bending them backwards and forwards gently, to cool the man who sat between them.

Tables were piled high with gold and jewelled dishes of exotic fruits, and silver-gilt vases of brilliantly coloured blossoms, so enormous that Allegra thought they could not possibly be real.

'Do not forget that you must call our master esteemed

Highness for that is his honoured title, and you must kiss the hem of his robe as a mark of respect. If you forget, then his wrath will be terrible and a thing which you will never be forgetting,' Husaina whispered, before pushing Allegra forward so that she had to run two or three steps to prevent herself from falling to her knees with an ungainly crash.

Through the cloudy silk veiling covering her face, Allegra saw the man she must address as esteemed Highness, or Saiyid, great lord, the man she had expected would be a gross and repulsive monster, his features snarling with cruelty, his mouth lascivious, his eyes narrowed and glittering with lust. Shaking, her heart thudding, she prostrated herself at his feet, as she had been ordered to do, and there she stayed, waiting for Adem Ali, Lord of the Incense Road, to raise her to her knees.

He was not ugly! He was not even obese! How could she put her plan into action when she had steeled herself to expect a vile and vicious old man, not a glowingly handsome princeling? How beautiful he was, healthy and young and good-natured; all of this she noticed in her brief glimpse of his face. Smiling good-humouredly, his eyes were filled with sparkling laughter, yet he seemed unaware of his mesmeric charm, for there was not a fraction of vanity in his expression. Richly dressed in emerald-green satin, with a collar thick with crimson rubies set in gold, and a ruby hilt on the crescent-shaped dagger tucked in his gold silk sash, he looked royal, magnificent . . . and refined.

Time passed and Allegra dared not move, yet her heart continued to thud painfully. All she could see were his feet encased in gold brocade slippers embroidered with green and scarlet silks. The toes curved upwards, in the Turkish style, and she tried to concentrate on these while she struggled to order her jumbled thoughts.

The fluting wail of the music, interspersed by the drumming of a *davoul*, rose and dipped, rose and dipped, and the smouldering scent of incense increased, wafting through her veil and numbing her senses. But she must not let it, she must stay alert and keen, ready to act . . .

The jewelled hand beneath her chin was like the touch of flame and ice commingled and she leapt with shock, her stomach turning. This man had destroyed the lives of those she loved most in all the world . . .

'Let me see the hair of which I have been told so much,' ordered Adem Ali, without any note of arrogant command in his voice. 'Come, to your feet, shy one, and let me see your face.'

Allegra felt herself being pulled gently by her hands, and then she was standing before the Lord of the Incense Road, the man whom she loathed and hated with all her heart for taking her from her beloved Nash, for stealing her precious sister.

She tried to gather her thoughts for what she wanted to say, while Adem Ali's hand flicked out to twist the veil away from her face. She heard his indrawn breath as he saw her hair. Washed and brushed repeatedly, it flared around her head, a glistening sunburst.

'*Saiyid*, Highness,' she began falteringly, her cheeks flushing. 'If I might ask a request of you . . . I have come so far and I – I must know something, or I cannot rest, I cannot sleep!' She pressed her hands together, gazing up at him entreatingly.

'What is it that you wish to know? If you please me, shy one? The answer to that is yes, you do please me.'

'Some months ago, my sister was captured by – by Arabs. They came to Cornwall where we lived and took my sister away. They showed your ensign, Your Highness, the flame-breathing dragon. I wish – that is, I must know, if Your Highness would please tell me: do you know the whereabouts of my sister, Elizabeth Pentrevick? They told me that a Christian girl had escaped into the desert a month or two ago, and, and, died there.' Allegra's throat felt as if it had been roughly squeezed and an icy chill was settling along her limbs. But she knew what she must do, and her plan was not yet complete.

'Elizabeth Pentrevick was your sister?' The Amir leaned forward, his eyes narrowed.

'You recognise the name? Oh, God be praised! Tell me, Your Highness, please . . . Where is she?'

'You spoke of her just now.' The Amir gave a sad, heart-rending smile. 'She fought against the life here. We tried all that we could to comfort her, but she would have none of it. She spoke of you.'

'She did?' Tears blocked Allegra's vision. She had known it all along. Elizabeth was dead.

'She said that she had no desire to live now that she was separated from her dear sister.'

'So, so, she – she was the one who fled into the desert?' Allegra choked on the words. There was a drumming in her ears, a frenzied madness spiralling upwards inside her.

'Sadly, it was she. It was the will of Allah.'

The Amir leaned forward to plunge his slender brown fingers into the mass of fiery curls, in what she took at first to be a tender gesture. Then as she realised that he was pulling her towards him to kiss her mouth, she did what she had planned if the news was of the very worst.

While he was leaning close, spellbound by her hair, she lunged towards him, her nerves seared with determination, to grip the ruby-hilted dagger from his sash and plunge it directly into his heart.

Youssef stormed up and down his chamber, biting at his cuticles with sharp white teeth. Rouhkia, his wife, was shaming him before Islam, making a mockery of the laws of the Koran and the sacred words of the Prophet. Yet he did not know what to do about it for he feared her brother beyond all men.

Adem Ali had the most vicious and destructive temper imaginable. From the age of two, when he had strangled his pet dog for urinating on his shoe, the temper of the Lord of the Incense Road had been as feared as the wrath of devils. Some said that he was the sire of Satan, that his mother had bedded with so many men that she had not recognised the Devil when she lay with him. Whether or not that was true, Youssef lived in terror of his brother-in-law. There was so much that he could be punished for . . . For one, his marriage to Rouhkia remained unconsummated. On the wedding night, when he lay on the flower-decked divan with her, the relatives standing over them to see that the deed was done properly, he had kissed

Rouhkia only to see, in his mind's eye, her brother, imagining the fate that would befall him if he did not accomplish the desired erection and penetration. Nothing could have been more likely to make him impotent, and so it was, to his shame and disgrace.

Next morning when he woke, there were the relatives again, closely watching, mouths grim, and yet again he failed to consummate the marriage.

At first, Rouhkia had loved him. She had been different before their marriage, gentle, sweet and shy, and how he had desired her. Because he could not accomplish the deed, and because it would mean his disgrace and vilification for not being a true man, Rouhkia had smuggled one of the palace's caged birds into her bedchamber and stabbed it to death over the bedsheet so that when the relatives returned to see the third attempt, she showed them the blood-stained bedsheet, her expression victorious. At once the eldest relative scooped up the sheet and strode out, beaming broadly, to convey the evidence to Adem Ali.

Rouhkia had been sweetness to him then, cajoling and tempting, kissing and caressing, but still he could not rid himself of the image of the fearful, murderous Adem Ali, and somehow, when he took Rouhkia into his embrace, she became the dreaded Amir.

It had been the dream of Youssef's parents that he marry Rouhkia. They were old and ill; how could he disgrace them? The weight of his shame grew and grew while the object which was desired to grow remained small and shrivelled and would not obey its owner. Still, Youssef had hope that he would succeed one day if his wife continued to be patient and loving.

Weeks and months passed and Rouhkia besought him to visit the physicians, which he did, swallowing their obnoxious potions with nausea, and sometimes prostration, yet still the small, shrivelled instrument remained infuriatingly quiescent.

When Rouhkia suggested that he might not truly find her rousing, and that he might in fact prefer the male sex, he denied it hotly. Others might have such inclinations but he, never! he cried, his thin face crimson.

'What are we to do, oh what are we to do?' Rouhkia had

sobbed in his arms. 'My brother asks if I am yet with child. He longs to be an uncle, to dandle our son upon his knee and yet we have not even joined our bodies.'

Mute with shame, Youssef cradled her in his arms and saw in his imagination an execution block, his head resting upon it, while his brother-in-law loomed over him, scimitar raised to behead him.

A few days later, a miracle happened. He became erect, and then so great was their hurry to join together that they clung like children. Alas, the erection crumpled the moment it touched the gateway, and so furious and disappointed was Rouhkia that she struck him in the face, over and over, and he did not resist, for he knew that he deserved his punishment.

Soon after, accusing him of deliberately denying her what she most wanted, Rouhkia took her first lover. Shamed, Youssef did nothing, said nothing. To make a public scene would ensure that his brother-in-law found out that he was impotent and he would be imprisoned, or beheaded, perhaps tortured for long, agonising weeks. To reject the sister of the Lord of the Incense Road was to reject Adem Ali, too, and to deny him the nephew which he craved. Wives should be with child and yet a year had passed and Rouhkia remained barren.

By now, she had discovered that she enjoyed taking lovers. She could take her pick of the male slaves and they would do whatever she ordered, unlike her husband. It was thrilling.

Seeing the new confidence in his wife's composure, and the detachment which was growing between them, Youssef panicked, thinking that his impotence would be broadcast, but no, Rouhkia stayed silent, confiding in none. She was revelling in her freedom, and a new husband might call a halt to her debauchery. There was nothing that Youssef could do without endangering his own security, and upsetting his ageing parents. His mother had suffered a strange wasting fever and she was now bedridden. His father wept whenever her name was mentioned, and wrote letters to Youssef begging him to get his wife with child so that his mother could see her first grandson before she died.

In despair, Youssef had gone to Rouhkia, beseeching her to

speak with him in private. He could see from her expression that she thought he was going to forbid her to take more lovers, and her face set in a grim scowl. How like her brother she had looked at that moment, and Youssef had wanted to turn and run away. Alone, he managed to say what was in his mind, that he wanted to be able to show his new son to his sick mother, and please could he try again to consummate the marriage?

Rouhkia had laughed in his face. She was not the same bride who had flirted, giggled and tickled him two years ago. Now she was obdurate, cold and self-seeking.

'My father and your father were loyal friends for thirty years, please, for their sakes, let us try again!' Youssef had begged, tears in his eyes.

'My father is dead,' Aliya said, in such a way that her words chilled Youssef. It was as if she were saying, 'You will be dead too if you do not watch out!'

'*Please!*'

'There is nothing more that we can discuss, Youssef. If your mother is sick then visit her, for the sight of her beloved son will cheer her, and if it is Allah's wish that she die without seeing her grandson, then who is to quarrel with the one true God? Certainly not I!'

'Rouhkia, you loved me once!'

'Yes, once, but not a second or a third time. You had your chance and you ruined it. If you were aged and old and ill, I would be able to forgive you, but I loved you and you betrayed me.'

'No, that is unfair! It is not my fault! Do you not think that I would make love to you now if I could?'

'*If* you could.' Her eyes glittered venomously. 'But you cannot, can you?' Stepping close, she thrust her square jaw into his face. 'Well, can you?'

Glittering basalt eyes stared mercilessly into soft brown ones, and to Youssef it was like gazing into the stony eyes of a sphinx or a pitiless she-devil of the night. Unable to answer, he turned away, shoulders sagging, and went back to his chambers feeling that the weight of the world dragged behind him on a chain.

He had visited his mother and was shocked at her fragility. She had wept on seeing him and he had wept too.

'How is our daughter-in-law?' she had asked, her voice tremulous.

'She is with child, mother, is it not marvellous?' Youssef lied, for his father had taken him aside before he went into the sick room, telling him that his mother had only a few weeks left to her.

'With child! Thanks be to Allah, the one true God!' his mother sobbed brokenly, clutching Youssef's hands to her bosom. Three days later, she died in her son's arms a gentle smile on her lips, as Youssef described to her, for the dozenth time, how she would dandle her grandson on her knee in just a few months' time.

After the burial, Youssef returned to his wife's palace. He should have known, when she refused to move into his residence, that she would prove intractable, for it was a wife's place always to go where her husband ordained. In Rouhkia's favourite palace, she was both master and mistress, as she had been since her brother had given her the residence when she was thirteen years old. For Youssef to declare otherwise would be tantamount to his attacking the authority of Adem Ali. Had he, Youssef, been a prince or *sherif*, then it would not have been impossible for him to assert his authority over his wife. As it was, he was worthy only to kiss the hem of her robe and not to kiss her hand as her equal.

For a time, he could find no compensation for his humiliation. He grieved for his mother, who called him her 'lion of lions', a fondly flattering term usually reserved for those in the highest positions. He grieved for his lost happiness and the carefree years of his bachelor life. As befitted a wealthy Muslim male, he was allowed to have a harem, and gifts of voluptuous and intriguing women frequently arrived in his audience chamber, sent by those who wished to win the favour of the brother-in-law of Adem Ali.

If only they knew that he treats me with contempt! Youssef thought, as he surveyed these gifts, not one of the women appealing to his senses. Perhaps he was more captivated by young men, as Rouhkia had said?

One day, he returned from a hunting trip to find that his entire harem had been disbanded and the women sold into slavery. When he demanded to know where they had been taken, no one would tell him. There was a conspiracy of silence. Rouhkia would only smile and yawn, and her servants were blank-faced, out of fear of her wrath; he did not blame them. He rode out into the desert, following the tracks for long hours, and on the morning of the second day, he saw a caravan in the distance. Spurring on his horse, he approached the caravan.

Nothing. Only hides, spices, salt and bolts of poor-quality material. His heart twisting savagely, his belly empty with dismay and distress, he rode to a hollow in the sand and there flung himself to weep.

Six weeks before, he had found out that he was normal, that the right woman could rouse him magnificently. It had only been a question of his finding the right woman, for, unlike most lusty Arabs, he was selective.

The slave girl, Mudija, was a gift from an old boyhood companion, and she was a delight. Dainty and glossy-haired with wide, violet-coloured eyes inherited from an English grandfather, she had a dark bronze skin and ebony hair which flowed thickly and glossily to her ankles. Shyness. He had never met a truly shy girl before, and it was entrancing. Mudija blushed when he spoke to her, and her voice faltered when he asked her questions about her homeland and family. His heart was moved for her plight and the unhappiness she had suffered since being torn from her mother's arms when she was seven.

That first night with Mudija, Youssef reached paradise a multitude of times. Virginal, gentle and sighingly tender, she responded wholeheartedly to his tentative, doubtful love-making.

Realising that they loved one another, Youssef spent every spare moment with Mudija. Within three weeks, she was with child, and Youssef rejoiced. He had been foolish, he knew. What did he expect his spurned wife to do when she found out that his slave was to bear a child before she did? The disgrace, the insult, of it! Blissful, Youssef and Mudija kissed and held hands and smiled rosily at one another, until the day came when Rouhkia's spies told her the news.

Her husband's concubine, who had been in the harem only a mere five weeks, was with child!

'Then she was with child when she came here and concealed it from him!' Rouhkia cried, her fingers curving into claws.

'No, she was virgin,' the spy explained.

'How did you know, fool? Did you examine her yourself?' Rouhkia hissed.

'No, *Ya Sitti*, but, but, *ya m'allmi* he say she virgin!'

'Allah preserve me from Turkish idiots and imbeciles!' Rouhkia spat, kicking out at the man. 'What else would the master say, you dupe, if he wanted to prove that he was not impotent?'

'Aiee, *Ya Sitti*, but you are right!'

'I know that, you blundering knave, I know that!'

It had taken Rouhkia little more than a few minutes to decide what she would do. Poison was beneath her, although it was a popular method of disposing of rivals. She could order one of her female spies to bring her some of Mudija's hair and nail parings and recite a charm of evil and destruction over them, but she did not know how long it would take to work. She could not tolerate the thought of Mudija's belly swelling, of everyone seeing that her husband had sired a child while she remained barren. Whatever she said about the slave having been with child when she arrived at the palace, there would always be many who would realise the truth: that she was sick with envy.

To pinpoint one concubine would draw attention to the reason for her destruction, and whatever Rouhkia's other failings, she had never dabbled in murder. Whatever her behaviour when she was enraged, Rouhkia liked to think herself above jealousy, regarding it as undignified, unbefitting her rank and position.

Not one fertile concubine would be removed from Youssef's reach but the entire harem! Abidullah, the slave dealer, was due, bringing Rouhkia new lovers (she hoped), and he would receive, in exchange, on condition that he never spoke one word on the matter, the entire harem of Youssef ibn Akhbal, thirty-two beautiful, self-indulgently plump females from all parts of the world.

Having invited Abidullah to peer through the secret spy hole which she used to watch her husband at his sport (a tedious waste of time until Mudija's arrival) she turned to the slave dealer with a broad and wicked grin.

'A fair exchange, would you not say?'

'Fair indeed, oh Exalted One, yes, fair indeed!' Abidullah salaamed, bending very low, hearing his old spine clicking ominously, but knowing full well that obeisance before this woman was more important than being bedridden.

And so the women were parcelled up, like sacks of exotic spices and, under heavy guard, sent on their way, with Abidullah red-cheeked with delight and disbelief at his good fortune. Thirty-two females and one of them with child . . . He would be able to retire on the proceeds of their sale.

'Thanks be to Allah the beneficent, the omnipotent!' he mumbled to himself, as the caravan of women and guards ribboned its way into the desert towards the coast.

Sobbing in the desert hollow, the wind moaning through the little shelter of flints and smooth, shiny stones which shepherds had built for their goats, Youssef wept until he was empty of tears. Long deserted, the shelter contained nothing but a dustball of tangled grasses and parched twigs, but Youssef hid inside, wanting to die. Eventually he slept, not hearing the windstorm which howled around him during the night, his mare covered by his blanket and standing on the sheltered side of the hut. Next morning, not knowing whether this had been the breaking or the making of him, he stepped out into the wind-cleansed desert.

He was not himself. He did not feel like Youssef. He was different, another man inside the same body. Uneasy, he licked his dry, dusty lips and patted his mare, shaking out her blanket and making comforting little noises in her ear, yet without the warmth of feeling to support his actions. He had loved Anuka, his mare, yet he felt no emotion when he looked at her now. She was a dark shape against the light, the usual shape for a horse, yet she might have been stone for all he cared.

He did not want to go home. He had no home. Allah, if only

he had never loved Mudija! To have her and then be parted like this, what punishment this was, what had he done to merit such agony?

His mind raced through the scriptures, seeking for a solution, but none came. He recalled having heard that a man should go for slave girls, for they have 'minds and intelligence'. Musa Kazim had said that, and how right he had been! Intelligence in a wife was nothing but a trial, but in a concubine it was a delight.

Hariri, who had lived in the eleventh century, had said, 'A virgin is like a hoarded pearl, an egg that is covered with a sitting bird, a first fruit ready for gathering or a vintage wine in store, a fragrant bed of flowers, or a necklet that is rare and valuable, one unsoiled by a touching hand, uncovered by a body that might clothe it, one free of the trifler's fancy, unsullied by the defiling hand. A modest visage has she, a bashful gaze, a flattering tongue, a pure heart, being a playful doll, a coquettish toy, a frolicsome gazelle, a girl of unblemished beauty; a bejewelled sash that is shining and pure, a bedfellow that shall never age.'

Every phrase reminded him heartbreakingly of Mudija! How could he bear this agony?

'I cannot go on,' he sighed into the bleak terracotta wastes of the desert. 'I cannot go on. There is no life left for me.'

Some hours after, he set out having smacked Anuka's rump and ordered her to return home to her comfortable stable.

On foot, he trekked into the arid, dusty wasteland which was called the Forgotten Desert because no man in his right mind would go there alone; yet Youssef wished to do nothing but lose himself in that stony isolation, lose himself until death.

'A virgin is like a hoarded pearl . . . She has a pure heart, she is a frolicsome gazelle, a bejewelled sash that is shining and pure, a necklet that is rare and valuable . . .' Like a litany, he muttered these phrases to himself, until his parched throat denied him words. Walking until darkness fell over him, suddenly and relentlessly, as happens in the desert, he collapsed unconscious.

Chapter Sixteen

Laughing, Adem Ali intercepted the death blow, his slim, powerful fingers closing round Allegra's fist so swiftly and skilfully it was as if he deflected assassination attempts every day. Gasping with shock, she found her wrist clamped in such a merciless grip that she felt as if her skin were burning.

'So, not such a shy one, eh? Allah, did you think that you could kill me so easily? If it were that simple then I would have been murdered a hundred times! A man who has many enemies must teach himself the art of side-stepping them . . . If you had drawn so much as a sequin of my blood, little *nasrani*, you would have been hacked to death by those eunuchs over there. They are skilled at torturing their victims so that death comes slowly. Would you enjoy seeing your intestines held up before your eyes while you were still breathing? Or would the torture of a thousand cuts suit you better? Do you see this casket here? It is covered in gilded leather which is very beautiful, but once this was human skin and it was stripped from a man who tried to murder me towards the end of Ramadan last year.'

Allegra gaped at the casket, her eyes refusing to focus properly, her body chilling with shock and dismay. Human skin, that casket was covered in human skin! Putting a hand to her mouth, she struggled to repress the urge to vomit. Would they hack her to pieces if she vomited all over their Amir's beautiful, gold-stamped slippers? Having conquered the nausea, she looked Adem Ali squarely in the face, noting with grim delight how his eyes flickered at her forthright gaze. No doubt only his most favoured concubines looked at him like that, for the newcomers must avert their eyes from the wondrous god who was their master. *God?* He was a devil, a vile and cruel man masquerading as a charming and debonair princeling!

'Devil,' she muttered, her heart fluttering, then her voice louder, '*Shaîtân, shaîtân!*' It meant demon or some such, for she had heard the slaves use it as a term of abuse to those who behaved badly, and she had noted how it resembled the name Satan.

'You are a devil, a vicious, cowardly devil! You buy and sell women as if they are spices or hides! You do not care about their sufferings as they travel in the desert or on board ship. Do you know how many of them die while coming here? Do you *care*? What of the children snatched from their mother's arms and the mothers snatched from their families, never to see them again? How would you feel, Adem Ali, if you were never to see your loved ones again because some avaricious and powerful lord had decided that he wanted to sell them for his own gain? Well, how would you feel, *shaîtân*, tell me, tell me!'

Feet planted apart, hands on hips, Allegra almost screamed the last few words while a shocked hush descended on the room and its occupants. None save the Amir could understand what she was saying, but all could tell that it was angry abuse. No one, not even his dearest, had ever spoken to their master in this way . . . He would have the she-devil executed, there was no doubt of that . . .

The black eunuchs stepped forward, gripping the hilts of their scimitars, ready to obey their master's command.

Allegra continued to rant and scream, until, drained of emotion, she sank to her knees, eyes glossy with tears, palms to her face. What had she done, how had she dared speak like that?

'You – you will have me killed now?' she stammered, shaking violently.

'No,' he replied, his voice gentle and rich, flowing into her mind like molten silk. 'You are a Christian, and a woman, and as both you know no better. Time will change your mind concerning matters on which you are ignorant now. Take the *nasrani* to her apartment . . .' Adem Ali, having said all that he planned to say, sat down again, the musicians began to play their reedy, gyrating tune and Allegra was led away by two of the guards.

In the simple chamber where she had spent the last day or so, she paced up and down unable to relax. Food was brought her, lamb roasted in herbs, thick with butter and rice, and strange, exotic fruits. How could she eat when Nash, if he were still alive, might be starving at this very moment? Oh Jesu, what had she done? She did not know whether to regret her outburst, much as he had deserved it, or whether she should scream at him continually, if she were ever given the chance to be in his presence again. If she ranted and would not stop, and went on and on, would they kill her then? It would be a blissful release from her inner torment, the grief and heartache, but did she have the courage to be tortured to death, hacked to tiny pieces by those glinting, silvery scimitars? Jesu, find me a way to die without pain, she begged, on her knees, as she began to sob into her folded arms.

Traffic in slaves . . . It was the vilest trade, the most loathsome and merciless thing on earth and yet she had become a part of it and could not escape . . .

She prayed urgently, asking for courage and strength, for release from this iniquitous place where Satan reigned. Yet her prayers failed to comfort her. Eventually, she slept, her throat aching, only to wake in the shadowy dark of the night, ravenously hungry. Snatching at the food on the tray, she crammed some of the cold, congealed stew into her mouth, barely chewing, swallowing eagerly, only to think of Nash again. Somewhere, he might be chained to some dank prison wall, fed on slops and foul water, or dead, his body rotting at the bottom of the Arabian Ocean . . . If only she knew, if only she knew!

Retching, she picked up the tray and flung it and its contents across the room so that they smacked against the far wall with a clattering crash. It was just unfortunate if it woke the entire palace, just unfortunate.

Youssef was carried into his wife's palace by Beduin tribesmen who had found him raving with fever and burnt dark as chestnut by the sun. Unable to speak, he could not tell them who he was, and they, having failed to cure him with their limited medical skills, were preparing to bury him, that being Allah's will. Then the coin fell from his neck, its chain snapping as he twisted in fever. Had they thought he was anything but a sunstricken pauper, they would have searched him for gold and jewellery. The coin, engraved with the emblem of the flame-spewing dragon, filled the Beduin with terror. Only the Amir Adem Ali and his close relatives wore this emblem, so if they allowed this man to die, they would incur the fury and revenge of the Lord of the Incense Road, and he was not a friend one would cherish, let alone an enemy . . .

Moving with inordinate speed, they transported the man on a stretcher borne between two horses, and thus they brought him to the palace of the Lady Rouhkia, sister of the Amir Adem Ali.

Rouhkia cursed her husband, standing over his sickbed and pouring insults on his head. She called him dullard and moon-fevered, poltroon and knave and many other words which were unrepeatable, before she stormed from the room, her face crimson.

Finally the day came when he was able to croak,

'Do you not mean sun-fevered, oh foul-tongued daughter of Hades?'

Eyes widening, Rouhkia bent close.

'So you are not going to die?'

'And cheat you of your greatest desire? No, I shall live for another hundred years and you will never be free of me.'

'What makes you think I want your death?' Rouhkia bent closer, staring into the seared and parched face.

'Would it not make matters so much easier for you, oh daughter of a thousand corrupt desires?'

'You are wrong, husband. Your presence gives me all the freedom I need. Without it, my brother would marry me to some autocratic lord who would shut me in his harem and keep me from the world. That would be punishment indeed, foolish husband.'

Rouhkia perched at the side of Youssef's bed, and leaning towards him let the folds of her silk gown fall open to reveal her heavy, rounded breasts, their glossy flesh glowing in the lamplight like moonstones.

'What do you think of my body, in truth, husband? Is it so repugnant that you cannot mount it and get me with child? Is there no hope for the fertility of our union?'

Reaching out, she picked up Youssef's hand, placing it on her breast where it sagged limply, while, with her other hand, she caressed the equally limp object between his thighs.

'Can we not manage it just once, enough to produce that nephew which my brother wants so much? Do you know what they call you in Arabia, my husband? Youssef-without-a-pizzle. Youssef-without-a-pizzle. What say you to that?'

'I say that Mudija will bear my son wherever she has been taken, and wherever she spends her days, that is what I say!' Youssef croaked, tears filling his eyes. 'Allah forgive you for what you have done, she-devil, for I cannot!'

'Aiee, you swine, you low, cunning swine!' Rouhkia leapt to her feet, cheeks crimson, and bent over Youssef's bed to smack him in the face, first his left cheek and then his right, her robe bursting open and her breasts swinging free. Then, muttering the foulest curses beneath her breath, she sped from the sick man's room.

Rouhkia was obsessed by the Christian slave, but she could not understand why. To all intents, he was useless; he never responded to her urgent attempts to arouse him, nor would he so much as kiss her tenderly, nor be drawn into arguments or discussions upon his needs. Yet this was no weakling like Youssef; this man's determined jaw, his hard, straight back and gritted teeth told her of power and an omnipotence of spirit which was new and tantalising to her. To win him would be the greatest moment of her life; she wanted nothing more, believing that her own soul would in some inexplicable way be renewed and revived through sexual union with this golden-haired *nasrani*.

She dreamed of him at night, waking with his name on her

lips. She had him brought to her chamber, shackled and chained, the dragging clank of the chains making her senses fizz. As he approached, she would turn, her expression stony, while her heart pounded.

Always she would be splendidly robed, in bright, priceless silks edged with black or pink pearls, their glossy hue a reminder to him of her brother's power and wealth. Low-necked, her robes would reveal the moonstones of her swelling breasts, her slightly parted knees allowing the silk material to fall in suggestive folds between her thighs. No matter that she was plain, and had never possessed beauty. With pearls in her hair and fabulous silks draping her body she could be the most radiant and unforgettable queen ever born, descended directly from the Prophet . . . Aha, if only she were, if only she were.

Would the Christian bow to her then, recognising in her the pure and holy blood of Mohammed? Perhaps he would; she did not know.

'Nash,' she whispered his name, reaching out to touch the broad expanse of darkly tanned chest where the brightly gilded hairs sprang and coiled as if they breathed as he did. 'Nash, did you sleep well?'

She saw his jaw clench. How he loathed small talk, rejecting her every attempt to engage him in conversation, but she was desperate to know everything about him.

The woman who had been indulged and pampered all her days, receiving all she ever wanted, faced the man who would give nothing that was not lovingly received, glittering dark eyes, almost evil with lust, staring into blue ones which reflected the sky so richly that it was more pleasing to look into those eyes than into the azure expanse of a bright summer's day. Her heaven was in his eyes, her heart in his, yet both were closed to her. How could she make him open them?

'Nash, tell me of the woman you loved, the one who turned your heart to myrrh. Was she English like you? Was she fair and fertile?' Her heart pinched as she said that last word. Fertile. In her mind's eye she saw Mudija, with child, staggering out into the desert to die of thirst and heartbreak.

'She was English, the daughter of sea-farers who have made the oceans their own over the centuries.'

'Not like we sand-wedged Arabians, you mean?' The lust-filled ebony eyes twinkled with a mild humour. 'The thought of being sea-borne fills me with alarm, the tossing waves, the wild storms, the sea dragons . . . My brother saw a monster at sea, a dragon which breathed foam flame and from which he took his emblem. He fought the beast single-handed and killed it.' Desperately she sought some admiration in the bright blue eyes, but there was none.

'We all have to face our dragons at some time or another,' Nash said, his voice meeting her gaze with a directness which snatched the breath from her lungs.

'If I told them to take away your chains, would you try to escape, Nash Hamilton?'

She wanted him to say that he would stay by her side until the end of destiny, that he would love her and worship her for ever. Allah, how she needed such assurances from this god-like man with the paradise-blue eyes and the thick, gold hair!

'Escape from silken cushions and the scent of incense? Who would wish to do that if they had their right mind about them?' he parried.

'And have you your right mind about you, Christian man?'

'I do.'

Her smile of response was simpering and opportunist, the dark eyes gushing with passion as they swept over him from head to groin, to thighs then feet. He wore only a white linen cloth bound around his hips in the Egyptian style, for that was all the clothes she allowed him. Instinctively, when she stared, he drew back, at which she moved closer, her lower lip falling open a little. At least she had good teeth, straight and clean, and her breath was not offensive. She chewed violet lozenges, which made her mouth sweet. Had she reeked of oily pilaf, rancid butter or any of the other Arabian foods, her proximity would have been even more distasteful.

He did not know that she spied on him at night, when he lay naked on the hard pallet. The nights were hot in the small chamber where he slept, and he lay on top of the coverlet, twisting from side to side as he fought for sleep. When he closed his eyes, he talked in his sleep, murmuring names and sighing as if his soul were escaping from his body. Allegra was a word which he sighed in his dreams, sometimes four or five times a night. She would watch that beautiful sun-bronzed body turning first to the left then to the right as he suffered his nightmares, one knee raised, then the other, then an arm flung out, then a hand. Towards morning when she watched, she would see what happened to all men save her husband: the male organ stiffening, raising itself away from the flat muscular belly. Then she would grip the concealing trellis until her palms were slippery with sweat and the dampness of her own desire would make her thighs wet. How she would yearn to fling herself on top of him, impaling herself on that hard and magnificent implement, yet she did not. At that point, her courage failed her. She could not understand why. She was monarch here; all she had to do was unlock his door and fling herself on to him. Why did she not do it? Was she afraid of his rage, his withdrawal, of the implement shrinking, as Youssef's did whenever she went near him? On the surface she might appear to be fearless and bold, but inside there was a limit upon the amount of rejection she could endure. Sister to the powerful Amir Adem Ali she might be, but she was, after all, a woman first . . .

Ah, the Christian! If only she knew how to tempt him into her arms. Time might be her only strength: surely as the months passed, he would forget his lost woman and lust after her? But what would she do while she was waiting? She found it impossible to starve herself sexually for more than a day or so; indeed why should she? Yet she did not wish to lie with another man while she waited for the Christian. Could it be that she loved him?

Nash saw the lust-dark eyes fill with some indecipherable emotion, as a pale-rose flush swept up Rouhkia's cheeks. What was she thinking about, or need he ask, for her mind appeared to be obsessed with sexuality and her physical needs? Here in this one woman was embodied every mystery and perplexity of the East, the passion, the arrogance, the complexity and the enigmatic, unfathomable whimsy. Lord God, if only he had his Allegra with him again, with her direct honesty, courage and the impulsive tenderness which did not shelter behind any creed, cant or dogma out of fear and uncertainty.

The wrong women were enslaved in Islam. The haughty and the merciless were free, the generous, loving and selfless were in shackles . . .

Youssef took many weeks to recover from his sunstroke. He seemed to strengthen, sat by the window, but then became pale and lethargic and once more took to his bed. His body wished to be healthy again, but his heart wanted to die, that was the truth of it. A life of bitterness, a screaming wife who hated him, the knowledge that he was a failure as a man and that the one woman he had truly loved was lost to him for ever . . . How did a man live with the knowledge of this?

Entertainers were sent for, and they spent many unsuccessful hours trying to make him smile. Their riddles and jests were sharp and clever, but Youssef might have been listening to a shopping list being read out.

'Tell me, *Effendi*, if you know the answer to this riddle, which was written by Majd Ad-Din Al-Mubarak Ibn Munkid, he who was called The Sword of the Empire and the Glory of Religion? The riddle goes, "There is a race whom man is permitted to slay, and which profanes the blood of the pilgrim even in the sanctuary, yet when your hand sheds their blood, it is not their blood but your own which is shed" . . . Do you know the answer, *Effendi*?'

'I cannot answer it.' Youssef's voice was faint. How could he find the solutions to riddles when he could not find the solution to reality?

'It is fleas, *Effendi*, fleas!' The riddler grinned, slapping his knee. 'They bite you, they suck your blood, *Effendi* and then when you kill them, you shed your own blood, you see, *Effendi*?'

Youssef raised his brows and sighed. Yes, it was clever, but he was not in the mood for banter.

'Tell the Effendi some proverbs, for he is not in the mood for verses!' snapped the riddler, ushering forward his two assistants.

'For every Pharaoh there is a Moses,' one of the men said, nodding as if he had uttered a great wisdom, 'and he who picks up a bee from kindness shall soon learn the limits of his kindness!' The three entertainers snickered.

'What is it that has no sound, no shape and no form and yet when it manifests, none can resist it?'

'Aiee, that is a riddle, you nincompoop!' The riddle master glared at his assistant.

'So what is the answer?' Youssef sighed.

'The power of Allah the all-merciful, the beneficent, *Effendi*. See, it is invisible and has no substance and no sound and yet none can resist it.'

'There is no need to explain everything to me, I am not a simpleton.'

'No, no, of course not, who would dare say such a thing, such an insulting and gross thing, *Effendi*? Not I, no, not I, never, never, never!' The assistant riddler salaamed repeatedly, the tassel on his *tarbûsh* swinging up, down and round until it slapped him in the eye.

The corners of Youssef's mouth twitched, very slightly, and then became downturned once more.

'Youth is a madness of which old age is the cure,' went on the man, blinking his bruised eye. 'Three things cannot be taken back, the arrow once it has sped from the bow, the word spoken in haste, and the missed opportunity . . .'

'No more, no more!' Youssef commanded. 'I am weary now. Leave me.' The tears were funnelling behind his eyes; he could feel them surging and pressing.

'The missed opportunity . . . The missed opportunity . . .' Mudija was the arrow which had sped from his bow and which he would never see again. And his son, his only son, where would he be born, and when? *Billâh!* If only he knew the answers to these questions.

As his strength returned, Youssef took to writing poetry, unschooled and clumsy, it was true for the most part, but broken hearts and tearing passions are not neat and tidy. He poured his heart on to parchment and studied its broken, bloody pieces.

He read the saddest of verses written by Ibn Zuhr, who had

been a learned Muslim teacher and physician in twelfth-century Spain. Separated from his child, he had written:

'*I have a little one, a tender nestling, with whom I have left my heart. I dwell far from him; how desolate I feel in the absence of that little person and that little face. He longs for me and I long for him; for me he weeps and I weep for him. Our affectionate wishes are weary with passing from him to me, from me to him.*'

Tears burst out of him, unstoppable. He wanted his son, Mudija's son. He wanted Mudija! When he had finished weeping, he struggled to gather the courage which he would need to confront his wife, but he shook inside at the thought of facing her. He did not have the strength to reprimand her, to remind her that woman was beneath man, as Allah had willed it in his wisdom, and that she must obey him, Youssef. *Billâh!* Why had he agreed to marry her?

How different from his blessed hours with Mudija, every one of which he could recall in the sharpest detail! Her mouth silken and honeyed against his, her arms gentle silk cushions encircling him, her breasts rounded velvet fruits to suck, her thighs pale and curving as they hooked round his hips, her hair fluffy and warm, scented with oil of lilies and jasmine.

Mudija! His soul cried out for her.

PART THREE

All the Perfumes of Arabia

All throughout the garden you'll the glory of the
Prophet see,
Leaves of green are his disciples, tulips are his
progeny.
Servants of Mohammed, now's the season of felic-
ity.
Taste their pleasures while you're able; pass they
must these days of spring.

While at daybreak clouds cast jewels in the garden
scene below,
While each morning, breezes, scented with the
musks of Asia blow;
Be alert to the occasion, while the world has joys to
show,
Taste their pleasures while you're able; pass they
must these days of spring.

So much has the garden's fragrance scented the
embracing air
That the dew's a distillate of roses when it settles
there.
Overhead the Sphere has stretched an awning
cloud against the glare;
Taste their pleasures while you're able; pass they
must these days of spring.

Mesîhî, (d. 1512)

Chapter Seventeen

The *hammam* was of palest marble, ghostly walls, ghostly floor, and the baths were deep-set in the stone, the whistling rush of running water pronouncing that it was safe to bathe here for, according to the Muslim religion, it was unclean to bathe in still waters. Even rinsing must be done with fresh water, jars being poured over the bather seven times, an almost holy and ritualistic event.

The Amir himself had installed the *hammam* in the palace, in modest emulation of those belonging to the Grand Turk in Constantinople.

Allegra bobbed in the waters, her mind empty. She had found that bathing was soothing, although her previous experiences of it in England had never convinced her of this. How different were hasty all-over washes in a cold metal hip-bath placed before a roaring fire, with the bather's back chilled to the spine and a howling draught stabbing at one's extremities! No time in damp and wintry England to savour the delights of running warm water, the delicate scents of attar of roses, violet and lily oils, the sweet odours of jasmine, marjoram, narcissus and lotus-flower.

The attendants were devoted with their labours, scurrying here and there, fetching oils, unguent pots, linens, embroidered slippers and warm robes, jewelled combs, pins, antimony and henna pots, and all the accoutrements of the lady. The ritual of the bath was indigenous to life in the harem, and Allegra had adopted it swiftly, employing these hours in the *hammam* as a haven, a time to think, or not to think, as she chose. It was necessary for the maintenance of her sanity.

In a few hours time, a man would be visiting her in her chamber. She would not be alone, of course, but surrounded by at least a dozen women, and she would be heavily veiled for this first occasion.

Adem Ali had sent to a neighbouring estate for a poet whose voice was bright as silver and coaxing as a bird of paradise, for this man Hafez, the Songbird as he was called, was to convince her that Adem Ali was the greatest, gentlest and kindest man in the world.

There was no subtlety about it, she thought as she relaxed in the shimmering water, enjoying its twirling silkiness wrapping round her limbs before it swept on its way. No mystery, either. She was told outright what the man planned to do, and that was that. As if anyone could convince her that Adem Ali was anything but a villain!

'*Ya Sitti* wish dress now?'

She could, with difficulty, now understand a few dozen words of Arabic. It was a throaty, glottal language and she did not care to speak it. Nonetheless, she was trying out her minute expertise whenever possible, for muteness had never appealed. The *halaik* was kneeling at the side of the bath, hands clamped together, head bowed, as if she, Allegra, were a queen or goddess. How worshipful these women were. What would they be like when their esteemed Amir finally rejected her as he surely must when she refused to be swayed by Hafez's eulogies?

Allegra missed the company of intellectual equals. She knew Adem Ali had wives and concubines, yet she saw little of them, and those who vanished hastily in the distance at her approach looked plump, dark and foreign, so she could not easily have engaged them in conversation. There was much celebration one day when one of the wives bore a daughter, and then tears and ear-splitting wailing which went on for hours when the child died three days later.

Adem Ali, Lion of Arabia and Lord of the Incense Road, wealthiest man after the Sultan of Turkey and the Caliph of Baghdad, so it was rumoured, continued to be without an heir. It was the custom for concubines who bore a child to become wives through that production alone, without any ceremony, yet the children were never considered bastards, as they would have been in England. That she could admire, having always thought that condemning a child and making it an outcast because of an accident of conception was barbaric and heartless.

She had heard now and again from Husaina of the Lady Khadija Nur, the favourite wife of Adem Ali, for whom he had divorced his first wife. When she was told this, she could not comprehend what was meant. Divorce? How could that be when it was forbidden by God and the Church? How could a man cast off his wife and take another in her place? she had asked the old mistress of the slaves.

'The ways of Islam are the ways of God, and thus it is as God ordained,' Husaina replied, touching the side of her nose with a jewelled finger.

'It is a different God from mine: a false idol!'

'Naiee, not so, not so! The same God, 'tis the very same and you are a sharp-tongued *shaîtan* to speak so cruelly.'

'Nonsense. If the God is the same, then the laws and the customs are the same. One marriage and only death shall part a man and his wife, that is the law. Here, you have a licence to fornicate.'

'What is this for-na-kit?'

'Lying with another outside marriage . . . begetting children when their parents are not lawfully husband and wife.'

'Huh, not so, not so! You are wrong in the thinking of this, misguided, but then so are all *nasrani*, and one day you will be knowing the truth,' Husaina nodded sagely.

'No, one day *you* will be knowing the truth!' Allegra riposted, her cheeks flushed.

She had tried out all the bathing rooms, for the *hammam* was enormous. There was a changing room, a cold water room, one with hot water, one in which to sweat and free the body of impurities (perhaps they hoped that her Christian beliefs would be sweated out, too?) a massage room, and a chamber to rest and recover . . . which was certainly needed if one had tried out all the various stages. Too much heat could be very draining, as she had discovered the first day she had soaked too long in the hot, bubbling waters. Shock at her crinkled skin was to remain until it smoothed itself out again an hour or so later.

Musicians were entertaining the Amir's harem, playing on flute and davoul, the eerie convolutions of the Arabic music echoing through the chambers of the *hammam* like the wailing of tormented spirits.

There was no cause for her to be alarmed by the presence of the musicians, Allegra was told, for they had all been blinded and so could see nothing of the naked bodies.

'They have had accidents, how terrible!' she had cried, at which Husaina had shaken her head.

'No, not accident. On purpose, to cause taking away of the sight so they are safe for the harem, the forbidden sanctuary of the women. It is the custom in Turkey and so here also.'

'Whose custom? Yours or that of Allah?' Allegra gritted her teeth, but there was no answer forthcoming. 'It is the custom' covered a multitude of sins.

Continuing to soak in the water, having told the attendant to return later, Allegra tried mentally to recapture the girl that she had been only a year ago. It was impossible, but an exercise which she felt duty-bound to attempt at regular intervals. Cushioned in this exotic, scented palace, where servants flung themselves to the floor in obeisance before her as if she were a queen, and only the gritty-tongued, acerbic mistress of the slaves dared speak her mind, it was difficult to recall that country called England which existed in another part of the world and where she had grown up. England, lush, green, stormy and wet, by turns cosseted and savaged by the sea. The emerald haven where she had been raised, and where she had learned how to be a loyal, virtuous and obedient subject of Queen Elizabeth.

Recalling her sister's face had become frighteningly challenging. The colour of the hair, bright primrose, and the soft blue eyes, not dissimilar to hers, these could be remembered, but the features, the expression, the curvature of the bones, the smile . . . These were lost to her for ever, as was the real Elizabeth, yet they had been raised together, they were sisters of the same flesh and blood, the same ancestry, birthed of the same mother . . .

She had tried to sketch her sister's face, scratching with a flinty piece of charcoal from a brazier, covering her fingers in smudgy soot but determined to recreate Elizabeth's features. She had failed. The face which appeared, sharply black, sooty and bold, was that of a stranger with broad cheekbones, button eyes and a crooked mouth. It was like losing part of her own body, her soul, an unnerving feeling which made her look down at her hands and arms, her legs and feet, to reassure herself that they were still there.

No one else in the harem appeared to have any memory of the past. All were either obsessed, possessed or repressed by their lord and master, Adem Ali, life revolving round his many wishes and whims. Never mind that some of the women here, beautiful, voluptuous, bejewelled and repeatedly bathed as they were, had not seen their master for many months. If he should become captivated by a new concubine, sleeping with her regularly and ignoring the others, then that was *kismet*, fate, and the will of Allah. Sometimes this neglect bore fruit, and the favourite, as with the Lady Khadija Nur, now the revered chief wife, found herself with child very quickly.

Now and again, Allegra had brief glimmerings of the reasons for such able adaptations by the women here. If one's home and family, loved ones and country were all snatched away, there were two choices: madness; self-destruction, or adjustment. Disorientation was unnerving; for its effects to be truly understood, it had to be experienced personally. However brave and hardy a spirit was before everything was taken from it, there would be shock and confusion, and an intolerable amount of mental suffering.

When she had learned of Elizabeth's death, something inside her had died too. Hope and faith were washed away. For a few days after hearing, she had been so bemused that she could not eat or sleep or speak properly; it was as if her mind were numbed. She dreamed of following her sister into the desert and dying there, and she had tried to escape, thinking that she had carefully eluded the guards only to discover that Husaina had suspected what was in her thoughts and asked for extra ones to be on watch.

She had changed. Her heart did not feel the same, nor her

thoughts. She would not eat, but Husaina would come and sit on her bed and force spoons full of milk and rice down her throat, sweetened with honey and wine.

Whenever she closed her eyes, she saw her sister's bones parched and bleached by the sun, the flesh picked away by carrion, and she longed to be with her again, even if death were the only pathway to such a union.

The Amir had not expected her to take the news so badly. Startling everyone, he had come to visit Allegra in her sickbed, bringing her sweetmeats which she could not eat, and holding her head while she drank wine. She could not understand why he was doing this: did he not have hundreds of fresh and lively women to entertain him?

He told her that he wanted her life to be saved. He could not take the deaths of two sisters upon his conscience. His enemies misunderstood him, as enemies always do, but he was a man who wished only the best for his people.

'Allah will make you well.' He smiled gently.

'I do not want to live!' Allegra had sighed.

'You will live . . . Live for me, white dove, live for me!' Tenderly he had taken her fingers and kissed each one, his ebony eyes limpid with feeling. He had forgiven her for her stupid and unsuccessful attempt to kill him . . . When the guards had rushed to take her in their grasp, he had waved them away before they could harm her. So, in a strange way, she owed him her life: the life that she did not want, the life that was a grevious burden to her now.

Today, she was much recovered and weighted down with an unsettling sense of gratitude to the Amir. She did not want it; she had done nothing to encourage it, yet there it was, haunting her.

Husaina insisted that the Amir had done everything to make her dead sister happy, but it was futile: the girl had not wanted to be happy. She had resisted all the comfort offered to her, and brought her tragic death upon herself.

'Do you think it possible that he loved my sister and that is why he is being so kind to me?' Allegra had asked, her heart torn.

'The Amir did love her, yes, of that I am sure. He is deeply devoted to his favourites and wishes nothing but the very best for them.'

'Was my sister a favourite then?'

'Ah, yes. She was so fair and lovely, so delicate. A tender plant, too fragile for the arid heat of the desert . . . The Amir gave orders that she have all she wanted, that we treat her with the loving gentleness of a daughter, but she herself refused to accept our love. It was the will of Allah.'

'Maybe it was. At least she has no suffering now.' Allegra closed her eyes. How many hours she had prayed for her sister's soul since learning of her death, begging the Blessed Virgin to take her into her arms like a mother.

And so time had passed and Allegra began to recover a little of her spirits. Some days she woke feeling sick and ill with grief. Nonetheless, she had begun to notice those around her, and how tenderly they had cared for her while she was grieving, and to them she felt gratitude. They were, after all, the ones who had tried to heal her sister. That they had failed was not their fault.

She had begun to listen to the harem chatter, much of the gossip lively, some spiteful, some protective. There were others with problems here: perhaps she could repay some of their help. That was how she felt on good days; on bad days, she wished that she were dead.

Despite his wealth and omnipotence, Adem Ali could not purchase himself a healthy living son, even though he had a harem of some two hundred concubines. The problems here appeared to be very much the same as in England. Infants, when they were conceived, died within a few days of birth, or before their first birthday, slight fevers sweeping them away, or defects becoming apparent as they grew, and there being no one sufficiently skilled to correct these. One of the Amir's infant sons had suffocated, so Allegra was told, yet he had not been feeble. They had found him dead in his cradle one morning. Husaina said that he might have been murdered by another favourite who had lost her own child.

Allegra was half asleep now, lulled by the teeming warm waters. Her mind filled with the golden memory of Nash. Thankfully, even after all this time, she could recall him in her mind's eye exactly as he was, handsome, tender, stalwart and passionate, his brilliant blue eyes glowing with adoration as he gazed down at her.

'My sweeting . . .' she heard his caressing voice as if he were next to her. 'There were so many things that I wanted to tell you, and fate forbade it, but I have not forgotten you . . . How could I? You were my heart, my soul, my guiding star.'

His arms encapsulated her, so that she was buoyant in the waters, held closely in his ardent embrace and kissed over and over until her lips grew hot and rosy. They were in the pool, bathing on the heavenly island, splashing in the glittering crystalline water as they made love, gripped together, heeding nothing while they were joined, so that their entire existence revolved round this blissful act of sexual union, for which their bodies were honed so perfectly that they could fit into one heart, one body and one soul, one kissing and kissable mouth . . .

Heat slid up her thighs and breasts, flushing her cheeks and she squirmed, feeling him driving deep inside her. Ah, she wanted this to continue for ever; nothing must separate them, nothing. He was so deep that he was hurting her, yet it was paradise and what she wanted more than anything else in the universe. Sense, control, loyalty, they had flung them all out of the casement, leaving nothing but the over-ruling desire of true lovers to be physically and spiritually one.

A harsh voice woke her from her earthly paradise, bidding her wake and be robed before Hafez arrived. Bemused, she gazed around her at the cutting white light, the dark, curious faces and the steamy, scented air of the *hammam*. Where was she, what was happening, where was Nash? Realisation slapped her in the face in the coldest, cruellest fashion and she broke into sobs.

The women gasped, jaws dropping, not knowing what to do or say. Hafez was waiting, Hafez who had arrived as ordered by their esteemed lord and master, whose commands must be obeyed at every second, every minute, yet the English girl was sobbing and wailing, throwing herself around in the water and looking as if she were trying to drown. Down she went into the watery depths, down deeper and deeper, and she was not coming out when they called her. Two of the women leapt into the *hammam*, splashing about hysterically searching for the *nasrani* and then a third and a fourth joined them, so that there was total confusion, and the raucous echoing of screams for aid.

The eunuchs were next in the waters, their huge muscular arms sweeping aside the screeching, flapping *hailaks*, their powerful brown legs kicking masterfully through the depths, but it was some time before the *nasrani* was carried to the surface and borne on to the marbled edge of the *hammam* where she lay silent, greenish-white and apparently drowned, while the women stood round her wailing and sobbing, and beseeching Allah.

The dancing girls were sinuous, curvaceous and skilful, their plump, shapely bodies the colour of ancient gold, their nipples and navels decorated with glittering gold beads. Their hair was a black forest whirling with shining scarlet and emerald silks edged with gold tassels, their eyes painted into almond shapes with green, scarlet and gold paints, their necks collared with simulated rubies and emeralds carved from glass, their *shalwar* worn so low on their broad hips that they appeared about to slip off.

Such a sight as this had rejuvenated the oldest, most jaded males, yet it did nothing for Nash Hamilton. What was lust without love, ardour without emotion? He had believed himself to be a perfect scion of the Elizabethan age, fearless, strong, modern in thought and deed, capable of living life to the brim without doubts and inner turmoils, and the journey on which he had embarked to rescue his betrothed, Elizabeth Pentrevick, had been a life voyage for himself. During it, he had found that he was not the man he had thought himself, and, in retrospect, he was glad. How could he have been proud of being such a man, one who had allowed others to dictate his behaviour, his ambitions?

'Marry a fair-faced, gentle bride who can manage your household with skill, bear you strong, healthy sons and embroider your shirts with her own hands . . .' So his elderly cousin had adjured him before his death, adding, 'Better still, why just the embroidery? Certes, find yourself a bride who can sew the entire shirt, every fine seam to perfection! That is what God made womankind for, and any who does not sew a perfect seam is suspect. What is above the neck does not matter, my boy, excepting that the features be comely and not offensive in any way. Black teeth are off-putting to husband and guests of the house! Methinks they also speak of a greedy belly, and women who put their bellies first put their spouses last. Hearken to me, my boy, you will find it to be thus. Your late mother, God preserve her soul, had a keen mind, but your father did not choose her for that. It was an additional attraction. Mark what I say, boy. Look at the hands. If they are clumsy with a needle, then beware!'

Elizabeth Pentrevick was a brilliant seamstress and embroiderer. By the age of seven she had embroidered an altar cloth of such exquisite beauty that a special service had been held in Pentrevick church to give thanks for its arrival there.

The dancing girls swayed past his eye, their faces seductive and suggestive, their mouths slightly parted to remind him of their skills in love-making, their hips gyrating at such a pace that the tassels of their *shalwar* spun outwards. The cloying scents of musk oil, ambergris, myrtle and palm-flower assailed his nostrils. Lord, what he would give for the scent of wild blossoms growing on an island paradise, with his precious Allegra crushed in his arms! Nothing existed for him now but her memory. Having lost her, all that part of him which she had created and roused was dead. It would never revive if she remained lost to him. Once, he had been a savage, and thought himself civilised. Now he knew that he was indeed a savage, wild, alone and despairing, primitive, lost to humanity as the most ferocious wolf mourning the loss of his mate. What was the comfort of religion at such a time? Allegra had become his religion, his beloved creed, and she was taken from his arms.

'Nash.' That wheedling, coaxing voice grated on his nerves whenever he heard it. Rouhkia had come into the room expecting to find him ready for love-making. Did Muslims believe in miracles, then? His mouth twisting, he turned his head away.

'Sulking, my heart? Why is that when you have the best food, silken clothes, a soft bed, and the most beautiful women to entertain you. A Muslim would know that he was truly in Paradise if he had all this . . . He would think that those girls were the glittering *houris* who dance for him alone.'

Rouhkia seated herself beside Nash, leaning close to kiss his cheek as he jolted his head away.

'Yes, I have everything except what I most want.'

'You growl like a wounded hound, my heart. *Ya Allah*, what is to be done with you? How many weeks have you been here, living on my charity, enjoying all the comforts of my palace and yet you will not make love to me?'

Nash raised his brows at the mention of charity and the enjoyment of comforts.

'Since when has enforced slavery been charity?' he snarled.

'Allah, you are so sulky and snappy! It would do you so much good to be shut in a dark cell for a week or two, then you would appreciate your freedom a thousand-fold.'

'My freedom! Jesu, what nonsensical talk is this? If I am free, then let me go . . . let me walk out of here!'

Rouhkia's mouth turned down at the corners. 'The guards would hack you to pieces if you tried to escape!'

'That is what I mean. Is that freedom? However, if *you* gave me my freedom, they would not touch me.'

'That has never been known. How could it be done? If I freed you, then every slave would wish for freedom!'

'Would they do that if they are as blissfully happy here as you claim they are?'

'You are the strangest, most discontented man I have ever known! I wish that Amid and Benguzi were here now. They were always so grateful for everything that I did for them.'

'Then why are they not?' Nash wished that there were sixty men here all clamouring to take Rouhkia's attentions from him.

'They die. Men always die. They are feeble and have paper hearts.'

Jesu, what did she do to her lovers? Nash inhaled deeply, struggling for composure, fighting back the urge to clamp his fingers round the golden, jewel-decked throat and squeeze until she was silent for ever. He had never wanted to kill a woman before, but then he had never been enslaved by one before. There was no choice in this, no freedom to leave when temperaments became heated.

'Look at me, *nasrani*, look at me!' Rouhkia rasped, digging her nails into Nash's chin and twisting his head round to face her. 'Why do you ignore me, am I so hideous? Do you not like my breasts?' Tugging at the lemon silk of her robe, she revealed the heavy, swelling moons of her bosom.

Nash did not see them. In his imagination, he visualised his hands round the jewelled neck, gripping, crushing, the delicate bones snapping, the eyes bulging, the head lolling brokenly, the tongue jutting, and then his escape to freedom, far, far away from this abominable prison. The lust to kill was so powerful that it consumed his thoughts and his feelings, crushing them tightly, impacting them beneath its single-minded desire, a murderous strength flowing into his arms and down to his hands so that they began to rise, slowly, slowly.

Rouhkia laughed with delight, thinking he was about to embrace her. Waving away the dancing girls so that she would have the Christian to herself, she leaned towards him, brushing her breasts against his naked, bronzed chest and fluttering her eyelashes seductively.

'Will you bed with me now, Nash? I cannot wait any longer . . . my body burns for you, here.' Taking one of his hands, she pushed it between her thighs, so that he could feel the fiery dampness through the fragile lemon silk. And then she was throwing herself on top of him, thrusting him back on to the velvet divan, while she murmured his name over and over, in that odd, broken way, her voice thick with lust.

Behind the smoky-silk curtain in the far corner of his wife's chamber, Youssef stood, the curving dagger in his sweating palm. It did not matter that it was an ornamental dagger, thick with pearls and rubies, for the blade was every bit as ruthless as a soldier's weapon. Unable to recover from his grief for the loss of Mudija and his son, he was about to have his revenge on Rouhkia. *Billâh!* There she lay, smothering her lover with her half-naked body, baring her breasts before a man who was not her lawful husband, opening her thighs, behaving in a vicious and shameless way! He would end her debauchery for ever. He would kill the yellow-haired slave who had been obsessing her for months now. Consumed by savage thoughts of revenge, he heard nothing, saw nothing, save his wife writhing on top of her slave, her clothing unfastened, her scarlet mouth opened like that of a slavering bitch.

Dead, the Christian would be no good to her ever again. Dead, he would be flung in a pit and his corpse covered with earth. No man would find fault with Youssef's act, for any man was allowed to revenge himself upon his faithless wife. Heart banging, throat scorched with hatred, Youssef leapt out into the room, a blood-freezing scream on his lips, dagger raised to hack the Christian slave to pieces.

The shock of almost drowning had affected her memory. When she tried to remember, there was nothing but a blur from which a figure would spring now and again, with the glaring colour and threatening countenance of a nightmare, so that she could not discern between what was true and what was imagination.

Hafez could speak seven languages, and his manners were superb. He had travelled all round the known world twice, so he boasted, and ventured to places where no white man had ever intruded. When she heard him saying this, a memory returned to Allegra, of another man like that, but so vague and nebulous was the recollection that it drifted away and she was too weary to snatch it back. She had slept a great deal in the past few days, and been treated by the Amir's famed physician, a man with a lazy eye which rolled towards his nose in the most disconcerting manner when he became absorbed in what he was saying. His powders and medicines were sharp and bitter, their acrid flavour lingering in the mouth long afterwards, and he had much to pronounce on Allegra's state of health, but as he spoke only Arabic, she would never learn what he deduced.

The ballads which Hafez had sung for her daily were colourful records of the bravery, valour and omnipotence of Adem Ali, Lord of the Incense Road. One concerned the winning of his flame-spewing dragon emblem, and when she had heard it, a little more of her memory returned.

The story went that there was once a nomadic people living in this land, who had worshipped a female god. Her name was Inanna and her symbol was a coiling serpent whose body wove its way round the feet of Inanna's statue.

'What did the female god look like?' Allegra wanted to know.

Grinning, Hafez curved his hands through the air. 'The way that all women should look, with heavy hips and full breasts for childbearing.'

'Did she have a gold necklace that curved round her throat and did not meet in the centre, called a torc?'

'That I would not know, white dove, for I never saw her. Shall I continue?'

The people were persecuted by a race who worshipped a male god of such ferocity and vengeance that the goddess worshippers could not resist his onslaught. Many died trying to rebuff the new patriarchal race, and the figure of the female god Inanna was carried in haste to a secret place. So valuable was it that there could not be any risk of the attackers finding it.

'So perhaps it was made of solid gold?' Allegra mused.

'Perhaps it was, white dove. That race, which conquered the ignorant, dark worshippers of the evil female god is the race from which the Amir himself sprang, his blood line. Their emblem for all that was most hideous and depraved of the people which worshipped a woman was a winged beast which breathed flame. They carved it on their pillars and in their temples and embroidered it on their headdresses and robes as a warning and a celebration of their own victory. Woe to a people whose god is a woman . . .'

Hafez looked not in the least apologetic as he finished the tale and his sharp, black eyes twinkled with malice.

Allegra was silent as she forced her thoughts back to an island paradise and an eerie statue of a voluptuous woman round whose neck was a gold torc and round whose feet coiled a great serpent. Inanna? Her followers were an evil and ignorant people? Oh, she could not believe that! She had learned a great deal since being flung into the patriarchal environment of the Muslim world. All that was female was to be mistrusted and despised, while all that was male was to be revered and venerated. So naturally males would not praise a goddess which they had conquered with great violence. They would see her destruction as justice being done. Women had been suffering ever since . . .

'What is in your thoughts, white dove?' Hafez leaned towards her so that she could smell the citrus oil dabbed on his throat and wrists. They were alone for one reason and one only: when he was eleven years old, Hafez, a French slave, had been castrated to preserve his enchanting singing voice.

'I remember a statue like the one you have just mentioned. But that is all I know.' Allegra pressed a hand to her forehead.

'If the white dove would admit that she is shaken with love for her exalted master, then she would heal herself more quickly. This shutting away of the self and refusing to recover is foolish . . .' Hafez smiled to soften his words.

'Have you no memory of your homeland, Hafez? Women there were sometimes downtrodden but they were never veiled and shut away like felons, nor were they insulted and reviled as a matter of course. With France, England and Scotland all being ruled by women, it is not fashionable to declaim that women are feeble and stupid!' Having said that, she realised that she was remembering more all the time.

'I do not remember any of this. I was only nine when I was captured, and I do not know why I was on the ship, whether as cabin boy or the son of one of the passengers. Nothing returns to my mind when I think of that time.'

'What did the Arabs do to blot out your memory?'

'That I cannot recall either, white dove, fair sweet bird of Allah.' Hafez smiled.

'Do you not bear any grudge for what has been done to you?'

'It was kismet, white dove. Allah willed it. What else? I was poor and unknown, and now I am wealthy and famed throughout the land. I was to be shut away, but Allah gave me a voice and a talent for creating verse and so I am free. A wise man knows when he is well off.'

'And what of woman? Is she to celebrate her captivity because it is in luxurious surroundings in the harem of a Muslim lord?'

Hafez missed the irony in Allegra's voice. 'All that Allah sends must be appreciated, white dove, for our future is decided upon the reactions we have to our destiny. If we are ungrateful, angry and rebellious, then further disasters will be heaped upon our heads until we learn how to accept with dignity and serenity.'

'I was told that Allah is the God of the Bible, the very same deity, and yet our God is loving and benevolent. He forgives and forgets. He does not preach war and greed.'

'Nor does Allah, who *is* the same God. He has many names. Before Mohammed, there were three hundred gods being worshipped in our land, with Allah only one of them. It was our great Prophet who elevated Him to His rightful place and taught that the worship of many gods was wrong. We call Him Allah the all-merciful.'

'Yet you say he deliberately punishes until his followers have learned their lessons?'

'Yes – and no. It is not exactly like that and yet . . . But we have strayed from the reason for my presence here! The Amir, the great prince who governs with authority and wisdom, who has the blood of the Prophet in his veins, decided that you would be accepted into his harem. It is an immense honour. His Highness has the world's choice of beauteous and virtuous females, of all colours and creeds, and yet he has decided upon you. You may remain here and your life from now on will be most blessed and peaceful. Never again shall you want for food and drink, for raiment, for warmth and comforts. And if you should bear a son for the Amir then your position will be of the highest, as with the Lady Khadija Nur. Blessings will be piled high about you and every jewel of the Orient will be placed in your keeping.'

Silence spangled the air between them as Hafez finished speaking. Allegra wanted to shut out his words, pretend that they had never been said, that she was in another time and place, anywhere but here. For a few moments she was unable to reply, and then she said, through gritted teeth:

'Do I have no choice? Is the Amir able to take any woman he wishes and add her to his harem without her permission, as easily as that?'

'He is, white dove. The Amir is Lord of the Incense Road, Prince of the Deserts of the Red Sands, Amir of Kabul and Mekbah, born of the Princess Kejia, direct descendant of the Prophet. He is Lord of the Pearl Lagoons, Lord of the Gold Mines of Amistra . . .' Hafez's voice droned on and on, as Adem Ali's titles and estates gushed from his thin, dark lips.

Allegra did not want to hear any more. Clamping her palms to her ears, she cried out so desperately that Hafez faltered to a shocked halt, his mouth hanging open.

'Is the white dove ill of a fever? Shall I fetch her women?'

'No, she is not ill! She is fit and healthy and there is nothing wrong with her *now*.'

'His Highness was generous enough to give the white dove fifteen days of the gentlest rest and care after her accident in the *hammam*, and he gave her the attendance of his own physicians. He has no wish to insult or upset the white dove, but only to show her how she will be revered and treated with the deepest tenderness now that she is part of His Highness's harem.'

A scraping at the door announced the arrival of an envoy from Adem Ali. Hafez let the man in with his own hand. The envoy was small, dressed in sumptuous buttercup-yellow satin embroidered with crimson silks and he wore a tiny, skilfully coiled turban of emerald silk. Seeing Allegra, he flung himself to his knees before her, making the deepest obeisance, which was almost as stately and reverent as the *temenah*, the obeisance made before the highest royalty. And then, with lithe grace, he leapt up and from a hidden pocket in his robe, produced a small flat casket, flinging open its lid and then placing it in Allegra's hands.

Amazed at this display of humility which almost amounted to worship, she stared down at the contents of the casket.

Eighteen rubies, each one the size of a thumb nail, set in thick, carved gold and supported by a delicate filigree chain of glittering gold.

For long seconds she stared at the dark crimson gems. They

were gloriously beautiful, passionate perfection, like tiny, radiant hearts throbbing with emotion. Lightly she touched them one by one, expecting to feel them pulse beneath her fingertips, expecting them to be as warm and soft as flesh. Then, she slammed the lid, and with the iciest of smiles, handed the casket back to the diminutive servant who looked stunned at her gesture.

He started to gabble, his voice, rising in pitch to a fervent squeak, but she could not understand his impassioned Arabic. Turning her back, she hoped to signify that she wished to be alone. After all, if they made deep obeisances before her and spoke of her being treated with respect and tenderness, should she not be able to give a command or two, now and again?

'White dove, blessed of the Lord of the Incense Road, will you return this bounteous gift which has been sent to you out of reverence and admiration?' Hafez pleaded, tugging at the hem of her robe.

Behind her she heard scuttling and commotion as the *hailaks* ran in, wanting to see what was happening, and why the envoy was wailing in that mournful, high-pitched tone. Silks rustled, bare feet padded on the tiles, voices hissed and muttered beneath gasping breaths, and the hem of her gown was tugged gently, again and again. But Allegra ignored it all. If she were going to be shut away in a harem, without the choice to refuse, without any hope of freedom, then she would set about making her wishes known to everyone here, including the Amir. She was grateful to them all for their attentive care during her unhappy weeks of illness, but she was not going to be ordered around, or won with gifts. She was already too much in the debt of the Amir, which she found most uncomfortable, and the knowledge that he had loved her sister made matters so much more complicated. She wanted to go on hating, loathing and despising him, as she had done from the moment Elizabeth was captured, but now there were other considerations to colour her impressions.

Turning slowly, she looked Hafez directly in the eye. 'Tell your master that I do want these rubies. They do not please me at all. I have no wish for gifts, and cannot be bought. I wish to see His Highness this afternoon concerning my future in this household. Will you please tell him that?'

'Aiee, how can I speak to him thus, white dove?' Hafez groaned, his cheeks pale.

'Sing it to him, Hafez. Turn into poetry and verse and let him hear it that way, what else?'

Chapter Eighteen

Husaina had ranted on about virginity and purity, instilling in Allegra that all women who went to the Amir's bed must be virgins. There had even been talk of an examination, but the old woman, whose reputation was unsullied, unlike her wits, had forgotten to examine her before the Amir saw her. Only after his interest was roused did she remember her shocking omission, and tremble with horror, especially when the result of the examination proved negative.

'Only for the first time do we have the trouble,' Husaina said, her voice trembling huskily. 'He must believe that he is the first, the one and only, then all will be well afterwards, *Mashallah*. Otherwise . . .' The old woman drew a shaky hand across her wrinkled throat, stark terror in her eyes.

And so they stared at one another glumly, unable to speak for long moments. Allegra had not realised what was expected, so she could suggest nothing. Then Husaina began to babble the solution in a breathless way and Allegra realised that she had done this before: tricked the Amir into thinking a new girl was a virgin when she was not.

'There are different methods of replacing the maidenhead,' Husaina's voice dropped low as she leaned conspiratorially towards Allegra. 'There is a root which shrinks and shrivels the insides so that they become tight and narrow once more, so that the esteemed male organ of His Highness cannot penetrate for some time and there is a struggle for entry. It is this which man enjoys and relishes. He wishes to conquer, always conquer, man, woman or beast. Then there is stitching . . .'

'Stitching!' Allegra cried in disbelief.

'Yes, the drawing of the female skin together with three or four stitches to give it the tightness and closure of the maidenhead. I have known women to ask for this so that they can present themselves as virgins and profit from it.'

'Not this one, never! Being sewn together like a shirt! Ugh!'

'Then there is the alum root, which is pounded with astringent herbs and placed inside the female passage. After some hours, when it is washed out, the insides are constricted, drawn together. *Ya Allah* the worst of it is the blood!' Husaina rocked backwards and forwards on her chair, a jewelled finger crooked against her mouth.

'The root will make me bleed?'

'No, I speak of the blood when the maidenhead is pierced. Men expect to see this, it is the sign. His Highness will look for it, but what will he see with you? Nothing! Aiee!'

'Is there some red dye, or . . .'

'The blood of some small creature. We need only find a rat or a bird and take a few drops of blood from it and these can be put in a tiny stoppered phial which you hide on your body somewhere, letting out the blood after the deed is done . . . Yes, that will be wondrous, thanks be to Allah!'

'After the deed is done? It makes it all sound more like a felony than a . . . a . . .' Allegra paused. What was it? A carefully-orchestrated deception. Madness, she thought it, and said so.

'Then will you watch my execution, white dove?' The old woman's voice cracked. 'If he discovers that I did not examine you when you first came here, then he will cut off my head! It is all set in motion now, *ya nasîb*, my fate, it cannot be halted. The Amir will take you to his bed and then my head will be sliced from my old neck and Husaina will die a terrible death because she did not watch what she was doing!'

Bending her head, the mistress of the slaves sobbed in the most pitiful way, hands to her face, her great, globulous, jewelled rings like brightly coloured tears dripping from her eyes. 'I am getting old, my memory is going. How could I forget that most important matter! *Billâh!* I want to die peacefully in my bed, not stretched out until my bones snap on the rack, and then be carried out to be executed! Do what I say, white dove, I plead with you on my knees! See, old Husaina is on her knees before you, and never has she done that before to any slave . . . *Istafarallah*, if the Amir finds out what I have done!'

Allegra helped the old woman to her feet, thinking of the lovers who had been horribly killed because one was a harem slave. She had grown fond of Husaina, who had cared for her attentively while she was ill, and now her heart went out to her. She also knew that Husaina would be punished if she, Allegra, tried to escape before the momentous night. How often she had thought of escape and explored every mental avenue, yet how did one get past the guards who had been doubled since her first attempt? And could she leave Husaina, knowing that she would suffer horrible punishment as a result?

How tortured were her thoughts. She did not know what to do for the best. She was trapped, unless she could turn her back on this old woman's pleas.

'You disappoint me,' Allegra said to Adem Ali when she stood before him that afternoon. 'I expected you to breathe fire and you do not.'

'I am sure that can be arranged.' The Amir's glittering basilisk eyes surveyed her with acquisitive humour. 'How gullible and foolish are you Christians, judging the entire world by your own narrow views. You speak of freedom as your right, yet how have you earned this blessed state? What have you done to deserve it?'

'If Christians are thus, then what are Muslims?' Allegra narrowed her eyes. 'You treat your donkeys and your camels with more compassion than you do your women!' Snatching up a carved gold tray, she flung its contents directly at Adem

Ali, sticky, sweet red sherbet staining the front of his immaculate silk robe.

Momentarily even she was shocked at what she had done, but the Lord of the Incense Road did not appear to be at all perturbed.

'How do you know that the fire-breathing dragon on my emblem is not yourself, my fiery one?' he said, his tone light, almost bantering. 'I had heard that there were devils in England, but I had never thought to meet one.'

Having recovered her bravado, Allegra leapt towards her captor, kicking out at him with the stiff points of her thickly embroidered slippers, knowing that she could not stub her toes this way. With all her force, she kicked, her mouth drawn back in a snarl. With one rapid, almost invisible move, Adem Ali grabbed her ankle and held it tightly, so that she lost her balance and, with a small scream, crashed heavily to the floor. Her fall softened by the luxuriant Eastern carpet, she was stunned all the same, the breath shaken from her, but she struggled to rise from this humiliating position, her face crimson with rage. But Adem Ali planted his foot on her breasts and pushed her back down so that she had to lie, gazing up at him, her teeth gritted, jaw jutting out.

'Man is stronger than woman, so he is master. That is how it is and how it always shall be, until the day of judgement is upon us, and even then, as Allah wills it, so shall man be lord and victor.'

For reply, Allegra bent her head, trying her utmost to bite the brown ankle which was directly in front of her face, but he moved too swiftly, continuing to pinion her, his ankle now out of reach of her teeth.

'Allah the all-merciful, but you are a devil of the most vicious breeding!' growled the Amir. 'Hafez called you the white dove. He said that you would bring peace and joy to our palace, but that I doubt. You grief is turned to anger now, I see?'

Now Allegra was digging her nails into the lordly ankle and scratching so deep that blood began to run. Adem Ali did not seem to feel any pain from this but gazed down at her with an expression of bitter disappointment.

'As you are a Christian, I had thought that you would be the gentlest and kindest here, and the most loving and forgiving, but I see that you are vengeful and violent as any heathen. What harm have I done to you since you came here and yet already you have injured me?' Shaking his head from side to side, the Amir surveyed his bloody ankle.

'I am not sorry! You are a fiend, a vile and cruel man who imprisons people against their will! If this is Allah's law, then he is equally vile and disgusting, a loathsome and repulsive heathen god! He is not the same God as mine, he is not!'

'*Haif-'alaîk!* Shame on you!' Her captor broke into furious Arabic, his face darkening with rage. 'Say what you will about me, but do not dare to insult my God! I can forgive anything but that.'

'If I wish to insult your god then I shall. He is a god of slavery and cruelty, a heathen devil who demands human sacrifice. He is as depraved and foul as the pagan gods who urged men and women to fornicate outside marriage!'

Adem Ali stepped back, reaching out to drag her up by the wrists and then, her eyes venomous with fury, he slapped her face, first one side then the other, so that pain stabbed behind her eyes and through her jaw.

Tears welling, she did something which no man or woman had ever done before to Adem Ali. She slapped him back, first one side of his face and then the other, just as he had slapped her. He was so taken aback that he did nothing to stop her but only stood there, eyes blazing, as if unable to comprehend what had happened.

Near to hysteria, sure that she would now be hacked to pieces by the guards outside, Allegra began to laugh, unable to stop.

Adem Ali looked at her as if he had never heard laughter, and then, before she knew what was happening, he was hauling her across the audience chamber in all its scented and lavish opulence and through a door at the rear which was concealed by screens lavishly embroidered with mauve, purple and gold peacocks.

Now her laughter faded and died for there before them was a massive bed, above which hung a canopy of blazing scarlet silks decorated with the emblem of the fire-spewing dragon. Lamps filled with aphrodisiac oils burned at every corner, incense braziers adding to the exotic, disorientating atmosphere.

The bed. The very bed where he had made love to Elizabeth, and where his children were conceived. Allegra wanted to burst out laughing again, in terror and dismay, but she dared not. The basilisk eyes were lacerating her very soul while the air was filtering into her lungs to steal her senses, its provocative stimulating essences filling her with a tumult of conflicting emotions. Fear and dread, disbelief and horror, passion and longing, but not for this man, only for Nash, her darling, lost Nash and their paradise island . . . There they had swum and made love amongst nature's blossoms and ferns, the piping birds, the honeyed skies. Here, there was decadence, corruption and subjugation.

Picking her up before she could protest, the Amir flung her on the bed, crushing her into the soft, downy mattress, the scarlet silk coverlet rising like the wings of an exotic firebird before drifting down around them.

'Rape is all that I would expect of a heathen madman!' Allegra cried, banging her fists into Adem Ali's face.

'Your country was forged by such rapes, when the Vikings and Saxons invaded your land centuries ago . . . Now those heathens are part of your country's heritage, their very blood is in your veins . . .'

Nash had said much the same to her.

Yet again the Amir startled her with his knowledge of her land, just as when he had spoken to her in his fluent English. There was one advantage in this latter skill: it meant that she could insult him roundly in her own tongue and that every barb went directly home. Knowledge sometimes makes one very vulnerable.

'I would rather be raped by the roughest Viking than by you!' Allegra countered, feeling her nails bend and break against his back and shoulders as she stabbed at him with arched hands, but he did not wince, nor raise his hand in return. Panic swept through her, a billowing wind, so that she could not think or speak. She looked round wildly, but could see no weapon with which to kill him. Laughing, having guessed her thoughts, he brought his mouth down on hers with such force that she was dazed by it.

For Allegra there was to be no escape. Cold and fearful though she was at the start, determined to fill her thoughts with Nash and refusing to allow this monster to arouse her, she could not help but be carried along by his ardour. But her submission was not rapid, for she fought with courage and energy, pinching, scratching, biting, kicking. Somehow her captor seemed to be able to clamp her in his arms and hold down her legs at the same time, yet with little effort on his behalf. He was not even slightly out of breath while she was already panting.

'Christian women are the most passionate . . . They have been taught that the union of a man and a woman is wrong, a defilement, and so they battle with their sexual urges. Once they realise that there is no such attitude here in my country, they fling off their gowns and throw themselves into my arms . . .'

'So flattering for your highness. No doubt it ensures that your highness believes himself to be a king among men, and possessed of the godliest attributes,' Allegra jeered.

'Christian women have beautiful complexions, such fair, soft faces and glowing eyes. Even without kohl they are radiant,' Adem Ali continued as if he had not heard her.

'It is the result of fighting their sexual urges. Wrong though it may be, it makes the skin beautiful and the eyes bright!' Allegra managed to tear a long rent in the burnt-orange silk of the Amir's robe.

'Eyes darkened with kohl are considered the zenith of beauty in my country, yet you have no need of such artifice. Women have been rebuffed because they did not wear kohl round their eyes . . .'

'Yet I am here!' Allegra jutted her jaw. She had refused to apply the thick black glutinous paste which the other concubines and dancing girls wore so liberally, for she thought it a device of the Devil.

'Allowances are made for non-believers if they are comely enough. Your hair is a bewitchment, such bright colour, such glowing, gilded-red lights . . . and your eyes are the blue of honeyed dreams. No *houri* could be more dazzling . . .'

'Have you not forgotten my failings? I am a non-believer! I have an outspoken tongue. I argue with men, despite their amazing wisdom and genius . . . And then of course there is the other little failing . . . I hate, loathe and despise *you*, Adem Ali!'

Whatever gratitude she had felt towards him for not having her cut to pieces when she tried to stab him was gone now. To protect Husaina, she had come here, thinking that she would be able to sustain the encounter, but the moment that she had been brought into his presence all the old hatred had welled up, like a sickness. He might have tried to make Elizabeth happy, but she was dead because his men had abducted her and exposed her to heartbreak and suffering which she was too delicate to survive.

Coming into this room could do nothing else but remind her of Elizabeth, yet he said that he had loved her . . . Pain speared through her head. She had trapped herself, by her own soft heart. Who would help her escape this now?

'You will use my title as do others. My name is not for your tongue. *Saiyid*, you will call me *Saiyid*.' Adem Ali's face had darkened.

'No, I shall not! I shall call you whatever I please. How can you stop me? You are a knave, a debauched monster . . .' Allegra's bunched fist caught her captor on the right temple, and this did make him gasp. Next his hand was chaining her wrist so tightly that her skin flamed, and then he was spreadeagling her on the bed and kneeling over her, his eyes flashing with fury.

How could she resist? Her breath was gone, her strength evaporated in the struggle. Her hands were aching where she had hit him, legs throbbing with the strain of keeping him away. Oh, she had not realised how desolate she was, and how she was grieving for Elizabeth and for Nash, not knowing whether he was alive or dead, Nash, who had made her a woman, who had revealed to her what it meant to love and be loved.

She did not want this assault to be happening. She did not

want to be here in this place, with this devilishly attractive, overwhelming Arabian making love to her . . . No, not love. Lust, only lust and . . . Ah, she had not realised how alone she had been in the past months, closing the door on her shock and grief without allowing it to heal slowly but surely. Now the door was opening, and bright, blinding light was streaming through, to bring with it all her hopes and dreams and longing for Nash Hamilton.

The urge to scream had gone and tears came in its place. She shut her eyes for she wanted to see Nash's glowing gilded head above her, his rich blue eyes twinkling with loving humour and adoration, not this smug, arrogant and assured Arabian who did not have to woo and win his women, but only buy them.

Never was there a man so artfully skilled in the practice of love as the Amir Adem Ali, his every caress and kiss and sigh so sophisticated, so coercive that it was not for a mere woman to resist him. He had begun learning the skills of love-making at the age of nine when his father had given him his first concubine, a slave woman twice his age and renowned for her abilities in bed. The woman was retained for the purpose of rewarding those who had pleased the father of Adem Ali. It was an original arrangement which worked superbly.

There was a single-minded resolution about the Amir which, unaffected by her struggles, frightened her. Ruthless and chilling, it was unlike any quality that she had encountered before. This was no ordinary man. This was one who believed he sat at Allah's right hand.

The nostalgic scent of incense was in her nostrils, as if a brazier was newly lit close by. Myrrh and frankincense and all the perfumes of Arabia . . . Would she ever blot them out of her memory, or were they burned into her very soul?

The Amir's kisses were sips of exotic, spiced wine, a brew more powerful than any contrived aphrodisiac. There was little that she could do now to resist, for there was something in the air which was making her respond to him; that, and her desperate loneliness. If his arms did not comfort and hold her, then whose would?

His kisses made her neck tingle. One, two, three, four sensual kisses down the right side of her neck, to her breast where he lapped her silky white flesh, stabbing gently at her nipple with his tongue. The effect was electrical, and she squirmed. Laughing, he repeated the daisy chain of kisses down the other side of her neck to her left breast, where he sucked gently, then with more passion, until tiny trickles of desire swam beneath her skin, from her breasts to her thighs, and back again. She had never had her earlobes kissed and nibbled before, and his tongue seemed capable of most miraculously arousing response in her . . . She could not help but squirm and reach out for him, wanting more, so much more.

Next he kissed the insides of her arms, with an exquisite finesse, nibbling between each kiss so that her flesh became fiery, then down to her waist and stomach, nibbling and caressing with his lips, her mouth opening to gasp with delight as his tongue dipped into the triangle of red-gold hairs between her legs. She could not believe what he was doing. Was such a thing possible? And yet he was doing it, and she was groaning with delirious delight. His tongue was like a thousand tiny, silver-tipped daggers, probing, piercing, rousing her, lapping deep between her thighs amidst her most soft and tender flesh, and then he was taking the little bud of desire between his lips and sucking it with such skill that she cried out with intolerable ecstasy. Again he sucked, then lapped, then sucked, so that the most frantic electrical impulses were flaming through her body, wild, uncontrollable, heavenly.

What was going to happen next? She could not believe it! He was bringing her to the summit of passion with his tongue alone. When she could bear it no longer, he thrust his mouth against her soft pink centre and kissed it ardently, so that dancing shivers coruscated along her spine, before he returned to the miniature rosebud, the source of all sensuality . . .

She could feel him stabbing against her legs, his male hardness both fearful and yet infinitely desirable. She wanted him and yet she was taut with anxiety. Would he know that she was no virgin? Would he despise her after he had made love to her? She thought of the drops of blood cached in the tightly fastened pouch so that they would not congeal. Her head spun, her senses danced the most dizzying whirligig . . . there was nothing she could do to hold out any more, nothing . . . He was kissing the inside of her thighs in the most tender places, places which she had not even known were so wildly sensitive, each kiss springing to life beneath her flesh, as if it could live and breathe on its own, scoring itself into her memory, doubling and trebling its impact until she shuddered with the most voracious desire.

Yet there was a bitter realisation about it. Now, she knew that she was born to betray; that she was weak, malleable, in the hands of men who stirred her senses. Perhaps fate was only being kind to her in matching her to Adem Ali; perhaps they were twin souls, far more alike than she would care to admit. First she had betrayed her sister, dear, trusting Elizabeth, and now she was betraying her beloved Nash with this ardent and exotic Arabian prince . . .

Kill herself if he touched her? She would kill herself if he did *not* touch her now!

Looking down at his glossy dark head was exciting beyond belief. How did he know exactly what would despatch her into tremors of passionate joy? Yet know he did, and he was showing his knowledge in the most direct manner possible.

Her face was flushed a rosy pink, her eyes dewy with desire. She felt as if she were melting into molten, glowing gold, a liquid star, yielding yet coruscating. It was Heaven: a miracle of the senses. Now he was trapping her, crushing her in his powerful arms, strong, sunburnt arms from all the hours that he spent hunting with his falcons in the desert, or riding one of his superbly sculptured Arab horses.

His measured air of indolence was entirely deception. Seeing him swathed in dazzling silks, the edgings of thick and lavishly embroidered brocade, the autocratic *Kuffayiah* and *aighal* on his head, and plum-sized jewels on his brown fingers, one could be forgiven for thinking him the most indolent of hedonists, yet there was a fierce source of energy coiled deep inside him, so that even as he lounged on silken cushions, he looked as if he might spring to his feet at any second.

Now the coiled energy was about to strike deep into Allegra, piercing, conquering. Her senses were desperate for the coupling.

'Now, *now*!' she gasped, her face and breast blazing with heat.

'Wait.'

To her surprise, he was pulling away from her, reaching to a small jewel-enamelled cabinet at his bedside. He pressed it lightly in a secret place and a tiny drawer flew open. Smiling to himself, he lifted out a golden phial from which he took the stopper, emptying some of the contents into his palm.

'What is that, *Saiyid*?'

'We call it *rakta-bol*. It is a love tincture, a mixture of gum Arabic and herbs.'

'A love potion? Then it is witch's magic! We do not need that!' Allegra tried to pull him back on to the bed, longing for the feel of his satiny brown skin beneath her hands.

'You and your witches! The English are obsessed with them. It is well known, this substance, and there is no magic in it. See, I will show you what we do with it.'

Grinning, his eyes glittering like French jet, the Amir began to rub the ointment into his thighs and the base of his stomach, then, to Allegra's astonishment, he massaged it thoroughly into his sexual organ. Next, he was emptying more of the ointment onto his palm and massaging it into her thighs and between her legs, so that the delicate skin in that area began to flame and tingle. It was thrilling, disturbing, almost intolerable. Gasping, she bit her lip, trying to hold back her cries of passion. The heat was increasing, she was being swept into a vortex of delirious desire, her arms were open wide for the Amir to plunge deep into her body . . .

It was difficult to remind herself of what she must do now, for her mind was whirling and dancing, but somehow the tiny, stoppered phial was at hand and in a few minutes she would empty out the blood, so that the drops fell beneath her buttocks, staining the silken sheet. Later, at the first chance, she would drop the tiny phial into the nearest brazier.

Conjunction with the Lord of the Incense Road, the Lion of Arabia . . . It was a fabulous experience, and as her delicate tissues seared and throbbed with the *rakta-bol*, and the frenzied plunging of the handsome Amir, Allegra's inflamed senses swept her away on to a glittering magic carpet, twisting and swaying through the stars, with the silver-honey moonlight bathing them both in a scintillating glow . . .

'White dove, do you want to fly away and leave me?' he whispered. 'You cannot. You are my slave. You were virgin until I took you and made you my own, and now you shall belong to me for ever. Allah sent you to me and Allah decrees that you shall stay.'

How did he know that she was flying away through the stars? Yet – there was a little of the old Allegra remaining, despite the onslaught on her senses.

'You may have my body, *Saiyid*. Allah may have decreed that, but my soul remains my own, and my heart,' she informed him.

'What good would they be to me if I did possess them, white dove?' The gleaming basilisk eyes surveyed her as if she was a new purchase which pleased immensely, obtained as it had been at a bargain price.

'Whatever men may say, they always want to possess their woman completely.'

'The white dove knows too much, or thinks she does. It is the will of Allah that you become my willing and devoted slave . . .'

'Yes, Allah the all-merciful. Then why has he not shown any mercy to me and your other slaves?' Allegra was doing her utmost to behave in the old intractable way, yet she was so relaxed and cosy from the fierce love-making that all she truly wanted to do was be wrapped in the Amir's arms and sleep.

'This *is* his mercy, ignorant one. But for his beneficence you would have been dead of starvation now, on your barren island.'

'But it was not barren, *Saiyid*! We had everything that we needed.'

'We? And who was with you?' The dark eyes narrowed menacingly. How swiftly his moods changed, from passionate to enraged, to glacial.

'My – brother.' Her heart banged.

She had almost revealed the truth. Husaina would have been horribly punished; herself, too. It was against her nature to mislead, yet the alternative would be purgatory.

'You had a brother?' His tone was lacking in curiosity. He did not require a reply. It was plain that he did not care if she had lost eleven brothers.

'I lost him . . . I lost everything when your men came for me!'

'Lost everything?' He laughed harshly. 'So what is this splendour here? Women have no judgement; they are both impure and deceiving. Woman follows the road of deception and sloth; she desires all to be placed before her; she does not wish to work for her needs. All must be given in generous quantities. We men have known this for centuries. It is why we put our females in the *harem*; why we guard them closely; why we rule them firmly.'

'I wonder why your women are like this after all these centuries of such close attention and guardianship?' Allegra arched her brows. The effect of the *rakta-bol* was diminishing; she was beginning to feel her old sharp-witted, disputatious self again, and ashamed of her submission. 'It seems strange to me that Muslim women should still be thus after all these years. Are you telling me that Muslim men have no influence with their women, that they cannot ever care for them as they would their falcon or their mare? Do you men simply stand by and allow your women to behave so badly?'

The Amir's handsome face darkened, the lines deepening on either side of his voluptuous mouth. Thrusting out his hands he pushed Allegra away from him as if she were foul, then leapt to his feet with the agility of a young gazelle.

'Your words prove what I said, what we men have always known. Woman causes trouble and conflicts. She has no logic, no conception of reality.' The dazzling features were fixed into an expression of autocratic zeal.

Watching, Allegra knew that these beliefs had been instilled into Adem Ali when he was a young boy, perhaps instilled with beatings, or harsh lessons, for he repeated them as if they were engraven on his mind, memorised like prayers. Briefly, she felt a spark of compassion for him and his narrow mindedness, after which she told herself that she was being stupid. Compassion was not what he demanded. And why pity a man who was without pity himself?

Her body ached from his savage and determined onslaught. She felt, at one and the same time, weary and satiated, unclean and ill-used. Never more than at that moment had she wanted her darling, strong and comforting Nash, yet she was confronted with this volatile, despotic Arabian prince.

'*Mashallah*.' It is the will of Allah.

The words rang in her head like the anklet bells which the slave girls wore to dance. Pulling on her robe, she got slowly to her feet, pausing when her head whirled, waiting for it to clear. Even if she could ever assume the tranquil fatalism of this perplexing man and his countrymen and women, would she want to? Her head was starting to throb and she wished that he would dismiss her, but he was silent.

Do not leave until you are commanded, Husaina had said, so she stood there, feeling slightly sick, her body bruised and sore, cold even though the night was clammy, and when all she longed to do was sob heartbrokenly in her bed away from the tigerish eyes of this tempestuous and quixotic man.

Chapter Nineteen

Stabbing wildly, his eyes dilated, his mouth twisted in a grimace of savage revenge, Youssef wielded the knife as if he were fighting off a host of *jinns*. Over and over he plunged the blade into his victim's back, knowing that he was commanded by Allah, that this was *Mashallah*, the will of God, and that he would be blessed for killing his wife's lover. He had survived the humiliation and the agony for too long but now it was over. Now she would be faithful to him for ever more. Never again would she betray him. Never again! He would have the body of the dead Christian preserved and if Rouhkia threatened to misbehave then he would show it to her as a reminder.

Laughing hysterically, he continued to plunge the dagger's blade until there was nothing to see save for a bloody mesh of gore. He was splattered with blood but he saw nothing, felt nothing, but his blessed, heart-lifting revenge on the filthy Christian slave.

Guards rushed in, mouths wide, faces ashen. Youssef felt himself being restrained, his arms clamped to his sides. Laughing, he threw back his head, crying '*Mashallah! Mashallah!*' and then he looked at the bed where the body of the Christian slave lay, scarlet and bloody, and he laughed again, and shook as if he were fevered.

There was pandemonium, guards and slaves running everywhere. No one knew what to do, for their master was crazed, his mind had left him, he was possessed by *jinns* and their mistress . . . *Allah*, what were they to do?

Not stopping to survey the events nor asking himself why he had been spared, Nash fled. If it was *Mashallah* that Youssef in his madness had stabbed his own wife to death while shrieking out his, Nash's, name, then it was also *Mashallah* that he escape while the palace was in uproar. Without their mistress, the slaves were terrified children, shocked and stunned. Sobbing and wailing, they were tearing at their clothes and their hair. He passed two eunuchs slumped to the floor, tears rolling from their eyes, their huge bodies heaving. Down narrow twisting corridors, he ran as far from the death chamber as he could. He had walked in the gardens with Rouhkia so he knew the way there, and through the little low gate which led to the outer court and then, while servants and slaves were tearing past him in the opposite direction, he slipped out through the main gates as easily as he had entered.

The desert perimeters greeted him. Out there, if he wanted to stay free, he must face the swirling, baffling and murderous wasteland. The desert of a thousand painful deaths, that was what they called it. He had no food, no water. It was madness to flee out into this terracotta wilderness and yet it would be mad to stay.

He had done nothing before he left except pick up his white

bernouse and now he paused briefly to fling this over his head to protect him from the dust as he ran and to conceal what he wore round his neck. Rouhkia was generous while she was in love. It had been her habit to decorate him with jewels to try and coax him into a response. She had taken valuable gems from round her own throat and looped them over his head. Rubies, emeralds, flesh-coloured and rosy-pink pearls, two glossy black pearls almost evil in their dark, slumbrous hue; diamonds, sapphires and amethysts, all clasped in gold.

Dusk was crowding in, almost palpable in its efforts to assert itself over the heat and glare of day. Hearing an eerie, echoing scream, Nash turned. Behind him, in the distance he saw the low white palace with its perpendicular turret and the tiny dark shape of a man falling from the tower, leaping, jumping, as if desperate to die. Youssef. Clenching his fists, Nash ran on.

Muslim men made their own hell on earth with their rigid beliefs. God alone knew how Youssef and Rouhkia had destroyed themselves with their strange and tragic marriage, but he wished that he had never been a part of their life.

He rested in a dark gritty hollow, stabbed by tiny sprigs of tough greenery. The night was ghostly and silent, no wind, no movement, nothing but the low, scintillating stars just above his head, so low that it seemed he could reach out and grasp them. How they pulsed in this clear dark sky, pulsed and fibrillated, teeming with cosmic energy, glowing with diamond-sharp light.

His dreams were stormswept and confusing. He dreamed of a bloody corpse, reached out to touch and it rolled to face him. It was Allegra . . . Heart thudding, he leapt into wakefulness. The dark night was clamped round him, a stifling blanket, and yet at the same time he was chilled and uneasy.

An animal scampered by, then there was a brief agonised screech as it became another creature's supper. The years had never reached this place. There was nothing here to mark out time, to impress itself, except Nash himself. He slept again, the jewels digging into his neck and collarbone. He would disguise himself as a desert nomad, darken his skin and hair with berry juice, find some ancient ragged robe to hang over his silken one and keep the gems concealed. He might buy a horse if he could pay for it with a jewel without arousing suspicion. Otherwise, he would manage on foot. He would steal if necessary, for he intended to make his way to the palace of Adem Ali, to discover the whereabouts of Elizabeth and Allegra. He would buy their freedom with the jewels, and take them back to England, and, God forgive him, he would answer to his conscience and their hearts when that time came.

Two days in the desert was like a month. Footsore and aching, barely able to focus his eyes in the flaying heat, his mouth, throat and ears packed with sandy grit which blew at him every time there was a tiny gust of a breeze, he persevered. On the third day he dined on roots, crushed locusts and cactus milk. On the fourth, he sat at a camp fire with hospitable merchants and devoured an oily and rancid pilaf. The merchants had their own dancing girl and she wobbled and swayed round their fire with a lascivious smile on her rouged face. Nash felt sick for it reminded him of Rouhkia. The Eastern way of displaying sexuality, of thrusting it in a man's face, was nauseating, choking. He could not stand much more of it. Thanking his hosts in fluent Arabic, he bowed courteously, declined the slave girl's arts, saying that he was ill, and went to the rough bed of goatskins which had been spread for him. Arabs were generous hosts, especially in the desert. He hoped that they would be equally generous when they discovered their best horse and some of their equipment had vanished during the night.

Having escaped so stealthily that the snoring, bibulous Arabs did not hear him, Nash slipped and plunged his way through the sand, the horse following obediently. It was a dainty animal, but strong, with powerful muscles and sharp, perceptive eyes. Not until they had three sky-sweeping dunes behind them did he mount the beast and make haste through the turgid, clogging sand. Then, having ridden for something like two hours, he dismounted, wrapped himself in skins and rolled into a ball to sleep, the horse standing beside him, its rein twisted tightly round his wrist. The desert night was cold,

Antarctica after Africa, and he shivered, curled up like a scarab in its shell.

At dawn, a vapid icy light piercing his lids, he woke with a start. A blue man was standing watching him, blue face, blue hands and neck, blue feet and ankles, even the calves where they disappeared into the shabby bernouse were bright, alarming blue.

Leaping to his feet, Nash prepared himself for battle. There were others behind this strange and frightening entity, and as he stood, knife at the ready, they advanced towards him, their own glinting daggers lifted to strike.

Allegra had been watching the dancers for weeks now. Trained from infancy, they were adept at their art, for art it was, the extraordinary, voluptuous and sinuous dancing which was nurtured by Islamic courtesans. Allegra, accustomed to the stately, rigid and proud dances of Spain which Katherine of Aragon had introduced to England, and the graceful, sophisticated movements of Paris, first displayed so superbly at Hampton Court by Queen Anne Boleyn, was taken aback when she first saw the frank, seductive and sensual way these courtesans performed.

Muslim women did not lace themselves into the unwieldy wooden corsets which were considered the height of Elizabethan fashion. Their robes were soft and silken, flowing loosely, draping their voluptuous curves like caressing hands. They liked bright shimmering materials and colours, decorated with glittering beads, spangles of silver and gold, gold fringes and tassels. They painted patterns on their hands and feet with henna, the deep terracotta powder which was made into a thick paste. The Prophet considered it imperative that female hands be painted with henna, the finger nails particularly. A woman's hands must always be decorated to differentiate them from a man's.

The henna was applied for a number of reasons, including purification and protection against evil, along with the beauty it brought. Hair too was plastered with the messy henna, the scent of which was redolent of hay newly cut. When it was washed out, even the blackest hair would have a reddish tinge.

The dancers decorated themselves elaborately, and applied pungent scented oils to their bodies so that, as they whirled past their audience, they left behind a fragrant aroma. For dancing, they bared their stomachs, wearing tiny bolero tops in the Turkish style which only just covered the breasts, and low-slung harem trousers in transparent silks. Belts, ornate, and hung with bells were popular, and even if they were nothing more than a length of cloth twined round the hips, they seemed to be obligatory.

The rippling muscles of the dancers were astonishing. So were their snake-like fingers and swaying necks, which moved from side to side as if they had no bones. Eyes were thickly painted with kohl, the black antimony which was considered imperative for beauty as well as a protection against eye disease. With arms gyrating and eyes glittering like black-enamelled crescent moons, the dancers undulated, shook and swayed their way around the chamber to the reedy, ululating noise of the lute and tabor.

Allegra was not bashful, but she did not wish these accomplished women to watch her early hesitant attempts to emulate their sophisticated movements. In England, she was considered an accomplished dancer, but those were stately movements, with the body tightly parcelled in a corset, farthingale and stiff, starched ruff. Here, there was very little to separate a dancer from the eyes of her audience, not even a yashmak.

Adem Ali appeared unperturbed by these girls when they swayed and shimmied before him, even the sinuous and stunning snake dance leaving him unmoved. He had seen it all before, a thousand times, yet these displays of wealth and grandeur must be maintained. The Sultan had troupes of dancing girls, so he must have them too. When he was entertaining important guests, these girls were valuable, and afterwards, his guests may choose one to take to their beds in true Arabian style. Always a generous host, he himself would never lie with one of these women; they were strictly for show.

There was something about the snake dance which made the hairs on Allegra's neck prickle. Ancient and primeval, it spoke silently of primitive passions and long-ago but not forgotten times. She could not help but recall the statue of the goddess on her paradise island, with the serpent coiled so happily at her feet. Perhaps this dance had once been an offering to the goddess? She felt that this was quite possible, but if so, it was incredible that it had survived all these centuries.

Slithering along the floor, the dancer seemed to eschew her human shape and become coiling, slender and undulating. One could hear a hissing sound and almost imagine the leaping, darting bifurcated tongue of a snake jutting from the dancer's carmine lips. Only one performer executed this display. Tahia could not speak English or Arabic, and although Allegra could make out some of her words as sounding French in origin, much of what she said could not be translated by anyone.

Tahia's inability to communicate verbally only added to her mystery; yet the *Saiyid* had never glanced in her direction, or so said Husaina. Allegra found herself captivated by Tahia's performances and wondering why the *Saiyid* did not admire such skills. Tahia could say only two sentences in Arabic: '*Alla ykûn ma'ak!*' (God be with you) and '*Alla ysallmak!*' (God save you!).

Young, loose-limbed and dark-eyed even before applying the antimony which gave her a Byzantine look, Tahia had enormous, round doe eyes. Her fingers were strangely long and pointed, her feet thin and spiky-toed. Her hair was dyed orange-brown with henna.

'Will you show me how to do your snake dance?' Allegra asked her one day, at which Tahia fluttered her eyelashes and turned her head away. 'Will you, please? I think it is very beautiful.'

'She cannot understand you, she is fevered in the head.' Husaina tapped her left temple.

'Can you translate for me?'

'I do not speak her tongue. No one knows where she comes from. She arrived with slaves from the great ocean, but does not speak their language.'

'How long has she been here?'

'Many moons, many suns. She is happy.'

'How can you know, if she cannot speak with you?'

'I know.'

'The *Saiyid* will not take notice of her, yet still she is happy?' Allegra's eyes glittered. 'How can this be?'

'It is thus. *Mashallah*, the will of God. She dances, the visitors are made greatly happy. The *Saiyid* is weary of such exotic and obvious display. He has seen it all.'

'Then why does he not get rid of his concubines? Should he not be weary of them too?' Allegra's voice was tart.

For five days now she had not been called to Adem Ali's bedchamber. The other women were smirking and whispering behind their hands. They had known her glory would be short. The chosen one was now the rejected one. Soon it would be their turn in her place. She was conscious of the secret malice, the triumph gleaming in the dark eyes which scrutinised her so intimately. It was unnerving. Here, she was totally subservient to the whim of Adem Ali. If he became bored with any woman who had attracted him, and if she had not borne a son, then back she would go into the ranks of the harem, from which time her lot would be as before: endless hours to be spent bathing and applying henna to her hair and body, making the pungent, dark-brown smoky brew which the Arabs called *kahwe*, sewing and embroidering, or replacing oil in the lamps or incense in the braziers.

Allegra shivered. The most disturbing thing had happened since Adem Ali had taken her to his bed. After her horror and revulsion, the nausea, the tears, had come a profound and eerie calm. And then, as if she were looking only for him, her anchor in this strange and perplexing land, she had found herself longing for the Amir's company. She understood that it was because of the suffering she had endured, the loss of Elizabeth, and the desperate loneliness and disorientation she felt, a prisoner in a hot and arid country where nothing felt dear or familiar, where there was no solace.

How many months had passed since she had last seen Nash? She had lost count; she had forgotten her own age, her surname . . . Her mind was indeed different. She was beginning to think and reason differently, like these quixotic and temperamental women who were her fellow slaves.

In such conditions, it was not unexpected that she, too,

begin to look to the Amir as the source of all things. She was a survivor, her spirit steely, yet if she fought with and offended these people, she would create her own destruction. Surprised at herself, she reined in her thoughts, kept her lids lowered, bit her tongue when hasty words leapt to be free. Was this cunning? She could not say as yet, but if it were, then it was alien to her impulsive and impetuous nature.

The *Saiyid*, the lord; all life, happiness and joy revolved round him. When he was pleased, then his women were overjoyed. When he was angry or melancholic, then his women wept. They did not need minds of their own, nor wills with which to reason. They need do nothing save echo the moods of their prince and master. They were the breath of his mouth, the beat of his heart, the blink of his eye, the click of his fingers, yes, most of all that, for when the Amir clicked thumb and middle finger together in that impatient and imperious manner, women would come rushing to fling themselves at his feet.

Allegra had felt disgusted when she first saw this display of devotion, the women scuttling to their master's summons like panting puppies; yet now, for her own preservation, for the peace of her mind and the ease of her heart, she too needed to be the same.

Having overcome the mountain of objection and revulsion, the determination never to behave like those witless, simpering slave girls, having found herself able to put aside pride and stubbornness, she had discovered that the Amir did not want her again. This was the ultimate degradation. After the preparations, the excitement of being the chosen one, surrounded by envy and hostility, mingled with good will and rejoicing, only to find that she was not summoned again.

Was it rejection like this which had made her sister run into the desert? Would she ever know the whole truth of it?

So she devised a plan. Soon the Amir was to hold the annual celebration for the anniversary of his parents' marriage, an odd thing to celebrate each year, Allegra had thought when first she heard, but then everything about Arabia was strange and different. Perhaps it was the anniversary of his legitimacy, the reminder of the Prophet's blood which flowed in his veins.

The harem always arranged an entertainment for this event, singing, dancing, the reciting of love verses, a great feast at which they would all sit with their lord together, this being one of the rare times such a communion took place.

Once there had been a visit by actors, men and women who had dressed themselves as famous historic figures in Arabic history, speaking their words as if they were reading them stiffly from a verbose and weighty book. That had not been popular with the Amir, so there would be no actors this year.

Hafez would sing, as he always did, and he was even now composing new verses, as well as adapting some of the ancient and well-loved verses of Islam. For Allegra, he translated them, and, for the first time, she heard the passionate and soulful words of Pir Sultan Abdal, the mystic poet from Shivas.

'Whatever your faith shall be my faith,
Though Judgement Day break me tomorrow,
If I may kiss your milky throat,
Come near, my lovely one, come near . . .'

And, the verses of Kadi Burhanettin, who had lived in the fourteenth century:

'My lord, could I but see your face, then gladly would I die.

'To feel your long-desired embrace, how gladly would I die.

'The darkness of your hair conceals the lips I seek; I ask,
"That fount of life, where is its place?" for there I'd gladly die.

'Last night I saw you in a dream, and we two were as one.
The meaning is not hard to trace – so I must shortly die.

'Since first creation when His beauty moved my soul to love,
I've sought for it in futile chase. To find it I would die.

'Ah, were heart mind and soul not so entangled in your looks!
I'd comb them out, were such the case, and, rid of them, I'd die.

'How long still will my lover, kindling fires of longing, make me burn?
And still how long must I keep watching for a sign of his return?'

'Why do you weep, white dove?' Hafez leaned towards Allegra as his fingers fell from his lute, the only English instrument at the Amir's court.

'What does the writer yearn for, Hafez, his beloved or his God? How moving are those words, so full of entreaty and longing!'

'The beloved and God can be one and the same . . . especially in the religion of Islam, white dove. In England, religion does not have the passionate glow, the intensity which Muslim mystics experience. Let me finish and then you can tell me who the song was written for.'

'With love my heart set out upon the road which leads to him;
Will not that door be opened which is knocked on in love's name?
'The fire of love which burns the lover burns the loved one, too,
Who else is it was praised but he from whom the praises came?'

'It is a woman he writes for?'

'Maybe. Maybe. I do not know. Maybe for a man, who knows?'

Hafez's eyes twinkled, and Allegra blushed. One could not live in a harem for as long as she had now and not learn of the love which could exist between two men. Indeed, some men went so far as to declare, 'Women for bearing sons, and young men for love,' so Husaina said. Some of the most virile leaders of Islam, with packed harems and enormous families, indulged in much dalliance with beautiful young boys, considering this more beneficial, romantic and beautiful than any relationship which could develop between a man and a woman. The enormity of this information, the strangeness and the shock of it, had given Allegra disturbed dreams for a night or two. Men loving other men, sleeping with them like lovers, kissing and embracing them . . . and doing other things which Husaina had described in detail, as if it were an everyday occurrence, which, for all she knew, it was. She did not know whether to blush or pale, or remain silent.

' "*The fire of love which burns the lover burns the loved one, too . . .*" Do not forget that, white dove. Do not get your wings scorched by flying too close to the flames.'

Hafez was speaking in riddles again, but then Islamic poets frequently did.

Two black eunuchs appeared. It was time for the evening meal, the main meal of the day, for the food eaten at midday was only a light repast. The heat, dust and aridity were apt to steal the appetite, but it returned with the cool of the night.

Allegra sat with crossed legs amongst the other women who dipped their hands freely into the large silver bowls and ceramic platters filled with rice and mutton cooked in butter, which always tasted rancid to Allegra. Mixed with this were aubergines, and colourful crescents of pepper which nearly tore the roof off her mouth, and beans and onions, or whatever vegetables were in season. Spices were used liberally for the flavouring of the dishes, cinnamon, cloves, saffron, turmeric, cardamoms and ginger being added so indulgently that their taste would frequently eliminate all others. Dates, almonds and figs, honeyed pastries, apricots, and slabs of the enormous, bulbous, rosy water melons were welcome finales to the rich, fatty and spicy *entrées*. The poor, Allegra was told, survived on couscous, a cereal, mixed with whatever vegetable was available. Only on the most special occasions did the labourers sacrifice a lamb or sheep, yet here in the palace of Adem Ali lamb was eaten every day, with poultry, veal, rare smoky truffles from the Arabian desert, delicate preserves made with flower petals, both delicious and fragrant, pastries, and sweetmeats of sesame seeds, carob, honey and almonds. Alcohol was forbidden by the Koran, and so the Amir drank *nabidh*, a mild, fermented concoction made from raisins or dates, and water, which the Prophet had imbibed heavily. Allegra preferred rosewater *narguile*, which was light and refreshing, despite the fact that it was usually lukewarm.

Oh, for a drink from a rushing, icy Cornish stream, then to bathe in it, flinging off her petticoats and lying in the chilling, stony depths, washing away the sticky, humid heat and dust of Arabia!

Husaina did not eat with the rest of the harem, for she had her own sacrosanct dining area. She had never invited another to share it with her, nor would she change this. There were enough squabbles and disputes on petty matters without arguing over Husaina's showing favour. Sitting in her corner, on her favourite Turkey rug, its ruby, sea-blue and deep gold flamboyant against the ivory tiled floor, Husaina watched the women out of the corner of an eye. Such young, foolish and greedy girls, each one so desperate for favour, and each cursed and yet blessed by her womanhood. So many dark heads and ebony eyes, such soft skin the colour of *kahwe*, and all of it draped in jewel-coloured silks and scented with pungent, heady, flowered oils . . .

Would she, Husaina, wish to be so young and beautiful again, to be chosen for the Amir's bed? No, never! There was pain and heartbreak along with it, and she was too old, too fragile now.

The women were dipping their fingers into the bowls and platters of food, cramming it into their mouths greedily. She would not complain about their over-eating. Her master liked his women plump. Thin women meant a lord who was lacking in wealth; everyone knew that. The wives of those who lack wealth and power shall never wax fat . . . That was what people said and it was true.

The English girl ate with more grace. She had taken some time to accustom herself to the hectic scramble for food, the plunging of the fingers into the buttery pilaf or lamb, and she always showed relief when the rosewater and the napkins arrived so that she could wash her fingers. Husaina chuckled to herself. Perhaps they sucked up their food through tubes in England, not caring to soil their pretty fingers? The English were very contradictory. They spoke of Godliness and cleanliness, yet they only bathed once a year and they wore the same clothes month in, month out, so Hafez had told her. No wonder they suffered such dread diseases.

'The white dove.' It was an apt name for her, and yet doves could be broken. What resistance did they have to the eagle or the falcon? Love alone could not protect, yet she, Husaina, had felt compelled to try and soften the blows with a little white lie or two.

She wanted to warn the white dove, tell her that the Amir was worldly wise, yes, more than any other man, that he had been born thus. Women were his *jijims*, toys which meant nothing to him beyond a moment's passion. He was debauched and cynical; he did not believe in eternal love nor any emotion similar to it. Lust meant everything to him, a pure, greedy and violent lust which he must slake regularly. Now that Lady Khadija Nur had borne him a son and heir, he was a little more at ease. The good Lord Allah must not think for one second that she was finding fault with her Amir, but she knew these things about him and, being old and venerated, could ponder upon them. Age gave a protection which youth, beauty and love did not.

The Amir's permanent favourite naturally would be the woman who bore his first surviving son. Husaina had always known that and, deep in her heart, she had longed to be the one who would bring that woman to the bed of her master. But it was not to be. The favoured wife had needed no training, no improving. Perchance, the Amir's eye had fallen upon her the day she arrived at the palace, and he had swept her into his bed that very night, before Husaina could get her busy fingers on to her. Such haste had happened only once before, and that *odalik* had died giving birth to a daughter which had also died. The new favourite, the Lady Khadija Nur, was healthy and strong, and so was her son, Prince Zühl Ibn Adem Ali, who would one day rule in the Amir's place. The little boy, even though only a few weeks old, showed every sign of being healthy and bright-eyed. His mother had spent many weeks in bed towards the end, for she became faint and dizzy when she stood up. Now that the Prince was born, she was recovering, for the birth had been long and difficult. She did not mingle with the rest of the harem, for she had her own quarters, a sumptuous suite of rooms retained for the mother of the Amir's heir, which was separated from the ordinary harem quarters by long corridors and arrangements of walled gardens and tiled courts. Only the *selamlik*, the men's quarters, were further away from the harem.

When Hafez said that fidelity was the way of things in England, and that men did not lie with other women when their wives were with child, Husaina had listened in disbelief. What a waste of man's seed that he should remain chaste while his wife grew big with child! She could not comprehend such a damming up of passions. Why did the Englishman not bury his seed in the bodies of other favourites while he waited for his favourite wife to recover?

Hafez had laughed. 'He takes one wife only, and none but God and death can part them. She will bear his whole family.'

'Even if that family be as large as two hundred children?' Husaina had squeaked, thinking of the usual size of an aristocratic Muslim's family.

'Not exactly. More like eight, ten, sometimes fifteen children. Englishmen do not wish to have two hundred sons.'

'They do not? But God has given them the seed to make many, many sons and daughters. Why do they waste it?'

'It is not the custom to have such large families or to collect women in a harem. Such are the ways of the Western world.'

Husaina could not believe it. For days, she had gone round muttering, 'The waste! Oh, the waste of seed! All those sons and daughters never to be born, *Mashallah*, the waste!'

The dishes and jugs were being cleared away now and the women were preparing to entertain themselves for the evening. They would dance, one after the other, as was the custom, and applaud each other vigorously.

Allegra disappeared, to return with three veils of shining silk. Husaina watched with interest, what did she plan to do? For an English girl she had innate suppleness and grace, and such dignity that she might be royal herself, of the proud blood of the Amir's race. Now the girl was draping herself in the veils and as the music increased in tempo, the reedy, nasal sound of the lute and the cracking and banging of the drum, she began to dance, watched open-mouthed by the harem.

Courage had been plucked from somewhere, but it had taken her days. These women were experienced at dancing. They had spent hours at their craft. She was new to the sensuous and suggestive Eastern movements yet she must begin somewhere, so why not here? If they laughed in her face, then she would practise and practise some more, until they did not laugh.

The beat of the music was primitive and rousing, yet there was no discernible tune. All the same, she liked the Eastern music; it struck a chord inside her. As her mother before her, she had always been affected by rhythms. Now twirling and twisting before the gaping harem, she found her feet were light and seemingly propelled by forces other than her own energy. She could even sway her neck from side to side like a cobra's, while bending up her arms and cupping her hands, one beneath each ear, before twisting them, palms to her face and forefingers extended. Then elbows rising, to be followed by the cupped hands, she swirled round and round so that the veils billowed out, a sunset cloud of ruby-coloured silk glittering with silver sequins.

The music slowing, Allegra launched herself into more voluptuous movements, hips swinging to left and right, the muscles of her strong, slender legs beautifully coordinated so that nothing moved except what she ordered to move. There was fire in her arm and leg movements, a magical flame in her head commanding her to dance as she had before the effigy of the serpent goddess on the paradise island.

Her performance was bringing everything back to her. The enchanted island, the eerie yet beautiful carved goddess, the primitive, unleashed urges which she had felt as she knelt before the goddess, but most of all the loving and longing, the aching, heart-breaking yearning for Nash. How resolutely she had buried her misery, but now it was rising, returning, flooding her, sweeping through her so that tears burst from her eyes, and, blinded by them, she fled from the chamber.

PART FOUR:

The Dance of the Seven Veils

Worrying about our rivals drives away sleep from our eyes;
Watchfully we guard the hoard wherein love's mysteries remain.

Fuzuli, 1494–1556

We shall never have enough, my soul,
Of bread and light, of sleep and love.
Light is insatiable, love is voracious.
We shall never satisfy our privation.
We shall eat and be hungry, we shall thirst.
We shall never have enough, O my soul.

George Thémelis

Chapter Twenty

The blue men were the Beduin, wearing robes dyed with *Lawit*, wild indigo, which, in the heat and sweat of the day, wore off, imprinting itself like dusty paint against their flesh. His first alarm over, Nash stepped towards them, grinning broadly and speaking rapidly in Arabic, a colloquial tongue which they would understand. He saw the startled look in their eyes and the way their hands fell down, their jaws dropping. A white man speaking Arabic! They had never known it, nor ever would again. What white man came to this place of stony desert ghosts and short life, let alone spoke their own native tongue?

'Any whose native tongue is Arabic will be considered as one of you,' their great leader Mohammed had said, such being their respect for a stranger who could manipulate his tongue round their glottal and throaty language that they were prepared to count him amongst themselves. What was more, this isolated, nomadic tribe had never seen a white man before and so there was a double impact.

Letting Muslim phrases drop from his lips as they would from those of a native-born Arab, Nash engaged their interest and their hearts. How could they murder a man who said '*Mashallah*' and '*Inshallah*', as if he had been born mouthing those godly affirmations? But first they must learn why he was there and what he wanted of them, and they would offer him the boundless hospitality of the nomadic Arab.

The story that the white Arab related chilled their bones.

Sold into slavery against his will, subjected to the whim of a wealthy woman (wisely he did not name her), and forced to do her bidding, then freed by an act of the one, true, and only God, Allah the all-wise, the all-merciful, the beneficent, he had escaped into the desert, and now here he was, without the means of returning to his own country.

The nomads listened, nodding now and again, their thickly plaited hair swinging across their wind-scoured faces, gritting their grimy yellow teeth at the thought of any man being subject to the whims of a female. Now and again they muttered in heartfelt confirmation those praises to Allah which were indigenous to their souls and their creed. It was the will of Allah that this man had escaped and that he was here now, discovered by them before the assassin desert robbed him of his flesh and his life.

Taking Nash back to their camp, they brought out the gleaming burnished coffee pots, their pride and delight, which the women polished and cleaned reverently with ritualistic fervour. A rug was spread for Nash to sit upon, and a dish of dates brought for him to eat while the women prepared the coffee.

First the coffee beans were brought out of the leather bag where they were stored, and placed in a long-handled iron skillet to be roasted. A woman stirred them at frequent intervals, so that every side would be baked, and then they were put to cool in a wooden dish before being pounded in a mortar. The woman's actions were ornate and rhythmic, bringing grace and artistry to the preparations. Nash was enjoying watching the ceremony.

On the fire, a large metal pot was bubbling with hot water into which the coffee grounds were poured, to be brought to the boil three times. Nash had finished the first dish of dates and was into his second when the coffee was poured into the brass coffee pot with its curved handle and Oriental-shaped spout, a few cardamom seeds in its base for flavouring. Unsweetened and greenish in colour, the coffee was handed to Nash in a small cup without a handle, which he drained instantly, barely tasting the contents. Holding out his cup to be filled, he drank again, and again. Not until a guest holds out their cup in their right hand, shaking it between forefinger and thumb, will the host cease to refill it.

Squatting round the fire, drinking, and devouring more of the dates, and the yoghourt-like mixture called *Lében*, Nash and the Beduin relaxed contentedly. The woman serving the coffee had a face of the same darkness as the steaming, gritty liquid, yet thankfully without its greenish hue, as if the rising smoke from the hot fluid had impressed its colour into her skin. Like many desert women, she did not wear a veil. Imprisonment, *purdah*, was anathema to these indomitable females who survived on a wretched diet, their stringy bodies propelled by willpower and sometimes little else. They soon lost their youthful freshness and became tired and wrinkled. An existence in one of the most arid places on earth was hardly conducive to beauty. The killing of an oryx or a gazelle was a rare event, so major that lengthy celebrations accompanied it.

Sipping the coffee was an important and ponderous ritual, a communion with the great and infinite, a reiteration of their faith, their hope, their very survival.

As they drank the bitter, chokingly rich liquid, Nash could not fail to notice that he was being scrutinised by piercing dark eyes all around him, the women, men, youths and maidens and the children all staring boldly, mouths gaping.

'Never try to speed up an Arab, never shout questions at him, or ask him why he is late. Leave him to his own speed, his own deliberations, for everything is beholden to the will of the great god, Allah. In this way, the best can be seen and observed.' Those were the words of the man who had taught Nash to speak Arabic, both the Arabic of the town and of the desert, for there were different colloquial dialects. He, Abdullah ibn Dullah was a merchant who had hired Nash's ship to carry his wares to Italy, after his own vessel had been sunk in a storm. During the long voyage, knowledge had been exchanged between the two men, kindred souls, free-thinking, adventurous, and with questing minds.

Abdullah, having seen his wares safely delivered, had taken up another cargoload, of silks, velvet, spices, Italian leatherwork and silverware, returning to England with them, again with Nash acting as his captain.

The friendly, intelligent and wise Arab had died soon after, of a fever contracted while in London, but he had left all his personal belongings to Nash, who treasured them.

'What is your will, *ya akhûyi*, my brother? You may stay with us for as long as you will it . . .' The words of the tribal elder summoned him back to the present.

This was not the first time that Nash had been stranded in the desert and he knew what was coming next. A young girl would be offered to him as a wife, and if he refused, then he would mortally offend these tribesmen. How much should one appreciate hospitality which gave one no choice of refusing it?

'I shall never forget your kindness, your generosity and your warm hospitality, *ya akhûyi*.' Nash made a gracious salaam to the speaker, one of the old, walnut-brown and wrinkled tribesmen. 'Ah, if I could but stay with you in your wondrous camp, but it cannot be, *Allâhu il'alîm!*, God knows it! I must find a physician, for I am a sick man, a very sick man. I have a disease which prevents me from taking a wife, nay even so much as touching a woman, for I would convey the miasma to her and she would sicken unto death. You shame me with your kindness, but I shall never forget it! *Alla ykâfik' 'an ni*, God reward you for me.'

It was such a noble, sincere speech, and Nash would have felt proud of himself had he not been forced to tell an untruth. He had made an impression on the tribal leader, that he could see, for the man's ebony dark eyes became fulgent with emotion. No doubt he was putting himself in Nash's position: visualising himself as a man forbidden to have consort with women because of a foul disease.

His horse had been fed and watered, and they had spread a colourful cloth across its back, handwoven and edged with a fringe of scarlet and indigo. With doleful eyes, Nash took his leave of the nomads, one of the women running to him with a package of food and a small cooking pot which she pressed into his hands in silent insistence. The reek of camels and garlic rose from her clothes. He supposed that she was beautiful in a primitive, exotic fashion, but he doubted that she had ever bathed, or cleaned her robe, although she might have washed her hair in camel's urine . . . Clamping his mouth on a sudden grin, he wheeled the horse round, affecting a mournful air as he bade his hosts goodbye, thanking them again, and telling them that Allah would reward them a thousandfold for rescuing him, and then he was galloping as rapidly as the hoof-choking sand would allow his horse to move . . . Away, fast, fast, to freedom.

The Amir was laughing at her performance! She could not believe her ears. After all the trouble she had taken, the repeated rehearsing, the careful selection of her dancing outfit, the early morning rising so that she could twist and turn and gyrate to the musicians' drum and tabor . . . What did he want of her, this quixotic, mystifying man? She would not accept that he had tired of her, that he did not want her again. What else did she have to live for but him?

Tears gemmed her lashes, living sequins, as she swayed and twirled before the Amir, yet she was determined not to run away this time. She wore *shalwar*, the transparent, baggy silk trousers, low-slung at the hips, a corded belt twined round the top, as was the custom for dancers, its bright gold colour blending with the gorgeous blue-green of the silk. Covering her breasts was a small, tight bolero richly encrusted with blue, gold and green sequins. The material was a thick, stiff silk which supported her bosom and when she stretched her slender arms upwards, the soft, plump ivory curves of her lower breasts were revealed, like snowy crescents. Her wrists jangled with silver and gold bangles, dozens of tiny silver bells tinkling at her ankles. Her feet, beautifully patterned with terracotta henna, were bare. Some dancers wore rings on their toes, but she could not move gracefully with such encumbrances. She had not been raised to walk bare-footed. Blue and gold hooped earrings shimmered in her ears, swinging as she moved, trapping stray strands of her bright silver-gilt hair, which she wore loose save for a *filet* of pearls, blue silk rosettes and tiny sparkling silver tassels which dangled enticingly on her forehead. Every now and again, she would shake the *daff*, the tambourine which she held in one hand, before banging it with the palm of the other as she dipped and turned.

The heat and the scent of lamp oil and myrrh were suffocating in the Amir's audience chamber. All the harem were gathered to watch the entertainers at his anniversary feast. One after the other there had been poets, singers, minstrels and acrobats, and then six of the concubines had danced. By the time it was Allegra's moment, the night was late, the air smoky with incense and steaming *kahwe*, the odour of hot, tired bodies vying with the more delectable aromas. Some were yawning, the Amir himself having the expression of one who, believing he is in Paradise, finds that it is Hell, and there had been a silly but fierce and noisy squabble between two of the younger girls.

'You are wearing my necklet!' one had shrieked at the other, seeing what she thought were her blue beads.

'*Ya* Allah, indeed. I am not! This was given to me by my sister many years ago. It is all I have to remember her!'

'That is *my* necklet! I would know that blue anywhere! You are a liar and a thief. I shall tell *Ya Saiyid* and he will punish you!'

Next, out came an angry hand to snatch at the beads and the two girls were rolling and kicking around the floor as Allegra made her entry, swathed in shimmering silver veils, to the low, gentle sound of the drum. Squawking and scratching, the girls appeared not to see her, and only when the Amir clapped his hands at them and shouted something abusive in Arabic did they stop fighting, burst into tears and beg forgiveness.

During the first five minutes of Allegra's dance, the girls were sobbing at the Amir's feet, he seeming to have eyes only for them. Short of air in this badly lit, smoky room, angry because no one was looking at her, Allegra fought for control and grace. Eventually the girls stopped sobbing and clutching at the hem of their master's silk robe, and his eyes rose, fixing on Allegra as if he had never seen such dancing before.

She truly believed that he was admiring her grace, that his heart was moved by her performance, for he stared so very fixedly, his mouth curving upwards slightly. It was not a leering smile, far from it, but there was more than a hint of lecherous acquisitiveness. Her spirits rising, she threw away the first of the veils, and then the second. This dance sprang from the very earliest of man's primitive beliefs. It was the dance of the goddess Ishtar who had gone to the Underworld in search of her loved one, and, at each door, must discard a veil as a symbol of penetrating more closely to the deepest and most forbidden mysteries. In later years, it was to become nothing more than a sexual and provocative performance, its true origins forgotten.

Three veils vanished and then a fourth. Could she do what she had planned so secretly for weeks now? None of the women had been told. How could she take such slow-witted foreign females into her confidence? Only with Husaina and Hafez could she talk, and she could not tell either of them what she planned to do.

The fifth veil drifted away, a glistening shroud floating to the far side of the room. Now there was a hushed and vibrant expectancy from all sides, but all that Allegra cared for was the reaction of the Amir himself.

He was sitting forward on his carved ivory throne, his hands gripping the finely wrought arms, his head extended slightly, dark eyes fierce with lust and reverence. Could there be both those emotions in his eyes? Yes, there were. Heart thudding, Allegra reached for the pin which held the sixth veil of ruby-red cloth-of-silver. This was heavier and more concealing, its edges heavily fringed. It clung to her breasts, encasing her in a shimmering shroud, like a tight fishtail, and then, as she loosed the pins, it began to drop down, catching on her breasts and hips, then slipping a little, then catching again, and then slipping, down, down past her thighs and to her bared feet.

A gasp echoed round the chamber. It was as if everyone had made the same startled sound at that very second. Sweat was beading Allegra now, her hair catching in sweat-dark tendrils at her forehead; her rouged lips parted slightly, the rose blush of her cheeks deepening. Half closing her eyes, she stood for long tortuous seconds, wondering if she dared continue. The only robe she wore now was the final and seventh veil, one of amethyst brocade encrusted with purple and gold sequins. It was adequate enough to conceal her worst blushes, but soon it must fall, or else she must run away, having lost her courage.

Then, as she whirled round and round, her hair flying out around her, she saw that the Amir was laughing, throwing back his head and laughing at her!

Hatred sang along her veins. She wanted to kill him, steal his curved dagger and rake it through his heart, his face and breast until he screamed and died. He was the cause of all her misfortune, all the pain and heartbreak. Because of him she had lost her beloved Elizabeth and Nash, everyone gone, ruined, destroyed *because of this despot*! That was when the tears began to sparkle on her kohl-darkened lashes, and she nearly sped from the chamber, head lowered, chest heaving, but she restrained herself just in time, quelling that cowardly urge to escape. In truth, where could she escape to? There was nowhere for her now and never would be ever again, save this accursed harem. How could he laugh at her when she had spent so much time on this dance, put so much effort into it and yearned for and dreaded this night? Ah, what was she to do? He was vile, a vicious, heartless devil and he had no more feeling than a beetle. A trader in human convoys, in death and misery and agony . . .

She must get away! *She must!* She never wanted to see or hear of him again, this omnipotent Amir, so darkly beautiful, so arrogant and powerful. Having bedded her, he had discarded her, just as he had with so many others. He was infamous for such behaviour. How could she have hoped that it would be different for her? And why, *why* should she want it to be different? She hated him, did she not, with every breath and beat of her heart? She hated and loathed him . . .

The truth, could she face the truth? She wanted him to notice her, to care for her, as Nash, darling, precious Nash had done. How could she have endured all these long, lonely months after his tender loving? She must make this Arabian notice her, really notice her. What other hope was there? To spend the rest of her life here, as sexless and unsexed as any eunuch . . . There was no other man with whom she could bed save Adem Ali . . .

Feeling as if her heart were being torn from her breast, she sank to her knees before the Amir, to see him laugh again, but it was at some word from his white eunuch, not at her performance. Oh Jesu, thank you, thank you! He was not laughing at her after all.

'There is one more veil, white dove.' The Amir's coaxing, richly modulated voice sang along her senses like the tinkling of cymbals, making the hair at the back of her neck stand on end, icy shivers of delight rushing down her spine.

'There is, *Ya Saiyid*, but I wish to retire now, if *Ya Saiyid* will give his permission?'

How subservient she sounded, how humble and prostrate at his feet! What had become of the proud and brawling fighter who had arrived here not so long ago?

'I wish to see the dance's ending. There is one, is there not?' The Amir leaned closer to her, reaching out a finger to trace it across her bare white neck, then lower, to slip inside and tug a little at the loosely-pinned brocade. 'This is the dance of seduction, for the wedding night of a great lord, yet you perform it here for me . . . I am honoured . . .'

'It is in celebration of the marriage anniversary of *Ya Saiyid*'s parents, Highness.' She bowed her head to hide her hot blushes as the finger traced across the top of one breast, pressing softly but firmly into the flesh.

'And shall I see the ending?'

'*Ya Saiyid*, I have not the courage to finish the dance here . . .'

How could she have humbled herself by admitting her fears to him? What had happened to her in these last few days? She was weak now, gullible, a fool, and she could not resist him. Oh, if he would but forget the dance and take her to his bed again!

'Then we shall finish it elsewhere.'

The Amir rose, at which the entire chamber leapt into movement. Having clapped his hands in dismissal, he stepped down from the dais and, taking Allegra by the hand, led her towards his private quarters, servants scurrying after them. Impatiently, he ordered them away with the wave of his hand and then he was closing the door firmly behind him and standing facing Allegra who was clutching at the fragile brocade, her heart juddering, the breath trapped in little choking bursts in her throat.

'*Ya Saiyid* . . . I . . .'

'Finish the dance. I command you, little scared white dove.'

Hesitantly, biting on her lip, she began to move once more, gyrating, curving her body, shaking her hips, encircling her hands in a twisting movement round her face, swaying her neck to left and right and fluttering her lashes at the Amir who watched, silently, and with the predatory air of a wolf who knows that the lamb will soon tire and drop into its mouth.

With trembling fingers, Allegra reached for the restraining pins, trying to open them without stabbing her fingers, without letting all the material fall in one clumsy swathe. Banging the tambourine above her head, she attempted a mysterious and enticing smile, before trying again to free the pins which had somehow become trapped in the stiff material. Eventually, blushing hotly, she threw the tambourine aside to make an all-out attempt on the pins which were twisted into the fragile threads of the brocade.

Next moment, the Amir himself was feeling for the pins, plucking them free with the panache of a man who undresses exotic dancing girls every night. Shocked at his touch, at his closeness, and at the effect of the fiercely burning ebony eyes staring into hers, Allegra could barely breathe. There was no air. She was going to faint . . . He . . .

The seventh veil, freed of its pins, dropped to the floor in a soft susurration of sound, like the distant, gentle swish of the ocean.

Unable to speak, unable to think, Allegra stood there naked, the soft, plump white curves of her breasts and hips so tempting that any man would need to be a eunuch to resist them. The Amir was not. A hedonist, he was a voluptuary of the highest degree, a debauchee. In Tudor England, he would have been a rake and profligate but here he was a God, living his life as Allah had ordained it, fully supported and revered by his people. Even his slaves appeared to worship him. How could they, when she hated him so much?

The nut-brown hands cupping her breasts made her moan, the sound coming unexpectedly from her lips, surprising her. Ah, he knew what to do to rouse a woman in seconds, and she melted at his caresses. Insistent, his hands swept over her plump flesh so that her entire body tingled as if tiny silver bells were ringing beneath her skin, a thousand of them, a tintinnabulation of joy, of love, of victory . . .

No, not love! She hated him, she hated him! She could never ever love a man like this!

His mouth was jasmine, incense and roses against hers and all the entrancing and magical glories of the East, and she could not resist, nor did she want to . . . Oh, to have the strength to thrust him away, but she was not the same girl who had first come to this palace of indolent enslavement. There was something powerful and intoxicating in the air here, some great enchantment, and she was bewitched by a man whom she knew to be a devil and yet she could not spurn him, nor close her heart to his advances . . .

How lonely she had been, desperately, yearningly lonely and she wanted, needed, strong arms around her, to cosset her, to take away the pain and suffering. It must not matter that he had caused them, for who else did she have now but him? She was his slave in truth.

She was on the broad, silk-clad bed with its looped hangings to keep out flying insects, and he was unhooking the gold cords which would free the curtains to swing down around them so that they were safe inside his silky, scented love nest.

His naked body crushing against hers, she realised that he had removed his clothes but so swiftly and silently that she had not noticed. She was bewitched, entranced, bemused. This man was God, and she was his willing eager minion . . .

Without his ruby-studded *samade* and *aighal*, his thick black hair framed his strong, aristocratic face like a lion's mane. The Lion of Arabia . . . was that not one of his many florid titles? Lord of the Incense Road, Lion of Arabia, yet it was as Prince of Passion, that she knew him . . . His glowing nigrescent eyes transfixed her, caging not only her gaze but her soul, her heart, her very will. Anything he wanted she would give him. Anything.

Again his rose and jasmine-scented mouth enslaved hers, crushing, coaxing, reviving. He was bringing her back from the plains of desolation and grief to the joy of belonging, of hoping. She found herself clinging to him violently, as if she thought one of the ominous guards might burst in and drag them apart, her knees clamping his sides, her lids fluttering. If she died tomorrow, then she would die happy now that he had shown he cared for her.

The harem would not laugh at her anymore. The Amir loved her, he had taken her back into his bed. Now she would be his *odalik*, which was what she wanted more than anything, for the *odalik* was next only to the wife, and so had every opportunity of displacing her. She seethed with furious jealousy whenever she thought of the Lady Khadija Nur, the pampered mother of the Amir's son, for rumour had it that the Amir was delighted with the Prince, and the mother of that Prince. Allegra wanted to tear out the woman's eyes and stamp on them, for *she* wanted to bear the Amir's heir . . . She wanted to recreate here the ways of her own country and have the Amir to herself, bear his sons and make him so content that he did not need the titillation of the other concubines. She knew now that she would succeed.

She had changed, and yet perhaps not. In Cornwall, she had dreamed of marrying, of finding the man she would love for all time. Now she wanted that here, in Arabia, the formation of her own safe, contented and legal little world: her protection and her soul's nourishment.

Nash was being forced to the back of her mind by the need for survival and love. She could not help it, for it must be done. She was thinking and behaving like an Arabian woman because there was no other way to survive here.

'Little passion flower, you were not like this last time . . . you were so cool, so fearful at first . . .' The Amir's eyes burned through her flesh, making her tingle, slowly and luxuriantly, from brow to heel. 'What has changed you in just a few short days?'

'I have not changed, *Ya Saiyid*, I am myself. I was . . . too grief-stricken to respond before.'

'Ah, you cool-hearted ones of *Ingiltarra*, so retiring, hiding so much behind those aloof expressions . . . I should have known . . .' There the Amir halted suddenly, as if breathless for her kisses, and then he clamped her so powerfully into his strong brown arms that she felt helpless with joy.

Was she not a woman after all? Must she always be impervious and indomitable, sturdy and self-supporting? Could she not indulge in blissful moments of loving delight such as this . . . and would the world come to an end if she did?

'Your skin is smooth and shiny like polished silk, and your hair is not oiled . . . No one will know that I have slept with you tonight, for there will be no stain of oil of roses or jasmine on my pillow in the morning . . . Do you not like our custom of oiling the hair? It thickens and improves the condition and . . .'

'Do not speak, *Ya Saiyid*, I beg of you! Make love to me!' Allegra begged, pulling his head down to hers and kissing him rousingly.

'Ah, now we have the truth of it . . . the virgin is a *bintilkha-'ta* at heart . . . Carry on, little *bintilkha'ta* and do what you will to me.'

Allegra did not know the word he used, nor that it was a derogatory term for a woman of low repute, a fallen women, and perhaps she would not have cared had she realised. The barriers of fear and desperation were gone, and she was beginning to live again, because of this quixotic and fascinating man.

Outside, the desert night was becoming colder and darker, the stars flung out in a glorious silver celebration, the moon a curving snowy icicle, lustrous, pearly and mysterious. Desert creatures skittered here and there, or slept in cosy burrows in the deep-dug sand, from which at dawn they would slither, or rattle or scurry their way out to feed. The palms of the nearby oasis were framed against the indigo sky like sternly-hewn ebony, stolid, implacable and enduring, their leaves splayed into hooked, scaly fingers, while below, the water which preserved life in this place, lay silent and black as if it were paralysed into immobility, make-believe water in an enchanted oasis.

Inside, the luxurious chamber was darkening as the untended oil lamps burned low, their pale light dipping so that the curtained bed became shrouded in shadow.

Slow, tender, cajoling kisses were not the Amir's way but on an earlier occasion, for this shy English girl he had made a little gesture, holding himself back as best he could. For a man who had never practised such restraint, he succeeded rather well, but not well enough to prolong the romantic aperitif beyond minutes.

Allegra gasped as he tore into her body with all the vigour and zeal of his Arabian blood. Now there was no holding him back. Over and over he plunged into her, deeper and more urgently, biting at her throat, her lips, so that blood rose to the surface there in scarlet blotches, while he groaned and panted as he increased his speed, no longer seeing the little white face beneath him, the eyes wide and startled, almost mesmerised, the breath stilled in the lungs.

The shrieking sound of a nightbird of prey pierced the steamy, throbbing air. It was a merciless, taunting noise, which meant death to some tiny helpless creature, who, clamped in the bird's beak and struggling fiercely to escape, would slowly become exhausted and then cease to move . . .

The analogy was sharp and clear in Allegra's mind yet she thrust it away, out of sight. Other women had captivated the Amir, and so would she. It could be done. She had heard of concubines who had ousted entire harems because of their own beauty, wit and character. She would do it too, no doubt of that. By tomorrow, he would be hers and she would be safe again, just as in the halcyon days with Nash . . .

Deep into the night they made love in the most ardent and frenzied fashion, Allegra shrinking from some of the more oriental and exotic demands of the Amir and yet wanting to comply even as she said no. In time, she would say yes, she told him, but he must have patience with her for she knew so little and was too young.

'Girls are younger in our country,' she told him, 'they are protected and chaperoned until they marry. Here it seems to be the custom for infants to learn the arts of dancing and coquetry.'

'All the better to please their lord and master,' the Amir grinned, his beautiful unblemished teeth glowing in the dimness. 'Are not the men of your country restless and bored with such unschooled wives?'

'Not in the least.'

'Do they not visit courtesans in secret?'

'If they do, I have not heard of it. Perhaps as wild young men they indulge, but very few do this after they are married and have families.'

'Sons are the greatest comfort and delight, God willing.' The Amir smiled to himself as if he were revelling in some secret glory. 'I have waited many years for a son and now the Lady Khadija Nur has given me my heir.' Slyly he watched Allegra's response, his eyes slanting.

Fury tore down Allegra's veins and whipped through her mind. The Lady Khadija Nur! The newborn heir who should have been hers!

Allegra who had thought that the favourite considered everyone else beneath her and so closeted herself away like some haughty queen, had to rearrange her opinion. Fear of poisoning was what kept the favourite shut away in her own suite of rooms, with her tiny baby son. What a terrible way to exist, to live in fear of one's life . . . but how sensible, for she, Allegra, would be the first to harm the baby infant if the opportunity arose . . .

Shock made her blink. She, harm an infant? What was she thinking of? How could she ever do such a cruel and heartless thing? But to pave the way for her own son, as concubines had done so many, many times before. Could she do it for that? Turning to look at the man lying as if lightly dozing beside her, she pondered on this. He was handsome in a marvellously devilish way, dark, glossy, virile and stunning enough to rob her of breath each time she saw him. She had never known a man with such hard, muscular shoulders, with such a proud and despotic spirit, so confident of his own superiority.

She had come to his palace ready to attack and denounce him for being a vicious, ruthless potentate. Yet, when she had found her worst fears realised, seeing that he had not a scrap of compassion or tenderness in him, she had allowed her emotions to overrule her common sense. Where was her own heart now? In his keeping. That was why she could contemplate poisoning a child to make way for her own. Favouritism was everything here. Everything. The favourite wife. The favourite child. The favourite servant. The favourite slave. She wanted to oust them all, have him all to herself, see his dark eyes brighten for her alone, share his body with no one else, be his Amira, if such a thing were possible, and rule beside him, not be shut away in the scented depths and anonymity of his harem.

The slumbrous dark eyes were open again, his muscular arms reaching out for her. Willingly she went into them, flinging herself against him, holding him tightly, quiescent as the white dove after which they had named her. There would never be a time like this again, so bright and sweet and passionate, but oh how she wished that every night could be the same, in the Amir's arms, crushed against his hard chest, thrilling to his love-making. It must be like this, it must go on for ever. Nothing would make her return to the tedious ennui of her early days here, when she had long, lonely hours to fret and grieve.

Shut out the past, her mind clamoured. Shut out the agony and the loss, make this man love you and all will be well, all will be well.

Nash had always believed that the desert was a lonely place where one might travel for miles and not see another soul, but it seemed that the entire nomadic nation had come out to hamper him. Seeing a camel train's camp fire glowing in the distance, across the landscape of undulating dark-honey dunes, he decided to settle for the night tucked away behind his own mountainous hill. His horse standing exhausted with head lowered, he fed it battered figs and a lump of hard, unleavened bread which the nomad woman had given him, then he munched on a chunk of the same bread, which was as stiff and unyielding as leather parched by the sun.

He had set about disguising himself. If men could turn blue because of the indigo dye of their robes, then he could darken his own skin and his hair, too. Not for the first time he wished that he had black hair, so that he could pass more easily for an Arab. He experimented with dyes, boiling dark berries in the pot which the nomad woman had slung over his arm, and then rubbing the juice into his skin. The result was streaky, but after three applications he was pleased. Now his skin had the appearance of years of having been weatherbeaten and sun-parched. Next, his hair. The berry juice was not so successful there, for the texture of hair is more resistant to primitive natural dyes. Out there, he had little choice, however, and it was only by good fortune that he had found the berries growing at the oasis. It might well be the last oasis he ever saw, for he had tracked his way by the stars, believing that he would be at the Amir's palace by now, yet he was not. He could follow the camel train, which would surely be going in the same direction, yet something made him resist that idea. With one exception, he had always worked alone.

His hair felt stiff and sticky now, oddly thick and heavy upon his head, like black icing, and his skin was taut and stretched. None of this mattered, nor did his parlous state of nourishment. Grit and valour would get him through to his destination, as they had innumerable times before.

Night arrived swiftly, the idyllic cerulean sky darkening as if a black curtain were being pulled across it. Soon came the cold, which made the skin prickle after the relentless heat of the day. Sand was everywhere, in his eyes, his ears, his mouth, collected in every seam and drape of his bernouse, clogged between his toes. All he had to slake his considerable thirst was cactus juice, freed from its fat, dull-green and pulpy shell by the sharp blade of his knife.

Sucking on the juice, wrinkling his nose, he thought of the women whose lives had changed his. Elizabeth, his fair and sweet-natured betrothed, and Allegra, the passionate heart, the one whom he loved and always would, to distraction. He intended to find them both, and buy their freedom with the collection of gems which he had concealed in his boots. They made walking a strange limping affair, but then he was mostly on horseback thanks to his undaunted steed. The gems were too valuable to risk their loss, so what was a little discomfort? The Amir's hunger for slaves was exceeded only by his hunger for jewels and gold, and the ones which Nash would offer him should persuade the most rigid man to accept them in exchange for two women. He had no idea where the Amir would have sent the girls; they might be anywhere, but at least *he* would know, or one of his slave-buyers would know, what had become of two white-skinned women, one with pale yellow hair and one with red-gold tresses.

He had no fears that the Amir would recognise the gems as belonging to his half-sister, for they had only come into the possession of Rouhkia a few hours before she hung them round Nash's neck, a camel train having brought them from some distant land. Rouhkia had spent the day trying them on and delighting in their fabulous beauty.

He would not think of her. The memory was like bitter aloes biting into his soul. More than anything he needed to be free of the frightful female who had tried to subordinate him and who had cared only for her own lascivious physical needs. In England, she would have been burned as a witch, or drowned in some village pond. He shuddered at the recollection of her name. How could a woman be at one and the same time so callous and yet so lustful?

The more autocratic Arabs were like their own desert, blowing hot and cold, their warmth strangely and unexpectedly superseded by chilliness, their pride like ice, their hauteur like flame.

He did not want to think of Rouhkia, her poor, murdered corpse crushing him. He needed silence, oblivion, so he slept curled into a tight ball, his cloak tugged tightly round him to block out the cold.

In his dream there were many voices, some with guttural, lashing tones, others shouting and fierce. Someone was kicking him, boots were stabbing into his back. He leapt awake, covered in icy sweat, to see *Ruala* tribesmen gazing down at him. No noble desert dwellers these; they looked like bloodthirsty freebooters or slave traders. Perhaps they were. Fifteen of them or more. How could he escape such a number? His heart plummeted. Smiling, he began to speak rapidly in Arabic, expecting to see surprise and respect appear on their faces, but it did not. Their leader, a squat and brutal-faced man was dark-skinned, possibly Egyptian. They were not *Ruala* Beduin at all, but in disguise. Had they been *Ruala*, he would have been sipping *kahwe* with them now and parrying offers of young virgin wives.

The leader, accustomed to subservience, bristled at the sight of the straight-backed Arab who showed no sign of respect for him. Growling something to his men, he watched, grinning, as they circled Nash, launching into him with savagely butting boots and fists. His horse was led away, for it looked a good mount despite its owner's obvious poverty, then for good measure they kicked the tall, ill-mannered Arab in the head as he lay sprawled in the sand. It was satisfying to take their venom out on a man, for usually they must expend it upon animals, women and children.

Nash was unconscious long before the final kicks struck his head, his eyes and his senses closing as he saw his horse being led away by a grinning thief. He had tried to launch himself at the man, but there was no strength in his limbs and his back felt as if he had fallen on to rock from a great height. Perhaps they had smashed his spine? It felt as if they had. God! Tears swelled in his eyes as the dawn and the pallid sunlight darkened, his vision darkening with it, until there was nothing, no sound, no movement, no breath, only the bruised and battered body of a Lord Nash Hamilton lying lifelessly in the sand like some stricken Arab peasant who would never walk or see sunlight again.

Chapter Twenty One

So this was what it was like to be possessed by the demon of lust.

Allegra lay on a daybed of scarlet silk embroidered with emerald and gold peacock tails. It was a beautiful object, brought from a far-off land, probably France, which was famed for creating such exquisite furniture. Two weeks had passed since her heavenly night with the Amir and she had also spent the previous night with him. She could think of nothing but him, of his kisses and his lovemaking. She burned with longing for him, her body yielding and moist with desire. She could not bear to hear the name of the Lady Khadija Nur mentioned in her presence, nor did she mingle with the other concubines now. They were not favourites, but she was: chief favourite. From being an *ikbal*, favoured by the Prince, she had risen to being an *odalik*, the one closest to the prince save for his wife.

Save for his wife! How that phrase tortured her, darting in amongst her contented thoughts and making her both restless and uneasy. The Lady Khadija Nur had achieved all that she craved: security, motherhood, the devotion and gratitude of the Amir. It was these last two which she, Allegra, wanted most. Women raised as Muslims might be capable of surviving the insecurity of life with their demanding and self-seeking men, but she could not do it. Greater proofs were needed by her than the knowledge that Adem Ali, the Lion of Arabia and Lord of the Incense Road was sexually roused by her body, for had he not been similarly roused by dozens of others?

What did he care for her feelings, her emotions and her mind? Did he even know that she had a mind, that she could be deeply, irrevocably hurt?

Nash had known and from the first he had tried to protect her. By remaining coolly distant, he had guarded her most of all, but their sojourn on paradise island had destroyed that distance, forcing them into one another's arms. He had been so much more perceptive than she, realising that if they acknowledged their feelings for each other then it would mean disaster. Yet it need not have been disastrous but for Adem Ali's slave dealers!

Tears pearling her cheeks, she brushed them away furiously. Weep for Nash, a man whom she would never see again, melt at the memories of his blazing yet tender kisses, his ardent, scintillating embraces? She must not do it. She must vanquish her memories of him and cleave unto what she had been given by God, or by Allah, the deity who was worshipped in this pagan land; she still could not believe that they were one and the same. She must strive for the accepting fatalism of the Muslims here, for she had noticed very early on that the happiest slaves were those who had adapted to the Muslim way of life. Even Hafez, once a Frenchman he said, had adopted the creeds of Allah and the Prophet Mohammed as his.

The tears were persistent, and she could not understand why she was shedding them. She had not asked them to come, nor had she received warning of them. Last night, in the heat and passion of the Amir's attentions she had felt like a princess, so important, so favoured, so appreciated, only to find, within a few hours of leaving him, that all the reassurance had fled. She did not know what he did while she was in the harem, and she did not possess the authority or the courage to intrude on his private hours. Besides, she might fall from his favour for ever if she became so intrusive. Muslim wives were obedient, subservient and pampering. They did not accuse, question or berate their men. Ah, if she lived to be eighty years of age, could she assume such long-suffering behaviour and smile sweetly along with it?

Sometimes she felt more of a pagan than the women with whom she shared the harem. They were not Christians, and yet they exhibited more self-control, more obsequiousness than she could ever muster. She knew what she wanted and needed; it was her nature to take these things, and yet she had not known, until she fell in love so ardently with Nash that she could hurt a loved one to achieve her own desires.

'Never have I touched such soft white skin,' the Amir had said, stroking her thighs. 'Your hair is slippery as silk and your mouth is warm as sunshine. Was there not some man in your own country who wished to make you his bride?'

'No, *Ya Saiyid*,' she had whispered, her heart pounding as the strong brown hands caressed her limbs, stroking so persuasively, so coaxingly.

'I find this impossible to believe in one so rarely beautiful, Allegra. Even your name is fragrant and lively as a flower . . . Never have we failed to select a fresh name for a new arrival in the harem, yet yours was so attractive I let you keep it. Allegra . . . how it dances on the tongue!'

Blushing with pleasure, Allegra thought of all the long years that she had despised her name, thinking it silly and affected when she would rather have a queenly name like Elizabeth or Anne. Now, for the first time in her life, she began to like Allegra, and accept it.

'And I am grateful, *Ya Saiyid*, eternally grateful. If you had taken my very name from me, then I would have been so bereft. As it is, I find it difficult to remember who I am at times, so much has happened.'

'You are not sad any more?' The glittering basilisk gaze penetrated deep into her soul.

'No, *Ya Saiyid*, hardly at all now. Sometimes, when I think of my loved ones, then I am sad, but so much time has passed and one cannot grieve for ever.' Was this truly Allegra Pentrevick speaking, she who had been so proud of her heritage and her family?

The Amir's highly skilled hands were reaching higher now, palming the tenderest and milkiest flesh inside her upper thighs, gently slipping his fingers through the pelt of redly-gilded hair between them. It made every nerve tingle, acute little shocks of delicious delight spearing her. He knew well how to rouse her, and it never failed. As her mouth opened to gasp, he clamped his lips to hers and there was no more breath for words.

He made love savagely and impatiently, catching her up and suspending her in his fury so that she could not fail to respond. It was to be compared with watching lightning strike, with seeing the torrid golden kaleidoscope of jagged light arcing to the earth and being speared by it, stabbed, trapped, set aflame. There was a violent primitive power unleashed during their love-making which sometimes alarmed her. How far could it go; what would happen to them if they both lost control?

When she tried to watch the Amir out of the corner of her eye, he seemed to know, even though he was transported in a delirium of passion. That in itself was unnerving.

He spoke to her in Arabic during the heights of their love-making, words which were so rapidly spoken that she could not catch them. Hafez had been teaching her more words and phrases in Arabic. Apart from the difficulty in pronouncing these in the required way, she was delighted at the speed in which she learned them. Arabic, like its religion, and its society, seemed geared to the male, for the rapidly-spoken guttural and hissing language was far from feminine. She had learned how to say simple words, Thank you, please, and such like, and she wanted to repeat carefully memorised phrases to the Amir, to surprise him. She wanted to say, 'I shall not forget your kindness for the rest of my life,' or 'I offer myself to you with all my heart,' or 'I cannot refuse you anything,' for such willing words of self-offering were, she knew, what the Amir most wanted to hear.

Sweat beading his dark skin like tiny topaz droplets, the Amir had grinned at her, speaking more slowly in Arabic.

'*Inshal'la bshûfak 'an karîb* . . . I hope I shall see you again soon, little passionate white dove?'

'*Fi akrab wakt inshal'la*,' Allegra had whispered, her cheeks rosy red, for she had been waiting for just that phrase so that she could reply with, 'Very soon, please God.'

Shivering, her tears forgotten, she wrapped herself round with her arms. He was a perplexing, complex man, her Amir, his mood changes as swift and startling as the desert which he considered his own. One moment, hot and arid, dazzling day, and then, within seconds, the sweeping, chilly shadow of night.

She had been fastening her rose-pink silk robe, a loose garment in the style of a hoodless bernouse, when he had spoken to her from the luxurious state of his great scarlet bed.

'You will learn to love my country,' he said, the nigrescent eyes scouring every part of her yet revealing nothing in their turn. 'You will learn to cherish the heat and the lack of water, even the choking red dust and the sand underfoot. You will dream of mirages and oases and you will not know the difference between them . . . The palms and the beasts of burden, the shimmering pools and the parched ferns desperate for water yet managing to survive year after year, all these will become dear to your heart so that, one day, you will forget where you came from, and how. Then you will know that you belong here, and you will be happy to die here.'

'There are many things which – which fill me with fear,'

Allegra had stammered, unable in the aftermath of such torrid passion to conceal her acute vulnerability.

'You will grow to love them all, white dove, that I promise you, as others have done.'

In one leonine, sinuous movement, the Amir was out of the bed and standing beside her, his glowingly healthy dark bronze body looking almost negroid beside her own pearly white skin.

'We are perplexing to Christians, that I know from my own experiences, for we can be autocratic and changeable as the desert winds, yet am I not human beneath it all?'

She had gazed up at him, into those shuttered ebony eyes and ached to see what was in his mind, but to no avail. He was the Lion of Arabia, the Lord of the Incense Road, the great and terrible Amir Adem Ali, and he had never had to answer to any man, let alone any woman.

'When my forefathers built this palace, they wished to make it the most beautiful and illustrious royal residence in my country. It took many moons to erect, the work went on and on, and all of it was done by Christian slaves brought here specially for the purpose, so you see we know much about the ways of the *nasrani*.'

'Why Christian, *Ya Saiyid*?'

'Do you not think it is fitting that Christians should bend their knee in labours dedicated to the Faithful? Is not Allah greater than Christ who was only His prophet?'

'Christ was Allah's prophet?' Allegra's voice faltered. What did he mean? She did not know that Jesus was considered to be one of Allah's prophet messengers, in much the same way as Mohammed, only to a lesser degree.

'He was, and so it was fitting that those who are of less importance spent their hours toiling for those who are greater, and shall ever be greater unto the ends of the world.' The Amir's eyes glittered fanatically. 'It was also thought suitable that those Christian slaves who died during the building of my palace should be plastered into its walls, a fitting tribute to Allah and a memorial to the feebleness of the Infidel . . .'

Allegra had gone pale, her stomach churning. Christian slaves plastered into these very walls! How could anyone have done such a terrible thing?

She must have voiced her words, for the Amir, gripping her by the shoulders, fixed her with his arid gaze.

'Not *anyone*! My ancestors, the Amirs who have ruled in this land for centuries, great and worthy men famed for their wisdom and their benevolence . . . They have brought my land out of the ignorance of the dark centuries and turned it into a land where men may flourish and wax fat . . . There are no poor here now, as there were before my family acceded. There are hospices and homes for the sick, places where women may bear children in comfort and ease. I have eradicated all fevers and deformities, bringing fresh water even to the villages in the most far-flung areas, and physic and healing with them. The people love me, they *love* me!' The Amir's fingers were pincers and she forced herself not to cringe. 'The sacrifice of the slaves who built this palace made all this possible . . . Blood sacrifice, dozens of them, to ensure that my house endures unto eternity, *Inshal'lah! Inshal'lah!*'

Then, the fanaticism was gone, his face gentle again, or as gentle as the Lion of Arabia's features could ever be, and he was crushing her in his arms for one last, lingering kiss before showing her to the door where a black eunuch waited to escort her back to her new suite.

That was where she was now, the favoured one, in her new quarters, a beautiful, white-walled living chamber hung with glorious scarlet, jade and deep gold carpets from the Orient, the shutters flung wide on to a tiny, exquisitely-pretty walled garden where brilliant blossoms flourished miraculously in the stifling heat. There were miniature palms, herb bushes, fruit trees and bright red blooms which looked exactly like Cornish roses, but surely they could not grow in this parched climate?

The tiles on the floor were bright lozenges of gold and delicate jade green, and the furniture comprised the elegant French daybed, a fragile table and stool carved ornately in a trellis-worked design, a bench of dark-honey wood, whose fragrance clung invitingly to the clothes, and the ubiquitous assortment of gleaming lamps and incense braziers. What was more, she now had her own personal servants, Ika, a young girl who obeyed her every word, and one devoted black eunuch who flung himself at her feet as if she were a goddess.

When he had first done that, she could not conceal her laughter. Clamping a hand over her mouth, she tried to look innocent, not that the man seemed offended. Far from it. He looked up, grinning broadly too. She was to find in the following weeks, that his notion of reverence was to emulate the mood of his mistress. When Allegra laughed, he laughed, when she looked sad, so did he; when she brushed away what she hoped was a secret tear, then he would look about to burst with sorrow. His name was Gazir and he had been a eunuch from the age of six, so he was on the heavy side, with a high-pitched voice, and passionately fond of dazzling colours.

Allegra responded with heartfelt delight, indulging Gazir's predilections. Now that she was a chosen one, with greater importance than her sisters in concubinage, she did not have to mingle with the others if she did not wish it, nor did she have to submit to orders. It was deemed now that she knew everything necessary, else how would she have caught the eye of their master? Along with the greater, yet still very limited freedom, went a larger purse. When merchants arrived with their goods, these would be brought in to Allegra by the eunuchs so that she might examine them and select what she desired. There was no hindrance in this; she could have whatever she wished and all would be paid for by the Amir.

'*Ya Saiyid* loves to play Sultan,' Husaina had whispered one day when Allegra declared that she could not spend so much money that did not belong to her. 'Indulge him, white dove, and he will be delighted.'

So Allegra selected delicate silks with which to make a new dancing costume, and slippers with curled-up toes which had come from Baghdad, and lengths of material for Ika and Gazir to make into clothes for themselves. For Gazir, there would be baggy *shalwar* in bright apricot, the very same colour as the fruit when ripe, and a sash of grape-purple, a turban of purple and apricot design, the colours interwoven like creeping vines.

For Ika, as well, there was to be something different. Having been raised from birth in the harem, she had seen virtually all that the known world had to offer, coconuts from that land where all the natives were black and shiny; scented carved boxes of sandalwood; elephants' tusks, huge, white and curving; fragile porcelain from Cathay; musk, ambergris, gold, frankincense and myrrh, so ancient and biblical to Allegra, and yet a part of everyday life to these people in the Amir's household.

The beauty of almond and citrus trees with their dark green sturdy little leaves, and the glorious riot of hues in Allegra's walled garden, these alone stirred the senses and yet it would seem that everything here was sensuous, exotic and worthy of its part in a great fable.

So what could she give the shy and obedient Ika, who was diligent, patient and loyal? She could not ask her, for Ika spoke only half a dozen words of English, taught to her by Husaina so that she could communicate with her new mistress, and Allegra's Arabic was still limited. In increasing number she found those phrases, 'As Allah wills it', 'So be it, for that is Allah's will', and 'As the Lord God Allah decrees', increasingly useful. Having found just how limited her Arabic was, she could at least pronounce these words and not only placate her listeners but express her own feelings of frustration in a way which was acceptable to all Muslims. If she clenched her hands, and gritted her teeth when she spoke these words, no one seemed to notice.

The gift for Ika proving evasive, Allegra decided that she would delay the pursuit. Something was bound to appear in due course. How could it not when treasures were being delivered to the palace constantly?

Three days had passed since then and she was not summoned to the Amir's bed. Had she not experienced her reactions to this, then she could never have described them. She had not known that the woman she now was existed; she had been, so she thought, carefully raised, well tutored, indoctrinated in the imperative tenets of the Christian religion. Surely any one of these should have been a protection against her present anguish? Yet, as time passed, she could not pray to Jesus and the Holy Family in this forsaken Muslim palace; it was as if there was a vast, thick and impenetrable barrier between her and Heaven.

Tormented inwardly, she could speak of it to no one, but she could babble on to Ika, who could not understand.

'You do not comprehend the agony I'm suffering!' Allegra said to her one morning. 'I am tormented and yet no one knows it, they all think that I am the favourite, that the Amir cherishes me and so I shall never be sad or lonely again. Certes, if his eye fell on you, Ika, you would be overjoyed, would you not? One night with him and you would ask for no more, that is true, is it not?'

Ika, who was stitching sequinned buttons onto a tiny bolero for her mistress, smiled and nodded as if she could comprehend, but all that she had understood was her name.

How could these women be so easily satisfied that one night with their lord and master would be the answer to their life's amibition? Ika was pretty and sweet-faced, small-boned, a little on the slender side for Arab taste yet so graceful and feminine. Why had she not risen above being a hand-maiden, to become the *mahbûb*, the beloved of the Amir?

Oh, this speculation was unfathomable. Why was she doing it?

'Ika, would you please fetch me some *kahwe*?' Allegra made a gesture to indicate the blowing on and sipping of a steaming liquid, and Ika, beaming, ran to obey.

The moment that Ika had left the beautiful chamber, Allegra felt nervous. There was something about this apartment which made her uneasy, a restless ambience in the air. Now that the Amir had told her so proudly of the Christian slaves whose corpses were plastered into the palace walls and foundations, she thought of them often. It was to be expected. How could a girl raised to be pious put aside such thoughts? Sometimes she dreamed of the men, seeing their limp white bodies being jammed into the palace walls as they were built, the glutinous white plaster being packed around them so that they were, literally, walled in. Holy Saints, but she hoped that they had been dead and had not died of suffocation! Something told her that some were far from dead and she would wake from a nightmare, imagining a skeletal, screaming face thrusting into hers. Once, the face was Elizabeth's and she wept for her lost sister, and the fate which had befallen them both. If she had arrived here sooner, she could have saved her life! Destiny. The Arabic for it was *nasîb*, but it did not sound as portentous and important as the English word.

Ika was back with the steaming, richly-brown coffee, its grounds thick and sandy in the base of the porcelain dish. There were tiny, almond-flaked cakes, gluey with sticky sugar, and sweetmeats made of almonds, figs, apricots and honey which she pushed aside. How the Arabs loved their sweetmeats.

What if the Amir did not send for her tonight? The thought cut into her mind so that her enjoyment of the rich, dark coffee faded, to be replaced by an icy chill. That was her worst fear, that he would tire of her, that she would have to return to the harem and become ordinary once more. If she did not become with child, then it was a possibility. Only those who bore sons were truly secure in this ruthless Muslim world. The Lady Khadija Nur would never have to worry again, nor have a sleepless night filled with frightening dreams, for she had a healthy son and the rumour was already circulating that she was expecting another child.

If Allegra had seen the favourite wife in the flesh, she could not have borne it. These separate quarters suited her ideally. She could forget that the Lady Khadija Nur existed, except when gossip reached her ears via Husaina or Hafez, both of whom she had repeatedly told that she did not wish to hear of the Amir's wife. They seemed to delight in bringing up her name, and saying how well she was, and how beautiful, strong and vigorous was her infant son, the Amir's heir.

Allegra clutched her fingers together, the coffee forgotten, the tray slipping to one side of her knee. She feared that she was barren, for she had made love so many times with Nash and now she was sharing the Amir's bed frequently, yet she had not conceived. She remembered how difficult it had been for Nash to take her maidenhead and she could not help but wonder if there was something else that was different about her: something more seriously wrong.

No, she must not think these crushing thoughts! She must concentrate on the bliss she had shared with the Amir, and give thanks for the good fortune which had already befallen her. He was fascinated by her, that she could see, and he had given her an apartment of her own, with unlimited luxuries. She could have anything she wanted, rich robes, silks and velvets, rubies and pearls, gold bangles and exotic, priceless scented oils and unguents to beautify her body and her hair. If she wished, she could spend all day practising her dancing while the musicians played for her. No doubt the starved and the ragged in the streets of every Arabian town and city would have given their hearts for such a life of indolence and hedonism, yet, without her loved ones, it was dross.

She would rest now, in readiness for the night. If he summoned her, then she would miss most of her sleep. Pray God that she did not have the nightmare again, nor see the hideous, suffocated corpses rising up to greet her in her dreams.

The beggar was tall yet he walked as if his spine were weak, with a strange hunching, limping movement, head bent low, his hood pulled down over his forehead. There was an excellent reason for this: his boots were crammed with jewels. Why they were there, he did not know, so his jaw had dropped when he discovered them. Staring at their brilliant, glittering beauty, he had racked his brains to remember where he had got them. Had he killed someone to steal them, or had he been taking them somewhere in secret for someone, his master perhaps? Rubies, emeralds, pearls, amethysts, citrines, diamonds, black pearls, pink and white pearls, sapphires, matchless, radiant and priceless.

Nash had been subsisting in the desert for some weeks now, ever since recovering consciousness. Bruised, aching and with a bloody head wound, he had woken to the world of the newborn child, knowing nothing, recalling nothing. Why he was there, who he was, and where he was going, these were just three of the questions which tormented him.

To live, he trapped and killed snakes, rats, lizards, birds, any creature which came into his view. For water, there was the sweetish-acrid cactus juice, or occasionally a low and sandy pool of water. Something told him that he had survived like this before, for he knew instinctively what to do. He was familiar with the desert, its changes of mood, its callousness, and its benevolence to those who understood and accepted its foibles.

His head wound was slow to heal and he had no water in which to bathe it until the third day, and then the amount of congealed blood which ran from the gash filled him with dismay. Now he could feel the jagged pulpy edges of the wound which was so deep that one finger disappeared into it when held lengthways.

At least the robbers had not stolen his bernouse, for which he thanked God. After he had washed the head wound, he noticed that there were streaks of white on his hands where the water had rubbed away some of the dye which was making him look brown. He could not see his hair, yet a closer inspection of the blood which had run into a sandy gummy pool revealed to him that it was too dark a brown for all of it to be blood. Dye . . . some sort of dark dye! But why had he done that? Why try to make his hair and skin look browner?

The unrelenting sun, the fine dusty drifts of sand which filled his mouth and nose and throat, the aching spine and limbs from trudging through the slipping, shifting sand, any one of these would have been more than enough on its own account. He found his mind filled with images as he tramped along, platters of steaming roast meat, juicy, dripping fruits, jugs of fresh frothing milk, of thirst-quenching ale and sparkling, icy water from the spring. There was a reassuring, familiar feeling along with these images: these were foods and drinks which he knew very well indeed, from somewhere, some place which he could not name.

Intead of the succulent roasts and creamy puddings, he was forced to dine on crisp-coated locusts, which settled during a stately fly-past. Having made a tiny fire with dried sticks, ferns and bracken, ignited by sparks from the friction of twisting and rubbing two sticks together (and how very long it took!) he roasted the locusts in the feeble flames, gently adding tiny fragments of anything handy which looked as if it might burn, sniffing the air as the insects crackled and heated. They smelt like strong green vegetables cooking, and he fell on them when he deemed that they were ready. There was nothing satisfying about their taste, no suggestion of meat or tender flesh, and yet he was so ravenous that he crunched and chewed them rapidly until none were left.

Lying in the sand afterwards, deep in a gulley which would provide some protection for the night, he wrapped his bernouse tightly around himself like a winding sheet and gazed up at the stars. This was not the first time that he had done this, he could tell, for he was familiar with the shape and design of the skies. He knew those stars intimately; he had navigated by them for years. Navigated! That word had dropped into his mind unheralded. So he was a sailor of some sort? Yet if so, why was he here in this desert, as far from the oceans as it was possible to be?

The stars throbbed and evanesced with spangled silver light. They were guides for the sailor, the traveller. Men tracked by the stars, braved the wild seas . . . Ah if only he could remember more, but he could not. The sudden tingling chill of a desert night was encapsulating him. Pulling the bernouse closer, he tucked in his head and searched for sleep.

Chapter Twenty Two

There would be no gift for Ika. The girl had complained of a pain in the head, vomited, and then begun to burn with fever. By nightfall she was dead. It was so shocking and so sudden that Allegra could not take it in. Her dear little Ika, so sweet, so willing, who had served her devotedly for nearly two months now, ever since she had been given her new chambers.

Husaina came, leaning on her stick, her face grave.

'The child showed no sign of any sickness, yet she is dead. *Mashallah!* So be it.'

'The will of Allah, is that what you say?' Allegra clenched her hands. 'Yet she was so young and healthy.'

'You speak suspiciously. Do you suggest she was fed some poison? It has been known, and there is much jealousy of the favourite.'

'Even jealousy of her servants?' Allegra was trying to analyse what Husaina had said. *Poison?*

'Yes, even that. You showed great favour to the girl, that you were happy with her services. There are many who would be angry and jealous of that.'

'I thought . . . when I was told that the Lady Khadija Nur kept herself to herself that it was only because she thought herself too good to mix with the underlings . . . Does she fear poison, too?' Allegra already knew the answer to this question.

'*Allâhu il'alîm!* She does. Just a grain or two of it and her son would be dead and so would she.'

'Could you not have warned me?' Allegra reproached, tears flooding her eyes. How often she had considered poisoning her rival, yet never understood that someone might wish to harm her or her servants.

'Allah, I did not think it would happen to you or yours!' The old woman looked deeply offended.

'No, no, of course you did not. Forgive me, Husaina, forgive me!' Allegra wiped away her tears.

If she could recall any Christian prayers to say for Ika then she would say them. The girl had died because she was the handmaiden of the Amir's favoured concubine, so she must blame herself for the tragedy. It was all her fault, all of it. Something terrible and destructive had been set in motion when her sister was abducted by the slavers . . . Nothing had gone right since, everything was going wrong, becoming twisted and inverted. Even that which she held dearest to her heart had been snatched away from her, and now that she had the Amir's attentions, she dreaded losing them in the same way.

Her very own pretty little maid-in-waiting poisoned! She flung her head into her hands. Of what value were riches and comforts when death came so arrogantly and took away the sweetest ones?

That night in the Amir's arms, she tried to forget the tragedy but it was impossible. Adem Ali knew what had happened. It seemed that there were no secrets in the Palace. He was shocked, yet apparently unsurprised. It had happened before, two years ago, he said, when his then favourite had died suddenly, after constant vomiting for two days. Since then, more care had been taken, and greater protection given to his loved ones.

'What care have you been taking of me, *Ya Saiyid*?' Allegra cried, knowing that she sounded petulant yet unable to help herself. 'It might have been me who took the poison and died! What would you have done then?'

To her dismay, he grinned, his eyes glittering. Was he thinking of the concubine who would replace her? Perhaps he already had his eyes on another girl . . . Her heart dropped, her stomach churned, and she tried to tug away from his embrace.

'Not so fast, white dove. Had you died, then I would have grieved deeply. That is the truth, I swear it in the name of Allah, the all-merciful. Who else dares to answer me back like you do? Who else insults me so successfully? Life would be tedious without my fiery little dove . . .' Gently he kissed the tip of her nose.

Placated, she sighed into his arms, resting her head on his hard brown shoulder, and soon he was moving on top of her, scything between her thighs and piercing deep into her moist body. Groaning with delight, she gave herself up to his passionate love-making, arching her hips and clutching at his hair.

How the Amir loved her vibrant response! Once he had heard a fool saying that all women were the same when the lamp was put out, but he could never agree. There were quiet, plump women from Turkey, who, despite their weight, could dance most seductively, and shy young slave girls from Cathay, with slanting eyes and skins the colour of pale gold; temptresses from Circassia, with white skins and patrician features; ebony-dark natives from Africa, with long, long slender limbs and enormous dark eyes. Some had silky hair, and some crisp curls; others shining tresses straight and long;

yet others thick, fluffy hair which settled like a cloud around their faces. How he adored them all!

There was an old saying: Mingle the arrogance and breeding of the Arab with the passion and intelligence of a slave girl and you will create the perfect son. If Allah was beneficent, this Christian girl would bear him a son, too, for the death of Ika had brought home to him yet again how swiftly life could be swept away. A man needed more than one heir; he needed six, seven or more, to ensure that if one died, there would always be a replacement. He was doing his utmost to right that situation.

That night, the Amir made love to Allegra three times. It was ecstasy beyond her dreams. She could not believe it when he barely paused after his crisis, continuing to kiss and fondle her, and thrust deeper inside her. Making tiny whimpering noises, she tossed her head from side to side, opening and closing her hands.

That night was the happiest since she had been brought to the harem. She slept beside the Amir whose love-making had eradicated her distress over Ika's death, and when he pushed her from the bed at dawn, she salaamed in the most subservient Arabic manner before hurrying to her own chamber to sleep for the next few hours.

There was to be no peace again. Husaina came into her chamber as she was sipping *narguile* and eating honeyed cakes for breakfast.

'A terrible thing has happened. It is hard to think that it was Allah's will and yet it must be.'

'*Mashallah*,' echoed Allegra drolly.

'The Amir's sister has died in the most terrible circumstances.' The old woman's voice trembled and tears slipped down her brightly rouged cheeks. 'It is family tragedy of the most dreadful and heartshaking kind and it will have to be kept quiet . . . Oh, how could he do such a thing?'

'Who has done what?'

'The husband of the Amir's sister . . . a weak and stupid man. He took it upon himself to sentence her to death for committing adultery. It is the usual punishment. Oh the shame of it upon the head of *Ya Saiyid*!'

'It is?' Allegra's brows rose.

'Yes. He carried out the sentence himself, with his own hand. Had she been any other then people would have said, "So be it, it is the will of Allah," but the Amir's own dear half-sister . . . He was very fond of her, even though they were only half-brother and sister. He showered her with gifts and jewels . . . He dreamed of her having a child and his becoming a beloved uncle. Ah, but it was not to be!'

'*Mashallah*,' Allegra echoed again. She did not think that she could bear any more news of death and tragedy.

'He will not get over this easily, white dove. He will need much comforting. You will cheer him best by getting yourself with child . . .'

The colour burst into Allegra's cheeks. Unseeing, she looked down at her breakfast.

'Now do not look so shy. I speak the truth. You would be wise to get yourself with child.'

'A son, of course!'

'*Aiwa*, of course!'

Allegra had expected general mourning, prayers and some sort of memorial ceremony for the Amir's dead sister, but there was nothing that resembled the Christian rituals. What had happened truly was the will of Allah, fate, destiny, and one did not berate the Lord God for carrying out His will. He knew best.

The Amir seemed morose, unable to accept the fact that he would never be an uncle now. Husaina's admonition rang in Allegra's ears as she tried to cheer her lover that night. If only she could have told him that she was expecting a child, but there was no sign, no sign at all.

'Guests will be arriving in a few days, Allegra,' the Amir said suddenly, his dark eyes bleak. 'Would you dance for them? They are very important to me . . . I wish to impress them and ensure that they have an enjoyable stay here.'

'They are eunuchs?'

'Eunuchs? Allah, of course not!'

'Yet you will let them see me?'

'It would be foolish to hide such an accomplished dancer, do you not agree?'

'But I dance for you, lord, not for other men, certainly not for strangers!'

'I know. But you will do this to please me will you not? They will be delighted with your performance and I want them to be very happy. Afterwards, if they wish to spend some more time in your company, then you may stay with them. It will not be forbidden.'

'Stay with them? What do you mean? Will you not be there, *Ya Saiyid*?'

'I shall leave early. You may do as you please. Keep them happy. As I said, they are very important men.'

Tears were rolling down Allegra's cheeks. Now she knew what he meant. He was weary of her; he would order her to sleep with his guests, to please them!

'You are cruel to me! How can you offer me to other men? It is against your custom! I shall not do it, I shall *not*!' Bunching her fists, she beat him about the neck and chest.

'I am too sad to argue tonight. You are gazing upon one who will never be an uncle. Can you not find compassion in your heart for this heartbroken man?'

'What of me, lord, what of me? I am no harlot, I am your devoted mistress . . . Tell another girl to entertain these important guests!'

'You. It must be you. Would you disobey me, your prince, your master?'

'If you make me do this then you are not fit to be my master, not fit, not fit, I tell you! I shall kill myself first!'

'Your heart is ice, white dove. You do not care for me but only for yourself. Leave me now. I commmand it.'

Stunned, Allegra obeyed, sobs racking her breast. Why had he said this, to hurt her so much? Now she could not comfort him for she was in terror. He was tired of her. He was going to give her to his guests . . . She would have no say in it and what would become of her when they had used her body?

'Lord, please do not make me do it, I beg!' Sinking to her knees at the side of the Amir's bed, she sobbed out her entreaty.

'Leave me. I said leave me! I wish to be alone. Tonight I am a man of sorrow. Go!'

*

Arab poets have been known to refer to the desert night as the lover, but there was nothing lovely or loving about the nights the amnesiac was spending as he attempted to navigate himself out of the desert's cruel heart. He knew, most powerfully, that he should have been able to employ those lucid, beckoning stars to guide himself to his destination; at times, the memory would be so overwhelming that he was sure he had remembered who he was and where he was going, and then there was nothing save blankness.

Half way to sleep, verses would dance into his mind, where from he did not know.

'*My spirit's nightingale will find the vales of Paradise a cage.*

'*Unless therein the vision of the Beauty shall delight its stay.*

'*How shall the uninformed perceive what satisfaction love affords?*

'*For love, with all its agonies, to base men seems a trifling play.*

'*Oh Seyhi, give up chasing midges, hunt the mighty falcon down!*

'*To those whose zeal soars heavenward the world itself's a paltry prey.*'

Seyhi. That was the name of the author of those verses. He had remembered it. His friend Abdullah's favourite poet, Seyhi, who had died in the early fifteenth century, having been born and educated in Kutahya, in north-western Anatolia, had been a student of medicine, and eventually become physician to the Bey of Germiyan and afterwards to Mehmet I . . . All of this he could recall, sharply, brightly, as if he had just come from the poet's school. Abdullah, his friend, the one who had taught him how to speak Arabic. When and where?

It was no good. His head was splitting and the stars taunting in their ebullient light. Clamping his eyes shut, he searched for sleep. What came instead was the memory of love. Rich, warm, rewarding, surely the reason for living? Life was brittle, sour and futile without love; yes, he could recall that fact and know it to be true.

'*How shall the uninformed perceive what satisfaction love affords?*'

So he was not uninformed. He knew what satisfaction love afforded. But how, and with whom?

Oh God, and all His Saints, why was he here? Why, *why*?

Ika's graceful little ghost seemed to haunt Allegra's chambers flitting here and there just out of the corner of her eye. There had been something about the slave girl which reminded her of her sister Elizabeth. That was why she had taken to her so swiftly, warmed to her and felt at ease in her company even though they could barely communicate. After so many years being a sister, it was impossible to think like an only child, if indeed she wished to do that. She was accustomed to having Elizabeth nearby, sitting with her embroidery, or riding on the wild moors swept by the sea mists and the hurling rain, exchanging gossip, discussing the latest modes, wondering what their father would do next, and quarrelling mildly on occasion.

Three weeks had dragged clumsily by and the Amir had not sent for her, yet she knew that she could break her head against the wall and scream and smash every ornament and piece of furniture in her apartment and no one would listen to her unless *he* commanded it.

Each hour, heavy, suffocating, was a crushing burden. She wanted to run from her rooms, flee outside into the open air, find a horse and ride out onto the blissfully rainswept moors of Cornwall, but there was nothing beyond these whitewashed walls except sand and yet more sand.

The view from her window, which had seemed so pretty, so perfect, now mocked her every time she glanced at it. She was not allowed to walk in the miniature walled garden, and her request that she should was met with shocked looks.

The garden, she learned, was private and belonged to the Lady Khadija Nur. When she was resident in this section of the palace, she had used that garden daily in which to exercise.

'Then why am I forbidden to do the same?' Allegra cried.

'Because it is the Lady Khadija Nur's garden and she may one day wish to walk there again,' Husain explained.

'Do you think that my presence will defile the air or the

ground? That is nonsense! She need not know that I have ever been in it.'

'She will know.'

'*How* will she know?'

'Her servants will tell her. Servants gossip, it is their nature. There will be talk of trespass and intrusion. The Amir will be furious and we shall all be disgraced for allowing it.'

'Then let me ask the Amir myself!'

'When next he summons you, then you will be able to ask him, will you not, white dove?' Husaina's earrings jangled.

'I want to see him now!'

'That will not be possible. *Ya Saiyid* will decide when he wishes to see you. That is the custom. That is how it is done here and always has been done.'

'Yes, I know. *Mashallah*, etc, etc!' Allegra swung on her heel, anger tearing through her body. What now? Oh Jesu, what now?

'Gazir cares for you well?' Husaina was staring at Allegra, thinking that she looked thinner and pale. This incarceration did not suit all women. Some grew buxom and smugly contented, others pallid and sharp. If the latter with this favourite, then she would soon be ousted by some wide-hipped, large-breasted slave, or one of the Orientals who were on their way now in a shipment from Cathay.

Husaina was extremely fond of the English girl, and felt sorry for her, but there was nothing she could say or do without being disloyal to her master, to whom she owed everything, all duty, all loyalty, all favour, all devotion. When she became too infirm to continue as mistress of the slaves, the Amir, Allah guard and nourish his soul, would send her to Aniyan, to the comfortable house which he had built for his retired servants: the most faithful ones, that is. Men spoke with fear and dread of the Amir, and she knew that he had done some terrible things in his time, truly dreadful and savage, but a man could not be Lord of the Incense Road and Lion of Arabia without being a strong commander. Had he shown weakness, then all would have crumbled and he would have been assassinated, his estates, his treasures, slaves and the entire harem misappropriated by someone else.

Better the devil you know . . .

'Husaina, do you not hear me? I said that Gazir is an excellent servant. He seems to know what I will ask for next before I speak. It is a little scary at times.'

'A good servant is always in tune with his master or mistress. You have been fortunate, white dove.'

'But for Ika dying . . .'

'That could have been you, white dove. Allah is watching over you, and so you live while the feeble one dies in your stead.'

'She was not feeble!'

'She failed to attract *Ya Saiyid*!' Husaina wrinkled her nose. A little rouge had gone astray and half of her nose was crimson, the other its natural brown colour. The carmine on her lips was crookedly applied, too. She was getting old, her hands were shaky.

'Ah, that would mean that she was feeble, of course! Any girl who cannot captivate a man, let alone the great Lord of the Incense Road and the Lion of Arabia, must indeed be feeble.'

'You have so much to learn, white dove. At times, you seem to be one with us and then suddenly, *shî 'ajîb*, you are so *inglîzi* again, just like that, like the desert lightning which strips the palms.'

It did not need a sharp observer to see that, Allegra thought, bowing her head. What did they expect, that she speak fluent Arabic and convert to Islam? She had been here less than a year, and at times it had seemed as if each month were twelve. She tried to count up the months, finding to her dismay that she could not recall the number. What had happened to her? What month had she arrived here, and how long ago was it? When she asked Husaina, all she got was Arabic names for the seasons and no more, for the old woman did not know the English versions.

It had been spring in Cornwall when she had set sail with Nash, and now it was . . . That was the trouble. The seasons here bore no similarity to those in England. Here there was no limpid, showery spring with sparkling bursts of crystalline sunshine, no summer that was blazing hot and shivering breeze by turn, no crisp, orange, gold and russet autumn, nor frosty, snow-spangled winter when there was little point in doing anything save sitting before a roaring fire to toast one's toes and sip a mug of mulled wine spiced with cinnamon.

Here, it was always chokingly arid, dustily dry, the air parched and the sun bleaching. At night, it went cold with the force of a northern winter and stabbed into the bones, making the flesh tingle strangely after the exhausting heat of the day, while there seemed to be no differentiation between the months. Husaina said that there would be rain, but only for a short time, and storms too would come, with terrible winds which piled up the sand into great mountains, but it was not the time for rain as yet.

'Is His Highness the Amir still mourning the tragic loss of his sister?' Allegra asked, not because she thought that he would have forgotten his dead relative, but because she knew nothing of the mourning periods here, their length, or if indeed they were employed.

'*Ya Allah*, he is still sad for her loss, and for the loss of his unborn nephew. Dearly and long had he wished to be the uncle.'

'Yes, that is sad. He has no other sister or brother?'

'None. They all die at birth or soon after birth, *Mashallah*.'

'Yes, it was Allah's will that His Highness the Amir Adem Ali rule here in Arabia. Allah knows what is best.' Allegra spoke with tongue in cheek, but Husaina never seemed to comprehend her irony. To make Arabians agree with one, it was only necessary to spout the phrases learned by rote: 'Allah wills it'; 'Thanks be to Allah, the all-merciful, the all-powerful'; 'Allah decides all, and rules all'.

When Husaina had gone, steering herself along with her stick like a drunken sailor, Allegra looked round her suite. The prison, that was what she should rename it. She could not revel in her privacy now, nor celebrate her success in her elevation. Advancement might be the whole world to the other slaves here, but not to her. She could not be so mercenary.

Frightened, insecure and disorientated, having lost everything that she loved most dearly, she had clung to the Amir as her raft in stormy seas, closing her eyes to his real nature, knowing that if she faced him as he truly was, then she would be destroyed.

All the same, she had no choice. He was lord and ruler here. If he had tired of her, then she would spend the remainder of her days making *kawhe*, sewing *shalwar* and boleros, refilling oil lamps and cleaning out braziers with nothing more engaging or riveting to pass the time.

She would never ride on horseback again, have a child of her own to love, or be an aunt . . .

Tears filled her eyes. It all depended on Adem Ali, for, without him, she would be childless, loveless, empty. He was the key to all things here, and the source of them too, the love, the generous gifts, but most of all the children.

It was terrifying to think that she would never have babies to cuddle and nurse because Adem Ali had wearied of her already. No wonder some of the women here looked beaten, and thought of nothing beyond their next meal! Would she be like that in a few more months, filling her belly with food to try and fill the place where her baby should lie?

More than anything, she had wanted babies with bright golden curls and Nash's sea-blue eyes, but Allah had willed it otherwise . . . Jesu, there she was thinking like a Muslim, much good may it do her! The urge for children had never been more powerful and overwhelming than at that moment, and she shuddered with the force of it.

Her very happiness, her motherhood, depended on the man who had not sent for her in three long weeks. There was no one else she could turn to, no one to comfort her or understand what she was weeping for, and how could she wail and mourn when others who had been here for years had never even been touched by the Amir, let alone bedded by him?

'It is the will of Allah. Whatever happens, it is the will of Allah!' she said to herself, over and over, fists clenched, trying to convince herself.

Chapter Twenty Three

The easiest matter was to redye his skin and hair. He grinned softly to himself as he completed this task, for he had no notion as to why he was doing it. Instinct told him to darken himself, not memory.

In the *Jahaliat*, the terrible old days of ignorance centuries ago, there had been a desert custom to bury girl babies alive, because they were considered useless. They could not wield a sword and fight the enemy, and enemies were many before the days of Mohammed. Sooner would the husband strike his wife a dozen times than do the same to his own beloved son, for sons were precious. When a son dies, the tribespeople say, 'He is gone, the Lord have mercy upon him!' but when a daughter dies, nothing is said and the grieving is over soon.

Abdullah had told him that; he could remember the very day, aboard a ship it was, with the glittering cloth-of-silver seas billowing in the background, the lucid sapphire skies hanging overhead like a veil suspended by the hands of God.

'If a son misbehaves, parents say proudly "My son is a kaffir" – that means of a nature which is heathenish – but if a daughter should misbehave, then she will be beaten and checked harshly. Even if a son should take a stick to his own mother, she will say no more than "My son is a kaffir" . . .'

He had remembered that women were ill-treated here, then? All women, or only the daughters of nomads and the poor? He could not recall more of that conversation and yet he felt it was of importance.

Before he reapplied the dark berry dye, he bathed in a

waterhole. Blackish and meagre, the water had been a blessing after his long, exhausting days of trekking. He did everything but drink it. Men had died from swallowing such ancient water, and he knew that it was imperative that he stay alive . . . if only he could remember why.

A handful of wet sand had been his only method of removing the ingrained dust and dirt, and it had left his body raw. Stripped, he was thinner, leaner, yet no less muscular. A diet of berries, roots, cactus pulp, small wild creatures and locusts was not one which added fat, nor were the long hours of walking, but they had not robbed him of vigour or mental alertness, he was pleased to find.

Twenty-five days had passed since he had woken to find himself with the head wound. Twenty-five days. He had counted it by the stars, noting each number with a solemnity that was almost a ritual. During that time he had seen no one, not one soul, nor did he know if he was travelling in a direction which would bring him to signs of life.

For all he knew he might be trekking round and round in circles, condemned unto eternity to trudge through the blazing, parching desert until he died. As the days passed, his beard grew, and it was dark, so dark that it could pass for black. He held it up to his eyes so that he could see the colour. Who would have thought that he had a black beard?

That night's supper was a snake cooked over the fire. Tender and succulent, it had a taste of chicken, he thought, then realised that he had remembered something else.

Chickens, squawking, pert birds which skittered around in panic when frightened, and which were kept for their eggs. He knew that he liked eggs, in syllabub and custards and other English dishes . . .

England!

He chuckled to himself. So he was English! Then what in the name of the good Lord was he doing in this God-forsaken, scorching desert?

Arabia. He knew that he was there, for he could not rid his mind of Abdullah and his extraordinary volume of Islamic knowledge, yet he kept thinking of death, too. Why? Because his own was imminent in this life-draining place? No, someone was going to die, someone he loved . . . Yet he did not know their name or even whether they were male or female. But he had to stir himself, keep pushing himself through the venomous heat, because he was going to save their life . . .

He dashed a sunburnt hand across his face. The skin felt taut and parched, his eyes gritty and inflamed with the frequent swirling gusts of sand. Now and again he would hear the eerie, singing sound which was caused by sand grains slipping down the sides of the high dunes. Desert dwellers believed the noise was made by jinns, the devils of Islam, and they wore blue amulets to protect themselves against the evil. Sickness, too, was caused by these demons and must be expunged by such violent methods as branding and the generous application of various unenlightened factors, camel dung and urine, spells, protective charms and burning feathers.

The Beduin belief in Paradise was profound, each nomad believing absolutely that he would go to Heaven after death. There was no doubt, no possibility of failure. In Paradise, the haven of flourishing crops, plump cattle and abundant rain, they would be youthful again, marry fertile wives and conceive children who would be born fully grown. Rich, never again short of food, they would be put in the delightful position of being able to raid the unfortunate ones who were consigned to Hell.

Why was he recalling Abdullah's words, spoken to him so long ago? Muslims. There was something important he must remember about Muslims.

'The dead Beduin is buried in a white shroud, a grave dug for him in which he is placed with his face towards Mecca, the great place of pilgrimage. Deeper graves are dug for women, not out of any conviction that more care must be taken for the female sex but simply because it is unthinkable that their breasts be bared when they rise from their burial ground on the day of Judgement.'

There was a chilling tale Abdullah had told him, about a nomad who was journeying with his pregnant wife. She was about to have her child, it could not be delayed, and so the baby was born in a mountainous valley, but alas the mother died of ignorance and neglect. Stricken, the father could do nothing to ensure that his son would live. He had no milk, and no way of feeding the baby, so he placed the child on its mother's breast, after he had gently laid her body to rest in a cave. Glancing one last time at his son, resting on his mother's arm, his mouth to her left breast, the father, with tears in his eyes, stacked stones against the entrance to keep away wild beasts.

It was months later when travellers, passing the cave, saw tiny footprints outside it. Wondering, they peered through the stacked stones to see, to their horror, the mummified corpse of a woman. What was worse, and what shocked them so much that they ran away wailing was that the corpse's left arm and breast were fleshy and coloured, and moving still, and beside it sat a baby boy . . . alive.

Preserved by the dry climate? Yes, it was ideal for that, but how had the infant fed off its dead mother's body for all those months and how had it got outside the cave to leave its footprints there? Even supposing it could have overcome that hurdle, it was too young to walk.

The father of the infant, hearing the tale, which passed like wildfire from Beduin to Beduin, rushed back to the cave. It was a miracle, Allah be praised! There was his son, and alive.

A reasonably happy ending. Having eaten all the snake's flesh, leaving only the spiny innards, Nash yearned for a mug of frothing amber beer, ice cold from the cellar of a Cornish inn.

Now he had thought of Cornwall. Obviously food was the way to bring back his memory! The grease from the snake was salve to his chapped, sand-and-wind-battered lips and he gently massaged it into his mouth. He wished he had a veil for the lower half of his face, like the Tuareg tribesmen who wore them to keep out the encroaching sand.

Night in the desert was stark black and white, the vivid technicolour of day having vanished. It was piercingly silent, too, in such a way that the silence throbbed against the eardrums. Ah, for the clatter of a teeming city, the shouts and barks of men and dogs, the creaking of timbers and clatter of footsteps, the swish, swish of the waves . . . Yes, for that sound he longed most of all.

His recollection of the mummified Beduin mother's corpse might have been precognition, for, next day, dragging his feet through the fierce, blasting heat which seemed to bounce off nearby rocks to smite him in the eyes, Nash found a deserted camp. A nest of twigs and bracken-like ferns, long parched to dusty fragments, a large, battered cooking pot hanging from a rusty hook, and nearby the skeletons of two men, the bleached ivory bones jutting sharply out of the dusty, ragged robes. They had made camp beneath a jutting shelter of rock and it was this which had kept their bodies exposed, free of the thick canopy of sand which might have covered them in a more open landscape.

Idly he kicked the battered pot, which swung and crashed from its rotted hook. It was rusted right through and his disappointment hit him heavily. No use for dry roasting, or steaming any greens or roots he might find. He had quite fancied a big snake stew . . . If he could find water and a snake.

The skeletons were like caricatures. He would not have believed that men could be such stupidly grinning idiots in death. His heart lurching, he sank down by the old long disused fire. Would this be his fate, his *nasîb*, as the Arabs called it? Nothing more than sun-blanched bones lying forgotten and alone in some isolated desert corner? At that moment, he felt that there was every possibility. Nearly an entire month driving himself on in the blasting heat and aridity, subsisting on a pauper's diet, racking his brains to try and remember his own name. Jesu, it was enough to drive a holy man into the wildest moonfever!

He had never been nearer to tears in his life, yet he had no spare fluid to make them. What an irony. Tears were eager, desperate to be spilled, yet he could not manage it! His belly felt as if it had been hollowed out by a knife and was lying empty and starved, exposed to the elements. Would that he had the sturdy leather belt, fashioned from interwoven leather strips, which the Beduin wear under their cotton gowns and which they would refasten more tightly to quell hunger pangs. A terrible, but a noble way to die, by starvation, lost and mindless in the primitive Arabian expanses . . .

He must have slept, for the silvery echoing of a bell shocked him awake. Church bells here in the desert? No, it was a camel train passing on the other side of the rock. Huddling himself beneath the stony overhang, he waited silently until they were well past and then, cautiously, he slipped out, to pad round the rock and see who they were. Dare he beg their aid?

The camel train was a lurching serpent undulating through the silver and terracotta sand, against a chiaroscuro backdrop of light and dark, the dunes which sang with cascading sandgrains. It was a reasonably long train, the beasts heavily burdened with carpet rolls, wicker baskets crammed with merchandise and borne amidst the trudging, uneven crocodile, two litters heavily veiled with scarlet and emerald silk: Wealthy ladies in their *purdah*, their portable harems built for travelling. They might die or give birth in those suffocating little boxes, and no one would dare rush to tend them save their husband or their sons, if they were nearby. If not, there would be a new wife to find. With four wives allowed by Allah, who needed to care overmuch for any one of them? All were easily replaceable.

His eyes lifted from the silk-hung litters to the pennants flying above them, twisting and tossing in the crisp desert breeze. They were painted with some bright emblem. In a moment, he would see it, fully stretched out by the wind, the venomous dragon with the pursed mouth and the bright-hued flames leaping from it like spears and he would remember everything.

He was not the only traveller keeping close to the camel train for safety and sustenance. There were a dozen more, trudging along behind with the grim, haggard expressions of those who exert themselves in great heat, sweat bubbling on their foreheads and drenching their black beards. No one uttered a sound as Nash fell in with them, dearly hoping that their next resting place would be near and that some kindly person would offer him food and drink. Fresh camel milk, succulent dates, seed-packed figs to crunch between the teeth, unleavened bread, freshly baked (for it went stiff and stale within hours), buttery rice heated over the fire, rare black truffles from the desert itself . . . His mouth ran with juices as he pictured all these coming his way, but it was to be another hour before they halted for the night at a *caravanserai*.

Bliss! An oasis, men and women, beasts and dogs, humanity, food, water, *life*! Nash wanted to run through the village yelling his head off with exultation. The left side of the street comprised an enormous building, solid, low and white-washed, with thin-walled compartments inside for all the occupants of the camel train to sleep. The villagers would stand guard outside, to watch the merchandise, and the gate would close at sunrest. This was the way that everyone ensured there would be no stolen goods, no raiders riding in to thieve and pillage.

Nash had not been ordered away, so he stood with the rest of the foot travellers waiting his turn as the litters were emptied. Six women, heavily veiled and with heads bowed, stepped into the building, servants bobbing round them in a rare panic in case a man's eyes might see an inch of their face below the clamping *yashmak*, or half an inch of bare brown ankle below the swirling hem of their skirts.

At the entrance to the *caravanserai*, one of the women stumbled. She had been walking in tiny hobbling movements as if she were injured, supported on each side by a servant. As she fell, tripping on her long veil, it was tugged from her face. Screaming, she flung up her hands, searching for the fallen silk, unable to find it and not knowing which way to turn.

Watching from the side, Nash saw a face of such exquisite, painted beauty that he felt a moment's pang, not of sexual lust but of avid admiration of such poignant perfection. She was creamy-skinned, the palest of pale ambers, with a heart-shaped, flattish face, snub nose, and slanting almond-shaped eyes, carefully painted so that they seemed to disappear into her hairline. The cheeks were rouged delicately, as was the rosebud mouth; the teeth were tiny and unblemished.

Minute, slender hands with fearfully long pointed nails peeped out of the heavily embroidered robe of tulip-yellow and jade-green satin thickly embroidered with scarlet roses and butterflies.

A faint scent reached his nostrils, mimosa, exotic, Oriental, unforgettable. Where was she going, this exotic beauty? To some lustful man's captive, on her way to a harem where she would be shut away from the world until her death . . . God did not fashion such perfection for the eyes of one man alone; surely he wanted all to see it? Thousands of miles she had been brought, from Cathay, an ordeal to incite both physical and emotional prostration.

Now that she had covered her face again and was being helped inside, he saw why she hobbled with such tiny, frightened steps: her feet were no more than three inches long, tightly bound in miniscule embroidered satin slippers which would have fitted a child of three years old. The people of Cathay believed that tiny feet were the apogee of beauty. Nash suspected that there was more to it than that. Bound feet kept women immobile; how could they run, escape from cruel husbands, or even walk freely on a summer's day when their feet were crushed into the size of a bunched fist?

Why did men plot to hobble their women, to veil and burden them, shut them away in *purdah* and swathe them in shroud-like robes? What were they afraid of? He liked a woman spirited and free, outspoken and bold, and he wanted her to choose him for herself, out of all the men in the world because she loved him and not because he had bought her for his harem and commanded that she adore him.

Where the delicate, amber-skinned girl had paused, there was a scarlet and gold fan lying in the dusty earth. Stepping forward, Nash swept it up and handed it to one of her servants, a scowling man with a sickly, mustard-coloured skin and a shaven head at the back of which hung a black plait tied with yellow ribbon. The man bowed, took the fan, then bowed again. He did not smile.

The amber concubine had servants of her own race with her, so she could not have been abducted by violence. Was she to be a gift for someone? Poor, unhappy, wild-eyed creature. God will that the man would be kind to her!

Speaking Arabic and assuming a nonchalant air Nash settled in with the other travellers. Outside the desert wind swirled with sand and slammed and crashed against the thick wooden doors of the *caravanserai*. From the direction of the amber concubine's room, Nash heard pitiful yelps of fear as the storm increased its velocity, and a mustard-coloured servant came running into the main hall, jabbering in a high-pitched, sing-song tone. By turns, he bowed at three of the men, his manner beseeching and eventually they followed him back to the amber concubine's room, much to his relief.

Later Nash heard that she had tried to cut her wrists. Her shame and humiliation had been so intense at accidentally showing her face in public that she wished to take her life, or was it something else? Was she only days away from the man to whose harem she was being despatched like a sack of merchandise?

Poor girl, no more than a child. He doubted that she would survive for long even if she did not succeed in killing herself. To commit such an act was a mortal sin in the eyes of his church, yet he could not condemn her for what she had tried to do . . . How would he feel if he was in her place?

'Where is she going?' Nash asked the man who seemed to know so much about his fellow travellers.

'To the palace of *Ya Saiyid*. She is a gift for his harem. He is the luckiest of men! Allah, what I would give to have her in my household! *Ya Saiyid* sent spices and incense to her father, and leather, ivory and pearls, and he has received her in payment.' The man leered, rubbing his belly and thinking about placing it on top of the painted concubine.

'Her father?' Nash could not believe his ears. 'Her father has given her in payment? His own daughter!'

'In their land they think little of girl children. I have heard that the poor drown them at birth, or strangle them. Some are left in the open to die of the elements. So she is fortunate to be alive and living in comfort.' The man shrugged.

'The Amir Adem Ali? That is where she is going?'

'Where else? Who but he could afford such a prize? There will be a furore in his harem when she arrives, such squabbling and jealousy and the tearing of hair and raking of nails. Women are like children, spiteful and envious. How they will envy this beauty!'

'The Amir has a large harem?'

'Of course. He is a wealthy and important man, a great prince and ruler.'

'Do you know of any other newcomers to his harem, foreign women perhaps, within the last year?'

'How would I know? Do you think I have a peep-hole into his palace? There are slave girls being taken there all the time, but not so many now that his favourite wife the Lady Khadija Nur has given him a son, the Prince Zühl. They say that contentment has made him lose interest in other women, but when he sees this oriental lily he will be revived, would you not say, oh tall one? Me, I would divorce all my wives in exchange for this lily . . .' The hand was rubbing again, the smile crooked with lust.

'What do you know of the mother of the Prince Zühl?'

'You ask too many questions, oh tall one! Where are you from, what is your name, why are you here? See, I can ask questions too.' The Arab traveller, who blew first congenial and then suspicious, narrowed his eyes at Nash.

Shrugging, as if he did not care what the man's reaction was, Nash turned his attention back to his meal. Rice cooked with greasy, rancid butter, into which were stuck rubbery vegetable strips, beady raisins and so much garlic that he wondered if the roof of his mouth would still be there when he had finished eating. A heavily veiled, plod-footed village woman was meandering through the diners with a large jug of water on her shoulder. A man with a deformed shoulder, which made his head poke downwards to the floor was following behind her with a smaller jug in which there was *nabidh*, the fermented drink made from dates and grapes for those who could afford his exorbitant price.

Nash chose water, for which there was no charge, drinking it down in one desperate gulp. Now at least he knew for sure where the camel train was going, not that he had doubted its destination. In this land, the Amir Adem Ali reigned as powerfully and with as much autocracy and despotism as if he were king . . . All merchandise must be offered to him for first refusal, and there were few merchants, traders and businessmen who were not connected with him in some way.

Nash was almost sure that the Amir would know where

Elizabeth and Allegra were . . . If he did not have them in his own harem then he would know to whom they had been sold, or gifted. Once he discovered that, then he would buy them back with the jewels which he had hidden in his boots and twisted inside strips of grubby material torn from his cloak and twined round his waist. He felt confident that he would achieve his aim. The Amir was infamous for his love of gems and if he truly were enamoured of the Lady Khadija Nur, his favourite wife, then he would surely free Allegra and Elizabeth if he had them in his possession? Nash could speak Arabic eloquently so he was sure that he could negotiate the exchange successfully. He saw the Amir as a greedy and acquisitive man who would not say no to the emeralds, rubies, diamonds and pearls which Nash would show him.

The guests who could not afford a private chamber were given flat rush mats for the floor and Nash settled himself for the night on his. He was not going to cause a furore, he, shabbily and simply dressed like a pauper or a pilgrim, by producing fabulous jewels to pay for a comfortable bed. After his nights in the rocky, sandy, hostile desert, this thin rush mat was paradise.

Outside the storm was throttling the palms which stood sentinel over the oasis, gripping and shaking them, blustering at their tough leaves and down, then whirling along the water's surface with a furious, petulant violence.

The plaster-walled building withstood the clamour magnificently, but the shutters rattled and juddered and the changing tempo of the wind kept up such a howling, squealing, blasting, hammering noise for the next six or seven hours that only the most exhausted could sleep.

Despite the solid walls and shutters, specks of sand found their way into the hall and fell on the faces of the sleepers so that they would find their mouths gritty when they woke.

Nash lay awake, preparing himself for the next few days. When he found the girls, as he knew he would, and bought their freedom, then he would take them back to Cornwall, their only guide and guard for what would be a long and dangerous journey, at least until they left the Arabian Ocean. Pirates, slave traders, storm, shipwreck, misadventure, how well he knew what long journeys offered! What would bring him the deepest embarrassment and unhappiness would be the way he must behave towards Allegra. He was a man of his word; a man who believed utterly in God, and his principles were high. Elizabeth and he were betrothed; after her ordeal, she would expect him to reject her outright most probably, for she, being virtuous and gently nurtured, would see herself as soiled goods . . . He gritted his teeth. He was prepared to find his Elizabeth deflowered, no longer the sweet, innocent virgin that she had been a year ago. He could deal with it, he was sure, but most of all he must let her see in every way that he would care for her devotedly and marry her the moment that they returned home. Should he abandon her, then she would have no opportunity of finding another husband, for who would have a girl who had been abducted by slavers and tampered with by Arabs?

He prayed ardently that she would still be virginal, but as much for her own good as for his. How chaste she had been when he knew her, so shyly innocent. He could not bear to think of her being forced by a dark-skinned savage . . . He did not believe that she could survive such a shock, such violence. She was pious; she believed in the holy sacraments; she had taken their betrothal so much to heart, and would be a faithful wife, he knew.

On the return journey he must show her, by every word and action, that he had not changed in his attitude towards her.

Yet he had. He knew that. A fiery, sparkling girl had snatched his heart and she still possessed it, wherever she was, his passionate, generous-hearted Allegra whom he loved as he had never believed love could be possible. Yet for Elizabeth's sake, he must do the honourable thing, be coldly courteous and polite to Allegra, but no more. If they smiled, or gazed into one another's eyes, he knew that he would be lost . . . lost entirely. When they got back to Cornwall, he would marry Elizabeth instantly and then he and her father would set about finding a suitable husband for Allegra, preferably a man who would live some distance away so that he need not see her again, or at least not more than on family celebrations and festivals.

Fist clenched, he pounded it against the matting until it ached agonisingly. Allegra, his beloved little She-Wolf! He had come all this way, trekked through the desert in a scorching heat which would have killed any other man and all so that he could find her and buy her freedom. She was a child of freedom, she would fade and die in some dogmatic Arab's harem, having to salaam and obey his orders, running here and there at his command and spending hours preparing her body for his love making ... At the thought of that, Nash raged inwardly, as he always did. This, most of all, told him that he loved Allegra and not Elizabeth, for where he was anxious for his betrothed's health and safety, he did not feel anger or distress at the thought of her lying with another man. His heart pounded when he visualised Allegra being trapped in a dark-skinned heathen's embrace. He knew how these Arabs made love: like savage, lustful, wild beasts. Why should they work to improve their manners or their technique when women were their slaves? They had not enjoyed the Renaissance which had taken Europe by beautiful storm over the last decades, reviving romanticism, finesse, and all that was most refined in man.

Not that he was excusing himself. He had behaved as immorally as any heathen by making love to his future wife's sister, God forgive him, for he would never be able to forgive himself.

Who would marry Allegra, for there would be the question of her immorality, too, oh, not the passionate love shared with himself, but the searching questions which would be directed at her: What happened to you while you were enslaved, did many men use your body? Her behaviour, through no fault of her own, would be labelled depraved and debauched; she would be considered no better than a harlot who had volunteered for such a life. However men and women viewed themselves as newly-enlightened, these old values did not budge. A woman who had lost her virtue outside marriage was a whore while a man who bedded many women was considered dashing and virile.

He had a good friend, a boon companion of many years standing, Sir Geoffrey Cleobard, who was still in search of a bride. He was intelligent, women would call him handsome, and he had a fine estate and a generous patrimony. Allegra would make him a superb wife; they could travel together and enjoy what he would have enjoyed with her had he been able to marry her . . . Growling, he punched the matting again. Why could he not have seen, dumb imbecile that he was, that he should have chosen Allegra as his wife and not the docile, bland Elizabeth? In some measure, he had his late cousin to blame for that, for he had taken to heart his guardian's description of a spouse, and Elizabeth suited it admirably.

What of the major importance of the spark which flared between a man and a woman when they were soul and heartmates? He had never felt that with Elizabeth; she was too demure, too cautious of revealing herself, but he had believed wholeheartedly that in time, as the years passed, she would open up to him like a rose, and that he would find her centre all the sweeter and more appreciable for it. Now he knew that he had been wrong, wrong, *wrong*, but that there was nothing he could do about it without behaving like a dastard and a coward.

At last he slept, drained of happiness, to dream of an ancient temple in the desert, its ivory ruins sparkling in the moonlight. Inside, knowing that he would find the mother goddess who had once been worshipped in this land, he stepped into the cool, glittering ruins, his heart thudding.

There she was, a gleaming figure veiled in moonstone silk. Joyously he ran to her, to sweep aside the veil, as he would in a Muslim marriage, so that he might stare at his beloved's face once more.

Allegra, the star of his soul, the reason why his heart was still beating, his blood still flowing. Slowly, she stepped down from the dais, moving towards him as if she were borne on a cloud, her arms were slipping round his neck and pulling him close, their lips were meeting, and a kiss was brought to life, one unforgettable, heart-twisting kiss. Then, tears in her radiant blue eyes, she pulled back, her face sad, returning slowly to the dais to step up on to it and become, once more, a statue of solid, unreachable stone, the coiling marble serpent at her feet, as if in reverent worship.

He knew what the dream meant. It was at one and the same time a reminder of their idyll on the Arabian island, a memory of the goddess statue there and a memory of their loving, yet it told him, too, that she was beyond his reach now, his lovely Lady She-Wolf, that he had lost her forever.

Chapter Twenty Four

The enamelled tray crashed to the floor with an ear-cracking clatter, orange sherbet spilling everywhere. The servant bearing it to Allegra had tripped on a crinkled Persian rug and now lay in the midst of the pool of sticky, sugary liquid. Her face was rigid with anxiety; she did not know how the lady *nasrani* would react. The mistress of the slaves, and Hafez the songster called her the white dove, but these days she could just as soon be the black devil.

'*Sumi!* Get up and clean that mess!' Allegra snapped, her command of Arabic now improved thanks to the patience of Hafez. The simple commands and enquiries could free her, she had found, for who wanted to be beholden to a translator?

'*Ya Sitti*, I do it now!' Sumi salaamed, shame-faced, and then stepped carefully out of the glutinous puddle to go in search of a cloth.

Allegra returned to the enormous, illuminated book that she was trying to absorb. Written Arabic looked like a host of tiny delicate black ants crushed on to the pages into squiggles, curves and dots; she would never be able to write it, she was sure, and yet she wanted to do so. She knew that the Amir would respect and admire her for such an accomplishment, and she needed his approbation so very much.

Closing the book, which was too heavy for her to lift unaided, she stepped to the window. It was a fine day (when was it not?) and the roses were lapping up the sunshine.

The keeper of the roses was delicately forking the soil around them before watering their roots, and sprinkling on some tiny grains which she could not identify. How cautiously he laboured, as if the roses might suddenly shrivel and die if he were clumsy. Now and again, he would glance over his shoulder as if observed by someone who made him uneasy. He was a eunuch, of course. It affected their nature, turning them into obese, simple children, with a predilection for bright colours and gewgaws, their high-pitched voices and disinterest in women making them oddly sexless. Only the Amir was male here: virile, and able to sire children.

Allegra wished that she could pick the roses herself, or simply bend down to smell them, but this request was always refused. The Lady Khadija Nur would be enraged at the invasion of her private gardens, Husaina would say, flapping a ring-encrusted hand back and forth.

'Yet that lady never walks into her garden!'

'She will, she will, when the infant is recovered.'

'The boy is ill?' Allegra's eyes opened wide, for no word of this had reached her and rumour was normally more efficient than anything else in the palace.

'A childish fever, not severe. He is over it soon.'

'Is the Lady Khadija Nur with child again? I heard that she might be so.' Allegra's chest tightened, a wave of dizziness gripping her. She could not bear to speak of the great rival on the other side of the palace, the one who had borne the Amir's heir and who had her own large and sumptuous suite and dozens of servants. The other day someone had called her *Ya Saiyida*, and Allegra's heart had twisted. She wanted to have that title and be chief wife here!

'Allah willing, she shall be brought to bed within the next six months.' Husaina made a praying gesture with her hands. Her nails, heavily stained with henna, were a bright and lurid orange. She had been treating her hair the same way and the increasingly white wisps and streaks were bright orange too, and quite incongruous.

'What does the Amir's astrologer say of the coming child. Will it be a boy or a girl?'

'A boy, *Mashallah*, a boy, what else? Allah has kept the *Saiyid* waiting overlong for sons and now he is bestowing them generously. Shall you add to their number?' The slanting old eyes stared piercingly at Allegra.

'It would not appear that Allah has ordained this, for I am not with child. My woman's time is here.' Fists clenched tight enough for the nails to mark her palms, Allegra assumed nonchalance.

'Ah, so that is why there is so much commotion here the last few days! Poor Sumi. She fears you.'

Silence reigned. Next they will be calling me the despot, thought Allegra. How ironical.

'The *Saiyid* has important guests arriving in three days. Shall your woman's time be ended then?'

'Why do you ask?' Awful suspicion chilled Allegra.

'The *Saiyid* told you what would be expected of you? That you entertain his . . .'

'Yes! It is unthinkable, hideous! I shall not do it! Tell the Lady Khadija Nur to do it, for *I* shall not!'

'Dance, you will dance that is all! The *Saiyid* has told his guests of your grace and beauty. He asks no more than that you dance for them.'

'That is all? What will happen afterwards?'

'You shall be free to return here to your apartment if you wish. But you may change your mind, for Shaikh Omar Hassan is young and very pleasing to the eye.'

Not even Allegra had been anticipating the rage which seared through her at those words. Almost spitting, she shrieked at the old woman, her face scarlet.

'You are a procuress, a filthy old procuress! Find yourself some street woman for I shall not sink to that level, no not ever, whatever you do!'

That night, she dreamt again of the Christian slaves whose bodies had been plastered into the walls of the palace. Husaina had said that none were in the walls of the harem quarters, yet Allegra felt sure that they were, and in her dream they were still alive, panting for breath, writhing and twisting in the swiftly setting plaster, their nails bloody from tearing and scraping, choking screams rising, sharper, sharper, until they were suffocated by the plaster in their mouths and noses.

She woke with a jolt, sitting up before her eyes had opened. The lamp in the far corner of the chamber had gone out and she was in darkness. Clamping her lids shut again, she called loudly for Sumi. If she opened her eyes she knew that she would see a hideous corpse staggering towards her, hands outstretched in supplication.

Sumi was there instantly, holding her hands and rubbing them.

'It is bad the picture in the dream? Never fear for your Sumi is here close to heal you, *ya sitti*.'

Tears burst from Allegra's eyes at the loving words of the young girl who had replaced her dear Ika. She had treated Sumi despicably, part of the reason being that she did not want to grow fond of the girl and then lose her as she had the devoted Ika. Now she felt ashamed, and wanted to make amends, but she was too embarrassed to know what to do.

Sumi continued to rub and kiss her hands, her face a basalt shadow in the dimness. A servant was relighting the lamp and the scent of ambergris filled the chamber for Sumi had put some drops of the oil on the lamp's surface. Fresh air, oh, what she would give for the heartening, purifying air of Cornwall and the sea!

'The bad picture of the dream has gone now, *ya sitti*?' Sumi asked, her filibert-shaped eyes soft with empathy.

'Yes, Sumi,' Allegra sighed.

'I had a sister at home who would have the bad pictures in the dreams. Now I cannot comfort her any more, so I comfort you, *ya sitti*.'

Never had Allegra felt more wretched. Sumi had been abducted too, never to see her family again. What point was there in being unkind and thoughtless to anyone? It was a failure of the imagination, but most particularly of the heart. In the coming weeks, when everyone avoided Allegra, Sumi and Sumi alone would stay beside her, gentle, devoted and affectionate as a kitten.

Allegra had undergone what she silently called the persecution of a thousand jinns, referring to her state of hysteria during the past two days. At first she was so confident. She would execute the dance for the guests, keeping it tame compared to the one that she had performed for the Amir, and then she would hurry back to her chambers. However, as the time approached, she became sick with anxiety, suspecting deception on the Amir's part. If he commanded her to lie with the Shaikh, could she refuse before such an important guest and still retain the Amir's affections? Shame and pride were so strong in these Arabians. If she ignored his command before guests, then he would be viewed as a weak fool who could not control his slaves.

Between the shaking fits, she had practised, while Hafez sang or the musicians accompanied her. All the exercise was tiring, so she did at least sleep better and if she did have nightmares she did not recall them on waking.

A bolt of precious, perfumed silks and a jewelled collar and anklet bells had been delivered to her, a gift from the Amir. She was unable to look at them or touch them for hours. If they were a bribe, she wanted none of it . . . Finally she examined them. The silks were diaphanous, softly imbued with a silvery grace, their edges trimmed with gold and emerald sequins. The collar was thick, heavy gold studded with emeralds, rubies and diamonds, the anklet bells matching, with tinier gems. Such beauty, such value . . . She could not imagine that they were real gold. They must be some sort of imitation. Even in the twelfth and thirteenth centuries kings had worn artificial jewels of bright coloured glass. These could not be real stones, not for her.

Having tried them on, she felt excited. Sumi held the polished handmirror while she twisted and turned, trying to see every angle. The silks were cerise, tulip-red, tulip-yellow, rose-pink, midnight-blue, silvery-white and apple-green, and she was thrilled with them . . . until she realised that they numbered seven. Her heart plummeted. The dance of the seven veils . . . Was he expecting her to do that for strangers? How could he betray his principles, his *credo*?

'Keep your wives veiled, hidden from the world and other

males. Let no man but yourself see their faces.' That was what the Amir had told her of the teachings of Mohammed in the Koran, the Muslim Holy Bible. Hafez had chortled when she asked if this were indeed true.

'It is what they would like to read, white dove, so they believe it implicitly. The truth is not quite so exacting.'

'All the same, when His Highness speaks of this, he speaks emphatically, truly believing it.'

'Yes. Yes, His Highness would do that.'

Hafez had refused to be drawn any further on the subject for he considered himself virtually Muslim.

Sumi was beaming as she helped her mistress try on the silks. But for her own slight physical disability . . . a limp . . . she too might have danced for the Amir at some time. He did not like women who lacked physical perfection, and indeed why should he waste his time with them when he could have the most beautiful and majestic concubines that the world had to offer? Emphatic that her *nasrani* mistress was the loveliest in the palace, she was positive that the Amir would soon elevate her to an even greater position. She had never seen the Lady Khadija Nur, for she kept herself to herself in her own lavish suite with her own bevy of slaves and attendants, but she did not believe that the mother of the Amir's heir could be as radiant and comely as her mistress. If only the fair *nasrani* could get herself with child . . . Sumi prayed to her god every morning and every evening that a child would be conceived very soon.

She had heard gossip which worried her. Two days previous, a messenger had arrived, sandy and parched, as they always were when reaching the palace out of the torrid expanse of the desert. He had been riding with a caravan, animals laden with precious wares, ivory, diamonds and sapphires, gold plates and goblets, purple silks and velvets from Genoa, salt, camphor chests crammed with snowy lace and linen from the land of the Franks, and slave girls too, some captured, and one a gift from a great prince of Cathay who wished to exchange her for more of the myrrh, frankincense and *kahwe* which the Saiyid had sent him earlier.

Alas, one day out from the *caravanserai* where they had

spent the night, their train was set upon by brigands. Oh, no, not the noble Beduin or any tribe which he could identify, but vicious men masked in black and intent upon murder.

Taken by surprise, they would have been lost but for a traveller who was with them, a tall man who had suddenly begun rasping orders. Soon they were formed in a circle, the animals acting as a solid barrier against the brigands, and one of the baskets had been wrenched open to reveal weapons, daggers, bows and arrows, short spears, even catapults. Boy-sized weapons which were being taken to the Amir's court as a gift for his newborn son. And so, under the guidance and sharp-thinking of this tall traveller, whose name no one knew, nor whence he had come, the brigands were beaten off and many of them killed by the stranger himself, whose hand was surely guided by Allah . . .

The amber-skinned concubine had all but fainted away during the skirmish, and was still shaken when the messenger left to inform the Amir of what had happened.

Listening, the Amir had gritted his teeth. Nearly lost, the treasures on which his power depended . . . So nearly lost.

'What has become of the stranger who saved your lives?' he questioned.

'He is well, *Ya Saiyid*, or was when I left, thanks be to Allah. The train will be a little slower for there must be time for the lady of amber to recover herself . . . She is very delicate, *Ya Saiyid*, and radiantly her beauty encompasses the stars and the moon.'

'You have looked upon her face?' The Amir's arms gripped the carved arms of his chair as he stared into the suncrisped, yet honest face of the messenger.

'Allah, *Ya Saiyid*, only when she was overcome and she must either die or be brought round with burnt feathers! Allah forgive me if I entertained one thought in my head but for her safety!'

'Yes, I understand. She is very beautiful, you say?'

'None lovelier, *Ya Saiyid*. Her skin is the very colour of the palest and most rare of ambers, her hair is black as shining ebony, her eyes slanting like this . . .' The messenger dragged up the corners of his own eyes to demonstrate.

'What is the lady's name? Were you told?'

'Her servants bear her story and her message with her, *Ya Saiyid*, but I believe that her name is the Lady Mu Lan, which means magnolia blossom, or so her servant said, *Ya Saiyid.*'

Skin like amber, ebony hair, slanting eyes . . . the Amir felt a delightful frisson at the thought of this Oriental beauty. She would be here in time for Shaikh Omar's visit, *inshall'la*, please God, and the latter, with whom he was to arrange a most lucrative business arrangement, would be duly overwhelmed by the female slaves who would indulge his every fancy and desire while he was resident at the palace. The *nasrani* would dance (during which her mouth must needs be closed, Allah be praised), the amber concubine would entrance with her rare Oriental beauty, and the remainder of the women would serve and wait upon them.

The young Shaikh was the owner of land on which lay the fabled incense forest of Maqueda, named for the Queen of Sheba. It was said that Sheba and Solomon had made love one night, during that brief yet memorable time when they were enamoured of one another. When they continued their travels the next day, little shoots began to spring out of the earth at the very place where they had coupled. Soon, there was an entire forest growing, of rare and fabulous incense trees . . .

The Amir wanted that land, yet the young Shaikh was too important to be ill-treated or taken prisoner. There would be reprisals from his tribe and their allies if Omar did not return to his domain at the expected time.

So the Amir must dazzle with friendship, to ensure a treaty forged under the most amiable and hedonistic circumstances he could create, so that Omar would not forget his visit here. At first, the Amir would appear willing to buy the fruit of the incense trees of Maqueda, or exchange goods for them, a voluptuous concubine perhaps, to strengthen the treaty, and then, little by little, he would encroach upon the Shaikh's lands and eventually possess them all, as he had done with so many others before now.

Every major trade route, every port, every caravanserai and trading station, every ship and train from Dhufar to Shirh and further, either belonged to him, or was so deeply in debt that they must consider him their master.

From the Bible days and before, the Incense Road had carried spices of the south and the riches of India, ebony, dyes, rubies, silver, coconuts, sandalwood and other spices, to Islam and the Mediterranean. Three thousand, four hundred years before, antimony had been carried to Egypt from Carmania, transported by what were called 'Asiatics of the Desert'. One of the major incense routes had touched Tabāla, where there was a renowned temple dedicated to the Venus-God, Dhu-l-Halasa, and from there had stretched into the heart of Arabia in the days before Mohammed.

In the time of Pliny, the Mineans, a race of 'new' Arabians, who may well have originated in Crete, had been overlords of the myrrh and frankincense trade. Teak was used for the most ancient buildings in Yemen, revealing that trade with India was flourishing even then. In later times, there would be disputes as to which of the Biblical countries were actually in Arabia. The famous Land of Punt, where Pharaohs despatched their fleets, might have been on the African coast, or the Arabian, but to the Amir such arguments did not matter. He and his ancestors had been overlords of these trading routes for generation after generation. These were the facts which mattered.

Bonds with Africa and India, Ceylon, China, the East Indies, the Red Sea ports, the Persian Gulf, had been unbreakable for centuries. From Persia had come backgammon, polo and chess, from the Far East, porcelain and rag paper, exotic new foods which were eaten from tables whereas Arabs hitherto had eaten sitting cross-legged on the floor. From Baghdad had come the fashionable trousers in place of the robe, and mattresses and cushions, primitive ovens and frying pans as well as priceless silks.

Allied with this had been the unceasing quest for knowledge of the Mohammedan, who believed that he who sought for knowledge was holy, and the integration caused by trade and travel, allied with the wide sweep of Mohammedanism, that served to create an empire greater and richer than any which had gone before. Not only pearls, rubies, silks and frankincense, but philosophy, medicine, wisdom, astronomy, chemistry, mathematics, logic, metaphysics, music and poetry spread out through the Islamic empire and thus to the rest of the world.

This was the Amir's heritage, and he had no intention of doing anything other than increasing it for his son and heir.

After the fabled incense forests of Maqueda, there would be other lands, other countries, other peoples who could come under his sway, for the truth was that the Amir Adem Ali had designs upon the world.

If Omar, young and lusty as he was, became enamoured of one of the concubines whom he would see during his visit, then the Amir would give the girl to him instantly. There were few gestures which bonded friendship more firmly than the giving of beautiful slave girls as gifts.

Omar would see only the dancing skills and the physical voluptuousness of the *nasrani*, not having been forced to listen to her pestilential diatribes on the fiendishness and viciousness of men. Allah, but he would not care if the girl were taken to Maqueda. Indeed, he would encourage it. He was hungering for skin the colour of the palest and rarest of ambers . . .

Sumi had been told what was afoot, for she was a close friend of Lu Lu, a girl whose name meant pearl in Arabic, yet without there being any reason for such a sobriquet. Lu Lu was sallow-skinned, lacking in curves, and had a poor complexion, yet she was a devoted and efficient servant and the Amir often sent for her when he wanted to ensure that a task would be carried out efficiently and without his being troubled again. Perhaps she was so named because she was a pearl of a servant? Lu Lu relayed to Sumi how she had heard a messenger telling the Amir of the besieged camel train and the advent of the amber concubine from the Oriental land.

Immediately that she heard of this amber girl, Sumi felt uneasy, a strangely disquieting dart of some disastrous portent intruding on her thoughts. The Amir was easily swayed by fresh and novel beauty; since Sumi's arrival, not so long ago, he had been enamoured of a black girl, a brown girl, two with pale skin, one with hair the colour of *kahwe*, and one with hair the colour of sand . . . As each new favourite ousted the last, the forgotten one would retreat into oblivion, never being summoned to the Amir's bed again. Only if she bore a son would she retain her position of power and influence, and as the Amir had only one surviving son there was only one favourite now. She would never need to fear a fall from power, and the Amir would visit her regularly to see his son and couple with her in the hope of fertilising her again. The Koran commanded 'Your wife is your field; go in unto your field as you will,' and so it became impious for the Faithful to disobey.

Lu Lu said that the slave girl from Cathay had feet so minute that they were smaller than a child's, barely the length of a woman's forefinger. Because of this, the amber concubine could hardly walk, but must stumble along on tiptoe, a few inches at a time, needing support to walk farther. The picture which these words brought to Sumi was one of a poor, shackled beast, hobbled by its masters so that it could not escape their tyranny, yet Lu Lu said that when the Amir heard of this physical deformity, he roared with laughter, his eyes twinkling, his face alight, clapping his hands in joy.

'So it is that the men of Cathay shackle their women! Allah, but we men of Islam should follow suit!' was his response, so Lu Lu told Sumi.

'He will not break our feet?' Sumi had gasped.

'It must be done in the cradle,' Lu Lu replied. 'The bones are tightly bound, like a wound is bandaged, and so they cannot grow and lengthen. They say the great court ladies of Cathay never move a step, but are carried everywhere in litters, even in the palaces. There are women whose work it is to bind the feet of infants . . . but only the girls. *Billâh!* but they sound like savages to me!' Lu Lu shuddered.

That night, the one before Shaikh Omar Hassan and his companions arrived, Sumi lay awake on her mat at the foot of her mistress's bed. She could not remove from her mind the horror that the picture of tiny, purposely deformed feet brought to her mind. All the agonies that she had suffered since her abduction by the slave dealers had crystallised into the mental image of little crushed feet which kept their female owners prisoners so that their men might have them at their disposal, night and day; so that they may never escape, never walk in the sun, never run in a moment of joy, or to catch a ball. Sumi could not bear her thoughts tonight, nor her fears for the coming visit.

Her mistress was the sister she had lost, and something of her lost mother, too, in a strange, comforting way. She did not want to be parted from her again, for she knew that she would be unable to tolerate the pain. If the Shaikh took her mistress away with him, back to the land of the incense forests of Maqụeda, then it would be doubtful that she, Sumi, so unimportant, would be allowed leave to accompany her. Yet she could not stay behind!

Gripping her little hands together and sobbing hushed tears into her pillow, Sumi decided what she would do if she could not go with her beloved mistress. There was a tincture which the concubines took for the tooth megrims . . . a dark cloudy mixture, bitter-tasting and which caused the deepest sleep if too much were taken. Sumi would take all she could find, swallowing it without thinking, and hopefully she would die. She could not bear to be parted from a loved one again, not ever.

Chapter Twenty Five

The evening began promisingly. The young Shaikh Omar Hassan was indeed stunningly handsome, with a smiling, friendly face and beautiful ebony eyes totally without guile. In his twenty-fifth year, he was wealthy, powerful and ardent. At home, he had a harem of forty concubines, all younger than he, and twenty-two of them were with child, which was extraordinary even for a race which prided itself on being lustful and fertile. So many slaves at home were not sufficient to ensure his 'fidelity', however, and he now watched the *nasrani* dancer with greedy, passionate eyes.

He wore a silk robe of peacock-green trimmed with glittering crystals, his *kuffayia* a deeper emerald, the *aighal* holding it in place looking rather like a corded halo. Like many Arabian chieftains he did not overdress; the pride which he and his tribesmen felt in the simple but ancient desert garb, the kerchief for the head, held on by the *aighal*, was more valuable than the most ostentatious dress.

Closer, and Allegra could see that the robe was trimmed with *kasab*, thickly encrusted gold embroidery in the shape of swirling piping, and that there was a black pearl on the Shaikh's finger which looked so enormous that it could not possibly be real, and yet of course it was.

She had made her grand entrance, preparing herself for the hubbub, clatter and careless attention which Arab men were perfectly capable of offering. Instead, there was such an attentive silence that she almost retraced her step, thinking that something was wrong. Then her music began, the piping, droning, chanting music which of late she had found to be far more rhythmic than she would have thought a year ago.

Slowly, sensuously, she shimmied her way into the chamber, the smoke from the braziers and the oil lamps lying thickly in the air, the scent of ambergris and jasmine, violets and patchouli vying with one another. The heat from the braziers was unnecessary for the packed chamber gave off a dense, humid heat of its own. There were eyes everywhere, mostly male. She had not realised that the Shaikh would bring dozens of his people with him, and that all would be goggling at her, mouths agape.

Her veil was in place most firmly – the veil which she loathed and which stuck damply to her face when she was hot, yet which might, she hoped, prevent the Shaikh from seeing her properly. Slowly, she swayed and twisted across the cool, tiled floor, her anklet bells, tiny, silver and delicately clashing as she moved, the tinselled tinkling echoing round the walls.

Twisting her arms upwards, she twined them round one another in the semblance of a snake, untwining, then twining them again, her hips rotating gently, her shoulders hugging her head so that she might have been a shimmering, multi-coloured serpent. A sound swept round the room from mouth to mouth, a low, startled, gasping sound. She did not know whether it was awe or dismay. Perhaps she was disappointing these men who were accustomed to seasoned dancing slaves?

At regular intervals, she crashed together the *sagat*, brass finger cymbals, one of which was tied to each thumb and one to each middle finger. With these, she was able to dictate the speed and beat of the musician's instruments, they, with practised competence following her superbly.

Out of the corner of her eye she could see the guests were being served *kahwe* in the tiny, fragile ceramic dishes, and platters of sweetmeats were being handed round by salaaming, or even more obsequious slave girls who flung themselves to their knees before His Highness and the guests.

Malban, made of pistachios, cornstarch, sugar and mastic pale-yellow gum resin, were piled high on the enamelled platters. Mastic was another of the aphrodisiacs beloved by the Amir. Sometimes, he would cram it into his mouth, insisting that Allegra do the same. She had never dared to confess that it failed to increase her desires.

Heads bobbing, mouths greedily opening, the guests were soon munching and chomping on the sweetmeats and reaching out for more, their coffee dishes being refilled, over and over, as was the custom, into infinity unless the drinker waved his empty cup from left to right as he handed it back to his host.

Twisting, her glittering veils flying behind her, Allegra clashed the *sagat* together with determined energy. How dared they munch, and gulp coffee, while she was performing her *pièce de resistance*!

The musicians' rhythm was increasing in tempo, gathering speed and vigour, as was Allegra, for this was the *takasim*, the music of the belly dance, never played exactly the same way twice, with soloists exercising their talents in between the long stretches when all the musicians played together. In all the months she had spent practising, Allegra had never felt that she could convey the convulsing passions of the other dancers she had seen, nor the willowy litheness of the serpent dancer,

Tahia, yet she could feel all eyes fixed fiercely upon her nonetheless. It was the aphrodisiac sweetmeat, no doubt.

Tossing her head backwards, she bent her spine agilely, her arms splaying out at her sides like glittering wings. She felt like a bird, some strange and ardent phoenix being brought back to life. If only the *Saiyid* would look at her as he had done the first time she had danced, then she would be reborn, for him alone. Please God let him look at me with love! she prayed silently as she moved.

The tempo of the drumming was faster now, and when she tipped back her head, her scarlet and buttercup hair swinging out like gilded tassels, she gyrated her body in a series of lively yet sensuous ripples, so that her hips and breasts shivered and undulated, yet her feet remained still, transfixed to the floor. Now she was reaching that moment of nirvana when she cared only for the music and the dance, euphoria sweeping through her veins and flooding her mind in a bright, sharp, velveteen sweetness. She felt that she could go on into eternity, that she would never tire, that she was made for dancing.

It was then the shout grazed her tranquillity. It was the Shaikh and he spoke in Arabic, so she could not understand. No matter, for the Amir was to translate. Then she knew.

'Take off the veils, little *gāzāla*, gazelle, take off all the veils and let us see your beauty unveiled!'

Flushing, Allegra continued, behaving as if she had not heard, and then the command came again, even more imperious. So, to placate her audience, she removed the sky-blue silk veil which was tied to her bangles so that it billowed when she whirled round. The blue veil drifted away, a soft cloud, leaving Allegra with more, for, wary of this happening, she had dressed herself thoroughly. They would think that they were getting their seven veils, but she would show them nothing of her nakedness . . .

The drum beat was increasing, the heat and the smoke suffocating; she was sweating heavily, the veils clinging as if they were damp. Head back, her arms splayed out as if in supplication to a goddess, and then the serpentine convolutions once more, so that she became, before everyone's gaze, an undulating, weaving snake, eyes slanted and flashing above the veil, fingers darting like the tongue of the creature she was emulating.

The euphoria was swimming back into her veins when the command came again, more insistently, so she loosed a second veil, one of claret silk beaded with gold and silver, and flung this as far from her as possible.

It drifted across the chamber, borne by a silent breeze, perhaps the breath of the watching men, or a desert wind working its way beneath doors, to land at the feet of the young Shaikh Omar Hassan. Grinning, he picked it up, held it to his face as if smelling the lush, flowery scents of Allegra's body, then tucked it in his sash, as if to say, 'She belongs to me now that I have this.'

Watching, Sumi bit on her lips until they were blotched and sore. She had prayed that the Shaikh would take a dislike to her mistress but she felt that the matter could not be averted: it would come to pass and thus become a part of that destiny which was allotted to each mortal. Brushing away tears, biting-hot as acid, she lowered her gaze, unable to watch the shimmering, swaying loveliness, the radiance that was her mistress, knowing that it would very soon be lost to her for ever. For the Amir to send her with *Ya Sitti* to the palace of the Shaikh would be considered an insult. She was deformed, her limp an incurable blemish. One did not despatch blemished servants to the households of allies.

How she wished now that she had agreed to the making of a curse. If she could have obtained parings from the Shaikh's nails and strands of hair from his head, then she could have taken away his lust. If she were Arabic, then she might have been able to put the evil eye on him, *lāmma* they called it here; she was not quite sure what it meant, or how it worked, but there was much talk of it when evil befell anyone. If only she knew how to work it, then she would put it upon the Shaikh at this very second and he would be taken ill, or collapse, or die, anything, anything, rather than becoming enamoured of her mistress . . .

Now the third veil was twisting away, and then the fourth. The heat was suffocating, Allegra's muscles felt leaden and yet there was a weightlessness, a compulsive motivation to excel at this dance, to complete it in perfection. Avoiding the lascivious gaze of the young Shaikh, she seemed to float across the floor, barely touching it, while the crescendo of music was interwoven by the silver clash of her finger cymbals.

She was not unaware that the Amir was sitting forward, eyes narrowed, his dish of coffee chilling in his grasp. It was he whom she wished to enchant, not the brash youth by his side. The Lord of Maqueda held no attraction for her; it was the Lord of the Incense Road who had locked away her heart in his keeping.

It was no accident that she removed the fifth and sixth veil while dancing only a few feet away from the Amir, but, at that moment, spoiling it all, the young Shaikh began slapping his hands together and shouting loudly. Soon, all the men were doing the same, while the concubines, concealed behind the grille which comprised a section of the wall of the chamber, clamped their arms to their sides, wishing that they could applaud similarly. Sumi, fighting back the tears, bent her head and tried to swallow her fear and despair.

The audience believed that she now wore one veil only, when in fact she was expediently draped in flesh-coloured silk beneath indigo. When she shimmied to the door and threw off the final veil, they would think her naked and she would have vanished before they could see the truth. Not even for her Amir would she disrobe in public. The fact that she had accustomed herself to wearing loose robes instead of the wooden corsets, farthingales and numerous underskirts of Elizabethan England was an accomplishment in itself. More, she would never do, not in public.

Just as she was about to discard the final veil, when the Amir's eyes should have been gazing at her with fierce intent, he looked away, holding out his coffee dish to a servant, and cramming a piece of sticky almond paste into his mouth. As if to confirm his total disinterest he then turned to the Shaikh to watch his reactions during those last, breathtaking moments.

Allegra ached to run across the room and command the Amir to love her, pounding his chest and shouting her commands in his face so that he had to obey, but she knew how futile such actions would be. He would have her shut away in the punishment room kept for scolds. It was a bare, stone hut with a hole in the floor for nature's easement and food was pushed through a shutter once a day. Husaina had told her of it. Madwomen went there, for who but a madwoman would shriek and scold their generous Amir?

The indigo veil billowed away as she whirled round and round, like a dervish transfixed in a wild, religious ecstasy, her hair flying out, her face heavenwards. When she knew that they thought her naked, she fled, out of the door, and into the interlocking corridors which led out of the *selamlik* – the men's part of the palace and into the main harem. There, snatching up a bernouse, she flung it over her head, pushed back her sweat-streaked hair, and sped back into the network of corridors which would lead to the room behind the grille, where the women were allowed to watch the entertainments in the audience chamber.

Gasping, her heart thudding, she peered through the mesh of the grille, ignoring the women, not seeing little Sumi doubled over amongst the throng, her hands to her ears.

A trumpet was sounding. Unexpected visitors were arriving. Next moment, a tall man walked into the audience chamber, and then there came a little company of people. Six men, in strange clothes and with amber-coloured faces and sloping eyes. They were bearing aloft a litter of the sort that Queen Elizabeth herself used for her excursions through the streets of London. On the litter, sitting cross-legged, and robed in peacock-blue and buttercup-yellow satin, richly embroidered in silver, sat the most exquisite girl that Allegra had ever seen.

She could feel the women around her straining to see through the grille, hear them muttering beneath their breath. The amber concubine with the tiny, child-like feet, this was she, even lovelier and more entrancing than her description had led them to believe.

The Amir leapt to his feet, moving to greet the company, his face alight with excitement. Allegra recalled that look. He had worn it the first time that she danced for him; she had not seen it since. Not until now. Reaching up, he took the hand of the slave girl, which had, Allegra saw, enormously long nails, like slender, miniature spears. Now he was pressing kisses upon the hand in the most familiar way and above her veil, the amber cheeks of the girl were blushing to the prettiest rose.

Such a fury reared up inside Allegra then that she thought she might choke of it. Scarlet, wanting to scream and lash out, she found that she could not even move her feet. Long, long minutes passed before she could turn from the grille, by which time the amber concubine was out of the litter – lifted out by the Amir! – and he was carrying her to a cushion on the opposite side from the Shaikh. There she sat shyly averting her gaze, while the Amir tilted up her chin with his finger, just as he had done to Allegra, and spoke gentle words of comfort and welcome to her.

No, she could not bear it! He had rejected her. He was ready to take another to his bed, not the wife who had borne him a son – and God knew that was intolerable enough – but a newcomer, a foreigner, yellow-skinned, with deformed feet and vicious, claw-like nails.

Allegra tore out of the room, a low wail coming from her lips, while the women, half-suspecting what was wrong, tried to pull her back. Many hands clutched at her, tugging, restraining, but she fought them off. She was driven by demons now. She was possessed. She would kill that yellow-skinned hag, kill her!

Racing, she went the fastest way, not pausing when she came to the guards who stood to attention outside the door to the audience chamber. Seeing her, the Amir's *odalik*, they stood aside. She was their master's favourite; she danced for him.

Bursting into the chamber like a whirlwind, a low growl in her throat, she made for the girl sitting beside her Amir. He was *hers*, not the foreign girl's! Claws outstretched, she lunged at the amber concubine, who screamed piercingly, gasping and choking as if she could not get her breath. Allegra's fingers were round the girl's neck, tighter, tighter, digging deeper and deeper . . .

It was the Amir who leapt to his feet, thrusting Allegra away so that she fell to the floor, wrenching a shoulder and moaning with the pain, and then, to her disbelief and horror, he was kicking her, his embroidered slippers with their hard toes feeling like hammers on her tender thighs. Once, twice, he kicked her, after which, having rattled out something in Arabic, he stared down at her with such contempt, such loathing, that she was too shocked for tears, for anything save the iciness which crept along her flesh in the most paralysing way.

The guards reached for her, dragged her to her feet and bore her out, her head lolling. She was too stunned to look back, to scream or insult the one she loved, had loved, and who had spurned her in the cruellest way possible: in public.

That night she was ordered to be alone in her room, not even Sumi was allowed to be with her. Lying on her bed, she chewed her knuckles, tears washing over them in a salty gush, her face burning, her body sore and stiff and aching.

He had rejected her. He was tired of her; it was true what they said, he was fickle. He did not have it in him to be faithful to one woman, nor to love any. Ah, why should he? He was not her sweet and loving Nash, who was fashioned from a far more superior mould, so different, and so much what she needed . . .

She had been willing to kill for the Amir, yet he had forgotten her already. She had been dazzled by his beauty and his love-making, so torrid and impassioned, so artful and untiring, believing this to be the love that she needed so desperately. Yet he was worshipped here as a god, had been raised as a god, and he treated women as the lowest slaves, obsequious creatures who must prostrate themselves at his feet and obey his commands, rush to do his bidding. Why should he persevere when he could have thousands? That look she had seen in some of the other women's eyes. They knew, yet if they could have told her in her own language, would she have listened to their warnings? No! She would have put it down to their jealousy of her favoured position.

What had she become, a Christian struggling to survive in a Muslim world, her old self – her real self – being contorted with bitter and murderous jealousy because she could not cope with sharing her man in the Muslim way? She was not made for promiscuity or the pains of infidelity. The good old-fashioned virtues were the ones she needed and wanted. But it was too late for that now. She had offended the Amir, before his prized guests. She had attacked his new favourite, and might even have choked her had she not been prevented. For nearly a year now, she had cared only for herself and where had it brought her? To a point of such shame and anguish that she could not face herself.

This was the end. She knew it totally, completely. This was her destiny, this terrible, lonely despair and shame. Her soul, languishing in some earthly purgatory, was lost to her. There was nothing she could do; nothing.

Chapter Twenty Six

Nash was treated like a prophet by the people whose lives he had saved. He was not allowed to walk the rest of the journey to Adem, but was forced to sit in a litter on a camel, just as if he were a woman. He found it frustrating and annoying to be hampered thus but his objections were waved away with broad grins. Food and drink were fed to him at intervals, with much salaaming and humility, and it was not until they reached the outskirts of the desert city that he was allowed to step down. Following this, there was another performance of the salaaming and gushing Thanks-be-to-Allah-that-he-sent-you-to-us, etcetera etcetera, and he was told that His Highness the Amir would wish to thank him in person.

'I shall come later,' he said, and then he was off on light feet. He had no plans to confront the Amir while dressed in dusty, filthy robes and with the appearance of a beggar. In the narrow, labyrinthine streets of Adem he would find somewhere to bath and buy clothes and then he would go to the palace.

The bath transformed him from exhaustion and squalor to

the level of princes, and his new robes, richly hemmed with goldwork in the Arabic style, the *kaffîyi* and the *aighal* standing out boldly, for he was tall compared to those whom he passed in the streets, he headed for the palace. There, he had but to send in the message that he was the saviour of the Amir's camel train, and he was rushed into the palace with a dazzling speed, servants kneeling before him offering *nabidh* or *kahwe*, almond sweetmeats, nuts, melon. He had eaten after his bath, but the fruit was enormous and looked temptingly juicy so he bit into it eagerly.

The servant who came to take him to the Amir was small and dark-skinned. He could not stop himself from glancing up in curiosity at this tall man wearing the clothes of Arabia yet not looking like an Arabian.

The Amir rose to his feet as Nash was shown into his private audience chamber, a signal honour indeed. Next moment the Amir was giving thanks to him, in carefully measured English, quite astonishing Nash, who answered back in kind. (Not knowing how useful his knowledge of Arabic might prove, he kept it secret.)

Now more refreshments were brought. Delicious chilled lemon sherbet, a sickly concoction of date syrup and ginger, and dozens of assorted sweetmeats, every colour and flavour imaginable. Musicians began to play as Nash sipped his sherbet, and then, before he knew it, the room was filled with dancing girls, laughing, twirling creatures, all very beautiful but flauntingly sexual. Some were bare-breasted; some wore their silken trousers so low that he could see their black pubic hair. Others had painted their nipples green or orange; one wore a pearl in her navel, another a diamond.

Nash knew well enough that pinning down an Arab to discuss the important business in hand was far from easy. There must be the ceremonial refreshments, the elaborate rituals of making and serving the *kahwe*; interspersed with the aimless, meandering and frequently eulogistic chitchat. All the same, Nash found it difficult to conceal his impatience; there was also the matter of the unstoppable flow of gratitude.

'Shall we not speak of business, Lord Hamilton? The trick is to deceive Allah, is it not? We are relaxing pleasurably, are we not? Should you have some business to discuss with me then we can do that later.'

'I do have business which I must mention!' Nash insisted, his voice firm.

'Yes, later.' The ripe dark eyes were guarded even while the Amir exhibited his most dazzling charm.

And so, to placate the Amir, Nash bit on his words for the next thirty minutes or so while there was another round of refreshments, something which tasted suspiciously like wine, yet could not be, for it was against the laws of Islam, and luscious fruity delicacies of jelly in ginger, date, orange, lemon, spice and ambergris flavours.

Finally, his impatience exhausted, Nash began to tell the Amir why he was there, why he had come all this way and what he wished to know.

Silence reigned. The Amir had not heard? Oh yes, he had. His eyes were hooded and black when he raised them to Nash's.

'What payment can you offer for these women?'

'I have many priceless jewels. They will not disappoint you, I do assure you, Your Highness. Do you know where these women are, then?' Nash persisted, sorry if he was offending Allah with his directness.

'One is here.' The Amir bit into a green spicy jelly, smiling a little as if the flavour delighted him.

'*One?* Which one, Your Highness?' Nash's heart leapt into agonised beating.

'The one you call Elizabeth; here, she is known as Fatima,' the Amir lied, enjoying the Englishman's discomfiture. Had the *Kaffir* not saved his camel train and the life of the amber concubine who had so delighted him in bed the previous night, then he would have been dead by now, hacked into numerous pieces. No *nasrani* had ever reached these parts alive, except in slave shackles.

Nash's heart dropped. He tried not to let it but how could he help himself? His beautiful, adorable Allegra was not here; his bright-faced child of nature, so vulnerable, yet so proud and brave . . . Gritting his teeth, he forced himself to remain calm.

'Do you know anything of the girl called Allegra Pentrevick, who was captured by your slave traders from an island in the Arabian Ocean about one year ago?'

'I know nothing of this one. I do not deal in slavery!' the Amir hissed. 'Tell me, do you love this one, this Allegra?'

'Very much.'

'You *nasranis* are all the same. You blab of love when it is lust that you mean and lust that you practise. Women's bodies are for two things only, pleasure, and the bearing of sons to carry one's name and house.'

'We must agree to differ on that.' Nash managed a pallid smile. Even if he could buy Elizabeth, how could he trail her around Arabia while he searched for Allegra? Jesu, what was he going to do!

'So stubborn, so resolute, you bring down disaster upon your own head.' The Amir appeared to be musing aloud as he sipped his *kahwe*. 'You may have this Elizabeth for all the gems which you bring with you. *All* of them,' he reiterated. 'I am not accustomed to haggling, especially not with *nasranis*, even though they be lords in their own lands. In the morning, you will see Elizabeth. On this you have my word.'

Heart heavy, Nash could see no way out of this dilemma. He would have Elizabeth, at least, and where he would go from there must be considered on the morrow.

'I will have the gems now,' the Amir interrupted his thoughts.

'When I see Elizabeth and not before, *Your Highness*,' Nash's azure eyes met the nigrescent ones of the Lord of the Incense Road, Nash knowing that he could be put to death at one command from this man, who could take his treasure and have him tortured and killed if he so chose.

'I will have them *now*.' The Amir leaned forward threateningly.

'Not until I see Elizabeth.' Nash gritted his jaw.

'What is to stop me having you killed this instant, *Kaffir*?'

'Nothing. Do it if brutal, needless murder is the sort of activity which brings you satisfaction, your Highness.'

The Amir jerked as if stung, the coffee dish almost falling from his grasp. He had met his match; this man could see right through him, to the deceptions and the avarice, the ruthless chicanery. Sitting there, where usually he was god and prophet in one, he felt transparent and vulnerable. Yet he knew that such a sensation was inane, for this Englishman could do him no harm, not here in his own palace surrounded by his stalwart guards.

There is a time when even the cruellest despot feels exposed, and the veil must fall away, just as it had fallen from the voluptuous body of the *nasrani* dancer the previous night. Now was that time for Adem Ali, yet such was his inexperience of vulnerability that he floundered, unable to find words, having to search desperately and in the most cowardly fashion for the correct reaction. But he would have his revenge for this humiliation, oh yes, and in plenty!

'When I have Mistress Elizabeth, we shall need horses and victuals for the journey to the coast. These must be included as part of the bargain.'

'So be it, Lord Hamilton.' The Amir clapped his hands, instructing his servant to take Lord Hamilton to a guest chamber in the *selamlik*, where he would spend the night before seeing Elizabeth. When the boldly foolhardy *nasrani* had gone, the Amir sent away his servants and his guards so that he could be alone to meditate, to try and regain his shattered equilibrium.

Nash barely slept in the small but pleasant chamber allotted him. Bare of excess furniture, yet picturesque because of the blue and gold tiles on the floor, the view of distant terracotta sand hills through the latticed window, he thought longingly of the cluttered home which he had left, of the maps and documents, the rolls of parchment and navigational equipment, the books and mementoes of his many sea journeys which were scattered throughout his mansion, Hamilton House. When Elizabeth became his bride, all that would have to be cleared and the place made habitable for a young wife, who would no doubt have strong ideas of her own about running his home.

What would she be like after this long, long year? How would life in this place of exotic corruption and debauchery have altered her? She might well be broken and sick at heart. He was prepared for anything, would forgive anything. How could he do otherwise when he had spent long weeks fornicating with her sister, even if their shipwreck was through no design of his? Guilt lay leadenly in his stomach; he would make it all up to Elizabeth, all. She would be the most treasured and indulged wife on earth, and he would never let her know that he did not love her, nor ever had.

Clenching his fists, he lay on the narrow pallet bed while night swooped down with the sudden all-encompassing ebony of the desert spaces. Blackness was an excellent companion for such dark thoughts as his, for they were dark whatever excellent intent was nourishing them. His life would be ashes without his lovely Allegra, without that flame which burnt so brightly and beautifully within her; even to have loved her for a few weeks had been paradise, but now he must face the fact that his paradise was lost.

Allegra had wept for hours, until she could weep no more. Now, gripped with a steeliness which had arrived from some unsuspected centre deep within her, she prepared herself for the only possible finale. Talk of poison had always been rife here; that was why the mother of the Amir's heir kept herself away from the riff-raff who might slip some deadly tincture into her drink, or into her son's. There was a woman in the harem who professed to know about such matters; she was something of a wise woman, or so she would have been called in England. Beautiful in a heavily painted, exotic way, she would suggest remedies for various female ills, for the pain of nature's courses, for the toothache, the troublesome back, the megrims in the head, the lack of sleep. She was considered a vital part of the harem for she could give hope to those who had most need of it, and who might create unrest if they were not treated with nostrums and kindly words. For more serious matters there were the Amir's physicians, but these were only summoned in extremity, for the eccentric and superstitious treatment of illness was indigenous to Arabian life, the wearing of charms to avert the evil eye often being considered more imperative than proper health care and the prevention of illness.

Allegra had visited the woman, Zoula, for the treatment of a strained muscle when she first began dancing. The woman was helpful, excessively polite, making decorative salaams, after which she had produced an unguent which did indeed help the strained muscle to heal rapidly. The woman could not speak English, but she knew a little French, for she had been a Frenchwoman's housekeeper in Tangier before she was captured for the Amir's household. As Allegra also knew a little French, learned from her one-time dancing master, the two women were able to communicate haltingly.

'You need great help, come me . . . I cure all ills when pain too much. Amir, he care not, lose interest soon. You will need me one day, so come, and I help. No need to suffer alone. Zoula will give release out of this world.'

Allegra's flesh had tingled when the woman spoke those words, for there was a bright, prophetic gleam in her dark eyes. Allied with the effect of being able to converse in a more or less straightforward fashion, even if the French was clumsily and ineptly spoken, Allegra found that exchange unforgettable. At the time, she did not believe a word that Zoula said . . . the Amir was never ever going to be weary of her, she knew that. She was going to oust the Lady Khadija Nur and bear many sons for his Highness . . .

How time had destroyed all her hopes and heartfelt dreams. Now she had nothing, no one. She was in disgrace. Now was the time to visit Zoula. She could not continue after this; too much had happened to her, too many shattering, heartbreaking events; she had found herself far from strong and invincible as she had thought a year ago, able to experience anything and survive. She was vulnerable, frail, mere woman. Perhaps it was this, as much as anything, which directed her towards Zoula's tiny cubbyhole of a room.

Inside there was the scent of sandalwood and verbena, and behind these the acrid odour of more unpleasant tinctures. Zoula sat there waiting, as if she had known that Allegra would come. Her eyes were thickly painted with antimony, her cheeks brightly rouged, her lips coated with a strong cerise colour. She wore these concealing cosmetics in the hope that when the day of judgement came, she would not be recognised as the purveyor of death for eleven concubines who had come to her for the final release from an intolerable situation.

Now here was the twelfth, and now must the business of release be repeated again, and for the last time. After this, she would never do it again; she had sworn to her god. It had become too much; too terrible – especially this time.

Her hands were large, the fingers knobbly, the nails chewed. In them, the phial looked minute, filled with blackish fluid, yet it would be enough, she told Allegra.

'Drink all down, deep, then close eyes. After, there will be no more to remembering.'

Taking the phial in a shaking hand, Allegra could not speak. The moment was here; she would never suffer again; she would pay the price for her guilt and shame, all of which she had brought upon herself. Croaking a thank you to Zoula, and paying her with a piece of delicate gold silk material trellised with emerald beads, she began the long, slow journey back to her own suite.

Inside, she closed the door. Sumi still slept on her pallet, the heavy, comatose sleep of a child. First she would pray, asking for forgiveness, knowing that she would die without being shriven, damned until eternity, yet willing to pay that price for the crimes she had committed, the greedy self-indulgence, the ruthless ambition, the betrayal of her sweet, innocent sister . . .

Kneeling, waves of heat rolling through her body, she began to pray. Before Sumi woke, she would be dead, freed of the agony which she had suffered in the palace of the Lord of the Incense Road.

Chapter Twenty Seven

Guards naked to the waist in emulation of those who attended the Grand Turk in Constantinople came for Nash the next morning. Barely dawn, yet he was ready, with that strained, unreal feeling of those who have hardly slept. Washed and dressed, he had paced up and down the room, wanting to pray yet being too unsettled.

Silent, with thick, squat shoulders and heavy, stolid features, the guards led him along corridors and through courts, across terraces and into the far section of the palace. Through an arch, he saw a pretty rose garden, almost as bright and lush as those in England, and then the guards were halting before a vast door ornate with scrollwork and engraved studs.

Three times they hammered on the door in what appeared to be a familiar ritual. A voice babbled from the other side, its tone questioning and one of the guards replied. Then the door was unlocked, heavy chains rattling, an iron key scraping. This was obviously the door into the harem, where the women were kept securely imprisoned. Poor Elizabeth . . . How she must have suffered!

Inside, the chamber appeared high-roofed for such a low-built palace. Bright Turkey rugs covered one wall, and lay scattered across the pearly blue tiles. A pile of scarlet, gold and amethyst silk cushions were plumped against this wall, and on them sat a woman, heavily veiled. A young infant lay beside her on a gold brocade cushion tasseled in scarlet.

'*Elizabeth!*' Nash leapt across the room, the guards following him closely as if he meant to harm the woman. Four attendants, all splendidly robed in bright, delicate silks stepped towards him, forming a protective circle before their mistress and the child.

'Elizabeth! Let me through!' Nash's heart was jolted, his body tingling with anticipation and also unease. How calm was her demeanour, despite the concealing veils, how confident, and so very much at home. And the child . . . Jesu, was the child hers? He swallowed. The Amir's son. Certes, the man would never let the mother of his son leave here! It was a trick, he had been deceived . . .

'Nash Hamilton, come closer.' The serene beauty beckoned to him, then clapped her hands at the servants who backed away, reluctantly, while continuing to stare penetratingly at the alien visitor.

He was not asked to be seated, so he knelt, staring unbelievingly into the heavily-kohled eyes of his betrothed. She was draped with jewels, soft satiny pearls which glimmered almost blue in the dawn light, rubies in her ears, just peeping round the edges of her veil, rubies and diamonds on her henna-painted hands. The scent of mimosa surrounded her, strong, evocative and yet somehow heartrending. She looked like an empress, regal, omnipotent, far, far out of his reach.

'I never expected to see you again, Nash Hamilton.'

Even her voice was different, deeper, more sensuous, and how eerie it sounded coming from behind that concealing veil. The hair on the nape of his neck tingled, and he flexed his hands.

'I have come a long way to find you, Elizabeth, I –'

'Not Elizabeth any more! I am the Lady Khadija Nur, chief wife of His Highness the Amir Adem Ali, mother of the Prince Zühl! Yes, I am she, the most important woman in these lands, and I intend to stay that way.' The imperious eyes glittered.

'Jesu, do not speak this way! I have come from England, all this way to find you . . . Our vows! We were to marry!' Nash felt lost. He had been preparing for anything except Elizabeth having the upper hand and not wanting him.

'Forgotten, with my English name. I am of Islam now that my son is born. He will be Amir here one day and I shall be beside him as first lady of this land. You find my ambition surprising? But did you ever know me truly, Nash Hamilton?

You saw only what you wished to see, like all men. Your eyes were painted with the pictures which were formed by your own dreams. I was an image of virtuous innocence, nothing more to you. Here, I am myself, here I have power and great position. Would *you* forfeit such riches for one of lowly birth, a foreigner?' The beautiful, china-blue eyes, so heavily painted with antimony, gazed fiercely at him, yet they were at one and the same time bright with contentment and security.

'So you will not return to England with me?'

She gave a little laugh. 'And leave my darling son? He would die! Who would feed him? I shall not trust him to any milk nurse. And what of my next son when he is born? No, I shall never leave here. But there is one whom you can take in my place.' The china-blue eyes flashed. 'Allegra. You would prefer her now, I think.'

'*Allegra* is here! But the Amir said not . . .' Nash could not hide the delighted gleam which came into his eyes.

'His Highness enjoys jesting. The *nasrani* is here, but she knows nothing about me. I am the Lady Khadija Nur as far as she knows. As mother of the heir, I have my own chambers and privacy, as you see. I chose not to show myself to her. At first it was because I could not reveal myself without shame . . . When she first came, I was with child, and yet in the ways of Islam I was merely a concubine and not married before God. I have changed since then, adjusted, and found myself to be the happiest of women. My sister has not been able to adjust, and so I begged His Highness to free her. She is barren, so he saw no reason to keep her here. She behaved disgracefully before valued guests and her punishment was to be cast out of the palace to beg her way in the streets for the money for her passage home . . . If she survived long enough to save it, that is.'

A blaze of jealous fury lit the antimony-painted eyes. It was then Nash understood that Elizabeth was no longer of his world. If she had ever been the gentle saint he had believed her to be then she was certainly not that now. He knew as well as she what begging in the streets meant: harlotry, being forced to give her body to the lowest, meanest men because she had no choice.

He shuddered. Elizabeth was not the woman he had idealised in his mind all these months. She was now a fatalist, a Mohammedan, different, almost repulsive. How could he ever have wanted her as a wife?

'Tell my sister that I am dead, for as far as you and she are concerned, I am. That is how I wish it to be. My father will not grieve so bitterly for a dead daughter as he would for an immoral one who is now a heathen in their eyes. Do you promise me?'

Nash nodded, knowing that his heart was no longer here in this beautiful yet chilly room with this ruthless woman and her dark-skinned infant. Where was his darling Allegra, where?

'As the mother of Prince Zühl I have considerable influence here. You will receive all that you asked for last night, the horses and guards to accompany you both to the coast. That gift is at my request. The freeing of a slave or concubine is rare for His Highness adheres strictly to the Sultan's ways. It happens only if she is infertile or grows old and too infirm to work. My sister has borne no child, so His Highness no longer has any interest in her and her behaviour here has been lamentable. Take her, and if you can be happy with her, then let it be so. Allah go with you.'

The expression in the eyes of the Lady Khadija Nur showed plainly that she thought no man in his right mind would take His Highness's leavings and expect happiness to follow.

With an imperious wave of a begemmed hand, the Amir's chief favourite showed that the audience was over and Nash was escorted from the chamber, not looking back, not wishing to do so. That part of his life was over, finished. Now he had Allegra, the woman he loved immeasurably. He could hardly believe his good fortune and yet he felt uneasy. Was Elizabeth telling the truth or was he to be made a prisoner again?

But no, the guards took him to the suite occupied by the *nasrani*, as Elizabeth called her, and there he himself opened the door and stepped inside.

Allegra, his beautiful spirit, lay on a pallet in the darkened chamber. His heart twisting, he flung himself down by her side, taking her cold white hands in his, calling out her name. Her face was white and still; her eyes grooved with shadows. She looked as if she were dead. Now he knew why Elizabeth had seemed so delighted about his taking Allegra. They had killed her, she and the Amir between them! As Elizabeth said, concubines never left here alive.

'*No!*' he cried, scooping her into his arms. '*No!* Jesu, I will do anything, anything if she still lives!'

The poison phial slipped from her fingers as he crushed her in his embrace, the poison which Elizabeth had taken care to put her way, with the help of Zoula. How could the latter have disobeyed the mother of the Amir's heir?

How cold she felt, and he wept over her, tears of bitterness and racking grief. This was all he deserved, but why did she have to pay the price? Oh Lord God, if he could turn back time!

Beside himself, he kissed the white face, hugged the cold, sad little form, and thought of joining her, so that she need not make the journey alone.

Then she stirred, a wisp of air passing out between her lips and touching his cheek so that he shouted her name again, and again. Ah Lord God, how he loved her, how he would love her, and she was not dead! He had brought her back to life with his kisses, his longing, for she was opening her eyes and staring at him in amazement. His love was unshakeable, unchangeable, as true love always is. He would forget her past the moment that they left this place. He would never ever insult or accuse. They would retrace their steps along the Incense Road to civilisation and their old life, neither being the same now, but united so closely in love and belonging. He did not care what she had done here; nor did he care that she might be barren, as Elizabeth had so maliciously put it. All he wanted was that she be alive, his own adorable, beloved Allegra . . .

'Nash, I am dreaming! Did the poison work so fast then? I am dead and seeing what I most longed for in all the world, that is it! But it is not the world, is it? This is Purgatory, the punishment for my sins. Nash, Nash, I wish it were really you, my heart!'

'My sweetest darling, this is Nash, I am really here, and I have come to take you home. We have horses and provisions, and we shall leave as soon as you are well. Do you have a fever, is that it?' He touched her forehead but it was cool.

'If only that were so, Nash, but I took poison. Can you not guess? I am dying now, can you not see? It is all I deserve, God forgive me. Elizabeth is dead, did you not know? I came too late to save her . . . She lost her mind and ran into the desert and there she died, alone, as I am going to die now.'

'Elizabeth dead? Who told you that?'

'The Amir. He told me what had happened to her. She died of a broken heart, Nash, like me!'

'You are not going to die! You are coming home with me, do you hear? Do you hear? Allegra, Allegra, do you hear me? This is Nash, and I love you! You are mine! We are free to leave here and we are going now, this minute.'

He loved her so much, so ardently that he could not take in the talk of poison. She was dreaming, or fevered, or both.

Gently he lifted her up, and her eyes opened, her legs steadied, though she clutched at his arms.

'I can stand up, Nash! Look, I can stand up!' Allegra's face was shining, her colour returning, her flesh warming. Joy was reeling through her veins and such a luminous, delirious happiness that she wanted to laugh and dance round the room.

The poison phial lay unheeded where it had rolled when she was lifted up. Inside it had been a sleeping draught, one strong enough to make her close her eyes swiftly, but not sufficiently powerful to prevent her from waking eventually. Zoula was clever. She had no wish to cause the death of the girl who danced like a goddess. It was to have appeared as if the *nasrani* had a remarkable immunity to the poison, sleeping for a few hours and then waking, a solution which would not cause Zoula to be punished by the vengeful Lady Khadija Nur.

Nash took Allegra's face in his hands, cradling it tenderly, gazing into her beloved eyes while her arms wrapped round his waist and clung.

'We are free, my sweetest darling, we are free. I vowed that I would find you and take you home and that is what I shall do. When we reach England, we shall marry. I want you as my dearest wife.'

'Nash,' she swallowed painfully, clutching at him even tighter. 'You do not realise what has happened to me here . . . I –I–you cannot like me now, let alone love me! When I tell you what I have done, how I have behaved, you will not want me, you will not! I am damned, beyond redemption . . '

'You, damned, my little one? If you are, then so am I, for did we not sin together on our paradise island? If you condemn yourself then you condemn me also, and that I refuse to allow!' He grinned broadly, looking down into her eyes. 'I have loved you far longer than I ever realised. Perhaps we have known one another before, in another life, at another hour, perhaps we danced together before the statue of the mother goddess in ancient times and vowed that we would meet again, and love again, and now we have.' He paused there to kiss her soundly, being a firm believer in actions speaking louder than words, certainly where love is concerned.

When he had finished, she spoke again of her fears, for how could she put aside so many months of inner torment? Some *jinn* had possessed her during these past weeks; she had not been herself; she had behaved like a *houri*, and yet she was baptised a Christian, and had never doubted her faith until the perfumes of Arabia had affected her senses.

'Nash, how can you want me? I am no longer pure: I have, I have shared the Amir's bed. He – he bewitched me, I could not resist . . . I would be burnt as a witch in England!'

'Then they would have to burn me, too. One day I will tell you what I have been doing while you were a prisoner here, my sweeting. Do you think that all are saints save you? That is not so.' He held her at arm's length, gazing into her troubled blue eyes. How lovely she was, yet the signs of strain were evident. And she was pale after being incarcerated here for so long. Sunshine and the air of Cornwall would soon restore her if the sea voyage did not accomplish that first.

'We are leaving here now, you and I, together. It is all arranged. There is nothing more to be said, no argument that would change my mind. I have trekked across the world to find you, Allegra, would I abandon you now because of a little bewitchment, as you put it? What manner of man would I be then? A knave, a poltroon!'

'Can we truly go now? Will he let us?' She glanced over her shoulder as if fearing that the Amir might be ready to pounce on them with his guard.

'Yes, as soon as you are strong enough.'

'I am strong now, Nash, now that I have you. Oh this is a miracle and I do not deserve it! Will you, will you never regret marrying me, Nash? Are you sure? If you changed your mind, I would understand.'

'But I would not! I would have to be moon-fevered to change my mind about you, my heart.'

Bending, he kissed the tears from her cheeks and stroked back her tangled hair. How delicate and vulnerable she was in his embrace; how could he ever have thought her independent and self-sufficient with a steely heart? She needed him, and he would be there to cherish her always, his lovely Lady She-Wolf. One day she would be restored to her old fiery self and they would quarrel and dispute, as lovers have always done from times beginning, but in future he would know that whatever they said or did, however fierce she appeared to be on the surface, she needed him desperately, and, more important, he needed and loved her.

He heard her whisper something. It sounded like '*Mashallah*', but he must have misheard. Why should she say that? 'The will of Allah, so be it'.

Having whispered that phrase, she would never say it or think it again. She had purged herself of Islam, accepting in that moment that the two gods were indeed one, yet with different creeds. She had now flung away the world of Islam, with a sure success, she knew. Love had overcome, her love and Nash's, conquering the despotism and the agonies of the last months and renewing her hopes and dreams.

'Take me home,' she sighed as he kissed her forehead and then the tip of her nose. 'Take me home to England.'

Lifting her up lightly into his arms, he strode towards the door where the eunuchs waited to take them to the horses. Within minutes, they would be riding from here, not looking back, never looking back, riding towards their Paradise regained.